THE
HOME
FOR
UNWANTED
GIRLS

THE
HOME
FOR
UNWANTED
GIRLS

A Novel

JOANNA
GOODMAN

HARPER

NEW YORK ▪ LONDON ▪ TORONTO ▪ SYDNEY

HARPER

HarperCollins books may be purchased for educational, business, or sales promotional use. For information, please e-mail the Special Markets Department at SPsales@harpercollins.com.

FIRST EDITION

Designed by Jamie Lynn Kerner

Library of Congress Cataloging-in-Publication Data has been applied for.

ISBN 978-0-06-283408-9 (library edition)
ISBN 978-0-06-268422-6 (pbk.)

18 19 20 21 22   LSC   10 9 8 7 6 5 4 3 2 1

For my Mom

To an Insignificant Flower Obscurely Blooming in a Lonely Wild

. . . And though thou seem'st a weedling wild,
Wild and neglected like to me,
Thou still art dear to Nature's child,
And I will stop to notice thee.

For oft, like thee, in wild retreat,
Array'd in humble garb like thee,
There's many a seeming weed proves sweet,
As sweet as garden-flowers can be.

And, like to thee, each seeming weed
Flowers unregarded; like to thee,
Without improvement, runs to seed,
Wild and neglected like to me.

—JOHN CLARE

THE
HOME
FOR
UNWANTED
GIRLS

PROLOGUE

≈∽∮∾≈

1950

He who plants a seed plants life. This is something Maggie's father always says, quoting from his prized *Yearbooks of Agriculture 1940–48*. He doesn't just dispense seeds; he is devoted to them the way a preacher is devoted to God. He's known in their town as the Seed Man—a vainglorious title, but it has a noble ring. Maggie loves being the Seed Man's daughter. It gives her an air of prestige—at least it did, once. Much like the province in which she lives, where the French and English are perpetually vying for the upper hand, her family also has two very distinct sides. Maggie understood early on that a stake had to be planted, an allegiance made. She aligned with her father, and he with her.

When she was very young, he used to read to her from his impressive collection of horticulture books. Her favorite was *The Gardener's Bug Book*. There was a poem on the first page, which she knew by heart. *The rose-bug on the rose is evil; so are those who see the rose-bug, not the rose.* While other children were lulled to sleep with fairy tales, her bedtime stories were about seeds and gardening—Johnny Appleseed carrying his seeds from the cider presses of Pennsylvania, walking hundreds of miles tending his orchards, sharing the wealth of his apples with the settlers and the Indians; or Gregor Mendel, the Austrian monk who planted peas in his monastery garden and studied the traits of each generation, and whose records, her father claimed, were the foundation of our current knowledge of genetics and heredity. Such triumphs, her father pointed out, always begin with a single seed.

"How do you make the seeds you sell?" she once asked him.

He looked at her as though he was offended, and replied, "I don't make the seeds, Maggie. The flowers do."

It's their potential for beauty he admires most: the graceful stem that has yet to grow, the shape of the leaf and color of the flower, the abundance of the fruit. Looking at the plainest seed in the palm of his hand, he understands the miracle that will come to pass as it fulfills its purpose.

He also appreciates the predictability of seeds. The corn seed, for instance, always produces a mature plant in ninety days. Her father likes being able to rely on such things, although occasionally his plants are imperfect or deformed and it troubles him deeply, keeps him up pacing through the night, as though the seed itself has betrayed him.

Always a source of comfort to her as a child, his stories mean even more to her now as she tries to quiet herself to sleep in this strange bed, strange body. At sixteen, Maggie has a seed of her own growing inside her and it's almost fully ripened. The baby moves and kicks with gusto, pressing its feet and elbows against the walls of her belly, reminding her of her terrible transgression, the shame it's caused and the way it's upheaved her comfortable life.

Outside, the sky has gone dark. She came up for an afternoon nap, but it must be suppertime by now and she's still wide awake. She lays a hand on her belly and instantly feels the unnerving acrobatics beneath her palm. At least she isn't alone in this place anymore.

Her aunt calls out for supper and Maggie stretches. She reluctantly turns on the lamp, eases herself off the bed, and goes downstairs to face them.

A platter of roast beef is set down on the table for Sunday dinner, alongside dishes of carrots, potatoes, peas. A bottle of wine is opened for the grown-ups. Fresh baked bread, soft butter, salt, and pepper.

Her parents are here visiting. Maggie is happy to see her father. She misses him, even though he's different with her. She can tell he's making an effort, but there's a shadow in his blue eyes now whenever he looks at her, which isn't often enough. His attempt at forgiveness lacks conviction. He can't quite overcome his sense of betrayal.

Maggie watches her uncle ceremoniously sharpen his knife and carve thin pink slices of beef that bleed onto the white porcelain. Her sisters blather and giggle together, excluding her. Someone asks if there's horseradish. And then Maggie feels a gush of warm liquid between her legs, just as her mother is saying, "*Tabarnac*, I forgot the horseradish."

Maggie's dress is soaked. Her cheeks grow hot with embarrassment. She wants to slink away from the table and run to the washroom, but the rush of liquid doesn't let up. "I peed," she blurts, standing. The liquid is still pouring from between her legs, surprisingly odorless, puddling on her aunt's wood floor.

She turns to her mother in a panic. Her sisters are all staring at her splotched dress with bewildered expressions. At last, Aunt Deda cries out, "Her water broke!"

Nicole, her youngest sister, begins to wail. Maman and Deda spring into action. The men slide away from the table, dumbstruck and meek. They wait awkwardly for instructions from the women.

"She's in labor," Maman says calmly.

"Now?" Maggie's father says, glancing over at the mighty roast beef sitting freshly carved in the center of the long pine table. "She's not due for another month."

"These things can't be conveniently arranged," Maman snaps. "You'd better call Dr. Cullen. Tell him we'll meet him at the hospital."

"What's happening?" Maggie asks. No one has prepared her for this moment.

Deda rushes over and throws her pillowy arm over Maggie's shoulder. "It's fine, *cocotte*," she soothes. "The baby's early, that's all."

No one ever says "your baby." It's always "*the* baby." Even Maggie thinks of it as "the baby." And yet in spite of all the havoc it's caused,

3

she's not quite ready to let it go. She's come to think of it as an ally or a talisman, though not so much as her future child. She's still too young for that, can't really connect to the concept of motherhood. She doesn't have to anyway. The baby coming tonight really only means one thing to her: she'll be free from imprisonment at her aunt and uncle's farm. She can finally go home.

She feels a contraction and lets out a roar of pain.

"It's coming," her mother says. *It's coming.*

PART I

⟞⟟⟞⟟⟞

Controlling Weeds

1948–1950

The growth of perennial weeds, particularly of a fleshy kind,
can be discouraged by allowing them to grow happily till just
about to flower and then harvesting them and laying them
back again thickly on the surface of the roots . . .

—OLD WIVES' LORE FOR GARDENERS

CHAPTER 1

---⌇⌇⌇---

1948

"Admit it, Seed Man, you voted for Duplessis!"

A boom of laughter drifts up to the attic where Maggie is weighing and counting seeds. Premier Duplessis has just been reelected and there's a buzz in the store. She dumps a handful of seeds on the scale, straining to hear what's being said downstairs. "Come on, Seed Man!" one of the farmers teases. "It's nothing to be ashamed of!"

Maggie abandons counting and crouches at the top of the stairwell to eavesdrop. She's been working for her father on weekends since she turned twelve two years ago, weighing and packaging seeds in small paper envelopes. It can be a tedious task, especially because the larger seeds have to be counted individually, but she doesn't mind. She loves being at her father's store; it's her favorite place in the world. She plans to work downstairs on the sales floor one day, and then take over when he retires.

His store is called Superior Seeds/Semences Supérieures, and it's about halfway between Cowansville and Dunham, the small town where they live about fifty-five miles southeast of Montreal. The name on the sign outside the store is written in French and English because her father says that's the way things work in Quebec if you want to prosper in business. You can't exclude anyone.

Maggie creeps down a few more stairs to get closer to the action.

The store is damp and smells of fertilizer, a scent she adores. Arriving on Saturday mornings, she always inhales deeply and sometimes digs her hands inside the cool dirt where new seeds are germinating in small clay pots, just so the earthy smell will stay on her fingers for the rest of the day. To Maggie, this is where happiness is found.

The store stocks basic things like fertilizers and insecticides, but Maggie's father prides himself on an impressive selection of rare seeds that can't be found elsewhere in the area. Vain enough to think of himself as a dispenser of life, he is redeemed by his sheer commitment to his work. He manages to straddle a fine line between ridicule and respect, and the farmers come to him not just for their seeds but also for his expertise in all matters rural and political. On a day like today, his store is as much a gathering place as it is a business. The back wall is lined with row upon row of tiny square drawers, all of them filled with seeds. There are giant barrels of corn, wheat, barley, oats, and tobacco for the farmers. On the floor, there are sacks of sheep manure, Fertosan, bonemeal, RA-PID-GRO. Beside those there is a wooden display rack for the trees and shrubs, as well as gardening tools, lawn sprinklers, and hoses. The shelves are crowded with powder packs and spray cans of DDT, Nico-fume, larvicide, malathion dust, Slug-Em. There is nothing a farmer or a gardener can't find.

"The day I vote Union Nationale is the day I close down this store," her father declares, full of bravado, the upturned ends of his moustache seeming to emphasize his point.

Her father has a magnetic way about him. He's as handsome as a movie star, with his blue eyes and Hollywood moustache. His hair is thinning—always has been, ever since his twenties—but baldness gives him a certain dignified air, somehow enhances his sophistication in her eyes. He wears linen suits during the summer and tweed jackets with fedoras in winter, and he smokes House of Lords cigars that stink up the house with that wonderful fatherly smell. Even his name, Wellington Hughes, sounds impressive.

Wellington thrusts his chin out in his stubborn, prideful way and says, "The man is a gangster and a dictator." He speaks in fluent French, being a great proponent of bilingualism as a business tool.

Maggie's father is a very influential man in the farming community, so it's expected he will support any politician who values, protects, and promotes agriculture the way Duplessis does. But he is also a proud Anglophone. He despises Duplessis and is quite open about it. He believes Duplessis is the one who's kept the French uneducated and living in the dark ages. He endures his customers' political views only because they choose to do their business at his shop and he respects their patronage and loyalty. Yet when the name Maurice Duplessis is dropped into the conversation, the color rises up in his usually pale cheeks and his voice goes up an octave or two.

"We know you voted for him, Hughes," Jacques Blais taunts. He pronounces it *Yooz*. "You need his farm credits. When we prosper, you prosper, heh?"

"My business would do fine without that egomaniac in power," Maggie's father states emphatically.

"Takes one to know one," Bruno Roy mutters, and all the men break out laughing.

"You Québécois have no loyalty to this country," her father says, uttering the word "loyalty" with reverence, as though it were the noblest trait a man could possess.

"*Maudit Anglais*," Blais jokes, just as the bell jangles over the front door.

The men turn to look and immediately fall silent as Clémentine Phénix enters the store. An unmistakable tension quickly replaces the jovial mood of moments earlier.

"I need some DDT," she says, filling the store with her husky voice and controversial presence. The way she says "I need" is not so much a request as a challenge.

Maggie's father goes over to where he keeps the pesticides. He picks up a can of DDT and wordlessly hands it to her. Something passes between them—a cryptic look, a communication—but then he quickly turns and walks away. Maybe it's nothing more than the old territorial grudge.

The Phénix family lives in a small shack on the cornfield that borders Maggie's property. This is very much a point of contention with her father. He feels the value of his own land is considerably diminished by its proximity to their impoverished shack. The Phénix kids own the cornfield, but it's all they've got. They earn their living from sweet corn and strawberries in the summer. In the winter, Clémentine's brother, Gabriel, works in a factory in Montreal. It's just the three siblings living together now—Clémentine, Gabriel, and Angèle—and Clémentine's four-year-old daughter, Georgette, from a marriage that ended in divorce. The rest of the family—their parents and two other sisters—were killed in a car accident several years ago.

Clémentine follows Wellington to the front counter, ignoring the snickers from the other customers, which she must be used to by now. Her divorce has made her a pariah in their small Catholic town, where divorce is not only a sin but also illegal. She had to go all the way to Ottawa to get it done, an unforgivable offense in the eyes of the self-righteous townsfolk like Maggie's mother.

"I need two cans," Clémentine says, folding her solid brown arms across her chest.

She's suntanned and freckled, wears no makeup, and lets her long golden braid swing out behind her like a skipping rope. Maggie thinks she's beautiful, even stripped of all the usual feminine trappings. She somehow manages to be feminine and tomboyish at the same time, her disarmingly pretty face not the least bit undermined by a hard expression, thick, muscular arms, or the unflattering potato-sack dungarees that conceal even the possibility of a figure.

There's something awe-inspiring about her, Maggie observes, a quiet defiance in how she handles herself with the men. She has none of the usual adornments that give women legitimacy—a husband, children, money—and yet she seems to do whatever needs to be done to manage her family and their livelihood.

"My crop is infested with rootworms," Clémentine explains. If she's uncomfortable with everyone's eyes on her, she doesn't let on.

Wellington crosses the store again and returns with another can of DDT, looking quite agitated. All of a sudden, the front door swings open and Gabriel Phénix steps inside. He swaggers over to Clémentine as all the farmers turn their attention to him.

Maggie hasn't seen Gabriel since last summer and her breath catches when he enters. He left for Montreal as a boy last fall—she remembers him running through the field on spindly legs, his shoulders slight, his face round and cherubic—but he's returned a man. He must be sixteen now. His blond hair is combed into a swirling lick, his gray eyes glint like razor blades, and he's got the same pronounced cheekbones and full lips as his sister. He's still thin enough that Maggie can count his ribs through his white cotton T-shirt, but his arms, which have muscle now and a fine thick shape, give his body a man's breadth and substance. Watching him from her spot near the stairs, she feels something strange inside her body, like the swoosh feeling in her belly when she dives off the high rocks into Selby Lake. Whatever it is about him, she can't seem to make her eyes look anywhere else.

"You okay?" he asks his sister. Clémentine nods and puts her hand on his chest, a signal for him to hang back and wait for her. He does, with clenched fists and a serious, insolent expression on his face, waiting to pounce in her defense if called upon.

Maggie's father puts the two cans of DDT into a brown paper bag and rings it up on the cash register.

"I need credit," Clémentine says.

More snickers.

"Credit?" her father echoes with contempt. Wellington Hughes does not extend credit. It's his policy. It is *the* policy, and his policies are like commandments. *Thou shalt not extend credit.*

"Our season starts in a couple of weeks," she explains. "I'll be able to pay you then."

Maggie wipes a film of sweat from above her lip. She realizes for the first time how hard life must be for the Phénix kids. The truth is she's never really considered it before, not even when she was friends with their little sister, Angèle. She's heard her parents talk about them—the divorce and the dead father's drinking—but she never paid much attention. Today, though, she finds something about their prideful audacity very compelling.

"If I let you take this bag on credit," her father says in his smooth French, "everyone in town will start coming to me in the off-season and promising to pay when corn season starts."

Gabriel pushes in front of his sister and unfastens his watch. He drops it on the counter and shoves it toward Maggie's father. "Here," he says. "Take my goddamn watch to show we're good for it. It was my father's. It's gold."

Wellington's upper lip twitches and he thrusts the watch back at Gabriel. "This isn't a pawn shop," he says, scowling.

Gabriel makes no move to take back the watch. After a moment, Maggie's father suddenly pushes the brown paper bag of DDT across the counter to Clémentine. "Here, then," he says. "Take it. But don't come back until you can pay for it."

"Thank you," she says, never once lowering her head or her eyes in shame.

Maggie's father looks disgusted. When Gabriel still makes no move to reclaim his watch, Clémentine grabs it and pulls Gabriel toward the door. On their way out, Gabriel looks directly at Maggie, as though he's known she's been here all along. Their eyes lock and her heart accelerates. His expression is defiant, full of hatred. His lips curl into an indolent sneer, and she realizes, with some shock, that the sneer is directed at her.

She notices her father watching her sternly. His warning is understood. *Thou shalt not date French boys.*

CHAPTER 2

⸺◈⸺

Maggie has taken to hiding in the Phénix cornfield for two reasons. The first is to avoid having to do her chores. The second is to observe and hopefully get noticed by Gabriel while he tends to his corn.

It's August and corn season is in full swing. She's sprawled on the ground between the rows, reading a *True Romance* magazine, ignoring the ants crawling all over her bare legs and tickling her skin. She's content here with the sun burning her back and the tall stalks sheltering her from her mother's nagging. She can hear Maman's voice all the way from their backyard. Ranting, ranting. Her sister Violet has knocked some clothing off the line and Maman is furious. Poor Violet, but better her than Maggie.

"You again?"

Maggie drops her magazine and looks up, pretending to be startled. He's standing above her, shielding his eyes. He's shirtless, wearing only blue jeans. His skin is brown, as dark as her father's cigars.

"I like reading here," she says.

He crouches down beside her. She holds her breath. A trickle of sweat moves slowly down the slope of his neck.

"*Tabarnac*," he says, examining an ear of corn. "The earworms are feeding on the silks."

"Have they penetrated the kernels?" she asks, knowing all about insect infestations from her father.

Gabriel shakes the husk of one of the ears. "Hopefully it's loose enough to protect the corn. They should be all right as long as the damage stays on the surface."

"Maybe you should have planted earlier," she says, sounding like her father. The condescension, the lecturing tone. She instantly regrets it. Gabriel gives her an annoyed look and stands up.

"Stick with your romance magazines," he scoffs. "Leave the farming to me."

Why did she have to open her big mouth? Maman always tells her she's got a big mouth and she's right.

Gabriel turns his back to Maggie, and her eyes are riveted to the jutting curve of his spine as he moves through the rows of corn, bending methodically to inspect the ears. As she watches him work, admiring him and reflecting with embarrassment on what she'd said, all the other dramas and obsessions in her life fall away like the corn tassels scattered around her.

"Maggie!"

She hears Violet's panicked voice before her sister even appears.

"Maggie!" Violet cries, shoving stalks out of her way. "Maman wants you home *now!*"

Maggie stretches out like a cat, acting as though she's not afraid of their mother, even though she's actually terrified. They all are.

"You better hurry or . . ."

Or she will beat them with the wooden pig spoon. Or lock them out of the house without supper. Maggie turns back around to give Gabriel one final longing gaze. He catches her looking and she waves, but he doesn't wave back. Violet observes this, but doesn't say a word. "Let's go," she says nervously, grabbing Maggie's hand and jerking her to her feet.

They trudge out of the cornfield just as the sun is beginning to set. "We better run," Violet says. And even though Maggie doesn't like to come off as wimpy as Violet, she knows her sister is right. They have to run.

Their house sits at the end of a long road that's lined on either side by a dense row of towering pine trees, and they run all the way up the dirt path that rises steeply from the cornfield and winds its way through the woods. When they get to the clearing where their gray stone Victorian sits nobly as the centerpiece of the property, Maggie and Violet are both drenched with sweat and panting like dogs. The screen door slaps shut behind them and there she is, Maman, standing at the stove with the wooden spoon in her hand. *"Où t'étais, Maggie?"* she asks, her voice soft but menacing. *Where were you?*

Geraldine is already setting the table, and two-year-old Nicole is on the floor playing with her British Ginny doll. Ever since their older brother, Peter, went to boarding school in Sherbrooke, it's just a house full of girls.

Violet rushes over to the table to help Geri, getting herself out of the line of fire.

"I was outside," Maggie says.

"I know you were outside. Doing *what?*"

"Reading."

Maggie attempts to hide the magazine behind her back, but it's pointless. Maman snatches it out of her hand and stares at it mockingly. "What does this say?" she asks.

Her mother can't read or speak a word of English. She is *pure laine* French and has never made any effort to absorb even the rudiments of the English language, not for her husband nor for the bilingual community in which she lives.

The Eastern Townships is mostly farm country, containing pockets of both French and English who live in relative harmony—that is, relative to Quebec, where the French and English tolerate each other with precarious civility but don't mingle the way other more homogeneous communities do. The same could be said about Maggie's parents, whose union has always been a point of bafflement for Maggie.

Her father earned his diploma in horticulture at eighteen and got his first job at Pinney's Garden Center in the East End of Montreal. He was the assistant manager when Maggie's mother showed up one day looking for a plant to pretty up her apartment in the slum of Hochelaga. She was a poor French-Canadian maid who had never stepped foot outside the slums, and he a literate, cultured Anglo, but he fell in love with her the moment he spotted her dark red lips and soft black curls that day at Pinney's.

Today, French is the official language of their household—a testament to their mother's stubbornness—but their father won on education. As a result, the children all attend the English Protestant school, making English the official language of their future.

The first time Maggie ever heard English was when she was five, on her first day of school. When she confronted her father about this sudden upheaval in her life—the switch from French nursery to English school—all he said was, "You're English."

"Maman's not," she pointed out.

"But *you* are," he said. "French is the inferior language. It's imperative that you're educated in English."

"What's that mean?"

"It means speaking only French will get you nowhere."

"But you speak French."

"That's why I'm successful. You must never forget how to speak French as your second language. It's a means to an end, Maggie, but it doesn't make you French. See?"

She did not. And when the kids at school started calling her "Pepsi" and "frog," she was even more confused.

"Why do they call me a Pepsi?" she asked her father one night, sitting on the floor of his cramped office.

The room was once the maid's quarters, but quickly became his sanctuary—not much larger than a closet, it's the place where he keeps his seed catalogues, books, homemade radios, tools, notes, and sketches of the garden he will one day plant in the backyard. There's an old mahogany desk and a typewriter crammed in there, too, and the room always reeks of cigar smoke. He can stay locked inside for hours with his music, his House of Lords, a bottle of wine, and whatever project he happens to be tinkering with at the time. He always keeps it locked because he says a man needs his privacy.

That night, he looked up from the Dale Carnegie book he was reading and removed his bifocals. He reached out and touched Maggie's knee. His hand was warm and comforting. "Because Pepsi is cheap and sweet and that's why the French Canadians drink so much of it, and why they have rotten teeth. But you're *not* a Pepsi. You're English, like Daddy."

After that, she learned English quickly, out of sheer survival. Nothing was more important than speaking perfect English—and not just speaking it, but *being* English. Fitting in at school required a complete transformation—including how she dressed. She traded in the baggy dresses her mother preferred for plaid kilts and crisp white lace collars and penny loafers that her father ordered from the Eaton's catalogue. She traded in her mother tongue for a new, more elegant language. Eventually, she began to feel English.

Nowadays, out of fear and obligation, they still speak French to their mother, whose presence in the house is mighty and unavoidable. But Maggie's allegiance is to her English side—her father's side—because he rarely raises his voice and he is the beacon of reason in an otherwise erratic household.

"What does this say?" her mother repeats, her voice rising as she points to the cover of Maggie's magazine.

"'*True Romance*,'" Maggie mutters.

Violet snickers.

"True romance!" her mother scoffs, shoving the magazine into the garbage. "Disgusting."

"She pretends it's her and Gabriel," Violet reveals.

"Gabriel Phénix?" Maman says, with interest.

Violet looks at Maggie with a flicker of guilt, even as she's answering their mother. "That's why she goes to the cornfield," she tattles. "To see him."

Maggie glares at Violet, silently letting her know she'll pay for this later.

"I never thought *you'd* be the one to fall for one of us," Maman says, grinning.

"What're you talking about?"

"Your father will say Gabriel's not good enough for you because he's French," her mother responds. "But I was good enough for *him*. Remember that."

She steps back with a satisfied look on her face and turns back to the stove.

Upstairs in her room, Maggie checks on her indoor garden. She's been planting seeds in her mother's old mason jars since she was a toddler. She keeps them in neat rows on the bureau beneath her window, which allows for plenty of south-facing sunlight and warmth from the heater behind it. Over the years, many of her most successful annuals—sunflowers, tall zinnias, marigolds, radishes—have been transplanted into clay pots and still thrive outside in their backyard all summer long.

Her father used to call her Joanie Appleseed when she was very young, and although the nickname was eventually forgotten, her passion for planting has never waned. It's the feeling of ownership she gets from the entire process, starting with the choosing and collecting of the seeds, the cleaning, sowing, and then constant nurturing to help coax them to their wondrous fruition.

Her newest endeavor, undertaken last year, is a collection of lemon trees, which she hopes will start producing fruit in another couple of years. She's fond of her lemon shoots—some as many as ten per jar—and enjoys observing their intricate root systems prepare for the lemons.

She's also got some wildflower seeds planted in her jars, but they've required a lot more effort and commitment than she'd counted on—a much longer drying time as well as rigorous cleaning to get them perfectly crunchy for sowing—and they still haven't yielded much reward. She had to use Ma's good rolling pin to crush their hard capsules, an infraction for which she paid dearly when Ma found out. Examining her wildflower seeds now, she can't help but feel disappointed with their pace of growth. She picked the seeds in May, despite her father's warning about how stubborn and temperamental they could be, and just as he predicted, most of them still haven't sprouted.

As she carefully pours water into the soil of the mason jars, she glances out her window at the cornfield. Gabriel is still there, wandering in the fading sun, detasseling his corn. She's full of marvelous feelings, watching him out there on his land.

She wants to hold on to this tingly resolve, this new exciting motive for opening her eyes in the morning when she hears Maman's voice barking her name or feels those hard, callused hands shaking her awake. Her parents say she's willful; that when she sets her sights on something, she doesn't relent. *Beware of the Démon Noir,* her mother often warns.

Gabriel pulls a tassel off one of the corn plants and sprinkles it on the ground. Maggie touches the dirt inside one of the jars to make sure it's just damp enough. She doesn't want to drown her precious lemon shoots. She packs the dirt down gently and then wipes her hands on her skirt, never taking her eyes off Gabriel.

CHAPTER 3

As quick and ordinary as an exhalation of breath, summer is over. The nights turn chilly and school resumes. Maggie starts ninth grade at St. Helen's School. It's an all-girls school, which suits her fine because she's lousy in gym and there are no boys to make fun of her while she's square dancing or playing Indian dodge ball. The school motto is *Loyauté Nous Oblige* and it's written on the crest of her tunic.

"Who can tell me where Napoleon suffered his first military loss?" Mrs. Parfitt asks, glancing anxiously outside. It's raining hard and the wind is rattling the windows.

Someone yells out, "The storming of the Bastille!" and Mrs. Parfitt lets out a burdened sigh. "Maggie?"

Maggie enjoys history because it's about facts, not interpretations. Facts are reliable, like seeds. "The invasion of Egypt in 1798," she responds.

Audrey scribbles *Teacher's Pet* across Napoleon's forehead in Maggie's textbook.

Maggie sits beside Nan and Audrey, her two best friends since third grade. They're both blond Anglo beauties who look nothing like her. Maggie has black hair and black eyes, inherited from her Huron ancestors.

Nan pokes her in the arm and whispers for her to look outside. A couple of the bolder girls are already at the window, squealing and pointing. In an instant, the sky darkens to black. Rain is falling in sheets and the wind is beating against the glass like fists. The world outside is a distorted blur.

Maggie worries about how she'll get her sisters home safe, knowing her mother will hold her responsible. That's the burden of being the eldest and having a mother who places no value on common sense.

"It's a hurricane!" someone yells.

"It's not a hurricane," Mrs. Parfitt reassures them, but her voice is submerged by the sound of two dozen screaming girls. She stands there helplessly as the classroom disintegrates into anarchy. "Everyone stay calm."

After a few more minutes of pandemonium, the students are released early. Maggie stops by Violet's seventh grade class to pick her up.

Maggie's mother doesn't drive and her father can't leave the store, so she knows no one will show up to claim them. It's Maggie's daily responsibility to collect Geri at the elementary school and walk both of her sisters home. Today will be no different.

When they get to the front door, Mrs. Parfitt is already there. "How are you getting home?" she asks, wrapping a plastic kerchief over her head. Her breath smells of butterscotch, from those candies she sucks all day.

"My father is coming," Maggie lies, too prideful to tell the truth. Mrs. Parfitt nods, opens her umbrella, and heads outside, where she's quickly swallowed up by the storm.

Maggie and Vi follow her out. The rain assaults them, their light-weight twill swing coats doing little to keep them dry. The combined force of the wind and rain almost knocks them to the ground. They cling to each other, linking arms and meeting the storm head-on, but it's senseless. Within seconds, their flimsy umbrella breaks and they're soaking wet. They look at each other and laugh helplessly, then plunge headlong into the storm.

They hold tightly to each other, pummeled and pulled by the wind as they flail blindly forward. By the time they reach the corner of Rue Principale, it feels as though they've traveled miles. Maggie can feel her sister's body trembling beneath the flimsy twill. She worries Vi will catch pneumonia or consumption, so she pulls her close and wraps an arm around her. Just as they're about to cross the street, the sound of a honking horn causes them to jump back.

With a burst of hope, Maggie searches the street for her father's Packard. The heavy rain has completely obscured the road and she can't make out any of the cars. She has to squeeze her eyes shut to keep them clear. A pickup truck suddenly emerges next to them and stops at the curb. With a sinking heart, Maggie sees it's not her father. As the window rolls down, Maggie glimpses Clémentine Phénix's face. Gabriel is in the passenger seat with Angèle sandwiched between them.

She hasn't seen them since the summer. Occasionally, she spots Gabriel working in the field. She looks for him there every day, before she goes to sleep at night and as soon as she wakes up in the morning. She knows he'll be leaving for Montreal soon and the thought of not having him around induces a palpable feeling of dread.

"Get in!" Clémentine orders. "We just came to pick up Angèle and saw you standing here—"

"I have to get Geraldine!"

"We'll pick her up on the way. We'll manage."

Maggie climbs in first and then Violet slides in after her. It's a 1939 Chevrolet pickup with only the one row for passengers.

Angèle smiles at Maggie, and Maggie smiles back with a swell of fondness. They were best friends once, until Maggie was sent to English school and outgrew not just Angèle but everything French.

Maggie's secretly thrilled to be crammed next to Gabriel, their shoulders pressed together. She manages to sneak a few sidelong glances at his profile, trying to absorb as much of him as she can— the angle of his jawline, the shape of his nose, the curl of his long dark lashes. He turns slightly and casts his gray eyes on her.

"Why didn't your father come?" Gabriel asks Maggie after they've collected Geri at the elementary school.

"Work," Maggie says. "He can't leave the store."

"Who would be shopping for seeds on a day like this?" Clémentine remarks.

Her father would say you can't just close up shop in the middle of the day. What if someone drives in from Granby or Farnham and finds the doors locked? You have to stay open, rain or shine. That's the nature of retail: the customer is the most important person in the world. Besides, it's catalogue season.

Her father works late through October and November, preparing his mail-order catalogue to be sent out in time for spring ordering. He puts it together by himself, starting in September by painstakingly clipping out the pictures he gets from his suppliers, agonizing over the layout, and then typing up descriptions of each seed. This year, he's introducing a brand-new grass, Prévert, which he invented himself after years of diligent experimenting. He spent most of last summer testing it at the Botanical Garden in Montreal, and now Prévert is ready to market. Peter says it sounds like "pervert." Peter is doing the illustrations to help out, but he's made it quite clear he's got no interest in his father's business. He wants to be an architect, not a "shopkeeper," as he put it.

"There's flooding all over the Townships," Clémentine says. "We heard it on the radio."

There's a deep blue vein pulsating in Gabriel's forehead as he watches the road. His knuckles are white from making such tight fists as they drive by a handful of cars overturned in ditches along the side of the road.

Everyone falls silent. Maggie can't help thinking about how M. and Mme. Phénix and two of their daughters were killed on this very same stretch of road. She wonders if Gabriel and Clémentine are thinking the same thing.

The road ahead is invisible. The wipers swish back and forth, utterly useless. The road comes into view for a second, only to become engulfed again. Clémentine starts praying quietly.

When she turns cautiously onto Bruce Street, Gabriel reaches across the front seat and rubs her shoulder. "Bravo, Clem," he says. He smiles, revealing the most gorgeous dimples. It's the first time Maggie's ever seen him smile. There's a tenderness between him and his sister that is nothing like Maggie's relationship with Peter.

As they approach the top of the hill, Clémentine suddenly jerks the truck to a stop and they're all flung forward. Geri starts to whimper.

"The road is flooded," Gabriel says. "It's practically a lake. We'll have to walk from here."

They pile out of the pickup and huddle together, Geri in the middle of Maggie and Vi. The sky is still black, and the earth is dissolving into a mucky lake. The water is up to their ankles. Gabriel reaches for Maggie's arm and holds on to her, chivalrously guiding the three girls toward the house.

Maggie imagines he's a brave soldier on the front lines of war, like Napoleon Bonaparte. In spite of the chill in her bones, she feels warm inside being so close to him. The grip of his fingers on her arm makes her tingle. She doesn't want to get home, doesn't want him to let go of her. She'd rather drown in his company than be separated from him.

He releases her arm at their front door, having the good sense to avoid their mother. Maggie turns to him, raising her hand to wave. "Thank you!" she says. But her words, absurdly inadequate, are swept away by the storm.

The front door opens and Maman is looming in the mudroom.

"They sent us home early because of the storm," Maggie tells her, still giddy from her encounter with Gabriel. Maman frowns, but even she can't ruin Maggie's good mood.

They come into the kitchen, where Nicole is sitting in front of the fireplace with her doll. Maman closes the door with her usual gruffness and quickly gets to work stripping off their wet coats.

"What are you smiling about?" Maman asks her.

"I'm not," Maggie says, pulling off her socks.

"*Tabarnac*," Maman mutters, not angrily. "You're all soaking wet. Go upstairs, take off all your clothes, and put on the *combinés* that are warming on the heater."

Maggie and her sisters look at one another, perplexed, and run upstairs before their mother remembers to yell at them. Three pairs of long underwear are draped over the heater in their room, which Maman must have put out there in anticipation of their soggy return.

Maggie pulls off all her wet clothes, tosses them in the hamper, and puts on her pajamas over the warm long underwear. She can't stop shivering. Their teeth are all chattering in harmony.

"Ma doesn't seem mad," Violet says.

"Why didn't she yell at us?" Geri asks.

"Don't worry," Maggie says. "She'll manage to find a way to blame us for the storm."

They laugh. Downstairs, they huddle in front of the kitchen fireplace wrapped in the patchwork wool blanket Maman made out of their father's old suits. She hands them each a mug of warm milk and keeps checking them for fever with a brusque touch to their foreheads.

It's turning out to be a perfect day, Maggie thinks, savoring the warm milk and heat of the fire, the memory of Gabriel sitting so close to her in the car, and then, afterwards, holding on to her in the rain.

"I told your father to go and get you," her mother mutters, clanging lids as she prepares supper. She's wearing an apron over a royal-blue-and-white floral print dress with buttons all the way down the front, like a doctor's coat. It's dowdy and unflattering. Ever since Nicole was born, she seems to have stopped caring about her appearance altogether.

She always complains that motherhood destroyed her beauty. She blames her children for the gray streaks in her hair, for the two back molars that had to be removed, and especially for her expanding waistline. She was pretty once—there are photographs to prove it—but not so much anymore. Having resigned herself to her fate, or rather dedicated herself to it, the transformation has been rapid. It began with a short unflattering hairdo that she parts on the side and combs over her ears, then the serviceable floral smocks and drab cardigans, and, finally, the total relinquishment of makeup as some sort of protest.

"Why am I surprised he left you there?" her mother natters, as relentless as the rain.

Violet rolls her eyes and Geri giggles.

"Well, but it's okay," Maggie says, trying to smooth things over.

"We're here. He couldn't just close the store in the middle of the afternoon."

Maman dumps a can of peas into her cast-iron pot and turns to face Maggie. "He's got you brainwashed, Maggie. Of course he should have closed the store and gone to pick you up."

"I'm not brainwashed," Maggie says defiantly, surprising herself. "The reason he cares about his business so much is because he cares about us."

"There's no point talking to you," her mother says, shoving the pot of stew into the wood-burning oven and slamming it shut. "You don't think for yourself. God only knows why you worship him so much."

Maman leans up against the oven door and pulls a cigarette from her apron pocket. She lights it and inhales languidly, eyeing Maggie. "One day you'll see him for who he is," she says, waving her cigarette. "Or maybe you're stupider than I thought."

A loud crash of thunder rocks the house. Nicole starts to cry and Geri squeals with delight. Maggie has a pleasant feeling of being cozy and safe by the fire.

"Maggie, Violet," Maman barks. "Set the table."

They both get up and do as they're told, making faces behind their mother's back while they lay out the plates and cutlery. There's a noise out in the mudroom and they all look up.

A door slams. Their father is home.

CHAPTER 4

Maman pounces on him before he even sets foot inside the door. His expression immediately sags in defeat, before he's even got his hat off. When Maggie first started working at Superior Seeds, she would observe her father's jovial moods with curiosity. At work, he's mostly lively and upbeat. Nothing like he is at home. In those early days, she felt privileged to be exposed to that lighthearted side of him, but as time passed, she began to wonder if his work persona was not slightly duplicitous. Why didn't his family make him that happy? Why was it he rarely laughed with his own wife and children?

Inevitably, Maggie came to lay the blame at her mother's feet. She is the one who robs them all of their father's true nature, draining him daily with her nagging and complaining. Her misery has a way of crushing even the most buoyant spirit. They all have to live around her, navigating her unpredictable temperament and her dark moods.

It's hard for Maggie to understand why he chose her to be his wife. She imagines he could have had any pretty girl with red lips and soft curls. Why did it have to be someone who'd had such a wretched life and was still so angry about it?

Hortense grew up in the slums, in a house with dirt floors and no running water that burned to the ground when she was eleven. It was her father who started the fire when he passed out drunk with a lit cigarette in his mouth, killing himself and the prostitute he was with. Hortense, the eldest, was pulled out of school and sent to work as a maid for a wealthy English family, which planted a seed of resentment against all English. In her own words, she married Wellington in the hope of being rescued from destitution, and yet what Hortense despises most about him today are the very things that first appealed to her: his education, his work ethic, his steady income, and his pride.

"Why didn't you just go to the school and pick them up?" Maman asks their father, jabbing him in the chest with the long wooden spoon farmers use to feed pigs.

Wellington shields his chest with his arm. "Let me in, Hortense." He speaks in a composed manner, which has the effect of riling her up even more.

"I would have gone to get them after work," he says. "They would have been fine until six." He winks at Maggie. She smiles to show her solidarity. Yet even as she tries to ignore the flutter of uneasiness inside her, her mother's earlier accusation reverberates in her mind: *He's got you brainwashed.*

"Don't you care about them?" Maman asks him.

As her father removes his wet trench coat and fedora with a look of resignation, Maggie questions for the first time if perhaps it *is* unusual that he didn't pick them up in the storm. "There's no need for all these histrionics," he says.

Maman slams the door to the mudroom. The children flinch.

Her father lets out a small sigh and settles at the table with shoulders slightly stooped and spirits dampened. Maman wordlessly dumps beef-and-pea stew onto his plate. He absently pushes the stew around with his fork, separating carrots and peas from the beef. He pours himself a glass of wine. The bottle is just for him. Maman rarely drinks. If she does, it's only with her friends and siblings.

"I'm trying to run a business," he says wearily. "I can't just close the store on a whim."

"A *whim*?" she cries. "You call that storm a whim?"

"Suppose a customer had shown up at my door and I was closed?" he says. "Suppose he'd driven all the way in from another town?"

"What moron would go out to buy seeds in a storm?"

Geri giggles. Maggie elbows her.

"Well, *did* anyone show up?" Maman asks him.

"No."

Maman slams a hand on the pine table and throws her head back, laughing victoriously. Violet and Geri laugh with her, but Maggie stays quiet.

"*Maudit Anglais*," Maman mutters. *Goddamn Englishman.* "What kind of father puts his job before his children's safety?" she continues, still not mollified. She is missing that innate sense of when to retreat.

"It's not a job," he corrects. "It's my business. It's our livelihood. I have a reputation."

"Oh, please."

"My family values are precisely what drives my work ethic," he says, and Maggie finds herself lulled by his eloquence. "If I didn't care about my family, I would close the store whenever I felt like it, and risk losing half a day's revenue."

Maggie looks from her father to her mother. It seems reasonable to Maggie. Surely it makes sense to Maman.

"You can't tease a strong work ethic out of a man's family values," her father continues. "And vice versa."

Maggie's father sips his wine, nibbles his stew. His fork clinks against the china. "Excuse me," he says, abruptly standing up and leaving the room with his glass of wine. As an afterthought, he returns to take the bottle and then disappears into his sanctuary off the kitchen.

"You can't hide in there all night!" Maman yells after him.

Maggie gets up and slips away. Upstairs, she wanders down the hall to her parents' bedroom and stands in front of her mother's bureau, staring at a photograph of her parents before they were married. Her mother keeps it in an etched silver frame on a doily right next to her box of Yardley face powder. Perhaps it's a reminder of happier days, proof she once wore crimson lipstick and had a slender, curvy figure. In the picture, Maggie's father is wheeling her in a push lawn mower. She's wearing a clingy, gauzy white dress and white high-heeled shoes with straps around the ankles. Her hair is a wavy bob, her lips a dark Cupid's bow, and her head thrown back in laughter. She looks gorgeous and happy. Maggie searches for some clue that it really is Maman. The woman captured in sepia looks so enchanting, prone to easy laughter, hopeful.

Has she spent too many years with a man she doesn't love? Or was it childhood tragedy that ruined her before she even met him? Even though Maman managed to get herself out of the slums and into a much better situation, maybe a tragic childhood is a thing that can't ever be overcome, like polio. It leaves a person crippled.

Maggie turns away and tiptoes out of the room, remembering what it felt like to be so close to Gabriel today, to hear him breathing beside her and feel his pulse beating; to have their legs touch, his hand on her arm as he walked her to the house. She can't wait to see him again.

As she fills a glass with water in the bathroom, she wonders if her parents felt this way about each other at first, or if they ever do now. She hears the noises coming out of the bedroom every once in a while when she goes to pee in the middle of the night. She used to think they were fighting—that her mother was beating her father—but Peter set her straight and told her they were having sex. Maggie was shocked that they could hate each other so much one moment and then make love the next.

She closes her bedroom door and goes over to the dresser to examine her lemon tree shoots and wildflower seeds. "Hello," she says, lovingly pouring water into the dirt of her jars.

The storm is still raging outside, and it pleases her immensely that, in spite of the howling wind and broken tree branches strewn all over the yard, her seeds are calmly, stealthily growing in the sanctuary of her indoor garden, and there's nowhere else she'd rather be.

CHAPTER 5

—◁ʘ/ʘ/ʘ▷—

On a Saturday afternoon in late fall, when most of the leaves have already abandoned the trees and winter is beginning to settle over the Townships in its typically irrevocable manner, Maggie gazes out the window of her attic at the seed store, lost in her thoughts. Smoke rolls out of the chimneys across the street, and she imagines living rooms full of harmonious families sitting around the fire, laughing and talking tenderly and respectfully to one another. Inside every house but her own, she imagines, life unfolds in a more amiable, civilized manner.

A man's voice at the top of the attic stairs interrupts her daydreaming.

"*Calice*," he says.

She looks up from weighing her seeds, startled to find Gabriel standing there in a red-and-black-checkered hunting jacket with a wool cap. He looks like someone who could survive out in the wilderness alone, killing bears and lighting fires with sticks and living off the land, she thinks as he takes off his cap, shakes out his blond hair, and leans up against her table.

"You have to count all those seeds one by one?" he says.

"What are you doing up here?" she asks him, her heart pounding. Her father must have been busy with a customer and not seen Gabriel slip past; otherwise he certainly would have forbidden him access. "The store's about to close—"

"Clémentine is buying bulbs for her garden."

It's that time of year, right before the earth freezes and the farmers go into hibernation, before the snows falls and the farms lie buried, silent, when everyone in the area floods her father's store to buy spring blooming bulbs for their gardens.

"You must get bored weighing those goddamn seeds all day," he remarks.

"I don't mind it," she says. "I like the work."

He looks at her strangely, but she doesn't elaborate. How can she explain that there's so much more to it than just weighing seeds, which, admittedly, can become a bit mind-numbing? It's the place itself that's special: the wonderful smells, the conversation and laughter downstairs, being with her father in this enchanted world he's created.

Gabriel scoops up a handful of seeds. "I wouldn't have the patience."

"It's really not so bad," she says, holding out her hand. "Smell these."

He smells the seeds in her hand and shrugs. She can't help giggling.

She's glad she wore her pleated plaid skirt and the blouse with the lace edging today. Her hair is styled nicely, too. It's wavy and parted on the side, held in place with a barrette. Her head is still throbbing from when Maman did her waves in the morning, not with bobby pins, the way most mothers do it, but with the side of her hand, jabbing relentlessly against Maggie's skull until the waves took. At least now she can say it was worth it.

"Anyway, I couldn't do it," Gabriel says. "Up here in this hot attic all day."

She stares deeply into his gray eyes and gets lost there for a moment. His cheeks are flushed from the cold outside. He's lovely.

"It's good preparation," she says.

"For what?"

"I'm going to manage the store one day."

"Why would you want to do that?"

"I want to take over from my father," she explains, as though it should be obvious to him. "He can't do it forever."

Gabriel is about to say something when her father's footsteps on the stairs silence both of them. "Mr. Phénix," he says in French. "Customers aren't allowed up there."

Gabriel brushes past him on the stairwell on his way down. Before disappearing from Maggie's view, he turns back once and grins at her. Her heart soars.

Her father remains in the attic for a few minutes without speaking, his presence warning enough. He's cautioned Maggie many times about French boys, always reminding her that they're mostly poor, don't finish school, and their teeth rot before they turn forty. One year, when her uncle Yvon got so drunk he threw the Christmas tree out the front door, her father pulled her aside and whispered a stern warning about French Canadians and alcohol. "That's why you stick with your own kind," he said.

"But you didn't," Maggie pointed out while Peter and Deda dragged the tree back inside, leaving a trail of silver tinsel and broken glass balls.

"That was my mistake. You can't change them, Maggie. Remember that."

His words have always stayed with her. *You can't change them.*

Her father leans back against her worktable with his arms folded across his chest. Maggie seals an envelope of prickly poppy seeds with her tongue and drops it into the pile.

"A new shipment came in yesterday," her father says. "There's Lily-of-Peru seeds, tiger lilies . . . Did you see them?"

"I didn't get to them yet."

He looks at his watch. "I've got some bookkeeping to do. Why don't you go home without me today."

She contemplates the long walk home by herself. "I'll wait," she says. She enjoys their walks home together. Besides, hanging around the store is better than being at home with her mother. "I can start on those new seeds?"

He looks at his watch again. "Those Lilies-of-Peru are worth an absolute fortune," he says sternly. "Be very careful when you're weighing them. I'll need about an hour, undisturbed."

She salutes him mockingly.

"Be *accurate*," he reiterates. "No rushing, Margueret." No doubt he suspects her of guesstimating how many seeds to allot for each envelope, which she does occasionally when she falls behind. "If you want more responsibility here, you can't cut corners."

She nods obediently, her face warm with pride. She can't suppress her smile. The stairs creak as he heads back down.

"Maggie!" he calls out. "*Accurately*, eh?"

"Yes, sir!"

She dumps a pile of tiger lily seeds onto the table and starts weighing them, paying close attention to the scale. Measuring, measuring, undaunted by all the seeds before her. The tiger lilies are thin brown ovals surrounded by papery triangles. They feel scaly between her fingers. She crushes one to see what it feels like. The paper wing disintegrates into dust, leaving just a seed the size of her pinkie nail. She flicks it out the back window, destroying the evidence of her wastefulness. If she stares at a single seed long enough, she can forget what it is. She can even forget it's a seed at all, the way when you say a word over and over again, it loses its meaning. Her mind does funny things like that up in the attic.

Time passes. Her hands move deftly while her eyes record the numbers on the scale, her vision seemingly unconnected to her brain. She finishes another sack of tiger lilies and then dumps out a sack of Lilies-of-Peru. She checks the clock; she needs to take a bathroom break. There's only one in the store and it's directly below her, tucked under the staircase.

As she reaches the main floor, she glances over at her father's office. His door is closed, a sign the accounting is not going smoothly. He probably needs some cheering up. Maybe she'll poke her head in and say hi. He likes it when she does that. He always smiles and says in his ultraserious voice, *All right, Maggie, enough tomfoolery. Back upstairs you go.*

She quietly inches open the door, expecting to see him hunched over a stack of papers on his desk, his bifocals balanced on the tip of his nose. Instead, she finds him standing behind his desk with his back to her and his pants down, his white buttocks exposed. Maggie realizes he's not alone; someone she can't quite see through the crack of the door is crouched down in front of him. She watches for a moment, horror-struck and captivated, until her father moans with pleasure and collapses against the desk. And then a woman's voice cries out, "*Your daughter!*"

Maggie lets out a loud gasp. Her father turns around; his face is flushed and sweaty. Whoever he's with tries to stay hidden behind the desk, but her head bobs up for a split second, and Maggie instantly recognizes her golden braids. Clémentine.

Her father quickly pulls up his pants and looks right at Maggie, struggling with his zipper and belt buckle. Maggie, shocked more by his hubris than by the indiscretion itself, turns and flees.

"Maggie!"

As he utters her name, she bolts back to the staircase. She hears him say to Clémentine, "I told you this was stupid!"

"You could have locked the door," she hisses back in French. The door slams.

Maggie dashes up to the attic, snatches a handful of seeds, and starts counting mindlessly. The seeds are slippery in her damp, trembling hands; all she can see is the image of her father with his pants down.

Moments later, Maggie hears her father on the stairs and contemplates ducking under the table. He steps into the attic with his hair smoothed back in place and the natural pallor returned to his skin. He paces the floor behind Maggie. She continues counting her seeds one by one. *Eight, nine, ten, eleven.* He paces back and forth, rubbing his bald spot with his fingers, sighing, silent, troubled. Still, he does not speak. *Fourteen, fifteen, sixteen.*

"What you saw—" he finally says.

"I didn't really—"

"It was an accident."

"An accident?"

"Mm."

"I didn't really see anything."

"It doesn't . . . It won't—"

"I'm not going to say anything."

He expels a breath. She isn't sure if it's a sigh of relief or remorse, if it's a sigh at all. He continues to pace behind her quietly for another few minutes before turning around and descending the flight of stairs.

She lets the Lily-of-Peru seeds slide between her fingers like sand.

They walk home together in total silence. Maggie's father makes no attempt at levity. There's none of their usual banter, only the weight of their shared shame hanging between them in the cold. When they finally reach the house, Maggie rushes inside.

The kitchen smells of cloves and allspice. She spots three sugar pies lined up on the windowsill. Her mother is at the stove, stirring a giant pot of *ragoût de boulettes*. They must be having company.

"You'd better get ready," Maman says. "Everyone will be here at seven."

"Who's everyone?" her father wants to know.

"I told you I invited the Dions and the Frechettes," she says impatiently, turning to give him a disapproving look. She isn't wearing her corset yet, which makes Maggie so furious she has to look away. She resents her mother's sagging breasts and loose belly, wishes she had made more of an effort to preserve her beauty over the years. What happened at the store today can only be her mother's fault.

"I'm in no mood to entertain," her father mutters, avoiding making eye contact with Maggie. "It's been a long day."

"Put the beer in the icebox," Maman says, ignoring him. "You walked right past it in the mudroom."

Hours later, the house is alive with music and raucous laughter. At the center of it sits her father, smoking a cigar and slapping a pair of spoons on his knee to the tune of "Les Filles du Canada," the humiliation of this afternoon seemingly forgotten. M. Dion is accompanying him with the fiddle, and the women are clapping and singing along. Maman opens a window to let in some fresh air.

"Hahaha!" they roar. *"Les filles du Canada!"*

Maggie's father helps himself to a long swig of Crown Royal. His cheeks are ruddy and splotched, his eyes glassy. Maggie usually loves it when her parents' rare good moods collide. It's pure serendipity when her father loosens up and morphs into a more vulgar, uninhibited version of himself and, at the same time, Maman relaxes and forgets to be miserable. It doesn't happen often, but when it does, it makes Maggie feel like their family is all right after all, that they're no less happy than other families. But tonight, Maggie's burden lingers, dampening her enjoyment. She can't get out of her mind the image of Clémentine Phénix hiding behind her father's desk and its greater implication on their lives.

Her father suddenly drops the spoons on the table, jumps to his feet, and pulls Maman to the middle of the room. He holds her tightly around the waist and expertly swings her around, as though they've done this before many times, and then he dips her, right there in the living room. To Maggie's and everyone else's astonishment, Maman kicks out her leg and tosses her head back blithely, laughing.

Everyone applauds, including Maggie, in spite of her confusion. Maybe it's best not to try to understand a thing like marriage, she reasons. Not yet. She's on a different path anyway.

CHAPTER 6

"Pass it over," Audrey says, reaching for the cigarette they're sharing. She blows four perfect smoke rings into the air.

It's early spring and Dunham is thawing. Maggie and Audrey are sitting on the front stoop of the Small Bros. building, where they make the equipment for producing maple syrup. Maggie blossomed over the winter. The onslaught of adolescence is fully upon her. Her legs are longer—she towers over Nan and Audrey now—and although she's still skinny, her breasts have swelled a full cup size. She wears her black hair longer, and instead of the waves curling around her ears in a sweet bob, they now fall to her shoulders, giving her what she thinks is a more sophisticated look. She's started wearing red lipstick, which she puts on after school and removes before going home.

Audrey hands Maggie the cigarette and she takes a long drag.

"I'm meeting Gabriel Phénix here," Audrey confesses.

"Gabriel? Why?" Maggie hasn't seen Gabriel since the fall, except for one brief glimpse when he came home to plant his corn.

"He invited me to go to Selby Lake with him," Audrey says, flushing.

"Like a date?"

"Yes, a date."

Maggie blinks. "You have a date with Gabriel Phénix?"

"Don't tell anyone, okay, Mags?" she says, flicking an ash into the slush at her feet. "He's so cute, but he's a frog." Her long lashes flutter adorably. "It's embarrassing."

Everything about Audrey McCauley makes Maggie feel deficient, from her golden curls to her shiny saddle shoes to her perfect WASP family. The last time Maggie was at her house, Audrey's mother was wearing a pink tweed dress with pearls, and her father, Dr. McCauley, was reading the newspaper in a winged armchair by the fire. Her little sister was playing the piano beside him. The whole tableau filled Maggie with inexplicable despair. How simple it must be to be one of them, Maggie thought to herself that day. In all the years she's been friends with Audrey, she's never once seen evidence of any sides or opponents, or even any noticeable undercurrents of animosity. They're just a family with a singular, common purpose: to be the McCauleys and thereby make others feel inferior. For Maggie to have lost Gabriel to Audrey makes the defeat all the more insulting.

"He's bringing a friend," Audrey says. "For you."

"I don't want to go."

Maggie's voice is drowned out by the roar of motorcycles. Audrey jumps to her feet. Gabriel and his friend pull up to the curb. Gabriel looks Maggie up and down, as though he's never seen her before. His expression reveals nothing. "Hey, Maggie," he says.

She glares back at him.

"This is my friend, Jean-François."

"Everyone calls me JF," he says, eyeing Maggie like he's just won first prize. He's not bad looking. He's got dark eyes and a bluish sheen to his frozen black pompadour. But when he smiles, she notices he's missing a bottom tooth. *Pepsis and their rotten teeth*, her father would say.

"Let's go," Gabriel says.

Audrey climbs on the back of his bike and wraps her arms around his waist. She grins stupidly, and Maggie wants to grab a fistful of her golden waves and pull her right off that motorcycle.

"You coming?" Gabriel asks Maggie.

Audrey gives her a pleading look. At least if she goes with them she'll be able to keep an eye on Gabriel. She gets on the back of JF's bike and notices that not a wisp of his blue pompadour moves in the wind.

Maggie's father has warned her about the apocalyptic possibilities of speeding down country roads on a motorcycle—careening into tractors, flipping over into ditches, slamming into utility poles. Last year, a St. Helen's girl died on the back of her boyfriend's motorcycle. Maggie closes her eyes. The wind is cold against her face, battering her cheeks until they feel bruised. She feels strangely exhilarated, wishing it were Gabriel she was holding on to.

Selby Lake is at the foot of Mount Pinnacle. Maggie has spent many summer days here grilling under the sun by the water, reading on the veranda of the canteen, chatting with the guests from Pinnacle Lodge. There's a dance at the dance hall every Saturday night and this summer she'll be old enough to jitterbug until the lights come on.

They park in front of the old abandoned Selby barn. The cottages stand empty and abandoned. The only people left after Labour Day are the farmers, who emerge only to cut ice or fish on the frozen lake. It's gray and mournful, and Maggie realizes she's never been here in the off-season. She follows the others inside the barn. The sky through the window is layered pink and orange, glowing like the inside of a pumpkin. "What's in your pockets?" Gabriel asks JF.

JF pulls out two bottles of Labatt Fifty and a long piece of black licorice. He tosses a beer to Gabriel.

"I'm cold," Audrey says. Gabriel unzips his leather jacket and hangs it over her shoulders.

Audrey reaches for Gabriel's hand and tugs him toward the loft. It's a famous make-out spot and Maggie realizes with a sinking heart that Audrey and Gabriel have been here before. Gabriel lets Audrey pull him away. He looks back once at Maggie, but she quickly turns away as he follows Audrey up the ladder like a puppy.

The moment they're alone, JF lunges at Maggie. There's a look in his eyes that reminds her of a wolf, but she holds her breath and tells herself it's her only chance to make Gabriel jealous. As his teeth clack against hers, she thinks about his missing tooth and has to suppress a gag. He manages to maneuver her to the ground and get her flat on her back. *My first kiss.*

JF unbuttons her coat. She doesn't stop him because she doesn't want him to report back to Gabriel that she's a prude. Besides, the more they do, presumably the worse Gabriel will feel. He flattens her breast with the palm of his hand. She closes her eyes and resigns herself to his grubby hands on her rib cage. "Ouch," she says.

He kneads her breasts, his fingertips icy on her flesh. She lets him grope her for a while before finally pushing him off.

"Heh?" he cries indignantly.

"Stop, please."

"*Maudite Anglaise,*" he mutters. "You're all prudes."

His breath smells like black licorice and cigarettes. They sit there sullenly, not speaking, until Gabriel and Audrey finally come down from the loft. By now it's dark, but she can see that Audrey's cheeks are red. She's disheveled and sheepish. Gabriel has an impassive look on his face. JF gets up and strides out of the barn, making a show of disgust. He doesn't even help Maggie to her feet. Gabriel doesn't seem at all jealous, which means she kissed that creep for nothing. She trails after Gabriel and Audrey, utterly miserable.

Gabriel suddenly turns to Maggie and says, "I'll take you home."

Maggie freezes. Audrey looks perplexed. "She lives next door to me," Gabriel explains.

"So?" Audrey has her hands on her hips.

"It's just easier," he says. "Get on, Maggie."

Maggie's spirits soar.

"Maggie!" Audrey says angrily.

Maggie hesitates. "We're going to the same place, Aud."

And then she climbs on the back of Gabriel's motorcycle and presses her chest against his back. He revs up his engine and they drive off, leaving Audrey and JF standing in front of the barn by themselves.

She doesn't even feel the cold. Gabriel's clean blond hair blows in the wind, the way hair should. She wraps her arms even tighter around his waist, inhaling the slope of his neck. Her insides are warm.

When they reach Bruce Street, her heart sinks. She wants to keep riding. She would go anywhere with him. But he comes to a stop and Maggie reluctantly gets off.

"Thanks for the ride," she says, trying to keep her tone light.

"Did JF try something?" he asks her.

"That's none of your business."

He turns to face her. "I like you, Maggie," he says.

She doesn't know how to respond.

"I just wanted you to know."

"What about Audrey?"

"You're the one I've always wanted."

Her mouth goes dry. Did she hear that right?

"Your father told me to stay away from you," he says, pulling her toward him.

"He did? When?"

"That day I came up to the attic to talk to you. Right before I left for Montreal."

"I didn't know."

"So, should I?" he asks.

"What?"

"Stay away from you."

"No . . . I mean. You don't have to."

He's staring at her, unflinching. His face is so close. She leans in slightly, their noses almost touching. Her lids close, and she feels his lips on hers, lightly at first, and then with more urgency. His hand moves to the back of her neck, the other one under her chin. He is a beautiful kisser. This will be her first kiss, she decides, erasing all memory of that barbaric experience with JF.

"*Maaaaaggie!*"

It's her mother. She quickly pulls away from Gabriel and looks toward her house. The kitchen window is open and she can hear her mother yelling her name into the late afternoon. "I have to go," Maggie says.

"Meet me outside the Small Bros. building tomorrow after school," he tells her.

Maggie nods, and he kisses her again. His tongue tastes sweet. She races to her house, not knowing what to expect and not much caring.

CHAPTER 7

———⁓⁓⁓———

Maggie loves watching Gabriel move through the field, tending to his corn, opening husks, pulling off tassels. If it gets too hot, he lifts his white T-shirt over his head and stuffs it into the back pocket of his jeans. She follows behind him, smiling, knowing he belongs to her now, as much as this land she loves so much.

"It's looking good," Gabriel says, relieved. "That cold spell didn't kill off too many seedlings."

He doesn't have to explain his concerns to her. She knows corn can tolerate some frost in the early seedling stage, but they're more vulnerable when the soil temperature plunges below freezing. This year, the cold weather dragged on well into March, causing the farmers much fretting over their crops. Gabriel kneels down on one knee and inspects the tufts of silk hanging out of the husks. A light breeze sweeps across the field, dusting it with pollen. The corn grows.

"Come," he says.

"Where?"

He pulls her by the hand and they head deep into the field, until they're completely swallowed by the stalks.

"Let's get lost in here," she says.

With school winding down and the weather finally warm, they've been able to spend more time together. Her father is always at work, and her mother prefers the kids to be out of the house as much as possible. Once the chores are done, Maman hardly cares where they go or what they do as long as they come running the moment her voice thunders across the field.

Maggie and Gabriel lie down side by side on their backs. Gabriel flings his arm out and she rests her head on his biceps. The leaf of a stalk tickles her thigh and she rolls closer to Gabriel. He's twirling her hair in his fingers, and when he accidently brushes her cheek with his fingertip, she shivers.

"I love it here in the field," she says.

"Me, too."

She props herself up on one elbow and gazes into his face. His eyes are silvery in the sun. "Why do you have to go to Montreal all winter?" she asks him.

He looks at her strangely. "Money," he says. "Why else?"

He's been working at Canadair, the airplane-parts factory, in the off-season since he was fifteen. It troubles Maggie, the thought of him returning to Montreal for the winter. It's hard for her to enjoy their time together now, to be fully present with him when the deadline looms large, casting its shadow over these precious days.

"There's nowhere else you can work around here?"

"I don't mind Canadair," he says. "As factory work goes, it's not the worst."

"What will happen to us in the fall?" she asks him.

"It's only June, Maggie," he says. "A lot can happen from now till then." He slides a strand of hair away from her eyes. "You're so pretty," he tells her.

"I am?"

He laughs. "You have no idea. That's why I love you."

She doesn't move. Just lets his words settle over her.

"I love you, too," she whispers.

Without another word, he rolls on top of her and they kiss for a long time. She can feel him growing hard against her thigh. Her shirt is coming undone, her bra being unfastened. She's the one doing the unbuttoning.

They've never gone this far before. Her heart is racing. He pushes her skirt up and then hesitates, so she's the one who leads his hand to her thigh. "You sure?" he breathes.

"Yes."

In that moment, she is absolutely fearless, her worries absent. It hurts fiercely, but beneath the pain, or entangled with it, one inseparable from the other, is such excruciating pleasure, she has to cry out with every thrust. When he finishes, he collapses on top of her. His jeans and underwear are down around his ankles. His backside is wet, his hair drenched. Her arms are wrapped around his torso. Suddenly he seems so vulnerable.

They lie there like that for a long time and he stays inside her. For no reason, she starts to cry. He lifts his head, alarmed. "Why are you crying?" he asks. "I'm sorry. I shouldn't have."

"No," she says. "I wanted to."

"Then why are you crying?" he asks her.

"Happiness."

"I really do think I love you," he says.

She knows boys lie, especially for sex. But she believes him. His eyes don't lie. His pounding heart is not lying. He drops his head back down, resting it on her shoulder. She closes her eyes and the afternoon slowly slips away.

And then as usual her mother's voice shatters the stillness, echoing throughout the field. *"Maaaaaagggggggie!"*

Gabriel jumps to his feet and pulls up his pants. "You better go," he says, sounding afraid. "She'll kill us both with that goddamn wooden spoon of hers."

Maggie laughs and fastens the clasp of her bra, buttons her shirt, pulls up her panties, and straightens her skirt over her bloodstained thighs.

He takes her by the hand and helps her to her feet, and they walk solemnly out into the world. The weight of it presses down on her. She's done the very thing she's been warned against since the onset of puberty—not just sex, but sex with a French boy. She's given herself to him and there's no turning back now.

She can see her mother waving the pig spoon, making wild gestures in the doorway, looking ridiculous.

"What are you doing with *him?*" Maman cries out, even though Maggie is still only midway up the hill. *"Vas t'en!"* she tells Gabriel.

"Meet me in the field tomorrow at three," he whispers, and her heart flutters. His motorcycle is parked in a clearing by the road. He gets on, revs it up, and speeds away. They don't even have time to kiss good-bye.

"I was reading in the field," Maggie says, approaching her mother. "Gabriel happened to be there. He's a farmer, remember?"

She manages to slip past into the kitchen. There's soup bubbling on the stove. The radio is on low, and she recognizes Tino Rossi's voice, which her mother adores. The butter, flour, and sugar are all laid out on the counter in preparation for Maman's Saturday baking. A pot of coffee sits on the pine table.

"Violet says she saw you on his motorcycle the other day," Maman says.

"So?"

Thwack—the pig spoon on Maggie's behind. "Stop it!" Maggie cries, knowing she's too old for these beatings.

"You're forbidden to ride on motorcycles, remember?" she says, her arm in the air, poised for another smack.

"I'm almost sixteen," Maggie reminds her. "He's my boyfriend, whether you like it or not."

Her mother steps back with a strange expression on her face. "You're just like him," she says, shaking her head.

"Who?"

"Your father. You're both English snobs who like to screw French Canadians."

Maggie is stung by the remark, but it bolsters her. "I love him," she says defiantly.

"Love him?" Maman repeats. "Who do you think you are? One of those dimwits from your romance magazines?"

Maggie's face blazes. She looks around the room for something to throw. Maman is watching her, knowing exactly what could happen next. Maybe they're alike in that way—the short fuse, the temper. Maggie's eyes light on the pot of coffee.

Her mother smiles. *I dare you*, her dark eyes challenge. But Maggie has enough restraint not to do the thing her mother would do. Instead, she runs upstairs to her room and slams the door, worried about how her mother will retaliate.

CHAPTER 8

=⧈⧈⧈=

They drive past miles and miles of yellow cattail grass growing wild on the side of the road, while the Yamaska River flows alongside them in perfect sync with the speed of Gabriel's motorcycle. It's the beginning of summer and Maggie appreciates all of it with fresh eyes today, this scenery she can sometimes take for granted—the barns with their rusted corrugated tin roofs, the silos and the cows, the endless cornfields glinting gold in the sunshine. Everything with Gabriel seems shinier, more worthy of her attention. Every smell is more fragrant, every color more intense. She loves this boy, whose solid torso she holds on to for safety; she loves this endless road and the wind whipping her hair into her face. In front of her lie miles and miles of possibility.

Gabriel is so much more than her father's narrow-minded caricature of French Canadians. He'll never understand the depth and complexity of Gabriel's heart, his loyalty. He fiercely loves Maggie, his sisters, his little niece. He would do anything for them. The other day, he beat up a guy who told Angèle she looked like an ape. And his eyes fill with tears whenever he talks about how Clémentine raised him, about their poverty and the mistreatment of the Québécois in their own province.

It hasn't been easy for them to be a couple. Gabriel's friends dislike Maggie. With her tartan kilts and penny loafers and her English Protestant father, she's the symbol of all the injustices and indignities they've ever suffered. In their world, there are two distinct sides and no one can ever fall in between or cross over to the other side. French and English. Catholics and Protestants. Maggie, with her mixed blood and incompatible religions, will never be one of them.

Gabriel points to the sign for Sainte-Angèle-de-Monnoir and turns off. When he brings the bike to a stop along the side of the river, he turns to Maggie and says, "My mother was born here."

"You must miss them."

"I guess so," he responds, tensing. He rarely talks about his parents. Every once in a while he mentions how young his father was when he died, usually in reference to his own mortality, but never more than that. Everything Maggie knows about Gabriel's father is from town gossip.

He gets off the bike and helps Maggie off. She hands him his knapsack and he pulls out a blanket and a bottle of wine in a brown paper bag. They sit cross-legged on the blanket. He pours them each a paper cup of wine.

"What do you want to do when you grow up?" she asks him, realizing they've never talked about it before. "What do you want to be?"

He looks at her blankly. "Be? I don't know. I'd run our farm if Clémentine wasn't such a pain in the ass. I'll probably wind up a foreman at Canadair."

Maggie smiles, covering her disappointment.

"I know I don't want to die with nothing," he adds. "My father died with nothing. And he left us with nothing."

"You could be anything," she encourages. "You're smart enough."

Gabriel shrugs. "I love working the field," he admits. "But Clémentine is in charge and she's too bossy. She treats me like a kid."

"Maybe you could have your own farm," Maggie suggests.

He doesn't answer.

"Whatever you decide, you'll be successful," she tells him, wrapping her arms around his neck.

They make love. Afterwards, they lie lazily under the sun for a long time, ignoring the ants crawling all over their legs.

"I pulled out," he mentions. "So you don't have to worry."

She looks at him and smiles, relieved. "I'm so happy here with you," she says.

"Mm. Me too."

When the sun finally begins to drop and the sky fades to pink, they head back to Dunham, silent and content. Gabriel pulls over at the gas station outside of town. "There's a rattling noise," he explains. "I'm going to leave the bike here to get it checked out."

As they approach the corner of Principale and Bruce Streets, walking hand-in-hand, Maggie notices a gang of kids from Cowansville High milling around in front of the Small Bros. building. Now that school is out, they mostly hang out in the street, waiting for something to happen.

Maggie spots Audrey in the middle of the pack and her heart sinks. They haven't been close since Maggie started dating Gabriel. Audrey has a whole new clique of friends now and a new boyfriend from Cowansville High, though she's held on to her old attitude of entitlement. As Maggie and Gabriel pass, Audrey's boyfriend, a stocky redhead, says loud enough for Gabriel to hear, "Well, if it isn't Maggie Hughes slumming with her Pepsi beau."

"Oh, Barney, be quiet," Audrey scolds, mock angry. "Ignore him, Mags."

Maggie looks nervously at Gabriel.

"What did you call me?" Gabriel says, taking a step toward Barney.

"I'm sorry, I don't speak Pepsi," Barney says, puffing up his chest. His friends join in, egging him on. *Peasoup, Pepsi.*

Gabriel's eyes get that dangerous steely look and his hands ball into fists. Maggie steps back. Before Barney even has a thought of self-defense, Gabriel's right fist cracks into his jaw. Barney stumbles back, shocked. The Cowansville High boys encircle Gabriel and start throwing punches at him. Audrey and Maggie scream helplessly. Gabriel, dangerously outnumbered, is getting pummeled. He crouches down to deflect the barrage of blows, and then someone yells, "The peasoup's got a knife!"

The English boys suddenly retreat and disperse, leaving Gabriel standing alone on the street, holding up his dead father's pocket knife.

"What's going on here?"

Maggie turns to see her father getting out of his car. He marches angrily toward them. "What is going on here?"

"This degenerate pulled a knife!" Barney cries.

Maggie's father looks from Barney to Maggie in confusion.

"They ganged up on him—" she explains.

"He punched me in the jaw," Barney moans, rubbing his chin. "All my friends did was help me out. Then he pulled that knife."

Maggie's father turns to Gabriel, who hasn't uttered a single word in his own defense, nor seems inclined to. He makes no attempt to conceal the knife either.

"Get in the car, Maggie," says her father.

She looks over at Gabriel. He doesn't meet her gaze.

"Go," her father orders. Then, turning to Barney, he says calmly, "Son, I'm on your side, but you should know better than to taunt someone like him."

With that, he drags Maggie to the Packard and gives her a push into the front seat. She's so ashamed—of her father's bigotry, of Gabriel for pulling the knife, of herself for doing nothing—she can't even bring herself to look at Gabriel.

As she drives off with her father, though, she watches him standing there in the street, stone-faced, with the knife still clenched in his hand. His nose is bleeding, his lip swollen, his white T-shirt torn to shreds. He stays there for as long as she can see him in the rearview mirror.

Later that night, after everyone has gone to bed, Maggie hovers outside her father's sanctuary. She watches the cigar smoke curl up from under the door and knocks tentatively.

"Come in," he says.

She's always loved this room. It's such a man's world, the very essence of her father. There are radio parts on the table and homemade radios—some finished, others mid-dissection—all over the floor.

There's a stack of empty House of Lords cigar boxes on the shelf he built, alongside all his books—*Handbook for Gardeners, Operating a Garden Center, Native Trees of Canada*, Dale Carnegie's *How to Stop Worrying and Start Living*.

"What do you think of Petunia Colour Parade for the cover of next season's catalogue?" he asks her.

"I like it."

"Remember last year's?" he says, handing her the '48 catalogue. She opens it and leafs through the pages.

COSMOS MANDARIN First new all double cosmos. The large bright orange flowers have as many as 40 to 50 petals, making them really double, but even more impressive is the foliage.

Sixty-four pages of single-spaced typeface. She holds it with the kind of reverence one might reserve for a precious work of art, admiring Peter's hand-drawn diagrams of wooden pot labels, bamboo cane stakes, plant ties, and hose nozzles. "Next year I'm looking into using real photographs," her father says. "Wouldn't that be sophisticated?"

"Very," Maggie says, pulling down one of the tattered books from his shelf. "'Sow seed generously,'" she reads aloud. "'One for the rook, one for the crow, one to die, and one to grow.' I remember you used to read that to me."

She runs her finger along the spine of *A Field Guide for Wildflowers*.

"You can do better than a French Canadian," he says.

"You didn't."

"It's different," he says, putting the catalogue back on the shelf. "Your mother's not the one who had to earn the living." Smoke from his panatela fills the room. "Besides, I've acknowledged my mistake. You can learn from it."

She remembers: *You can't change them.*

"Why did you marry her?" she asks him.

He looks at her wearily and sighs, offering a single, defeated word by way of explanation. "Lust," he says. "She's always had a strange power over me. Still does."

As soon as he says it, Maggie understands the way Gabriel makes her feel. It's the reason her parents can sometimes hate each other and still want to dance together and have sex. Now it has a name. *Lust*.

"You're forbidden to see him, Maggie. Do you hear me?"

"Those English boys started it today."

"He's a hoodlum. He's not our kind and you deserve better. This is not how I raised you."

Her head buzzes at his hypocrisy. She wants to scream, *And what about Clémentine?* But she holds back, too terrified to crack the fragile wall of silence and denial they tacitly erected that day. It is the only way their relationship can be sustained.

"I'm not cattle," she says. "Why can't you let me be happy?"

"I of all people know you can't be happy with him."

"He's not Maman."

"Isn't he, though?"

She doesn't answer.

"Please don't cross me on this, Margueret."

"You can't tell me who to love," she says, daring to defy him for the first time in her life. "I can love whoever I want."

He smiles thinly, his lips disappearing, and she has the fleeting thought that the two things she wants most in the world—Gabriel's love and her father's approval—cannot coexist, and that one will eventually have to be sacrificed for the other.

CHAPTER 9

The next morning when Maggie comes downstairs, she notices a suit-case by the back door. Her mother is making bread, working the dough with her fists.

"Who's leaving?" Maggie asks.

"You are," Maman responds, giving the dough a hard punch.

Maggie opens the suitcase, and her heart plunges when she sees her clothes, neatly pressed and folded. She must have slept through her mother's packing. "Where?" she asks, panicking. "Where am I going?"

"You've got a summer job on your uncle Yvon's farm," she says.

Her aunt and uncle live on a dairy farm in Frelighsburg, about six miles away from Dunham. They don't visit very often because of Deda's weight. It's hard for her to move around. Alfreda—they call her Deda—must weigh close to three hundred pounds. All of Maggie's memories of her involve her elephantine shape moored into an absurdly small pressed-back chair. Even the most negligible movements leave her panting and spent. Maman rarely visits them because Deda is too fat to clean and their house is filthy. In spite of that, Maggie likes her aunt. She's affectionate and warm, with a robust laugh that emanates from the depths of her enormous belly.

Her father comes into the room then and Maggie turns to him. "Was this your idea?" she asks him.

"Settle down, Maggie," says her father.

"I don't want to work on Yvon's farm," she says. "I want to keep working with you at the seed store—"

"Yvon can pay you much better wages."

"I don't care about better wages! I want to stay here!"

"It's just one summer."

Her mind is whirling. What about Gabriel? What if he leaves for Montreal before she gets back? "Please don't make me go," she says. They don't understand. She can't be away from Gabriel, or the seed store.

"Yvon got a contract selling his milk to Guaranteed," her father explains. "It's a big deal for them. So you see, this isn't about you, Maggie. He needs someone to help out on the farm, and frankly, we could use the extra money."

"I was eleven years old when I started supporting my family," Maman says, wiping her hands on her flour-covered apron.

"Don't worry, you can keep some of it," her father promises, adjusting his Panama hat. "Now go say good-bye to your sisters."

"I'm not going," she says. "You can't force me." But even as the words leave her mouth, she knows she's already lost the battle. She's fifteen. What can she do? Run off with Gabriel and get married? Live in poverty in his shack or at his uncle's apartment in Montreal? She underestimated her parents.

"Go on."

Maggie doesn't move. She looks desperately from one to the other, silently beseeching them to change their minds.

"*I said go,*" her father repeats, raising his voice.

"I hate you both!" Maggie cries, running from the room. She climbs the stairs slowly, feeling a crushing sense of shock and betrayal. How can he do this to her?

She hugs and kisses her sisters, sobbing and clinging to them.

"Are you ever coming back?" Geri asks, wide-eyed.

"In the fall," Maggie says. "If they let me."

She kisses Nicole's plump red cheek one last time, grabs a few things her mother didn't bother to pack—notepaper, pencil box, makeup, a handful of romance magazines—and returns to the kitchen in defeat. "I know you're doing this to keep me away from Gabriel," she says.

Her father finishes his coffee and doesn't respond. Maman turns slightly, her expression unreadable. She approaches Maggie and pecks her on the head. "It's not forever," she says.

Maggie's exile is probably the first thing her parents have agreed on in years.

Her father takes her suitcase to the car. Gabriel doesn't have a telephone, so she can't even call him to say good-bye. She runs outside and searches Gabriel's property, hoping to spot him. "Can I just go and say good-bye?" she asks her father.

"There's no time, Maggie," he says. "I have to get you to Frelighsburg and then back in time to open the store."

"Please!"

"It's too early in the morning for all this melodrama," he says. "Stop fancying yourself Juliet and get in the car."

They drive the fifteen minutes to Frelighsburg in silence. Maggie stares grimly out the window.

"Gorgeous day," her father chirps.

She looks over at him, seething. He starts to whistle. He whistles the rest of the way to the farm, while she composes an impassioned letter to Gabriel in her head.

Frelighsburg is a small town nestled at the bottom of a steep winding hill and sandwiched between the Saint-François-d'Assise Catholic Church and the Holy Trinity Anglican Church. The Pike River flows right through the middle, clearly marking the town's boundaries: French on one side, English on the other. In the cemetery behind the Saint-François-d'Assise Church, the stones are marked TOUCHETTE, PIETTE, GOYETTE. At the Anglican cemetery there are the WHITCOMBS, BYRONS, SPENCERS. Even dead, the French and English remain segregated.

When they pull up to the farm, Deda is waiting for them outside in a rocking chair. She's wearing a loose, stained frock and slippers. She manages to get up and meet them halfway, already flushed and out of breath. Maggie's father doesn't even go inside the house. He unloads her suitcase, sets it down on the side of the road, pecks her on the cheek, and gets back in his Packard.

"Can't be late for work," her father calls out, rolling down his window. "Take care, my Black Beauty."

And then he drives off, his tires kicking up a cloud of gravel as he goes. Maggie watches him disappear, feeling abandoned, bereft. Hating him, but longing for him to turn back for her just the same.

"Come, *cocotte*," says her aunt, appearing next to her and putting a fat arm around her shoulder. "Let's go find your uncle."

The one thing Maggie can be grateful for is that her aunt and uncle are both easygoing and fun—especially Yvon. Even Maman melts when he's around, laughing at his jokes and fawning all over him because he was in the war. He still wears his soldier's uniform with the forest green wedge cap to all their holiday parties, even though he's been back almost five years. He sings war songs and always smells of wet wool, whiskey, and Brylcreem.

"You get more beautiful all the time," he says, pulling Maggie into his arms. "How old are you now? Sixteen?"

"Fifteen," she responds, barely recognizing him out of his uniform.

He shakes his head in disbelief. He has a glorious pile of wavy black hair that parts naturally in the middle and falls over his eyelids in the shape of a heart. He's very handsome in spite of the big stomach that now bulges over the top of his belt buckle.

Maggie looks around, remembering why her mother doesn't like to visit. Their house is dark and gloomy. The drab Victorian furniture is all in tones of maroon and deep brown, and Maggie can see that everything is dirty. There are dust *minous* floating around on the wood floors, cobwebs in the corners, mucky boots and shoes piled in a heap by the door, and discarded *Union des Producteurs Agricoles* newspapers stacked on the floor of the foyer.

Deda notices Maggie looking around and says, "It'll be nice to have help around here. It's hard for me to manage."

Maggie can't wait to give the place a good cleaning. Deda slices up some fresh bread and pours Maggie a glass of unpasteurized milk.

It reminds her of Nicole's spit-up. "You'll get used to it," Deda says cheerily.

They go upstairs to see Maggie's room, which is as dark as the rest of the house. There's one small lamp on the bedside table, which does little to brighten it up. "Do you mind if I lie down for a bit?" she says. "I'm tired."

"Of course, *cocotte*."

When she's alone, Maggie climbs into the iron bed and pulls the patchwork quilt up to her nose. It's scratchy and heavy and weighs almost as much as she does. Like all the quilts in her mother's family, it's made from the wool worsted remnants of men's suits— herringbone, houndstooth, pinstripes, tweed. It smells of cedar. Maggie cries softly. Everything is strange here. The darkness is darker, the air heavier. She misses her pretty wallpaper and fresh sheets that smell of soap, her sisters' warm bodies in the bed.

She can't stop thinking of Gabriel. After a while, she pulls out some notepaper and a pencil and writes out the letter she composed in her mind on the way here.

> *June 28, 1949*
>
> *Dear Gabriel,*
> *I'm sorry I couldn't say good-bye, there was no time. I've been sent to Frelighsburg to work on my uncle's dairy farm, under the pretext of my family needing the money. But we all know I've been banished here to keep me away from you. I will send letters as often as I can. Wait for me, my Love! They can't keep us apart!*
>
> > *Yours forever,*
> > *Maggie*

The days unravel quietly, without any of the tense eruptions she's used to at home. Maggie's job is to help with *"le train,"* which is what the farmers call their morning routine. She cleans the cow stalls, collects eggs from the coop, washes and plucks feathers off dead chickens. She also helps Deda with the cooking and cleaning, which isn't so bad because her hard work is always rewarded with praise and accolades. If she misses a grease stain on the stove, Deda never notices. She's just happy to have a clean glass and fork at mealtime. By the time Maggie falls into bed at night, she hasn't the energy to feel sorry for herself or lie awake mourning her separation from Gabriel. She just sleeps.

"Pluck the feathers right out," Deda instructs. She's teaching Maggie how to pluck a chicken. "Like this. Don't be afraid to hurt the bird. He's already dead."

They're sitting side by side on the porch, staring at the tender pink bellies of two chickens in their laps. There's a stream of sweat trickling down the side of Deda's face as she works. "That's good, Maggie," she encourages. "And then the feathers go right into this barrel. I save them for stuffing pillows."

Maggie tosses a handful of feathers into the barrel. A breeze sweeps across the porch, and some of them blow away and land in Deda's hair. She giggles and shakes her head. In spite of everything, there are still moments of pleasure.

"You must have a boyfriend in Dunham," Deda remarks, reaching for another chicken. "A girl as pretty as you. What's his name? I won't say anything."

"Gabriel," Maggie confesses, dying to talk about him with someone. She mailed her letter to him on her first day at the farm, and now she's waiting for his response.

"Gabriel was the angel who told Mary she would bear a son that would be Savior of the world," Deda explains. "I suppose it's his letter you're waiting for?"

Maggie looks away.

"I envy you," Deda says. "Having all that in front of you. You can still pick the right man, someone who will make you happy."

"I can't wait to go back," Maggie says. "They can't keep us apart forever. Eventually they'll have to accept us together."

"And he'll wait for you?"

"Yes, I think so," Maggie says, sounding more confident than she feels. She puts her chicken down and turns to her aunt. "Are my parents happy together, do you think?"

Deda gives her a bewildered look. "You live with them," she says. "You'd know better than me."

"I know, but they fight so much. And then they dance together . . ."

Deda laughs. "That's about right."

Maggie waits for something more, but that's all Deda says.

The next morning, there's a letter for Maggie in the mailbox.

> *I'm terrible at writing. I'm coming to see you. Saturday at noon in front of the Church.*
>
> *GP*

On Saturday, Maggie washes her hair and puts on the one Sunday dress her mother packed. She tells Deda she's going into town to buy stamps and have a soda at Freshy's. Deda smiles.

Gabriel is already waiting for her in front of the Saint-François-d'Assise Church when she arrives. He climbs off his bike and she runs to him. He pulls her into his arms and inhales the smell of her hair. They stand there holding each other for a long time before she even lifts her head. She can barely look at him, like not being able to look straight at the sun. "I miss you," she says, bursting into tears.

"It's only been a week," he says, stroking her hair. He leads her into the cemetery behind the church. "There's no cornstalks, but it'll do."

"I don't have much time," she says. "An hour maybe."

They sit down on the grass and she lays her head in his lap. "It's hard being here all alone," she tells him. "By the time I get back to Dunham at the end of the summer, you'll be leaving for Montreal."

"I can come home on weekends to see you. Or maybe you'll come with me."

"I still have school," she reminds him. "I have to finish."

"Why?"

The question startles her. The answer should be self-explanatory. She feels a slight dip of disappointment, but quickly shoves it aside. She wants their reunion to be perfect. He lies down beside her, and they kiss and nuzzle among the tombstones for a while.

"How is it here?" he asks her.

"Lonely," she says. "But my aunt and uncle are nice."

"Your parents must sure want to keep you away from me."

"After what happened with Barney—"

"You think that was my fault?"

"You didn't have to pull the knife."

"You didn't have to get in your father's car and leave me alone in the street."

She looks away.

"You're a lot like him," Gabriel points out, and he means it as an insult, just like her mother did.

"Well, from what I hear you're a lot like your father," she fires back.

"I'm not my father."

She shrugs, wanting to hurt him. "Anyway," she says, "I'm glad I'm like my dad."

Gabriel is quiet for a few minutes, and just when she thinks he's moved on and they'll be able to lie down in the grass and kiss and touch each other, he says, "You think you're better than me."

"I do not."

"I hate the way you looked at me that day in town."

"What way?"

"The way your father looks at me."

"That isn't true," she says. "You're looking for a reason to fight with me!"

"You were ashamed of me."

"You shouldn't have pulled the knife."

Gabriel lies back, pulling Maggie down with him. "Your father thinks he can stop us being together," he murmurs, running his hand up her calf, her thigh, between her legs.

"Is that what this is about?" she asks, as his hand inches closer to her panties. "Besting my father?"

He doesn't answer. And then she feels his finger inside her and she cries out. Turning her head to the side, she finds herself facing one of the tombstones. She closes her eyes.

The neighbors and farmhands start showing up around dusk for Deda and Yvon's party, which, they've warned her, happens every Saturday night. They love a good party. Maybe the loud music and constant clamor of people in their home fills the silence of having no children.

As the sky grows dark, the fiddle comes out of the closet, the gin and the cards are laid out on the table, and the floor begins to thump from the square dancing. Yvon hands Maggie the Crown Royal. She takes the bottle and swigs from it. Her chest burns and she feels warm inside. Yvon begins to dance her around the living room.

Deda is in her chair, clapping her hands. Yvon's arms are around Maggie's waist. He's looking at her fondly.

"I always wanted a daughter," he yells in her ear. He's holding her tight, dancing with her to the fiddle. The room is hot and swirling.

She's starting to feel nauseated from the whiskey and Yvon's tight grip on her. She's noticed lately the way he stares at her while she's performing the most banal tasks—hanging up sheets, squeezing lemons, chasing after chickens. Until now, she's taken his attention for paternal fondness, nothing more. But something about the way he's pressing up against her now makes her want to escape.

When the song ends, she slips away and goes upstairs to her room. She flops down on the bed, holding on to the mattress, willing herself not to throw up. She yanks the old quilt up over her face, hoping the weight of it and its coolness might be able to keep the liquor inside her. She prays for morning, for the nausea to subside, to feel like herself again.

Sometime later—possibly minutes, possibly hours—she hears creaking in the hallway outside her room. The door opens. She attempts to sit up, but her body doesn't cooperate. She lies there, paralyzed, wondering who's in the room with her. "Is it time to start *le train?*" she mutters.

A man's laughter. Yvon. "No, Maggie," he says. "It's two o'clock in the morning."

She groans. When he lies down beside her, she stares at him in confusion. She's so drunk she can barely move. He begins to murmur things in her ear: *So beautiful. Can't stop thinking about you. Can't control myself anymore. Want you.* She's lucid enough to know that what he's saying is wrong. Her body tenses. She wants to cry for help, but nothing comes out of her mouth. She tries to roll away, but his leg across her body is so heavy. Her stomach lurches.

Has she led him on? He's her uncle. She's always adored him. Did that give him the wrong impression?

His breath is whiskey and cigarettes. She remembers that afternoon with Jean-François at Selby Lake. The revulsion, the smell of licorice on his breath. She squirms while Yvon slurs in her ear. Dirty, inappropriate words that make her cringe. He's half on top of her now, his leg pinning her down. His arm around her, holding the side of her face with his hand.

"Stop," she begs. "*Mon'onc,* please!"

When his fingers begin to unbutton her dress, bile comes up in her throat. His hands move all over her, exploring parts of her body she thought only Gabriel would ever know. He presses his full weight down on her so she can't even raise a leg to knee him in the groin. Her panties come off. She attempts to twist away, but it's impossible. She hears herself crying and pleading with him, but Yvon doesn't hear. Or he doesn't care. Maybe the words aren't coming out. She isn't sure anymore.

He forces her to touch him, but she fights. She uses every ounce of strength she's got left to resist. Frustrated, Yvon unbuckles his belt and shoves his pants down. He's breathing hard, pushing himself inside her. She remembers making love to Gabriel just a few hours earlier. How pleasurable and sweet it was. The thought of Gabriel now is unbearable.

She makes herself focus on the usually comforting noises around her—the crickets, the pipes, the fading music from downstairs. On an ordinary night, all these can lull her to sleep with their soothing rhythm, but now she finds them deafening.

Finally, Yvon collapses beside her on his back, panting like the farm dogs after they're done chasing the cows. "You're not a virgin," he remarks, staring up at the ceiling. His tone is a blend of surprise and disappointment. "Lucky boy on the motorcycle," he says, lighting a cigarette. Maggie watches its orange tip crackle as it burns.

She rolls away from him. The room is spinning and her hand encircles the bedpost to keep it steady. She squeezes her legs together against the pain.

CHAPTER 10

Maggie's parents come to visit for the first time at the end of August—not to see her, but to celebrate Yvon's birthday. She's been in Frelighsburg all summer, and although she speaks to her parents on the phone every Sunday night, she hasn't seen them since the morning she was sent away. Their conversations are always strained. She quietly pleads with them to let her come home, but the answer is always the same. *After Labour Day.*

She knows they're waiting for Gabriel to go back to Montreal. Her anger toward them has dulled over the months and given way to hopelessness. She doesn't have the stamina for anger. When she hears their voices over the phone—first her mother, then her father—asking how she's doing, she wants to tell them what's happened to her. She wants them to know what Yvon has done. She blames them, and thinks they should bear the burden with her, but she says nothing. What if they don't believe her? What if her father doesn't come back for her?

Yvon came to her room one more time since that first night and tried to get into her bed. He was drunk and muttering about how he couldn't keep away from her, but she stopped him cold with her voice. "Don't come near me or I'll tell my father," she said. Sober, she was a much more valiant opponent.

She couldn't see his face in the dark, but she guessed from his silence he was surprised. He'd underestimated her. He backed out of the room that night, warning her not to do anything stupid, and hasn't come to her bed since.

Gabriel has been back only once since that awful night with Yvon. He knew something was wrong the moment he saw her in the Frelighsburg cemetery. She could barely look at him or touch him. She was quiet, distant. They did not make love. She had to lie and tell him it didn't feel right, doing it in the cemetery.

"Is something wrong?" he finally asked.

"No," she lied. "Just a stomachache." The thought of any man touching her or kissing her now filled her with revulsion.

"You know what they say," he said. "Out of sight, out of mind."

"It's not that," she said. Still, she had no words to express how she felt—as if iron bars had gone up around her body—or how her emotions had begun to shut down like some internal power outage.

She had planned on asking him to take her to Montreal with him, but when she saw him face-to-face and looked into his eyes, she found she couldn't go through with it. She knew he would ask her why she'd changed her mind and wanted to run off with him all of a sudden, and she couldn't bear the thought of telling him.

"You sure everything is okay?" he asked again. "Is this about what we talked about last time? Because I pulled the knife?"

No matter how many times she reassured him, she could tell he didn't believe her. He was perceptive enough to know that something was different. When they parted ways, it was tense. He looked troubled but was too proud to press her. She knew he would never want to come off desperate or groveling, and so he drove away stoically, unsure of what had passed between them. And she let him. The next time he offered to visit, she made some excuse about having too much to do on the farm. He hasn't offered again.

Her parents' Packard pulls up in front of the house and Maggie watches them approach with a feeling of detachment. She's on the porch, sitting in the wicker rocker where she plucks chickens with Deda. She realizes as her sisters—Violet, Geri, and Nicole—rush toward her just how much she's missed them, but she knows her parents are not here to rescue her. They'll eat roast pork, make small talk, and drink whiskey in honor of Yvon, and then they'll leave without her.

She greets Vi with a hug and they look each other over. It's the longest they've ever been apart. "I saw Gabriel the other day," Vi tells her.

Maggie wants to know more, but just then her parents join them.

"How have you been?" Maggie's father asks.

"Fine."

"You look tired," Maman says, studying her face. She's dressed up today and wearing lipstick. Her hair is done in waves, and she looks pretty, younger. Her perfume lingers on the porch as the screen door slaps shut behind her.

Maggie turns to Violet. "Where?" she asks. "Where did you see Gabriel?"

"In the field."

"Did you talk to him?"

"I told him we were coming to visit you today."

"What did he say?"

"He just said to say hello for him."

"That's it?"

Violet nods.

They go inside. Supper is already on the table. Maggie hasn't been feeling well all day, but now the smell of pork makes her heave. She puts her hand over her mouth and suppresses a gag. "What's wrong with you?" her mother asks, sounding more accusatory than concerned.

"I don't feel well," Maggie responds, slumping into one of the kitchen chairs. The longer she sits at the table, the more nauseated she feels. "Move the pork," she says, and then pushes her chair away from the table. She rushes to the bathroom, but it's too late. Halfway down the hall, she throws up all over the wall.

Maman comes running, with Deda waddling behind her. Deda takes one look at the mess and gags. Maman goes straight over to Maggie, grabs her by the shoulders, and stares into her eyes, searching for something. Maggie throws up again, this time all over her mother's brown oxford shoes. Maman releases her and heads back to the kitchen, returning a few moments later with a pile of wet rags. "Go into the bathroom," she says. "Kneel over the toilet and stay there."

Maggie does as she's told. When she's finally empty inside and the nausea has passed, she lies down on the cold floor and stares up at the ceiling.

"Are you done?" Maman asks through the door.

"I think so."

Her mother comes in and closes the door behind her.

"I must have a stomach flu," Maggie says.

"Stomach flu," Maman scoffs. "Have you been throwing up a lot?"

"Tonight was the first time. It was the smell of pork."

Maman rubs her forehead, looking agitated. "Did you have sex with Gabriel?"

The question is like a punch in the gut. *How does she know?*

"Yes or no?" Maman says sternly.

Maggie doesn't answer.

"My God," Maman gasps. "You did, didn't you?"

Maggie suddenly feels trapped.

"Mon Dieu," Maman mutters, closing her eyes and running her hand through her hair. She starts pacing around the bathroom like a caged animal. "When was your last period?"

Maggie realizes she hasn't had it since she's been in Frelighsburg. "Not since I've been here," she admits, panic starting to rise.

"Did you have sex with Gabriel?"

"Yes," Maggie cries. "But I love him. We're going to—"

Maman slaps Maggie across the face. "You're pregnant!" she cries.

Maggie shakes her head. *It can't be.* Gabriel pulled out.

"I knew it the minute I saw you today," her mother says. "You're pale and you have dark circles. You look the way I looked with all of you."

"It's just the flu," Maggie argues weakly.

"You've missed your period, you idiot. And the smell of meat . . . That's exactly what happens to me. Remember? When I was pregnant with Geri and Nicole? I couldn't cook meat for the first four months with all of you."

Maggie's mouth is dry. There's a thick lump in her throat. And then the horrifying realization. *What if it's Yvon's?* "It might not be Gabriel's," she manages.

"There were others?" Maman cries, her eyes darkening. *"Tabarnac!"*

"Not other boys," Maggie clarifies, her voice trembling. She isn't sure if she should tell on her uncle—what her mother will do to him, what *he* will do to Maggie—but she must protect Gabriel.

"Who then?" Maman's voice is like ice.

Maggie buries her face in her hands.

"Who?"

"Mon'onc Yvon!"

Her mother doesn't flinch. She just stands there, staring at Maggie. Maggie waits for her to react, but nothing comes.

"Maman?"

"He wouldn't do such a thing," her mother says at last.

"But it's the truth," Maggie says. "When I first got here."

"If it's true, you must have done something."

"Done something?"

"To flirt or seduce him."

"I didn't!"

"You can't mention a word about this to anyone," Maman says. "Not to Deda, your father, your sisters."

"I wouldn't."

"It would destroy Deda," she says. "If it's true."

"It *is* true."

Maman opens the bathroom door to leave.

"What are we going to do?" Maggie asks her.

"We'll do what all families do in this situation," she says, her back to Maggie. And then the door closes and she's gone.

Afterwards, the grown-ups huddle around the kitchen table and talk in hushed whispers. Everyone else is ordered to stay outside until her mother emerges, stone-faced. She pulls Maggie aside. "You'll stay in Frelighsburg with Deda and Yvon until the baby is born," she says. "And if you see that boy again—even *once*—if I get wind you've met him in town or he's come here—you will be thrown out of this house and into the street."

"You're going to make me stay here with Yvon?" Maggie cries.

"He's taken good care of you."

Maggie shakes her head, bewildered.

"We've got no other choice," she says. "This is Quebec, Maggie."

"What did Yvon say?" Maggie asks her. "Did you tell him it might be his?"

"Of course not," she whispers, cupping Maggie's chin. "Your father and Deda have no idea about that and it will never be spoken of, all right? Yvon is letting you stay here until you have the baby. We should be grateful."

Maggie pulls away, freeing herself from her mother. "I'm not staying here with him," she says. "I'll go back to Dunham and have my baby with Gabriel."

"And where will you live?" Maman asks her. "All cramped together in their little shack? All five of you in one bedroom? And how will he support you and a baby? Selling his corn? Will you live apart all winter while he's working in the factory in Montreal? It's a hard life for a couple of poor teenagers. Especially since you won't be able to finish school. That's what happened to me."

This shuts Maggie up.

"You don't know poverty like I do," Maman warns her. "Think about all that, because you'll be on your own if you keep this baby."

"What does Daddy say?" Maggie asks, brushing away tears.

"He says what *I* say. He's devastated. We can't have an illegitimate baby ruining our reputation. Make your choice, Maggie. We're going back to Dunham now."

"What will happen to the baby if I stay here?"

"It will go to an orphanage," she says. "Where all illegitimate babies go. No one except the people in this house will ever know the truth."

"Why can't Deda keep it?" Maggie asks. "She's always wanted children."

"We are *not* keeping this child."

We, as though Maggie's baby already belongs to them.

Maggie stays out on the porch, contemplating her choices. She still loves Gabriel. She could find her way back to Dunham, tell him she's pregnant and hope he'll marry her. She'd have to quit school and give up her dream of running her father's store—

And that's what stops her cold. The idea of abandoning the future she's always envisioned for herself is one she can't bear. Her life to this point has been organized around that very goal; it's galvanized her when everything else has felt bleak. Even contemplating quitting that path leaves her feeling empty and useless.

Exile here at the farm suddenly seems less unbearable. Perhaps it's the more noble choice to hide out and protect all their reputations, and then return to life as it once was. It wasn't a fairy tale, it wasn't without its hardships, but it was a good life just the same.

"Maggie?"

She turns around to find her father standing behind her. She didn't even hear him come outside.

"I'm sorry, Daddy—"

"We'll fix this," he says. "We'll get you back on track, Maggie."

She looks up at him, surprised by his gentle tone. "How?" she asks him.

He pulls her to him and holds her against his chest. She breathes in the smell of panatela on his shirt and lets herself cry while he strokes her hair. She doesn't deserve such kindness from him. She's disappointed him in every conceivable way, and yet here he is, consoling her.

"For starters," her father says softly, "you are forbidden to see Gabriel Phénix again. You'll stay here until this is over and you will have no contact with him. And if you do, if you choose to see him again, you will no longer be part of our lives. Understood, Maggie?"

Maggie pulls away and looks up at him, lips trembling.

"We won't see you, we won't speak to you. You will not be welcome in our home," he underlines. "And you're damn lucky I don't kill him with my shotgun."

Later, as her family prepares to leave, Maggie corners Vi outside and says, "You have to tell Gabriel something for me."

"What?"

"Tell him it's over. I won't answer any more of his letters and I'm not coming back to him." After their last encounter, she doubts he'll be surprised.

"But why?" Violet's eyes are wide. "When I got here, you were desperate to know what he said."

"It doesn't matter," Maggie says. "Just tell him I'm not coming back."

"Why aren't you?" Violet asks, seeming to relish the drama.

"You'll know the truth soon enough," Maggie tells her. "Just tell Gabriel we're through, will you?"

Violet nods obediently and runs off to the Packard. Maggie stands there and watches them drive away and then goes back inside.

CHAPTER 11

Sunday dinner. Her parents are here. Her uncle sharpens the carving knife. Maggie is about eight months pregnant. She's been in exile for longer than that. She's calculated she has to stay another two months. After she has the baby, she'll need to lose the weight before she can go back to Dunham, back to work, back to her previous life.

She tries not to think too much about the path she did not take—the path of Gabriel and motherhood. She's had a long time to make peace with her decision. It was not the romantic choice; it was more practical than that. She glimpsed her future as a poor farmer's wife, a sixteen-year-old mother stuck at home in that shack, turning fat and bitter, just like her mother. She glimpsed an existence without her beloved seed store or her father, and it was no existence at all.

Maman is right; life isn't a romance magazine.

"*Tabarnac*, I forgot the horseradish," Maman says just as a gush of warm liquid between Maggie's legs soaks through her maternity dress. Maggie stands. Everyone is watching her.

"What's happening?" Maggie asks.

"It's fine, *cocotte*. The baby's early, that's all."

Deda and Maman help her upstairs, supporting her on either side. In the bedroom she's occupied since the day she came to live with her aunt and uncle, Maman quickly throws some of Maggie's things into a small suitcase. "Get me some towels," she tells Deda.

Deda waddles out of the room. Maggie hears the linen closet door open and close, the water running in the bathroom, Deda's heavy footsteps creaking on the hall floor. Maggie tries hard to focus on the ordinary minutiae of what's going on around her; otherwise she'll faint. That's when the first pain slices through her, so sharp and abrupt she reels backwards.

Maman looks over at the clock on the dresser. "Tell me when the next one starts."

"The next *what*?" Maggie asks.

"Contraction."

Maggie sits down on the bed and waits. Deda stands over her, watching, while Maman continues to pack. Deda pats Maggie's dress with the towel. It's about ten minutes later when another pain shoots through her. Maggie screams and leaps off the bed.

"Nine minutes," Maman says.

Maggie has to walk it off. She can't stay seated. The pains start to get more intense and last longer. Every time another one seizes, she cries out, "It huuuuuuurts!"

Deda reaches for her hand and tries to hold it, but Maggie flings it away and grasps her fleshy forearms. When the next contraction comes, she squeezes, and this time, Deda is the one who cries out.

The trip to the hospital is a blur. Maggie writhes in the back seat of the Packard, sandwiched between her mother and Deda. Her father speeds all the way to the Brome-Missisquoi-Perkins Hospital in Cowansville. She's wheeled to a private room. As soon as she lies down on the bed, there's a sudden excruciating pressure in her lower back, the memory of which she will never forget. She can feel the baby in her groin.

Dr. Cullen appears next to her. He peers down between her legs, studying the situation the way she's seen her father study his seeds and bugs beneath a magnifying glass. "She's already fully dilated. It's crowning," he announces, grabbing her ankles and resting her feet on his solid hips. "Push hard," he instructs. "Press your feet into me and push."

Maggie does as she's told. She pushes until the pain becomes unbearable, and then she unleashes a scream that makes everybody jump back a few feet.

"Push, Maggie."

"I can't!" she cries, collapsing. "I can't do it!"

"You're doing fine," Dr. Cullen says. "I see the baby's head. A couple more pushes, that's all. It's *there*."

She pushes, grunts, and jams her feet into Dr. Cullen's immovable fortress of a body. She squeezes her aunt's hand until it goes limp in her own. She can feel it. *It*. The baby. It's coming. Push, collapse, push, collapse. "One more," Dr. Cullen encourages. "Don't give up now, Maggie. You're close."

And just when she thinks she can't stand another second of the torture, the baby is there. After all that heaving and panting, it just slips out and there's an explosion of relief that it's over. She can't see it, but she can feel it—slimy and squirming, like a reptile sliding out of a swamp. Then she sinks into the mattress, feeling suddenly weightless. She hears the baby crying from across the room, and it sounds like two wildcats fighting outside her window. Her body feels strangely empty.

Dr. Cullen takes the baby over to the basin. Deda and Maman leave Maggie's bedside. Maggie hoists herself up on her elbows to get a better look at what's happening. Dr. Cullen is holding the baby in the palm of his hands, a tiny bluish creature covered in blood. "The umbilical cord tore," he explains, holding it up for her to see. It looks like *boudin*, the blood sausage Maman cooks for supper on Thursdays.

Blood is everywhere. Her mother is gazing at the baby. "It's a girl," she says, her voice emotionless.

The baby is still crying when Dr. Cullen hands it—*her*—to the nurse. Maggie wonders if everything is all right. The nurse washes her methodically, without affection or fondness. Maggie can only glimpse the baby's flailing fists. She flops back against the pillow. *A girl*. She thinks about Gabriel and tears slide down her cheeks. She has no one to blame but herself. A name comes to her then, the name she would have given her daughter. Elodie. A type of lily whose buds open to reveal layer upon layer of lush candy-pink petals: a flower she's always loved whose name she can now give to the daughter she will never know.

"She's got jaundice," Dr. Cullen tells Maggie's mother.

"What's jaundice?" Maggie cries.

The doctor and her mother exchange conspiratorial looks, and Dr. Cullen comes over to her, needle in hand.

"What's that?" Maggie asks.

"Just the twilight to help you sleep."

"Her name is Elodie," Maggie tells them as the syringe penetrates her flesh. "Will you tell Daddy? Will you make sure he knows?"

No one responds.

"Elodie," she repeats, trailing off. "*Tell Daddy.*"

Maggie wakes to total silence. The hospital is eerily still; the only sound is the echo of the baby's crying inside her head. "Where is she?" Maggie asks.

Deda gets up out of the chair and shuffles over to her. No one else is around, but then her mother suddenly appears in the doorway.

"One of you could have kept her," Maggie sobs, looking from her mother to her aunt. "It's not too late!"

"It would ruin your family name," Deda says gently. "Your mother may not be Catholic anymore, but she still cares what people think of her. And your father has a reputation in town."

"I want to see her then."

"Drink this," Deda says, handing Maggie a glass of water. There's whiskey in it, which makes her gag. "It will help with the pain."

Maggie finishes the water and whiskey. She's exhausted and sore. "Can I at least see her before they take her away?" she repeats.

"It's too late," Maman says, her tone softening. "She's already gone. She's not yours, Maggie. She never was."

And then she turns and leaves the room without another word.

"Was she pretty?" Maggie asks her aunt.

"She was very small. Born too early. They're all ugly when they're that premature."

"What's jaundice?"

"It's nothing. Don't worry."

"Where did they take her?"

"To the foundling home in Cowansville."

"Why couldn't I hold her?"

Deda sits heavily on the edge of the bed. It squeaks and sags beneath her weight. "It makes it too hard," she explains. "This is what people do in these situations, Maggie."

"I wanted to say good-bye."

Deda touches Maggie's forehead, her fat paw grazing her hairline. "Your uncle would like to see you."

Maggie turns her face away, swelling with anger. "I don't feel well," she mutters.

Deda brushes her lips on top of Maggie's head, smooths her damp hair, and leaves. The door closes and Maggie is alone. She feels completely hollow, as though her insides have been scooped out and dumped in that enamel basin.

Feelings come in waves. Grief, relief, shame, guilt. She could have kept the baby. She's not blameless. Instead, her infant daughter is about to be hurled into the world all alone. She will grow up untethered, incomplete. They both will.

Maggie begins to drift off, lulled by the rain battering the windows. In that place between sleep and alertness, the name comes back to her. She whispers it into the night. *Elodie.*

I will find you, she thinks, slowly succumbing to sleep. It's a promise as much to herself as to her newborn daughter. *I will get you back and make it right.*

PART II

Transplanting out of Season

1954–1961

When for some reason it is necessary to transplant at a time
of year that is really too cold, puddle the plants in using
hot water instead of cold. This, surprisingly, really does not
damage the roots.

—OLD WIVES' LORE FOR GARDENERS

CHAPTER 12

Elodie

Tata's outstretched arms are what she sees first when she opens her eyes. Instinctively, she raises her own arms, and in one swift movement, Sister Tata lifts her from her crib and deposits her upright on the floor.

"Cold!" Elodie cries, dancing in place to keep her feet off the ice-cold wood. Tata laughs. Elodie loves the sound of her laugh.

Tata picks her up again and sets her down on one of the empty cots. "Soon," Tata says, taking a pair of wool socks from the drawer and slipping them on Elodie's tiny feet, "Elodie will be ready to move to a big-girl cot."

Tata lifts Elodie back onto the floor and takes her by the hand. Together, they go downstairs for breakfast. Elodie can almost manage the stairs by herself, but not quite.

Elodie is four years old. She knows this because she hears the nuns say it to the visitors all day long. She hears them say other things, too: "She's very bright. She's already talking. She'll be a beauty when she fills out."

People come to look at the girls to decide if they want to take them home. On those days, Elodie wears a pretty dress for the visitors. She has only one. She prefers to wear the ugly dress so she can play and get dirty, but it's very important to make a good impression on the visitors if she's ever going to get adopted. Tata says this is the object of the orphanage—to see to it that all the little girls are "placed" with good families.

Elodie is an orphan, which, Tata has explained, means she does not have a mother or a father. When Elodie once asked her why not, she was told quite plainly, "You live in a home for unwanted girls because you were born in sin and your mother could not keep you."

Which means Elodie *did* have a mother, at one time, and now she does not. She wonders sometimes about this person, this mother who gave her away. Where is she now? Why did she go? What does it mean to be born in sin? And why is it called a home for unwanted girls? If they all live here, she reasons, surely the nuns must want them.

The nuns don't answer those kinds of questions. They merely instruct her to behave and make a favorable impression on the visitors, reminding her again and again that nothing is more important than being chosen by a nice couple so that she can grow up in a proper family, instead of at an orphanage.

Occasionally, the visitors have other children with them and Elodie observes them with curiosity—the way they hold their parents' hands, and cling to them, and look at Elodie with pity.

The nuns say to the visitors about her: "She's small and thin, yes, but she's perfectly normal."

The visitors seem to like the fat, round kids with rosy cheeks and fat legs. Tata always tells her, "Eat, Elo. Eat. You have to get fat so a nice family will take you home."

The nuns are always telling her: "You're too small. You're too pale. The visitors want a healthy child."

But Elodie is happy here. She doesn't know any other kind of life. Besides, there's green grass for running around outside and toys to play with. And there's Tata, who makes her feel safe.

CHAPTER 13

⟨⟨⟨⟩⟩⟩

Maggie

"Isn't that Angèle Phénix?" Peter says as they turn on to Ontario Street with their bags of fresh fruit and vegetables from the market.

Maggie has been living in Montreal with her brother for several months. It's been a challenging transition from country life; she's had to catch on quick. She used to think the hostility between French and English was fairly palpable back home, but here in Montreal it's a perpetually simmering, volatile thing. There are no written signs telling you what language should be spoken where; you have to read between the lines and listen carefully. You have to simply *know* so as not to offend anyone.

"Angèle!" Maggie exclaims, genuinely happy to see her. She sets her bags down on the sidewalk and hugs her old friend.

"What are you doing in Montreal?" Angèle asks her.

"Working at Simpson's. I live with Peter." Peter waves hello, looking uninterested. "We live over on La Fontaine," Maggie says. "How's nursing school?"

"Oh, I love it," Angèle says. "It was the right choice for me. I wouldn't have made a very good nun. You look gorgeous, Maggie."

Maggie thanks her.

"I love your skirt," Angèle goes on, admiring the felt flowers Maggie's glued onto the fabric. She sets down her groceries to touch the flowers, and Maggie notices the front page of *La Presse* poking out of the paper bag. The word "orphanages" catches her eye. She reads the headline from where she's standing.

Quebec orphanages to be converted into mental institutions.

Maggie came to Montreal to escape the past. Yet here it is, taunting her from the front page of the newspaper. How quickly she can be wrenched back to that shameful place. Confronted all over again with the secrets and scandals she's worked so hard to forget.

"Horrible, isn't it?" Angèle says, noticing Maggie staring at her paper. "I was reading about it on the streetcar from work."

Maggie reaches for the paper and quickly skims the article. "*Every* orphanage in the province is going to be turned into a mental hospital?"

"It'll take some time, but yes, that's what they're doing."

"It's so they don't have to educate the children," Peter says.

"You've heard about it?"

"It's all over the news."

"They're starting with the Sisters of Charity of Providence next year," Angèle says.

"But where will all the orphans go?"

"Duplessis doesn't give a shit," Peter answers.

"Why are they doing this?"

"Duplessis is a monster, that's why," Peter responds. "Obviously the federal government gives more money for the nuns to take care of sick people than it does for orphans."

"It's barbaric," Angèle says, clicking her tongue.

A swell of dread settles in Maggie's chest. She thinks about that helpless baby in the palm of Dr. Cullen's hand and wonders if her daughter could wind up in an asylum. Whenever Maggie has allowed herself to think about Elodie, she's imagined her with a gentle, nurturing mother and a father who is present and attentive and doting. For the first time since she gave her up, Maggie considers that her daughter may not have been adopted.

She can feel Peter's eyes on her, and she knows *he* knows what she's thinking. Like everyone else in her family, he has cooperated in the surreptitious cover-up of her pregnancy.

"How's Gabriel?" Peter asks Angèle, changing the subject, and Maggie's cheeks heat up at the mention of his name. She tries to keep her expression neutral.

"He moved to Montreal a couple of years ago," Angèle says. "He had a falling-out with Clémentine over how to run the farm, and he hasn't been back to visit since. He's a foreman at Canadair."

He's here, Maggie thinks. She knew he would be, but the confirmation is like a jolt of electricity in her body.

"He's married," Angèle adds, not looking at Maggie when she says it.

Everything goes silent—the street noises, the shrieking children in the alley, her breathing. It takes Maggie a moment to recover. "That happened fast . . ." she manages.

"He's happy," Angèle says.

"What's his wife's name?"

"Annie."

Annie. A punch in the stomach. She has no one to blame but herself. "We should go," Maggie says, hugging Angèle numbly and hurrying away with her grocery bags.

"Put it behind you," Peter says, catching up to her.

Maggie looks at him, startled. "Put what behind me?"

"Gabriel, the pregnancy. Mum and Dad did a good job covering it up. You're here for a fresh start."

They finish walking home in silence. By the time they turn onto La Fontaine, a pretty East End street lined with trees and wrought iron fire escapes, Maggie is fighting back tears as she climbs the narrow stairs.

They live on the second floor of a triplex, with tenants above and below, whose noises she hears at all hours, whose odors she smells the moment she wakes up. She's getting used to it, learning to walk in socks or slippers, never shoes, so Mme. Choquette from downstairs doesn't bang her broom into the ceiling. Their apartment is bright at least, with hardwood floors and lots of windows. The kitchen linoleum is coming up in places, but the appliances are almost new. Maggie's room is practically bare, except for two cast-iron nuns' beds and a Salvation Army dresser. When she complained there were no curtains, Peter said, "You'll live."

She left her mason jars of planted seeds and lemon tree shoots behind in Dunham, knowing her mother would get rid of them.

She drops her bags and goes straight out to the balcony. She lights a cigarette and blows smoke at the city's unwavering skyline. Clothes hang on the lines that run from the balconies to the telephone poles, zigzagging across the sky so that pairs of long underwear and work pants connect the entire block.

What Peter said is true. She came here to start anew, to recast herself—not as some tragic failure and disappointment to her family, but as a self-reliant working girl. Maybe even to win back her father's affection.

The way they parted left her heartbroken. When she got back to Dunham after having the baby, Vi had already replaced her at the seed store. Maggie understood it was her punishment for having let her father down. She went back to school, caught up, and graduated on time. She knew better than to ask for her job back, let alone a chance to work on the floor, selling. There was a cloud over her now, and there always would be in Dunham, particularly in her parents' home. Even the locked file cabinet drawer in her father's office, which she knew contained all the information about her daughter's birth and whereabouts, taunted her. Finally, when school was finished, she felt she had no choice but to leave.

She stood outside Superior Seeds the day of her departure, staring at its facade with a mix of nostalgia and despair. She was nineteen. A woman. Yet being there still made her feel like the little girl who used to count seeds in the attic. It was Violet's job now, and one day Geri would take over, and then Nicole. How simple life had been on those Saturdays at the store, when she'd been her happiest and had known exactly how her life was going to unfold. Now it was a legacy from which she was excluded.

Her father was standing at the cash register, delivering one of his ubiquitous sermons to a young farmer. "You'll want to dust right down to the whorl with rotenone when the plants are young," he said with authority. "And try tying the tips of the ears together for the earworms."

"What about DDT?" the farmer asked.

"The great insecticide debate rages on," her father said. "But it's a remarkable insecticide as far as I'm concerned."

"Is it really a cure-all, though? How does it affect the birds and the fish . . . and *us?*"

"Pesticides are the only solution to the insect problem," her father countered. "They preserve the seeds."

Maggie wasn't sure if her father was sad or relieved to see her go. In any case, he did not try to stop her. She handed him a bouquet of bright yellow rosinweeds. "I picked them for you on the way."

He put them down on the counter. "Would you like some Bountifuls to get a garden started in the city? You always loved having your own."

"Sure," she said, knowing there would be no garden.

He handed her a brown paper bag. "I knew this time would come," he said. "You always were my wildflower."

CHAPTER 14

It's autumn, and the Townships are fully immersed in a kaleidoscope of orange, red, and yellow as the leaves migrate purposefully from branch tips to earth. Maggie, Roland, Peter, and his girlfriend, Fiona, are on their way to Dunham to visit her parents. It will be the first time Roland meets her whole family, even though it was her father who set them up.

Roland Larsson used to be the branch manager at the Business Development Bank in Cowansville, where her father does his banking. Roland has since been transferred to Montreal, which prompted her father to arrange the blind date with Maggie.

Her first impression of Roland was that he was extremely smart and sophisticated. Physically, he's tall and well-groomed, with perfectly straight white teeth and a long chin. He's half Scottish and half Swedish, which is something they have in common—they're both half-somethings. His blond hair is already beginning to thin and he wears bifocals, which makes him look much older than he is. Maggie would have put him in his forties, even though he's only twenty-nine. But what drew her to him was his mind. He's traveled places, and he reads textbooks for pleasure and knows interesting facts about many different subjects.

On their first date, he wore a suit and shiny black shoes that squeaked when he walked across the room to greet her. He smelled of cologne, something grown-up and fatherly, and he seemed very refined and worldly to her. Their first kiss was a little awkward, but that was probably her fault. She compared it to the way Gabriel used to kiss her, back when she was just a teenager, full of swirling hormones and erratic emotions. And although she's not that much older in years than she was with Gabriel, she's much older in spirit. It's probably a good thing Roland is nothing like Gabriel.

After that first date with Roland, she found herself hoping for another. She felt there was more to explore beneath his surface—some interesting texture or tender wound that might give him a bit more complexity and intrigue. She was thrilled when he called her again and invited her to see a show at the Palace Theatre. They've been together ever since.

"Did I mention there's an opening in the secretary pool at the bank?" Roland says, taking his eyes off the road to look at Maggie in the passenger seat.

"I like my job," Maggie says. She works in women's undergarments at Simpson's department store. She's a good salesperson, as she always knew she would be.

"But you might prefer secretary work," Roland says. "And you could eventually move up to credit officer."

"I'd hate taking dictation, sitting at a desk all day," Maggie says. "I like selling."

"We help people start businesses," Roland tells her. "It's really quite gratifying."

"Has a woman ever started her own business?" Maggie asks him.

"Not that I know of," he says. "Not in Cowansville anyway. Unfortunately, no bank would ever issue a loan to a young woman with no collateral, no credentials, and no one to cosign."

"It is the fifties, though," Fiona says from the back seat. "Things have improved since the war."

"It's more like the eighteen fifties in the Townships, though," Peter says.

"I suppose it's possible for a woman to get a loan," Roland reflects.

"It's a miserable life, owning your own business," Peter interjects. "Our father never has a moment to himself. He has nothing but worry and stress. It's a great big burden, is what it is."

"Daddy's happy at work," Maggie counters. "That's important. Enjoying what you do."

"What am I going to do with this girl and all her ambitions?" Roland says, squeezing her knee and smiling. He has long teeth and the bluest eyes Maggie has ever seen. "I think it's charming."

"I just want to do more than cook and clean and change diapers," Maggie says. "I want to contribute."

She heard recently that Audrey is engaged. Soon she'll be one of those housewives—grumpy and irritable, with her husband, Barney, hiding in his workroom, building things and smoking cigars to avoid her. Maggie would never tell any of the girls at work—who talk of nothing but babies and husbands—that eventually she wants to be promoted to women's apparel on the third floor, and manager after that. She's promised herself that no man will ever lock himself in a room to avoid being with her.

"Motherhood is the greatest contribution a woman can make," Roland says. "Don't you think so?"

Maggie grows quiet. She avoids looking at Peter.

"Can't a woman want both?" Fiona asks. "A job and a family?"

"One or the other would suffer," Roland states with certainty.

"Not with the right man to help out," Maggie says.

Roland looks at her sharply. "Most men want their wives to be home taking care of the children. And I should think most women want to do just that."

"My mother has five children," Maggie says, nonplussed. "And she's the unhappiest woman I know."

"That doesn't mean *you* will be."

Maggie turns away and stares out the window.

When they pull up, Roland comes around to Maggie's side, opens the door for her, and helps her out. She holds on to him for support, her heels getting stuck in the gravel as the four of them make their way to the house.

When they enter through the mudroom, Maggie can smell the simmering meat and spices from the kitchen. She finds her mother at the Commodore, pulling out a large casserole dish of rabbit potpie, one of her grandmother's recipes from Rivière aux Rats. Most of Maman's meals are traditional Mauricie specialties—*cretons*, roast pork, freshwater perch, venison, and hare stew. Under duress, Maggie's father can often be heard muttering, "If it wasn't for her cooking . . ."

Maman turns around and rushes over to Peter. "I forgot how handsome you are!" she gushes, tousling his hair. She's always boasting about how he won the Goutte de Lait Healthy Baby contest for being the cutest baby in the region; she still keeps the yellowed clipping from the twenty-two-year-old *Missisquoi Herald* in her pocketbook.

She completely ignores Fiona, whom she hates, and turns to Maggie. "What a pretty dress," she says.

"It's robin's egg blue," Maggie tells her, shocked by the compliment. Maman still smells of Yardley soap, which is somehow comforting.

"Linen after September, though?" Maman says.

Maggie ignores the remark and hands her mother a wad of crumpled dollar bills. "Here. For you."

Maman wordlessly slips the money in her apron pocket. "Your father's in his closet," she says. "Nothing's changed."

"This is Roland," Maggie announces, remembering Roland standing behind her, halfway between the mudroom and the kitchen. He's wearing a brown plaid sports jacket with a monogrammed white hankie neatly folded inside the pocket, which is begging for a snide remark from Hortense—either to his face or, later on, behind his back.

Roland hands her a bouquet of pale pink roses and a bottle of Pouilly-Fuissé. "*Por twa*," he says, in appallingly bad French.

Maggie's mother takes the flowers and wine without so much as a thank-you. She looks him up and down, probably noting with disdain his shiny tasseled shoes, his expensive gold watch, his impeccable posture, and his no-nonsense cologne.

Her sisters come rushing into the kitchen then, and Maggie hugs and kisses them all. She's only been gone about six months, but they seem so old to her all of a sudden. Nicole is almost eight now, with waves just like Maggie used to have at that age. Geri is as adorable as ever, even in the unforgiving vortex of puberty, with those scrawny legs and the blunt bowl haircut that Maman has given her. Violet still looks the same, only slightly glummer. Maggie hands them each a brown paper bag filled with cashews and Belgian chocolates from Simpson's.

Her father finally emerges from his office in a cloud of smoke. "You remember Roland," she says, secretly thrilled to present him as her date. The two men shake hands, and Maman bullies everyone to the table.

Sitting between Roland and her father at supper, Maggie can't stop smiling.

"I've never had a meal like this before," Roland raves, polishing off his plate. The wine is flowing and all the adults are flushed and jovial. Maggie translates for her mother.

"It's just an old family recipe," Maman says, her face pink with pride.

"I grew up eating haggis and herring," Roland tells her. "This is heaven."

He looks over at Maggie, grinning. Probably thinking she'll cook for him like this one day. She knows he's always tallying up her good points, contemplating her for marriage. He's almost thirty. His readiness for settling down is palpable. It makes as much of an impression as his soapy smell and his tasseled shoes.

While Maman and Vi clear the table for dessert, Maggie's father and Roland launch into a discussion about the federal election. The Liberals are in again, which means another term with St. Laurent. "He promised equal opportunities for all the provinces," her father gripes. "Where's he been throughout Duplessis's reign of terror in Quebec, eh?"

Every time Duplessis's name is mentioned, Maggie feels sick. She can't help think about what he's done to all those orphans—possibly to *her* child. Once again she can taste the old shame like bile in her mouth, sabotaging what could be a perfect night. She squeezes her eyes shut against the "if onlys"—*if only I'd kept her, if only I could find her*—and hopes they'll change the subject.

"We spend more time talking about Maurice Duplessis than anyone else," Maman complains. "What are you going to talk about when he's dead?"

"The idiot who replaces him," Maggie's father answers, his cheeks ruddy from the liquor, his blue eyes bright and cheerful.

He instructs Roland and Peter to wait for him in the family room, and then he gets up from the table and retrieves his bottle of gin. With a sly grin, he comes up behind Maman and grabs both cheeks of her behind, squeezing hard. He does it right in front of Maggie, which makes her blush. Maman shoos him away, giggling in spite of herself. "You want coffee in there?" she asks him, knowing his answer.

"We'll be fine with this," he responds, holding up the bottle.

Maggie joins the men in the family room, only half listening as Roland, Peter, and her father drone on about small business, CBC's poor programming, agriculture, architecture, railroads. Fiona is reading a fashion magazine. Maggie's lids grow heavy as they talk and talk into the night, but she's glad to sit back and let them entertain one another. She feels no pressure to vouch for Roland or try to win anyone over on his behalf. Before long, they disappear for a Scotch and cigar in her father's private sanctuary and Maggie returns to the kitchen.

She finds her mother alone, sweeping the floor. Her sisters have all gone upstairs to bed. She sits down at the pine table and her mother joins her. She's comfortable here, surrounded by all her mother's things. Maman likes order in her kitchen. She has a permanent spot for each utensil, pot, dish towel, and decoration. Whether it's an antique enamel pitcher or the framed picture of Peter as a baby, she's compulsive about keeping everything in its proper place. The room is filled with her—her scent, her style, her cleanliness, her perfectionism. The floor gleams. The stove sparkles. The windows are spotless. The curtains in the window are as pristine and crisply pressed as the day she hung them. Her world is as orderly as her father's sanctuary is chaotic.

"Congratulations," Maman says, pouring them each a cup of coffee. "You're dating your father."

Maggie has a sip of coffee, savoring its bitterness. She forgot how good her mother's coffee is.

"Does he build radios, too?" Maman teases.

"Model airplanes and trains."

"You don't love him the way you loved Gabriel Phénix."

"Gabriel wasn't right for me."

"You mean he wasn't right for *him*," Maman says, pointing to her husband's sanctuary.

"Now you're coming out on the side of love?" Maggie says, anger rushing to her temples. "Now you're rooting for Gabriel? That's ironic since you banished me from him."

"I'm not rooting for anyone," Maman responds. "I'm just stating the obvious."

"I love Roland," Maggie says spitefully, as though her mother just laid down a challenge.

"Your father sure loves him," Maman says. "Maybe that's enough for you."

CHAPTER 15

Elodie

1955

It's a bright September morning, and the sun is spilling inside the classroom through the open windows. Elodie is on the carpet, coloring. She uses the broken crayons that Sister Tata keeps in an old maple syrup can for the younger students. Elodie doesn't use coloring books, which are boring. Instead, she likes to draw pictures of families. She always draws herself standing next to her mother, holding her hand and smiling, with as many brothers and sisters as space on the page or time will allow before Sister Tata rings the bell for lessons.

The mother in her drawings always has blond hair, like hers. Elodie isn't sure why her mother left her with the nuns when she was born, but she's confident there must be a good reason. Whenever she asks the sisters why she lives at the orphanage, they tell her, "Because you were born in sin and nobody else wants you." Sometimes they say, "Because you were born in Scandal."

Elodie has no idea what any of it means, or where Scandal is, but she's sure her mother will come back for her eventually and she'll be reunited with her brothers and sisters. She likes to name them all in her head—Claude, Lucien and Lucienne (the twins), Linda, Lorraine,

Jeanne. At the top of her pictures, she writes *MA FAMILLE*. Sister Tata—whose real name is Alberta—taught her how to write the letters, and now they march across the top of every one of her drawings. Sister Tata says it's a miracle Elodie can sit still long enough to draw her families. One time she drew a family with seventeen kids.

Her best friend, Claire, doesn't color with her; she prefers to look at picture books. Claire is six, and she almost knows how to read. They've grown up together at Saint-Sulpice, and if Claire is still here when her mother comes to take her home, she's going to ask if Claire can come, too.

For now, Elodie is happy enough here, even though the nuns and the people who come to visit call it the Home for Unwanted Girls. Elodie doesn't feel especially unwanted. Her nickname is Elo, and even Mère Blanche calls her that. She shares a room with twenty other girls, all of them motherless just like her. There used to be only ten or twelve girls to a room—never more than that—but recently they've begun to cram in as many as two dozen. There are many, many rules at Saint-Sulpice, but Elodie finds ways to maneuver around them. The sisters tell her she has a rambunctious nature, and she's had her fair share of punishments for talking back—having to miss supper, losing outdoor privileges, or getting her knuckles hit with the ruler. But she likes school, and soon she'll learn how to read, and on her birthday she got a doll, which was donated by one of the families in Cowansville. She named her Poupée.

On this day, a knock at the door disrupts their usual routine. Sister Tata claps her hands to get everyone's attention. "At your desks," she says sternly.

"But I'm not finished," Elodie says, not budging from the carpet.

"At your desk *now*."

Sister's tone is enough to get Elodie up on her feet and back to her desk. Sister opens the door and a man enters the classroom. Unusual, Elodie thinks, looking over at Claire. The man is wearing a grey suit and hat, which he takes off and sets down on Sister's desk. He has a moustache and a glum expression. Elodie decides she doesn't like him.

"This is Dr. Duceppe," Sister announces. "He's going to ask you each some questions. Just answer as best you can. You will be called outside the class when it's your turn. In the meantime, you're to remain at your desks, eyes in front and backs straight, working on your lessons. No fidgeting, please."

Elodie raises her hand and also blurts her question before she's called on. "What sort of questions?" she wants to know.

"You'll find out when it's your turn."

With that, Sister Tata calls on the first girl. Elodie watches her make her way to the front of the class and follow the moustached man outside. The door closes. Elodie is beside herself with anticipation.

She has a hard time concentrating on writing her letters. She's supposed to copy the letter A from one end of the page to the other, but it's boring and hard to keep the A's neatly between the two lines. She can hardly wait for her turn with the doctor.

Finally, it comes. She jumps up from her desk and makes her way out of the class, where the doctor is waiting for her. She follows him down the hall to Mère Blanche's office, neither of them uttering a word.

"Sit down, please," Dr. Duceppe instructs, closing the door behind him.

Elodie sits in the chair facing the desk. The doctor sits across from her, in Mère Blanche's chair. She can see notes on his clipboard. *Elodie: 3–6–50.* There are some other words too, which she doesn't know how to read.

"Do you know what this is?" he asks her, holding up a square brown object that has a texture like the ball the boys play sports with outside.

She reaches out to touch it and discovers that it unfolds. Inside, there are rectangular pieces of paper with numbers on them. She shrugs. "No, monsieur."

He takes the thing back from her and scribbles something on the paper. "It's a wallet," he mutters.

"For what?"

He raises his eyes to meet hers without lifting his head. "For carrying your money," he says.

"What about this?" He holds up a picture of some oddly shaped silver things. And then another of a big machine she doesn't recognize.

"No, monsieur. No, monsieur."

"Keys," he says. "Stove."

"Do you know what the word 'compare' means?" he asks her.

"No, monsieur."

Scribble, scribble. "That's all," he says, not even looking at her.

She sits there for a moment, not wanting it to be over. "That's all?" she repeats.

"You can go back to your class now."

"I can almost tie my shoelace," she tells him.

He doesn't say anything. She goes back to the class. Claire is looking at her expectantly. Elodie shrugs. Nothing more is said about the moustached man for the rest of the day.

The next morning when they get to class after prayers, Sister Tata tells them to go straight to their desks. "But it's carpet time," Elodie reminds her.

"There's no carpet time today," Sister says, and Elodie is disappointed.

Before long, two more sisters show up in the classroom, followed by Mère Blanche. Elodie looks over at Claire. Something is going on.

"Girls," Mother says, standing front and center of the room, her hands clasped together, her back straight as a plank. "Today is Change of Vocation Day," she announces.

The girls begin to twitter. Elodie is excited. Change of Vocation Day! "Is it a holiday?" she cries out, not bothering to raise her hand.

"After today," Mother continues, "there will be no more school."

Elodie's spirits plunge. No more school?

"From now on, the orphanage will be a hospital," Mother tells them.

Elodie looks over at Sister Tata and notices tears rolling down her cheeks. Her head is lowered, and she won't make eye contact with Elodie or any of the girls.

"What does that mean?" one of the older girls asks.

"Just as I said," Mère Blanche responds sharply. "We are now a mental hospital. There's no more orphanage and no more orphans. From this day forward, you are all mentally retarded."

Elodie looks around the room. Everyone is dead silent. Some of the older girls are crying. Sister Tata's shoulders are shaking, her head still lowered, her eyes hidden. "What does it mean, 'mentally retarded'?" Elodie asks.

"It means you're mentally deficient," Mother explains. "Do you understand? You're mental patients now. This is how we go forward."

With that, she turns on her heels and leaves the room to its silent shock and heartbreak.

The next morning, three important things happen, all of which give Elodie an anxious feeling of terrible things to come. The first is the banging that wakes her up much earlier than usual. When she looks outside, she sees workers removing all the shutters from the windows and replacing them with black iron bars.

Next, when she goes downstairs to breakfast, she notices that all the sisters are wearing white habits instead of their usual black.

"Why is your dress white?" she asks Sister Joséphine, sitting down to her bowl of *gruau d'avoine*.

"This is the habit the nurses wear."

"Since when are you a nurse?"

"Since today."

The banging outside is deafening, and some of the toddlers are crying and covering their ears. "Why are they putting up bars on the windows?" she asks Sister Joséphine.

"It's a mental hospital now."

"But it's not a prison."

"It is, in a way."

Elodie can feel her lower lip begin to quiver. "Will we be locked inside?"

"Yes," Sister says, not making eye contact. "This is the way it is now, so you must stop feeling sorry for yourself."

"Why is this happening?"

"Because you were born in sin."

Elodie bites her lip. She stares down into her bowl of gruel and concentrates on not crying at the table.

"Do we have lessons today?" Claire asks Sister Joséphine.

Elodie's head pops up.

"No," Sister says. "Today we have to get ready for the new patients. Tomorrow you start working."

"Why?"

"No more school."

"What new patients?" Elodie wants to know.

"Stop asking so many questions."

"What kind of work will we have to do?" Claire asks.

"You'll have to help take care of the other mental patients," Sister Joséphine responds, and Elodie notices she's made a point of inserting the word "other"—"*other* mental patients."

"*We're* not mental patients," Elodie clarifies.

Sister Joséphine sets down her spoon and stares directly across the table at Elodie. "Yes," she says, her voice cold, her eyes unflinching. "*You are.*"

An hour later, while the bars are still going up in the windows, a yellow school bus pulls up in front of the redbrick building that Elodie has always known as home.

"The crazies are here!" someone yells.

The orphans crowd around the windows in the front room with nervous anticipation to watch as their strange new roommates pile out of the bus one by one. The children and nuns let out a collective gasp as the spectacle unfolds before them—old men and women shuffling clumsily up the walk in pajamas, some of them babbling and singing, others in stupefied trances.

"They're old!" one of the children cries out.

"And scary!"

This is the third disturbing thing to happen this day.

Elodie feels a knot of panic tighten in her chest. She's old enough and clever enough to understand that life as she knew it is over.

CHAPTER 16

———✥✥✥———

Maggie

On her way to meet Roland at L'Auberge Saint-Gabriel in Old Montreal, Maggie can't help glancing inside her purse to look at her new bra. It's not so much the bra that thrills her as the achievement. The department manager at Simpson's gives a free brassiere to the number one salesgirl every quarter, and this time it was Maggie. She can't wait to tell Roland.

With her job at Simpson's and Roland by her side, her life in Montreal is turning out not to be such a bad backup plan after all. They are creating a solid, fulfilling life together in the city, and Maggie experiences more moments of genuine contentment than she ever thought possible.

Roland is waiting for her at their table, sipping a Scotch. There's a bottle of wine for them to share chilling beside him. She smiles and waves.

"How was your day?" Maggie asks him, unfolding the white linen napkin on her lap.

"Far too boring to discuss," he says. "I'm reviewing a loan proposal for a small mining company run by two very charismatic and persuasive brothers. They've managed to establish a viable business out there, which I admire. If I don't subsidize them, they'll be swallowed up by Noranda mines. I hate to see that happen."

Maggie nods in all the right places. Roland's cleverness and business acumen still impress her a great deal, but she can't say she finds it interesting. She decides on the escargots and *suprême de volaille* for dinner.

"So it looks like I'll have to go out to Rouyn later this month," Roland finishes as the waiter arrives to take their orders. "What about you. How was your day?"

She reaches for her purse and pulls out just enough of the white lace brassiere to show him, without anyone else seeing what it is.

"You bought a brassiere?"

"No. I won a brassiere," she explains. "I was the number one salesgirl this month!"

Roland doesn't say anything. He finishes his Scotch and reaches for the second, which has appeared next to the bread basket. "Congratulations," he says, staring into his glass. No smile, no feeling behind it.

"Aren't you proud of me?"

"For selling the most brassieres?" he says. "I'm not sure that's an achievement on par with, say, raising children."

Maggie blinks back tears as the waiter sets down her ramekin of escargots. The smell of garlic and warm butter wafts around her, but now she can't enjoy it. "I'm a natural with the customers," she murmurs. "I've got my father's instincts—"

"Let's change the subject."

"I want to keep working."

Roland puts down his fork and looks straight at her. "You mean measuring women's breasts all day? Where does that lead, Maggie?"

"Women's apparel. Department manager. Maybe even to a store of my own one day."

Roland chuckles sourly. "Get your head out of the clouds," he says dismissively. "You haven't touched your escargots, dear. They're delicious. Very buttery, just the way you like them."

"I thought you'd be happy for me."

"How can I be happy when I haven't got a say in what happens in our marriage?"

"What does that mean?"

"A man needs a legacy, Maggie. Otherwise, what's the point?"

The waiter delivers Roland's third Scotch and asks Maggie if something is wrong with the escargots. She shakes her head and forces herself to smile up at him. She picks at the rest of her meal, tasting nothing. They finish off the bottle of wine, and then Roland orders a cup of coffee to pep himself up for the drive.

At home, he heads straight for his liquor trolley in the living room and fixes himself a nightcap. "Drink?" he asks her.

She grimaces, kicking off her pumps. She notices one of the heels is scraped from the cobblestones in Old Montreal. She kneels down in the vestibule and rubs the scuff with her thumb.

"I want you to go off your birth control," he says, sitting down on the brocade sofa.

"Now?"

He leans back against the plump cushions and crosses his leg. "Yes. Now. *When*, Maggie, if not now?"

She should have seen this coming, but the truth is she's still not ready. She's not over Elodie. The wounds have not healed nearly enough to start again. "You haven't said anything before tonight—"

"Well, I'm saying it now," he snips. "I thought you'd bring it up at some point, but apparently it's not at the top of your priorities."

"You're being a bully."

"You told me you wanted children."

"I said not right away."

"And it's *not* right away!" he cries. "I've waited patiently for almost three years."

"I don't feel ready."

"You may never feel ready," he says. "But it's like diving into a lake. It just has to be done."

"Easy for you to say," she mutters, remembering the nausea, the weight, the heartburn, the contractions. The loss. "We have a good life together, Rol. We're happy. We don't need to rush to start a family. Not yet."

"I'm not going to wait until they make you manager of brassieres at Simpson's," he says. "That could take decades."

"I don't like you when you're drunk," she tells him.

He stands up, crosses the room to his liquor trolley, and pours himself another Scotch. "Funny," he says, plunking ice cubes into his glass. "My father felt the same way about me when *he* was drunk. Couldn't stand me. He did everything he could to avoid me. I rubbed him the wrong way, I suppose. Especially when he was drunk." He sits down, swishes the Scotch around in the glass and takes a healthy gulp. "Every time I opened my mouth, he cringed. I once overheard him say that to my mother."

Maggie is startled by Roland's unexpected confession. He's not in the habit of sharing personal stories with her, even when he's been drinking. "I was more surprised to hear him say it out loud than I was to hear that he didn't like me," he continues. "I knew of course that he didn't like me. A child knows."

Maggie nods, thinking of her own mother.

"I just want the opportunity to do better," Roland slurs. "I'd like to try to be a good father, Maggie. Don't you see?"

His lids are beginning to droop, and Maggie feels sorry for him. "We can discuss this in the morning," she says. "When you're not so drunk."

He responds with a loud snore.

Upstairs, she sits down at her vanity and combs her hair. Maybe Roland is right.

Maybe doing better than her mother did would be healing. What if she could make up for every kiss withheld, every caress denied? Raise a child who feels treasured and adored?

The idea begins to blossom as she gets ready for bed. A baby to love, a life to shape. She could do it with kindness and affection, not anger; with a gentle voice, the balm of acceptance, and all the nurturing that would enable a living thing to thrive. It might even turn out to be redemption for the daughter she gave up.

CHAPTER 17

———✑/✑/✑———

Elodie

1957

"Stay still!" Elodie cries impatiently.

Big Abéline barks like a dog and chomps her gums together as though she's about to bite.

"You don't even have teeth, *imbécile!*" Elodie says.

More barking.

"Stop barking, or I'll get Sister Louiselle," Elodie threatens. Sister Louiselle is the meanest nun at Saint-Sulpice. She arrived with the crazies two years ago to manage the mental patients and teach the other nuns—who, previously, had only ever cared for orphans—how to run the place like a hospital.

Big Abéline growls. She weighs about 250 pounds and could crush seven-year-old Elodie like an ant. Still, it's Elodie's job to wash Abéline before bed, which means scrubbing her back and under her armpits and even her private parts, which Elodie always skips.

Some of the other crazies are easier to handle. P'tite Odette is tiny and gentle, always cooperative. She has droopy eyes and a slow way of talking—Claire says from all the medicine they give her—but Elodie isn't even sure why she's here. Mam'selle Philodora is another one Elodie doesn't mind taking care of. She's retarded for real—not crazy like the other ones—and everyone likes her. She's always smiling and laughing, happy. She doesn't seem to know or care where she is. She likes to hug and cuddle, which Elodie enjoys in return.

Big Abéline is the worst. Elodie hates her. Her barking and growling, her sweaty thighs that are always covered in a rash, her unbearable stink.

"Why is she still in here?" Sister Louiselle says, coming into the bathroom.

Abéline barks at her.

"She's not letting me wash her," Elodie complains.

"Go to the dorm," Sister Louiselle says. "Say your prayers and get to bed."

Relieved, Elodie leaves the room and escapes to the dorm. She drops to her knees and pretends to pray. Crosses herself, not meaning it, slides under the crisp white sheet and pulls the wool blanket up to her chin. The younger girls are already asleep, the older ones still working. Elodie lets out a long sigh. Another boring day is behind her.

The room is cold for October. She used to love the fall, but that was back when she still got excited about things. There's no more playing outside, no more singing or coloring. No more sunshine on her skin, fall leaves, books, crayons, or hope.

She presses her doll, Poupée, to her cheek and closes her eyes. The good thing about working all day—whether she's bathing the crazies or making their beds or washing their dirty clothes—is that by the time she gets into bed at night, she's too tired for sad thoughts or even for listing all the things that make her angry. But tonight, just as she's hovering on the precipice between deep sleep and semiconsciousness, she's startled awake by a brusque shake.

"Heh?" she cries, rolling away from the intruder.

"It's time to wake up."

Elodie blinks in the dark, trying to orient herself. Outside, it's pitch-black. "It's the middle of the night," she moans, recognizing Sister Tata standing above her.

"You're going somewhere, Elo."

Elodie sits up, confusion giving way to exhilaration. "I'm leaving here?" she says.

"Yes," Sister whispers, helping her out of bed.

She puts her feet on the ice-cold floor and winces. "Did my mother come for me?" she cries, her voice bursting with hope.

"Of course not," Sister says. "Get dressed. Put this on."

"That's not my uniform," Elodie says, studying the dress Sister Tata has laid out on her bed.

"You don't need your uniform. Just put on the dress."

"It smells funny," Elodie says.

"*Chut!*" Sister Tata says, exasperated. "You and your debating."

"Where am I going?"

"To a new place."

"Why?"

"Because we're overcrowded here."

"Where is this new place?"

"You'll find out when the time comes."

"When will that be?"

"I don't know."

"Why do we have to go in the middle of the night?" Elodie wants to know, her excitement giving way to dread.

"I don't make the decisions," Sister Tata answers, moving down the narrow aisle to one of the other cots and waking another girl, and then another. "Now go wash up and get dressed."

"But—"

"Stop with your silly questions!"

A parade of girls joins Elodie in the bathroom to wash and change. When she returns to the dorm, she counts six of them in total lined up in their donated dresses, as sleepy and bewildered as she is. That's when she realizes with a wave of horror that Claire is not among them.

"Isn't Claire coming, too?" Elodie asks, panic rising.

"No," Sister says, collecting some of the saved trinkets from their First Communions and confirmations and dumping them into one small suitcase.

Elodie looks around at all the other sleeping girls with a stab of jealousy, not because she's happy here but because it's the only place she's ever known and it's beginning to dawn on her that she's leaving here for good.

"Let's go, girls. The train is waiting."

"The train?" Elodie cries, always the one to speak up. The other girls are older by at least two years and know better than to argue. "Where are we going?"

Sister Tata doesn't answer.

"I have to say good-bye to Claire—"

"There's no time," Sister whispers. "And you mustn't wake her."

Elodie looks beseechingly at the mound of Claire's sleeping body. How can she not say good-bye? They've been inseparable for the past five years. "Why can't I say good-bye to Claire?" she whimpers, tears springing to her eyes. "She won't know where I've gone!"

"Stop whining, Elodie. You'll wake the others."

Elodie reaches for Poupée and clutches her to her chest.

"You can't take that," Sister says, taking Poupée away from her. "I'm sorry. Dolls aren't allowed where you're going."

"But, Sister—"

"Hurry up, Elo."

The moment Sister Tata turns away to console one of the other girls who isn't allowed to bring her mother's silver chain with her, Elodie crouches down and grabs all the drawings she's ever made of her imaginary family. She's been hiding them beneath her mattress since the orphanage became a hospital, and now she stuffs them inside her bloomers. She won't leave those behind.

With one last look at the room where she's slept for as long as she can remember, Elodie shuffles down the hall, tears rolling down her cheeks. *Good-bye, Claire. Good-bye, Poupée.*

The air of mystery only adds to Elodie's sense of impending doom as she follows Sister Tata and the other girls down the stairs, shivering in her thin dress. As they reach the landing, she feels someone's hand wrap itself around hers. She looks up, and one of the older girls—a pretty, redheaded ten-year-old by the name of Emmeline—winks at her and squeezes her hand.

Outside, Elodie can see her breath in the air. A station wagon is waiting to take them to the train station. All six girls climb in the back while Sister Tata sits in the front seat, her small black Bible pressed to her lap. A million questions are on the tip of Elodie's tongue: *Where are we going? How far is it? Why us? Is it a proper orphanage or a convent?* But she dares not speak them aloud. Part of her is relieved to be pulling away from Saint-Sulpice—it's never been the same since it turned into a hospital—but her heart still feels heavy for the ones she's leaving behind. She is not crazy. She doesn't belong in a hospital, and she assumes they've finally figured out their mistake. Elodie can only hope that Claire will come along shortly with another batch of girls.

When they reach the station a few minutes later, they silently pile out of the car and follow Sister Tata single file down the length of the platform. The station itself is in a squat redbrick building beside a track, somewhere in the middle of nowhere. "Where are we?" Elodie whispers to Emmeline.

"Farnham," she says as Sister Tata hands some papers to a man in a funny hat. He checks them carefully and invites them to board.

"Bon voyage," he says.

Elodie sits beside Emmeline, still holding her hand. She has the window seat and stares outside with her nose pressed against the glass from the moment the train starts to rumble and shake until it jerks forward and starts pulling away from Farnham.

The sun is just beginning to rise, giving Elodie her very first view of the world outside the walls of Saint-Sulpice. The train rolls past miles of bright orange and red trees, vast fields, farms, and cows. Elodie is mesmerized and pensive as she takes in the unfamiliar landscape, trying to imprint all of it in her mind. Her whole body is tingling with anticipation, curiosity, wonderment, until, with a sudden bolt of dread, something occurs to her.

"Sister Tata!" she cries.

"Lower your voice, Elo," Sister says sharply. "What is it?"

"What if my mother comes for me?" she asks, tears filling her eyes. "I won't be there!"

One of the girls in the seat in front of her snickers, and Elodie reaches out and smacks her head from behind.

"Elodie!" Sister says.

"Will my mother know where to find me?" Elodie wants to know.

"Yes, Elodie. There's a Record of Transfer. Now settle down."

Relieved, Elodie flops back in her seat and rests her head against the window, peering through the glass until her vision blurs and she dozes off.

The next thing she knows, someone is tugging on her arm and dragging her to her feet. "We're here," Emmeline says.

Elodie looks around, taking in the gray buildings, concrete, cars, dirt, and funny smells. "Where are we?" she asks disapprovingly. "It's ugly and it smells bad."

"*Chut.*"

"It's Montreal," Emmeline explains softly. "We're in the city."

The city. Elodie's heart starts pounding. Another car is waiting for them. It's shiny and new, with the letters B-U-I-C-K written on the back. Elodie can read now, thanks to Claire, who taught her whenever they had snatches of free time.

Sister Tata instructs the girls to get inside the Buick. The mood in the car is somber as Sister turns around to look at them with a troubled expression on her face.

"Are you going to stay with us?" Elodie asks her.

"I can't, Elo. I have to go back to Saint-Sulpice."

Elodie squeezes back tears, trying not to be a baby, but her lower lip won't stop quivering. They drive through the city streets in silence, past tall buildings and garish signs that loom above them on every corner, dwarfing the landscape. DRINK PEPSI! ASK FOR LABATT! DU MAURIER, THE DISTINGUISHED CIGARETTE.

Elodie can see Sister Tata's lips moving as she recites her prayers to herself. Elodie is spellbound and repelled at the same time by everything happening around her. "Look at the train on the street!" she cries, pointing out the window.

"It's a streetcar," Sister Tata explains.

Finally, the car comes to a stop in front of an imposing gray stone building with a cross at the top of its center colonnade. At first Elodie thinks it's a convent, but then she notices the words carved into the stone facade: HÔPITAL ST. NAZARIUS.

"Another hospital?" she cries. "I don't belong in a hospital!"

Sister Tata gets out of the car. The other girls follow, but Elodie refuses to budge.

"Get out," Sister says harshly. "This is your new home, whether you like it or not. You won't be any worse off than you were at Saint-Sulpice."

Elodie reluctantly gets out and shuffles miserably behind the procession of the other more compliant orphans as they make their way up the front steps. What she wouldn't give to be back at Saint-Sulpice.

Once inside the foyer, a heavy double door is opened for them by another nun and then locked with a single twist of a large, gleaming gold lock. Elodie jumps as it clicks, and then she cowers behind Emmeline.

Sister Tata hands over the suitcase and some papers to the other nun—a short, thick woman with a pinched face, thin lips, and small dark eyes like a bat. "The youngest is seven," Sister Tata tells her, pulling Elodie forward.

The nun looks Elodie over, inspecting her with her wide-set bat eyes, and frowns. "She'll be in Ward B with the older ones," she says in a cold voice that makes Elodie want to hide under Sister Tata's skirt.

"Very well then," Sister Tata says, turning to face the girls. "I have to go back now."

Elodie bursts into tears. "Don't leave us!" she cries, wrapping her arms around Tata's waist. "I don't belong in a hospital!"

Sister Tata kneels down and cups Elodie's face in her hands. "You'll be with other orphans," she whispers. "Don't talk back and you should be fine."

And then she stands up and straightens her habit and touches Elodie's shoulder. "Good luck, girls," she says, and Elodie can see that her eyes are watering. "Sister Ignatia is in charge of you now."

They all turn to look at the nun whose grim demeanor, cartoonish frown, and harsh voice have already put the fear of God in them.

"Good luck," Sister Tata repeats, unlocking the door and disappearing into the first light of morning.

Sister Ignatia moves quickly to lock the door again. *Click.*

"Follow me," she says, and the girls do as they're told, walking behind her up six flights of stairs and then single file down a long, eerily quiet corridor.

Where is everyone? Elodie wonders, but doesn't dare ask.

At the end of the seemingly endless hallway, Sister Ignatia stops and unlocks another door, on which there is a sign: WARDS A–D.

The moment they pass through that door, the place springs to life, assaulting them with the smell of bleach, the purposeful comings and goings of nuns in white habits, and a cacophony of wailing and distant screams. They continue to follow Sister Ignatia until she stops in front of yet another mysterious room.

"This is the dormitory for Ward B," she says, pushing open the door to reveal a huge room with six rows of ten white iron beds, each one placed head to foot with barely enough space between them for a stubby chest of drawers no bigger than a filing cabinet. A simple cross hangs above the first bed of each row. Ten crosses, Elodie counts. Sixty beds, sixty drab wool blankets. Six barred windows facing a concrete wasteland and gray sky as far as the eye can see. In the corner of the room, a terrifying statue of Jesus on the cross presides over them, keeping watch when the nuns can't.

Sister Ignatia doesn't give them much time to absorb their surroundings before leading them along the back wall to the bathroom. "You have to go through the bathroom to get to the common room," she explains, striding ahead of them on short but efficient legs. She pushes open the door to the common room, and Elodie gasps.

"What's the matter?" Sister Ignatia says, turning to her with black eyes and flared nostrils. "You've never seen a mongoloid before?"

Elodie swallows a thick lump in her throat and nods her head. There was Philodora, but she was different somehow; sweet and harmless, not frightening like these girls.

"Better get used to them," Sister Ignatia barks.

The room is organized in similar fashion to the dormitory, only instead of rows of beds there are dozens of rows of rocking chairs, most of them occupied by girls not much older than Elodie who are babbling to themselves or snarling like animals or staring at the wall with weird dead eyes. They all have the same chopped hair. It's hard to distinguish the mentally retarded from the mentally ill; here in the common room, they're all lumped together. Somehow, the sight of young mental patients is more terrifying than the old ones back at Saint-Sulpice.

"Why are some of them wrapped up like that?" Elodie asks, pointing to a strange white jacket with buckles.

"It's a straitjacket," Sister Ignatia responds. "And if you don't behave, there's one for you."

Elodie steps back, still hiding behind Emmeline, and notices a naked girl whimpering in the corner. She's curled on her side, the bones of her white spine prominent, her knees pulled up to her chest, shivering violently.

Elodie can't believe her eyes. The girl's wrist is chained to a pipe.

Sister Ignatia doesn't acknowledge the girl, nor try to explain or justify the reason for it. It all seems to be part of normal life here at Saint-Nazarius.

After the tour is finished, it's time for haircuts. A moonfaced girl—one of the other patients—chops the new girls' hair into a broom style above the ears with a thick thatch of uneven bangs. When it's done, Elodie stares at herself in the bathroom mirror and frowns. Now she looks like the crazy girls from the rocking chairs.

"Are they all as horrible as Sister Ignatia?" Emmeline asks the moonfaced girl.

"They got rid of the last Ward B supervisor because she wasn't mean enough. In case you haven't figured it out, you've arrived in hell."

When the haircuts are done, the girls are made to line up for inspection. Sister Ignatia rejoins them and gives them a disdainful once-over.

"Sister?"

Everyone turns to look at the girl who, with trembling voice, has dared to address Sister Ignatia. It's Emmeline.

Sister Ignatia approaches her with a curious expression. "What is it?" she says.

"I think there's been a mistake," Emmeline tells her, meeting her icy glare. "We're orphans. We don't belong in a hospital like this."

Elodie wants to cheer. At last, someone has spoken the very words she's been dying to scream from the moment they pulled up this morning. This place is a madhouse. A place for the severely retarded and the lunatics, patients much worse off than the old people from the orphanage.

"You don't belong in a place like this?" Sister Ignatia repeats, her lips curling into a menacing half smile. "Where *do* you belong?"

Emmeline looks down at the floor. "An orphanage," she replies softly. "There still might be a chance for us to get adopted. No one will ever find us here—"

Without any warning, Sister Ignatia's arm crashes down on the side of Emmeline's skull. The blow is so powerful Emmeline stumbles backwards and lands on the floor, stunned.

"This is exactly where you belong," Sister Ignatia says, standing above her. "You were born in sin, were you not?"

She paces in front of the frightened girls. "You must never question whether you belong here. You're lucky we let you have a roof over your heads and food in your bellies. It's more than you deserve. Your lives are worthless, and you will be treated as such."

She turns back to Emmeline, who is still crumpled on the floor. "And you," Sister says, prodding Emmeline with her black boot. "You will stay in Ward D with the epileptics."

"No, please," Emmeline begs. "I won't say another word."

Sister Ignatia grabs a fistful of Emmeline's freshly chopped hair and drags her down the hall. Elodie blocks her ears to drown out

Emmeline's screams and bites her lip hard to keep from making a sound. She can feel the girls on either side of her trembling, and when she sneaks a peek, she sees tears streaming down their cheeks.

The rest of the day is a fog. The meals are inedible—brown meat and soggy vegetables with a drop of molasses smeared on the plate for dessert. The afternoon hours are interminable. The girls are left in the common room to rock in the chairs with the zombies. They haven't been assigned jobs yet, so there's nothing to do but stare at the walls and avoid being noticed by the nuns.

At night, Elodie slips gratefully under the itchy gray blanket on her cot and closes her eyes. Sleep will be her only reprieve here; she already knows that. The moment she loses consciousness, she will be free.

"Sit up."

Elodie opens her eyes, startled to see one of the nuns standing over her.

"Open your mouth."

"What for?" Elodie asks, regretting it immediately. The nun slaps her face.

"Open your mouth," she repeats.

Elodie opens her mouth and the nun places a pill on her tongue. "Swallow it," she says, handing Elodie a glass of warm water. "It's to help you sleep."

Elodie lies back down as the nun moves over to the next girl. She lies there for a long time, thinking about Sister Tata and Claire, wondering what they're doing. Do they miss her? Has Claire asked where she is? Will she ever see them again? Her thoughts turn to Emmeline, and she worries for her on the epileptic ward. She doesn't even know what an epileptic is, but it sounds terrifying.

And then, out of the ghostly silence, she hears a little girl singing a lullaby from across the room, and she wonders if she's dreaming. "*Fais dodo, bébé a Maman; fais dodo . . .*"

Elodie tries to move her head to see who it is, but she can't; she's paralyzed. She can barely keep her eyes open, too. Her body is floating now and she feels strangely calm. The little girl's song is soothing, buoyant in this dark place.

She hears someone whisper, "*Shh!* Agathe. Sister will hear you." But the little girl continues to sing. Elodie drifts off. Her mouth feels dry and her tongue thick; her hands and feet are tingling. "*Fais dodo, bébé a Maman; fais dodo . . .*"

And she disappears.

CHAPTER 18

———— ✒ ————

Maggie

Maggie digs her hands deep into the soil and breathes in the smell of dirt, a smell she still associates with her father's store. She can practically hear his voice as clearly as if he were standing beside her. *Forget using a trowel and plant the bulbs deep, at least nine or ten inches for tulips and daffodils.*

She always follows his instructions to a T. As a result, her garden is the pride of Knowlton. *The depth will keep the roots cool and moist during our hot dry spring. Now mulch the bed with bonemeal and bulb fertilizer.*

It's 1959 and Maggie is almost nine weeks pregnant. Having already had two miscarriages, both around eight weeks, she's reluctant to get her hopes up this time.

The miscarriages feel like retribution for having given away her firstborn. Since Maggie started trying to have a baby, Elodie has been constantly in her thoughts.

She's nine years old now, no longer a baby. It's strange imagining her growing up somewhere possibly nearby, a complete stranger. Maggie can't stop wondering what sort of girl she is, whom she looks like. Gabriel? Yvon? Blond or dark? Plump or slender? Optimistic, charming, sullen, or sad?

After the second miscarriage, Violet said, "Maybe something got damaged when you had your baby."

Her mother said, "Maybe God is punishing you."

Both hypotheses are plausible. Motherhood—which so far has proven to be frustratingly out of her reach—seems to be the singular prerequisite for feeling valued as a woman or being of any worth whatsoever in the world. If she can't get this right, it's hopeless.

Her life these days is spent traveling back and forth between two grand homes—both beautifully decorated, both lonely. Roland bought the country house in Knowlton after the first miscarriage, hoping it would cheer her up or at least give her a project. She still works at Simpson's, but she hasn't been promoted yet.

Roland works long hours, and Maggie is alone most of the time. Even on weekends, he drives into the city to spend time at the bank, leaving her by herself to rattle around the house. She tries to ignore her percolating resentment—she knows he doesn't want to be around her sadness—but it doesn't work. Roland, in spite of all his assurances and promises of compromise at the beginning, has turned out to be slyly inflexible.

Still on her knees, Maggie reaches for the hose and tenderly sprays her flowers. Gardening is meditative for her. This season she planted creeping vincas, which have spread across the rocks like pink carpet. She's got vivid phlox and gentians and geraniums, and spectacular running strawberry bushes along the sides of the stone walkway. She's not afraid to try unexpected things. Sometimes they exceed her vision; other times they fail miserably. No matter what, she loves her garden.

Some nights, long after Roland has fallen asleep beside her, she sneaks outside to inspect her work. She'll stand here, with her bare feet planted in the dewy grass, admiring her beloved annuals and perennials. It's the garden her father has always dreamed of making as soon as he can take some time off work. He has notes about all the unique and breathtaking bulbs he'd plant; detailed sketches that include perches where he could sit among his flowers; elaborate plans for a stone birdbath, a fountain, a pond full of frogs. He's always dreamed of languid days in which he would do nothing but garden. His office is still full of old plans, lists of potential flowers—brilliant bluebirds, lavender Canterbury bells, snow-in-summer—but he's never had the time. Not with the store and the catalogue and the mail-order. He always complains he's too busy with other people's gardens to have his own, but Maggie suspects he derives more pleasure from the planning and the daydreaming than he would from actually working on the damn garden.

After an hour of toiling in the soil, Maggie stands up. The cramps start the moment she gets to her feet. Back down she goes, doubled over in the grass. She can feel hot blood between her legs even before she sees it on her white shorts.

She stays there for a long time, lying in the grass. Too numb to cry, too devastated to move. Roland eventually comes home and finds her staring up at the sky.

"Maggie? Dear?" He crouches down beside her. "What happened? What did you do?"

"I didn't *do* anything!"

"Were you gardening?" he asks, his tone accusatory. "Did you overexert yourself? You were to take it easy—"

"You make it sound like I'm doing it on purpose!"

Roland's lips are pursed. "You were just supposed to . . . You weren't supposed to push yourself . . ."

"It's not my fault."

"No," he says quickly. "Of course not. It's just another setback."

"This is the third one."

"We'll go to a doctor," he says. "We'll get you looked after. We shall not give up."

Comforting words. Heroic. *We shall not give up!* At least it's something she can latch on to.

A few days later, Maggie finds herself staring at the telephone. She's wanted to do this for months, maybe even years. With a sudden burst of courage, she reaches for the receiver and dials. "Connect me to the foundling home in Cowansville, please," she tells the operator.

"One moment," the operator says, her voice crisp and neutral. Maggie lights a cigarette, exhaling into her coffee.

Within seconds, another woman comes on the line. "Good Shepherd Sisters," she says pleasantly. "This is Sister Maeve."

Nothing comes out of Maggie's mouth. She's staring into the mouthpiece as though it's a foreign object.

"Good Shepherd," the nun repeats. "Hello?"

"Hello, Sister," Maggie manages, with the appropriate amount of humility and respect in her voice.

"How can I help you, dear?"

Kindness. Maggie relaxes. "I'm looking for information about a little girl," she says.

"I'm sorry," the nun responds, her tone changing. "I can't help you."

"Well, but she's my daughter."

"If you had a baby and she's here, then she's not your daughter. Unfortunately, you have no rights in this province, dear."

"But I'm her mother."

"Best forget her. You understand if she's illegitimate, you've no rights? That's the law."

"I'm not even asking you to tell me where she is," Maggie says. "I just want to make sure she's been adopted—"

"The records are sealed," the nun says. "No one here or at any orphanage in Quebec can give you any information. Pray for forgiveness, child—"

"Please. I'd be so grateful for anything you can tell me," Maggie begs, the receiver trembling in her hand. "I only want to know if she was adopted so I can stop worrying she's wound up in an asylum—"

She holds her breath, waiting for Sister Maeve to tell her to forget it and move on. The nun sighs. "Do you know the date of birth?"

The question catches Maggie off guard. She hadn't really expected to get anywhere. "March 6, 1950," she says, her voice shaky.

"And the day she was brought here?"

"The same."

"Hold on, please."

Maggie tries to stay calm. Deep breath, deep breath. Her heart is hammering her chest. Sister Maeve is gone for a long time, at least ten or fifteen minutes.

"No infant girl was ever brought here that day," she says, returning at last.

"What about the next day?" Maggie asks, confused.

"No babies arrived here in March of 1950," she says. "I'm afraid you've got the wrong foundling home."

"Are you sure?"

"I'm sorry."

"Is there another one in the area? Close to Frelighsburg?"

"The closest I know would be in Sherbrooke," she says. "And a good deal of unwanted newborns go to Montreal."

Unwanted newborns.

"I'm sorry I can't be of more help, dear. God bless."

The line goes dead.

Maggie doesn't move for a long time. She lights another cigarette off the last one. Deda told her that her father took the baby to the foundling home in Cowansville. Why isn't there a record of Elodie's arrival?

Maggie impulsively reaches for the telephone and calls her father at work. "Where did you take my baby?" she asks him.

"Maggie?"

"I spoke to someone at the Good Shepherd foundling home," she says, vibrating with adrenaline. "Deda told me that's where you took her, but there's no record of a baby girl that or any day in March."

"They told you that?"

"Yes."

"It's illegal for them—"

"Where did you take her, Daddy?"

"Calm down," he says. "You shouldn't be dredging this up, especially now. You're pregnant."

Maggie squeezes back tears. She hasn't told her parents about the latest miscarriage. "Where did you take her?" she repeats.

"I took her to the foundling home in Cowansville," he answers, his tone rising. "Just as your aunt told you. Which she shouldn't have, by the way."

"And I told you no infant arrived there that day."

"Where else would I have taken her?" he asks. "I've got nothing to gain by lying, Maggie. That's where all illegitimate babies were brought. There wasn't exactly an abundance of choice in the matter."

"You didn't take her to Sherbrooke? Or Montreal?"

"I did not."

"It doesn't make any sense."

"Maybe there was an error, Maggie. I doubt very much their records are foolproof. In any case, you have to put the past behind you. You're lucky to have such a good situation now." She can hear men's voices in the background. "I have customers," her father says. "I have to go. Focus on the baby you're carrying now. The other one is a dead end."

CHAPTER 19

———✦———

Elodie

1959

Elodie tries to lift her head off her pillow, but it feels like bricks. The pill they give her at night turns her into a zombie the next day. She rarely feels awake. Instead, the world unfolds through a foggy slow-motion filter. She knows from the nuns that the pill they give all the patients is called Largactil. Some of the older girls in Ward B call it the lobotomy pill. Even though Elodie is only nine, she already knows what a lobotomy is from a girl named Nora. Nora was transferred from the epileptic ward last spring. When she arrived at Ward B, Elodie wasted no time asking her about Emmeline.

"She hasn't spoken since the lobotomy," Nora said matter-of-factly.

"What's a lobotomy?" Elodie wanted to know.

"It's when they stick an ice pick into the front of your brain to make you less violent," Nora explained. "They do it all the time at the surgery."

Elodie gasped, not believing it could be true. She ran to Sister Alice—the only semihumane nun on the ward—and tugged at her habit. "Is it true they stick ice picks in patients' heads to stop them from being violent?" she asked, breathless.

"What are you babbling about, Elodie?"

"Nora told me Emmeline hasn't spoken since she had the lob . . . lob . . . the thing where they make a hole in your head—"

Sister Alice sighed. "A lobotomy is a perfectly respectable oper-ation," she explained. "With the dangerous patients, there's no other choice."

"But Emmeline wasn't dangerous—"

"If you mind your business and stay out of trouble," she warned, "you won't need to get one."

That afternoon, Nora was chained to a pipe because of her "big mouth." She blamed Elodie and never spoke to her again, right up till she was transferred to another ward.

Elodie lies motionless on her cot, still groggy and dry-mouthed. In some ways, she's grateful for the Largactil. Although she hates how it makes her feel during the day—slow and foggy and dim-witted—it does dull the pain immediately before falling asleep and upon awak-ening. In those few minutes of docile stupefaction, when her thoughts are a blur and her mind barely conscious, she can forget. Everything has a hallucinatory quality—the other patients, the nuns, the hope-lessness of her incarceration. The Largactil at least neutralizes the despair for a while.

I'm not crazy, she reminds herself. *I'm not crazy.*

The lights go on and the girls rise from their beds. They shuffle to the washroom, brush their teeth, and splash cold water on their faces, trying to shake off the effects of the drug. The best that can be said about Elodie's days at Saint-Nazarius is that she doesn't mind her current job sewing bedsheets in the basement. Her first job was cleaning the bathrooms on all the women's wards. Floor upon floor, toilet after toilet, she did that for the better part of a year. When she heard from one of the other girls that there was a job sewing, she lied and said she knew how. Somehow, she got away with it. By observing the other sewers—and with the help of one of the old-timers, a kind epileptic named Marigot—she was able to pick it up fast enough to keep her job. Apparently, she has a knack.

After breakfast and prayers, Elodie makes her way down to the basement—her refuge—and sits down at the sewing machine. It doesn't bother her to sit for hours at a time without a break; the back pain is a luxury compared to how scrubbing floors and toilets made her body ache. Besides, there are worse jobs, like carrying the dead bodies out to the cemetery behind the hospital. Patients die at Saint-Nazarius almost every day—not just the old ones, but children, too. Word travels fast through the wards, filtering down from the older girls to the younger ones. In this place full of secrets, there are no secrets.

She gets to work sewing her quota for the morning—a dozen sheet hems an hour, two dozen by lunch break—letting her mind wander to the hum of the machine. She loses count of the sheets as they pile up beside her, but somehow the correct amount always gets done. Sister Calvert's bell clanging next to her ear startles her out of her daze.

So goes the monotonous routine of her days. Lunch is some kind of brown meat drowned in thick, clotted gravy. Dessert is always a smudge of molasses on the plate. Afterwards, it's back down to the basement, where she is expected to meet her afternoon quota—the threat of a transfer always looms—followed by more indiscernible mush for dinner and then back to her ward to rock mindlessly in the creaky chairs with the real crazies.

By nighttime, when the nun on duty stops at her bed to dole out the Largactil, Elodie takes it with a mix of dread and relief. She's grown to like it when her lids get heavy and her head starts to float, the precise moment when reality falls away.

Tonight, her last conscious thought before peaceful oblivion is, *Oh, there's the moon.*

She wakes up shivering and disoriented, her bed soaking wet. It's still dark and everyone is asleep. She's aware of a pungent vinegar smell. It takes her a few minutes to realize she's peed the bed.

For a long time, she lies in her own urine, contemplating how she's going to navigate the maze of beds to the bathroom. Her row is the farthest from it, and she's still semidrugged. When she finally has a strategy mapped out in her mind, she slides off her cot, strips the sheets, and rolls them into a ball.

She creeps carefully along the narrow space between the wall and the first row of cots, but she's still very groggy. Her legs aren't doing what they're supposed to—they feel like cooked noodles— and the room is spinning. The Largactil is powerfully immobilizing, but she uses the wall to steady herself. What she hadn't counted on was the strewn boot sticking out from under one of the cots.

The boot is supposed to be in the cubbyhole at the entrance to the dormitory; every girl has her own cubby—a small shelf above a hook to keep her precious few belongings—but leave it to Elodie to trip over a stray boot and go flying across the room. Had she been more alert, she might have been able to stop herself from falling so hard; instead, she reaches out for something to hold on to and winds up knocking over one of the metal nightstands. The nightstand and the lamp go crashing to the floor, the glass of the bulb shattering around her.

She can hear some of the other girls rousing. *What's happening? Who's there?* The light suddenly comes on, and Elodie is momentarily blinded. Her knees hurt and she can see she's bleeding from the broken bulb.

When she looks up, Sister Ignatia is towering above her, frowning. Short and stocky as she is, from Elodie's vantage point on the floor, the nun is a giant. "What happened?" she roars.

"I had to go to the bathroom," Elodie murmurs. "I couldn't see."

"It smells like you already went to the bathroom."

Elodie tries to hide the wet sheets with her body.

"You've woken everyone up."

"It was an accident," Elodie says. "I tripped over someone's boot."

"Are you trying to get someone else in trouble?"

"No, Sister. It was an accident."

"You should have been more careful."

Elodie can't hold back a rogue sob that escapes her lips.

"Go wait for me in the bathroom," Sister Ignatia tells her. "And take off that soiled nightgown."

"But I didn't see the boot!" Elodie cries, unable to control herself. "This isn't fair!"

"Fair?" Sister Ignatia says, her lips pulling into a frightening smile. "May I remind you that you are a patient in *my* hospital? I am your judge, and I judge not only your transgressions today, but *all* of your sins, as well as the sins of your parents. Now go and wait for me in the bathroom."

Elodie scrambles to her feet and scurries off to the bathroom. She removes her nightgown and stuffs it into the sink with her sheets, running hot water over the whole pile. Shivering and exposed, she wraps her arms around her bare chest and crouches down to generate some body warmth.

Sister Ignatia enters the bathroom carrying a large bucket of ice. Her demeanor is calm. She dumps the ice in the tub and shoves Elodie into it. Elodie tries to be stoic, but it's freezing and she starts to wail.

Sister Ignatia reaches for the large wooden scrub brush under the sink—the one they use for cleaning the floors—and scrubs Elodie's thighs until her flesh is raw.

"That should do it," she mutters with satisfaction, and then she holds Elodie's head under the tap. "Next time be more careful."

Before leaving, she tosses a clean white nightgown at Elodie.

The door swings closed behind her. Alone at last, Elodie climbs out of the tub and puts on the nightgown. "I'm not crazy," she whispers to her reflection in the mirror.

If she stops repeating it to herself, she may forget.

CHAPTER 20

Maggie

Maggie watches her mother sweep a pile of dirt into her dustpan and then dump the whole thing out the back door. "Those beasts never stop tracking filth inside this house," she complains.

She means her children, the three youngest who still live in her house. Maggie has a sip of ice-cold lemonade and moans with pleasure. Her mother's lemonade is made with fresh lemons, heaps of sugar, and a touch of honey for extra sweetness. The apple cake melts in her mouth, and Maman's sublime cooking almost makes Maggie forget how miserable it was to live with her. It helps, too, that her mother treats her way better now that she's married and someone else's problem.

Maman pours herself a glass of lemonade, slices off an end of cake, and sits down facing Maggie. It's Sunday afternoon. Roland and her father are in the maid's quarters, drinking and puffing on cigars.

"How are you feeling?" Maman asks. "Still got the morning sickness? I had it for months. Terrible. Remember?"

Maggie's been dreading this moment. She looks away. "I lost the baby."

"Again?"

"Yes," Maggie admits. "I saw a doctor, though."

Roland arranged an appointment with a specialist, Dr. Surrey, in Montreal. He gave Maggie a D and C, which he claimed would at least clean her out. "There's definitely residue in the uterus from one of the previous miscarriages," he said. "Which would explain the trouble you had with the last pregnancy."

"So you mean the residue from the first miscarriage might have caused the second?" Roland interjected. "And so on?"

"Absolutely."

"I knew there was an explanation," he said, pleased with himself.

"Miscarriages are quite common, Mrs. Larsson. They don't mean anything is necessarily wrong. However, without a follow-up D and C to clean up all the tissue, there's a greater chance of another miscarriage."

Maggie's uterus is clean now. The first miscarriage—a common, random thing—had likely caused the others. There's nothing to worry about, Dr. Surrey assured her. All they have to do now is start trying again. Their chances are excellent.

"You'll probably have a grandchild by next summer," Maggie tells her mother, sounding more optimistic than she feels. "He gave me a D and C, which he said should fix everything."

"How's Roland taking it?"

Roland's way is to make model trains and compulsively toil over teeny puzzle pieces and mostly to work. He's started to leave the house a little bit earlier in the mornings and come home later than usual in the evenings. He often misses supper. Maggie has always known he's uncomfortable being around her when she's down. Her moods frighten him, make him squeamish. She's learned this about him over the years: he needs everything in his life to be orderly and pleasant. He wants his wife to be perky and accommodating. She tries, but she's discovered she's a terrible actress.

In some ways he tricked her, pretending to love her ambition. Really, he only ever wanted her to have children. He's very good at pretending, something she's discovered gradually over the course of their marriage, by way of little crumbs of information he lets slip, usually when he's had too much to drink. His father was a cold, stern Swede who did not like him. His mother tried to compensate and cover up the father's disdain, right up until she died, leaving the two of them alone. Roland became a master at cultivating a veneer of cheeriness and normalcy, especially in an atmosphere of tension.

She wishes they could go back to the way they were, before they got so fixated on having a child. Roland is way more determined than she is, and it's changed him. It's put a strain on their friendship and affected the quality of their marriage—the very things she treasured most about their life together.

"He's making you pay," Maman says, picking at her cake.

"Who?"

"God."

"Maybe I'm not supposed to have children," Maggie says. "I wasn't sure I wanted any at first."

"No one really wants them," Maman admits. "But what other choice is there?"

"Didn't you want us?"

"Who thought about such things?" Maman says. "We just got pregnant. It's what was done."

"Why didn't you keep my baby?" Maggie asks her mother. "You could have raised her as your own. You like babies."

Maman frowns but doesn't disagree.

"She could have stayed in our family."

"Imagine what people would have said? You disappear for nine months and then all of a sudden *I've* got a new baby? The immaculate conception! Everyone would have known."

"Everyone probably knew anyway."

"What are you bringing this up for anyway?"

"Maybe she was my only chance at having a child."

"Stop feeling sorry for yourself."

"I thought I could forget her," Maggie says. "I did for a while, until I got pregnant again. And now . . . I don't know. I think about her a lot lately. If it wasn't for what happened—"

"Stop it."

"Where did Daddy take her?"

"There was a foundling home nearby. It was the only place we knew of."

"No infant was brought there in March."

"How do you know?" Maman asks, her eyes narrowing.

"I spoke to a nun there."

"You'll never find her," she says. "Trust me. They don't want you to find her."

"Who?"

"The church. Your father." She finishes her cake. "Just have another one," she says. "The odds are much better."

After supper, Maggie goes outside by herself. She heads straight down to the cornfield, wanting to get lost in there. As she makes her way through the stalks, she's able to breathe again. The air has the musky smell of ripe corn, a smell that instantly transplants her back to a time of romance and possibility, when her future felt as limitless as the stalks that seemed to grow right up into the sky.

A voice in the night startles her back to the present.

"Is that you?"

For a split second she thinks she's dreaming. She hears the corn crunching beneath his boots. His keys jangling. She stands very still, waiting. And then she turns slowly and he's there, filling the field like some beautiful hallucination. Just like in her fantasies.

"Hello, Maggie," he says.

"Gabriel?"

He smiles at her as though they're still teenagers and meeting here in secret. The decade of their separation dissolves and it's just the two of them and the smell of the corn and the humid air and the tickle of husks and tassels against their ankles.

CHAPTER 21

—⊙⁄√⊙—

Gabriel is twenty-seven. There's virtually nothing left of the country boy he was. He's filled out—his jaw is square, his shoulders broader, his muscles more defined. He's paler, and his blond hair, once thick and long, is now shaved in a buzz cut that makes his beauty starker, more angular. He's also bulkier in the chest and arms, probably from years of lifting heavy airplane parts. Maggie finds it hard to reconcile him with the boy he was a decade ago, when they made love for the first time in this very spot.

She feels self-conscious, worrying about her appearance.

"How've you been?" he asks, his voice light and with no hint of a grudge.

She searches his face for a flicker of what he once felt for her, but there's nothing there. He's looking her over, the way men do. Nothing more.

"What are you doing here?" she asks him.

"What are *you* doing here?" he says. "This is my field."

She smiles and he smiles, too.

"I'm visiting my parents," she says. "I still come out to the field whenever I'm here."

"I know you do."

Has he seen her here? Watched her from a window? "What about you?" she asks. "Angèle told me you don't come home much anymore."

"That was a long time ago," he says. "Clémentine needed some help on the farm. It's harvesting time."

"So you two have patched things up?"

"We've made amends," he says.

"You're still at Canadair?"

"Where else? The stock exchange?"

She laughs, but it comes out sounding shrill. She's not sure he intended it to be funny.

"I'm also driving a cab at night," he adds. "It's extra money."

He doesn't ask her anything else about herself. They stand facing each other in silence, which magnifies the volume of the crickets around them.

"You're married?" she says, trying to sound light.

"Yep."

"Kids?"

"No," he says. "Not for me. I don't want any."

A million different things go through her mind. Would he have wanted to raise her baby a decade ago—assuming it was his—or would he have fled the moment he knew she was pregnant?

"Do you want to go for a drink?" he asks her. He still hasn't asked if she's married or has kids. Maybe he knows from his sisters, town gossip. Maybe he doesn't want to know.

Maggie glances toward her parents' house, thinking about Roland holed up in the maid's quarters with her father. "I'd better tell them," she says, not being specific.

Back inside, she pounds on the door of her father's sanctuary. It opens a crack and she's immediately engulfed in smoke. Her father thrusts his head out, looking put out. Maggie glimpses Roland sitting in the leather armchair, his legs extended in front of him, a cigar in one hand and a glass of Crown Royal in the other. Mario Lanza is on the radio. "I'm going into town to meet Audrey for a drink," she tells them.

"Shall I drive you?" Roland offers in a thick slur. Ready to jump in the car and take her wherever she needs to go.

He's a good man, she thinks guiltily. If only he hadn't changed. If only she'd met him first.

"You're in no shape to drive on the country roads," she says. "We'll sleep here tonight. I'll tell Maman to make up Peter's old room for us."

"Hard to believe it's been ten years, eh?" Gabriel says over a pitcher of lukewarm draft. "I like your hair like that."

He reaches out and touches it. Maggie sits very still as his fingers slide slowly down her natural waves. Then he pulls back and chugs some beer, as though the caress was a perfectly ordinary gesture. "So do you have kids?" he asks her.

"Not yet. We're trying. I've had some setbacks—"

He nods but doesn't offer any sympathy or encouragement the way most people do. She refills her glass.

"What's your husband do?" he asks.

"He's a banker."

Gabriel lights a cigarette and exhales a straight line of smoke. "The Seed Man must be proud," he says. "He's English, obviously?"

"Are you still angry with me?"

"Why would I be?" he laughs. "We were kids."

She doesn't believe him.

"Do you have a picture of Annie?" she asks him. She's curious, like wanting to stare at an accident.

"You know her name?" he says.

Maggie blushes. "Angèle mentioned it. She must be pretty."

He shrugs. They finish off the pitcher and he orders another. She reaches for one of his cigarettes and he lights it for her with his Zippo. He flicks it shut with a swirl of his hand.

"So, here we are," he says. "Married to other people."

She opens her mouth to say something, but she's not sure how to streamline all her feelings into a cohesive sentence. She looks into his eyes and is certain of one thing: she still wants him.

"As soon as I saw you tonight . . ." he says. "You still look so good."

"You sound disappointed."

"I was hoping you'd gotten fat."

"I wish it hadn't taken us ten years to run into each other again," she says, suddenly overwhelmed by an urge to confess everything— her pregnancy, the baby, the foundling home, even Yvon. She's *nearly* drunk enough to do it, but in a moment of clarity, she decides to say nothing.

"Now what?" he says.

She shakes her head and they stare at each other for a long time, neither of them flinching or looking away. Maggie feels a spark of hope. For a quick moment, anything seems possible, but then a waitress comes by and Gabriel gestures for the bill. Maggie's mood collapses. She takes another one of his cigarettes and leans in flirtatiously for a light. "Are you happy?" she asks him, holding his wrist to keep the flame steady.

"What kind of question is that?" he says, leaving some cash on the table. "Let's go."

She follows him outside and they head toward Bruce Street. Without uttering a word, he reaches for her hand and holds it as they walk. It doesn't feel the least bit illicit; it feels natural and right.

"I wish we could just stay in this moment," she says as they approach the Small Bros. building.

"Why can't we?" he says, pulling her into the alley.

"What are you doing?"

He pushes her up against the brick wall. Without warning, he kisses her. What shocks her most about it is not his presumptuousness or even her own recklessness in responding, but her excitement. She's kissed him so many times before, yet it feels as exhilarating as that first time.

He presses up against her, pinning her to the side of the building. Her arms instinctively go around his waist, one hand slipping under his shirt and sliding up his smooth back. But when his hand is suddenly under her skirt and traveling up her thigh, she pushes him away. "Stop."

He ignores her.

"Stop!" she says again, her mouth against his ear.

He looks at her, surprised.

"We can't do this," she says. "Roland will be wondering where I am."

"Roland," Gabriel mutters, his fingers slipping between her legs, tugging at her panties.

"Please don't," she says weakly.

He stands back, glaring at her.

"This isn't how I want this to happen," she says.

"How *do* you want it to happen?" he asks angrily, adjusting his pants. "We're married to other people."

"Not cheating."

"You'd like me to leave Annie so you feel better about fucking me?"

"Gabriel, don't."

"That's not an option, Maggie." He swears under his breath and then impulsively punches the brick wall behind her head. "Same old Maggie," he says, shaking out his scraped hand. "Leading me on, flirting. But when it comes right down to it, you don't really want to disrupt your privileged little life, you just want to know you can still get me. Go back to your goddamn banker."

"I'd give anything for it to have all turned out differently!" she cries, her voice reverberating in the narrow alley. And the truth—hurled out into the night like that, so stark and inexorable—stops him. They both stay there, not sure what to do next.

"I'm sorry," he says. "I'm drunk. This was a mistake."

The words land like knives. He walks her home, to the edge of the cornfield—the place they once hid together, made love and disappeared together, found and lost and found each other. She inhales deeply, not wanting to go inside. The air is humid and has that fragrance of high summer, a blend of dew, budding flowers, and fresh manure. The sky is starless. She realizes she's crying, but Gabriel probably can't see her tears in the dark.

Maybe this is for the best, she reasons. Lust is just a choke hold that renders the heart and mind completely powerless. At times, it has nearly destroyed her parents. She's better off with Roland, who is—or at least was—her friend.

"Good night," Gabriel says.

Without saying a word, she turns away from him and starts her climb up the hill.

"Hey!" he calls after her. "I work the day shift at Canadair till three fifteen."

A dare.

CHAPTER 22

⟨⟨⟨ ✦ ⟩⟩⟩

Maggie turns off the TV after *Gunsmoke* and goes upstairs to her bedroom. She removes her clothes, puts on her favorite white nightgown with the eyelet ruffle bib, and sits down on the edge of her bed to comb her hair. She gazes absently at the wallpaper—a red toile de Jouy depicting French pastoral scenes—and realizes she's already sick of it. She still loves the room, though; it was one of the main reasons she wanted this house. It has a fireplace and coffered ceilings and a breathtaking view of the backyard.

She can hear Roland brushing his teeth and she knows what will be expected of her tonight. He's going to emerge naked beneath his velour robe and peel the bedspread back in a neat triangle, just enough for him to slide under without disturbing it too much. Then he'll lean across the bed and give her a minty, utilitarian kiss on the lips. She can practically smell the Colgate on his breath. Years of obligatory, anxiety-filled intercourse in an effort to procreate has accelerated the unraveling of their sex life.

"Duplessis is dead."

"What?" she gasps, looking up to find Roland standing in the doorway of their en suite bathroom.

"I just heard it on the radio," he says, his tone excited.

Last night on CBC it was reported that Duplessis had fallen ill after suffering a cerebral hemorrhage. Having never considered that a man as powerful as Duplessis might be vulnerable to such mortal inconveniences as illness or death, Maggie is genuinely shocked. "My God," she says, overcome with some sense of vindication. She immediately runs downstairs to call her father.

"The dictator is dead!" he cheers.

"It feels strange in a way, don't you think? He's been in the background of my life for as long as I can remember."

"It took a brain hemorrhage to get him out of that office, but by God, Quebec is finally free."

"What if the next premier abandons agriculture?"

"Sweetheart," her father says, "as this province soars, so, too, will Superior Seeds."

He's in a boisterous mood. Maggie can already picture him at work tomorrow, gloating and puffed up with satisfaction.

She returns to the bedroom to find Roland tucked under the chenille bedspread, holding his transistor radio on his lap. He carries it around the house with him like a pet.

Maggie goes directly into the bathroom to brush her teeth. When she's done, she stares at herself in the mirror for a long time, trying to see herself the way Gabriel must have seen her the other night. Her face is rounder than she's used to—probably bloating from the last pregnancy. Or maybe cynicism and disappointment are already quietly undermining the beauty for which others have so often praised her. This may be what happened to her mother. Maggie remembers that photograph of Maman in the push lawn mower, how beautiful she was in her twenties. How different she is now.

Maggie is slightly closer to thirty than twenty. She shuts her eyes against the image of her future self—a clone of her mother with no discernible trace left of her youthful, lovely self except for a single photograph, framed and sitting on a doily in her bedroom, for her future children to ruminate over and stare at in bafflement. She switches off the bathroom light and joins Roland in bed.

"I still can't believe it," he says.

"This date should be a provincial holiday from now on."

"It's been a long time coming," Roland agrees, and sets his radio down on the bedside table.

Maggie snuggles up to him, resting her head on his chest. "What'll happen now?" she wonders aloud.

"Only good things, I expect. Let's hope his replacement can move us forward into the twentieth century."

"It's truly the end of an era."

"Your father must be elated," Roland says.

"He'll probably throw a parade."

They both laugh, and then Roland leans in to kiss her with all the awkwardness of a teenage boy making his first attempt. She gently pushes him away. "Not yet, okay?"

He slumps back against his pillow and stares off in the distance, looking hurt. "I thought we were going to start trying," he says. "The doctor said after the tubal washing we should start immediately."

"I'm just not ready, Rol."

Roland sighs. "I understand," he says, softening. "But soon, all right?"

She kisses his chest and her body relaxes. "Thank you," she says, relieved.

The holidays come and go without much fanfare, followed by a long, deep winter hibernation, in which Maggie spends too much of her free time trapped indoors, thinking about Gabriel and their dreamlike encounter in the field last fall. Curled up by the fire day after day, in the same wool sweater and thick ski socks, Maggie loses large chunks of time to her richly imagined fantasies.

And then one afternoon, shortly after winter has broken, Maggie finds herself in an unfamiliar part of the city. It's as though she's been holding her breath all these months and now, suddenly, she can't hold it for another moment. It's a new decade—the fifties are over—and she feels restless, brazen from the cabin fever. She needs to breathe.

Canadair is near the Cartierville Airport in Saint-Laurent. There's a bus that stops along Sherbrooke Street that will take her straight to Côte-Vertu. She walks purposefully, enjoying the mild March weather and the season's first strong rays of sun on her face.

When she was a little girl, Canadair was well-known for manufacturing airplanes during the war. A lot of the farm boys like Gabriel used to travel to the city and work shifts all through the winter. She remembers Gabriel bragging back in the late forties, when Canadair began making F-86 Sabre Jets, as though he himself were the one making them. He used to say that helping to build airplanes for the Royal Canadian Air Force was a privilege, even though he only made forty-three cents an hour and worked seventeen-hour shifts.

She's thinking about all of this as the bus comes to a stop at Côte-Vertu and the full magnitude of what she's about to do presses down on her like the airplanes landing on the Cartierville tarmac.

CHAPTER 23

———✦✦✦———

Maggie traces the blue-and-white fleur-de-lis tattoo on Gabriel's biceps with the tip of her finger. She imagines that making love with him now, as a woman, will be very different than it was when they were young. Their tender, tentative adolescent lovemaking—as well as the last few years of perfunctory sex with Roland—have taught her very little about sex or even about how to be in her body. Sex with Gabriel now, she fantasizes, will be more mature and free.

But not yet. This time she's waiting. Out of respect for Roland and a healthy fear of repeating past mistakes, she's told Gabriel she won't sleep with him until they're sure they want to make a commitment.

"When did you get this?" she asks him about the tattoo.

They're at his friend's bachelor apartment on Papineau. There are beer bottles and ashtrays everywhere, mice scurrying boldly across the linoleum and gusts of wind rattling the drafty windows. The friend who rents the place is never around. Maggie suspects he keeps it for sleeping with women who are not his wife. Gabriel says it's nothing like that, but never elaborates.

"Couple of years ago," he says. "Do you know what the fleur-de-lis stands for?"

"It's on the Quebec flag."

"It was the first provincial flag in Canada," he says. "One of the few good things Duplessis accomplished."

"So you had it tattooed on you?"

"It's meaningful to me," he says. "It was from a banner that was carried by Montcalm's French-Canadian soldiers at the victory of Carillon." He lights a cigarette and picks up an ashtray from the floor. "You probably can't understand."

After a long silence, she says, "You still haven't really forgiven me, have you?"

"Forgiven you for what?" he asks.

"For ending it the way I did."

"We were teenagers."

"What if we'd stayed together?"

"It would never have worked then," he says dismissively.

"Maybe this would have been enough," she murmurs, snuggling closer to him.

"Meeting secretly in this dump?"

"Being together."

"You're too much of a romantic."

"Am I?" she says. "What is this to you then?"

"I don't know. Me trying to have sex with you."

She playfully punches his shoulder.

"And to you?" he asks her.

"I'm hoping it's a second chance for us," she admits.

He runs his hand along her hair and then lets it drop back to his lap. "We're both married, Maggie. Is the future really an option for us anymore?"

"If it isn't, why are you here with me?"

"I told you. I want to sleep with you."

"And if I don't?"

Gabriel sighs, exhaling at the same time. "I honestly don't know," he tells her. "But I like being with you. It's easy. You know me."

"Doesn't your wife?"

He shrugs. "It's different. She knows part of me. The man I became when I moved here for good."

"And who is the Gabriel I know?"

"The insecure boy who pulled a knife on a couple of thugs," he says. "The farmer's son. The kid who fell in love with an English girl who ended up breaking his heart."

She reaches out and touches his face.

"But you made the choice for us, Maggie, and it wasn't me."

She turns her head away, unable to look him in the eyes. It's on the tip of her tongue to blurt out that it was her parents who made the choice for her, *her father*. But then she'd have to tell Gabriel about the baby and she's not ready for that conversation.

"Anyway," he says, "it's the best life for you."

"What is?"

"*His* life. The one you're living."

"Who? Roland's?"

"Your father's."

"It's not that simple."

"He always had you brainwashed, Maggie."

"My mother used to say the same thing."

"You couldn't have it all, I guess," he says, his tone lighter. "The big house, the banker, your old man's approval, *and* me."

"That's mean," she says, standing up to leave.

He grabs her arm, pulls her back down on the couch, and straddles her. She can feel his erection and it makes her weak. "Do we have to talk so much?" he asks, his breath warm against her neck. "Let's just stop talking. It only causes problems."

He kisses her on the lips and the hairs on her body stand up. She tickles his back under his flannel shirt, remembering that first time in the cornfield when he was just a boy. The sweat on his tanned skin, the way his ribs stuck out, the cocky way he would strut up and down those stalks. And now here he is with that same lean, strong back and the same erratic temperament that never could manage to conceal his inner struggle between pride and vulnerability, between who he was and who he aspired to be. That's what he meant when he told her she was the only one who really knew him.

"Let's just enjoy this moment together," he whispers.

"You mean have sex."

"Of course."

How can she enjoy their time together when her mind keeps leaping forward, strategizing and fantasizing, greedily wanting all of him? She dreads having to go home to Roland and his crusade to get her pregnant; to all the pretending and politeness, the smiling and fakeness. Gabriel is real; she wants their relationship to be real. She has no interest in embarking on some kind of illicit affair, filled with secrecy and guilt and uncertainty. She can't stand the thought of him returning home to Annie tonight, sleeping beside her, talking intimately the way couples do. She wonders how often he makes love to Annie and if he enjoys it, and it's killing her not to ask him.

He kisses her neck and she lets out a small cry.

"What now?" she murmurs, but he doesn't answer.

CHAPTER 24

—⁂—

Elodie

1960

One day at lunch, someone tells Elodie matter-of-factly that Emmeline from the Saint-Sulpice Orphanage is dead. "You were there with her, weren't you?" the girl asks, shoveling meat in her mouth. "At Saint-Sulpice?"

"How did she die?" Elodie wants to know, her appetite vanishing.

"Overdose of Largactil, I heard."

Elodie is outraged. She's used to keeping her anger inside, despairing silently so as not to get in trouble, but this is more than she can tolerate. She'll never forget how Emmeline held her hand the night they arrived, the way she spoke up for all of them by telling Sister Ignatia they didn't belong here.

Emmeline isn't the first one to die and she certainly won't be the last. Elodie has a thicker skin about it now, or perhaps a harder heart. She's ten now and takes things more in stride. Death waits in every corner of Saint-Nazarius, as real and ubiquitous as the nuns themselves, but never has it been this close to home.

A few days later, when strange itchy red spots appear all over her body, forcing Sister Ignatia to send her to the infectious disease ward on the third floor, Elodie seizes the opportunity to finally speak up on behalf of Emmeline and all the orphans.

"Chicken pox," the doctor confirms, taking a quick look at her neck and arms. "You mustn't scratch like that."

Elodie is studying him carefully, trying to assess whether he's one of *them* or someone who might be able to help her. He seems decent enough. His eyes are bright blue and she likes the look of his moustache and the pocket square in his white coat.

"I'm going to give you a bottle of calamine lotion," he says. "Stop scratching, young lady. You'll have scars."

She almost bursts out laughing. Scars! If he could see the scars she's already got from all the beatings. He thinks she cares about chicken pox scars? He has no idea.

He slathers her with pink lotion that feels cool on her skin and instantly soothing. "You should cut your nails, too."

"Doctor?"

"Hm?"

"A girl from the sixth floor died the other day."

"Yes," he says abstractly. "This is a hospital. It happens."

"But there was nothing wrong with her."

"She wouldn't have been here if that was so."

"There's nothing wrong with *me*," Elodie informs him. "And I'm here. Most of us up there are perfectly normal. We're just orphans. We're not crazy."

"Your records say otherwise."

"What records?"

"When you were transferred here," he explains. "We have your records."

"What does mine say?"

"I'm not privy to the psychiatric ward's records," he says. "But I assure you if you're here, there must be a reason."

"I'm normal," Elodie says adamantly.

"Stop scratching," he says.

"Can I see what's written about me?"

"Of course not."

"I don't want to die in here," she says. "They killed Emmeline giving her too much Largactil. She came here with me from the Saint-Sulpice Orphanage and she was fine. She was smart and normal and they gave her a lobotomy."

"It sounds like she was a very sick girl."

"But she wasn't, though. Not when we first got here. And now they've killed her."

"You're being very dramatic."

"She's not the only one," Elodie goes on. "Last year another girl disappeared in the middle of the night. I heard her body was thrown out back and buried in the cemetery. All she ever did was sing."

Elodie still remembers the little girl who used to sing herself to sleep every night, her sweet voice floating across the room. Her name was Agathe. She was only about five, but Sister Ignatia used to beat her to try to get her to stop. One morning when Elodie woke up, some-one said, "Agathe is gone."

Her bed was empty. Freshly made as though it had never been slept in.

Nothing was ever said about what happened to her. No explana-tion was offered, as though they weren't worthy of knowing.

"They do all sorts of terrible things to us," she tells the doctor. "Can't you help us? Does anyone know what they're doing to us up there?"

"Calm down," the doctor says, frowning.

"Were the crazy patients in my ward crazy before they got here?"

"How would I know that?"

"Will I turn crazy if I stay here?"

"Where are you getting these ideas?"

"Please help me," she begs. "We've been forgotten up there. And the nuns . . . they're cruel. They torture us. Please, isn't there some-thing you can do?"

The doctor places a hand on her knee. "I'll look into it," he tells her. "Calm down and I'll get to the bottom of it."

Elodie nods obediently, her whole body caving with relief.

"Take this," he says, handing her the calamine lotion. "And put it on when it gets too itchy."

"Thank you, Doctor."

He winks and she leaves the room, feeling lighter and happier than she has in years. She smiles at Sister Calvert, who's waiting for her by the door, and says, "Chicken pox."

"You seem awfully happy about it," Sister mutters, and shuffles off down the hall, her habit swooshing with every step.

Several days pass and nothing happens. Elodie waits for the doctor to appear, expecting his visit. He promised he would look into it. Maybe the nuns are giving him a hard time, she reasons, and she has to be patient. Wouldn't it be something if he exposed the whole situation here and the hospital realized there'd been a terrible mistake and set them free? Sent them back to Saint-Sulpice, where, to the best of Elodie's recollection, she'd been relatively happy?

Lying alert on her cot one night, about a week after her visit to the doctor, she realizes that no one ever came by to give her Largactil. Maybe the doctor said something about Emmeline's death after all and the daily tranquilizers have finally been outlawed. She has mixed feelings about not having her sleep medicine, but a surge of excitement at the possibility of freedom drowns out all other concerns.

The next thing she knows, rough hands are shaking her awake. She tries to sit up, but someone pulls a pillowcase down over her head, making it difficult to breathe. There are hands grabbing at her, pulling her this way and that. The world is black under the pillowcase, but she can hear the buckles of the straitjacket as they attempt to get it on her. She thrashes, her screams muffled by the fabric, terrified she's going to suffocate.

"*Calme-toi!*" one of them hisses, and she immediately recognizes Sister Ignatia's voice.

They're wrestling with her now, but she's making it very difficult for them to fasten the buckles. "Stay still!" Sister Ignatia says impatiently, and then punches her in the head.

Elodie's body goes limp. The straitjacket is tightened. Sister Ignatia is barking orders. Elodie realizes the other assailants are patients just like her, willing to comply, relieved it's not them. They carry her in total blackness to another room, where's she's dumped on her back on a metal bed frame and then tied to it like an animal. There's no mattress, and she can feel the sharp metal coils digging into her back where the straitjacket doesn't cover her body.

The pillowcase comes off her head, and Elodie realizes, to her great horror, that she's in a dark, airless cell with boarded-up windows. The heat is stifling. "What have I done?" she cries, pleading with Sister Ignatia. "Why are you doing this to me?"

Sister Ignatia does not answer, and her silence is more frightening than anything she could have said.

"Please don't leave me here!" Elodie wails. "Please! Sister—"

Sister Ignatia slides a bucket under the bed, and Elodie understands immediately that she's going to be here for a while; that she won't be untied, even to go to the bathroom.

"Don't leave," she pleads. "It's so hot. Please—"

Sister Ignatia turns sharply, the skirt of her habit swishing at her feet, and marches out of the cell with her lackeys trailing mutely behind.

Elodie contemplates screaming out, but quickly discards the idea. She knows no one will hear her; if they did, no one would come. She squirms around on the cot, trying desperately to find some shred of comfort—a slightly bearable position at least—but it's impossible with the straitjacket and the heat and the metal digging into her flesh. Sleep doesn't come either. Without a mattress or air circulation or the ability to move her limbs, she can only lie there, berating herself for not having tried to escape a long time ago.

Could she have? Not at seven years old. Not once she was locked behind the doors of Ward B. Agathe escaped. Emmeline escaped. Perhaps death is the only viable way out. She decides she will never again grieve the death of another Saint-Nazarius girl. Why should she? They're free, they're at peace, and she, Elodie, is the one left in hell.

She measures time by the meals they bring her three times a day—a purée of whatever was served in the cafeteria. The cell reeks of urine and feces and her own vomit. Once in a while, out of intolerable boredom, she prays. She bargains with God, questions how He can allow her to be treated this way, but no answer ever comes, only more of His callous silence, a void where there is supposed to be solace. She hates Him almost as much as she hates Sister Ignatia.

After nearly a week of imprisonment—exactly seventeen vile milkshakes—the door opens and Sister Ignatia appears, her expression smug. She unlocks Elodie's chains and wordlessly unfastens the straitjacket. Elodie winces the moment her arms are free. Her muscles are stiff, her joints ache, and her bones are weak. Every inch of her body hurts. When she tries to sit up, she lets out a cry and collapses. The sharp metal in her back was preferable to the pain of trying to move.

Sister Ignatia hands her a dress, wincing at the stench from the overflowing bucket, and then covers her mouth and nose with her hand.

"Is it because I told the doctor about Emmeline's overdose?" Elodie wants to know.

A flash of something gleeful—victory or amusement—passes over Sister Ignatia's bat-like eyes, but she doesn't give Elodie the satisfaction of a response.

CHAPTER 25

Maggie

Maggie wakes up from a terrifying nightmare, crying out so loudly she wakes Roland. She leans over and turns on the lamp with trembling fingers. Her heart is racing.

"What's the matter, dear?" he says, placing his hand on her shoulder.

"I dreamed I was drowning," she says, trying to calm down. "I was pregnant and we were both drowning, the baby and I. I kept thinking, *I can't lose this one, too.* Oh Roland, it was awful!"

She doesn't mention that the unborn baby's name in her dream was Elodie.

Roland pulls her close and they lie back together, leaving the lamp on at her insistence.

The next day, having barely recovered from her sleepless night, Maggie sits down in one of the booths at Fern's and orders a cup of coffee while she waits for Audrey. Maggie's got a driver's license now and a Ford Falcon that Roland bought her for her birthday. Now that she's finally quit Simpson's, she has even more free time on her hands, mostly to ruminate over the two lives she finds herself caught between—which is no doubt to blame for her recent nightmares. One of those lives contains her beloved homes, her treasured garden in the country, and her marriage to a wonderful man she can never quite love enough; the other—still mostly a fantasy—contains Gabriel, which, she believes, is enough.

She hasn't stopped thinking about him since their encounter at the apartment on Papineau. She's been telling herself a lot of things lately to justify her emotional infidelity, but the one that seems to assuage her most is that she should have been with Gabriel all along. She's only just found him again, but her feelings are as deep and un-yielding as they always were. Roland doesn't ask much of her. He works long hours and is generally happy when she's happy. His trust and complacency—or unwillingness to scratch beneath the surface of things—makes falling in love with another man almost too easy.

She lights a cigarette, still thinking about how things left off with Gabriel when she went to the apartment the other day. *Say hi to Audrey for me*, he said as she was leaving.

His tone had an edge to it. She'd made the mistake of letting him know she was getting together with Audrey in Dunham. Of course it brought back that incident long ago, with Barney and the fight in the street when Gabriel pulled a knife. He didn't have to say it, but he was angry—she could see it in his face at the mention of Audrey's name. Maggie regretted it immediately.

They didn't speak while she collected her things. A familiar ten-sion had wedged itself between them, and she worried fleetingly that maybe love could not surmount one's roots. She wants to believe love is irrepressible, but what if it can't hold its own against who a person is, fundamentally, at the core? It terrifies her that they would have to give up on each other after all this time and retreat to their respective sides, defeated by the complexities of language and class.

"Can I see you again Friday?" he asked her.

"I can't," she said. "Roland likes to see a show on Friday nights."

"*Qu'i mange d'la marde*," Gabriel muttered. *Let him eat shit.*

She kissed him and touched his face. His eyes were dark gray, angry.

"Another day," she said. "Any day but Friday. I want to see you again."

He looked away. She made him promise to call her. That's how they parted.

She glances up from her cup of coffee and sees Audrey waddling toward her. Audrey is seven months pregnant with her third child, rosy-cheeked from being outside, and more adorable than ever. Her blond hair is bleached platinum now, like a movie star's. They've continued to stay in touch over the years, politely and from a distance, just enough to still be able to count each other as an acquaintance. Audrey likes to send Christmas cards with photographs of her family, accompanied by long, self-indulgent letters detailing their achievements with exclamation points. *Barney was promoted! Lolly is finally potty trained! Davie won the Goutte de Lait Healthy Baby contest!* She also likes to get together once or twice a year for pie and coffee so she can brag in person.

"How are you feeling?" Maggie asks her.

"Not so bad," Audrey says, sliding her unwieldy body into the booth. "You look gorgeous. You've still got that figure. I envy you."

Maggie smiles, but she can tell Audrey does not envy her at all. Audrey orders a coffee and some apple pie and takes a drag off Maggie's cigarette. "Where do we begin?" she says, clapping her hands together.

"How are the kids?"

"Lolly is a hoot, and Davie is an absolute *mohn*-ster. I'm crazy to be having another one! I don't know what I'll do if it's another boy. Listen," she says. "Before we get into things, how are *you* coping, Mags?"

Maggie tips her head. "Coping?"

"I hear you're having a hell of a time getting pregnant," Audrey says, her voice turning sympathetic. She lowers her voice and whispers, *"The miscarriages."*

Maggie flicks her ashes into the ashtray. "Where did you hear that?" she asks.

"Oh, you know Dunham," she says. "Violet, I think."

"I've had a tubal washing," Maggie tells her. "The prognosis is good."

Audrey is obviously rooting for Maggie to get on the baby band-wagon. People seem to have so much invested in a married woman getting pregnant within the accepted timeline. It troubles them when it doesn't happen, as though some universally agreed upon contract has been tampered with or disturbed. Maggie can actually feel the unspoken championing of her success at fertility, the simultaneous panic if she were to fail.

The waitress brings Audrey's pie. "Do you think . . ."

"What?"

"Never mind," Audrey says. "Forget it." She has a bite of her pie.

"What?"

"Well, I wonder. Do you think . . . Is it possible there was some damage from the, um, first pregnancy?"

"Yes. That's exactly what the doctor said. There was scar tissue after the first miscarriage—"

"No, Maggie," she interrupts. "That's not the pregnancy I mean."

Maggie freezes. Audrey is rubbing her belly protectively, watching Maggie. "What are you talking about?" Maggie manages, her chest pounding.

"Oh, it's all right, Maggie. I've always known."

Maggie stubs out her cigarette and lights another one. Her fingers are shaking. Audrey reaches across the table and touches her hand. "It doesn't have to be a secret anymore," she says.

"How did you find out?" Maggie asks, trying to keep her voice calm and contain the waves of shame rising up in her throat.

Audrey gobbles another forkful of pie and burps. "I've got the worst indigestion," she says. "To be honest, I always suspected."

"How?"

"I know what Gabriel expected," she says. "I wouldn't go all the way with him, which is probably why he traded me in for you."

The remark stings and Maggie glares at her. "How did you know I was pregnant?"

"There's a reason girls get sent away for a year," Audrey says. "And, well, now you've confirmed it."

Their eyes lock. Maggie is suddenly confused about why Audrey wanted to meet with her today. Perhaps Audrey's been biding her time for years, waiting for just the right moment to pay Maggie back for stealing Gabriel.

"I wasn't pregnant when they sent me away."

Audrey's blue eyes widen. "You weren't?"

"No, my parents sent me away to keep us apart. Just like I told everyone. It was all true."

"And he came to see you there? He got you pregnant while you were *there*?" She leans back in the booth, looking very satisfied. "Don't be mad at me for bringing it up. I'm just curious."

Maggie is quiet as she tries to guess at Audrey's motives. Maybe she's just trying to be a friend. Before Gabriel, they'd been inseparable.

"I just want you to know that I'm here if you need someone to talk to," she says, burping into her napkin. "I know we grew apart when I started dating Barney, but I've always missed our friendship. I know you're going through a hard time right now. I wanted to reach out."

"Does anyone else know?" Maggie asks her.

"Not that I know of," Audrey says. "Does Gabriel know?"

"No," Maggie says. "Not yet. And please, no one else should know. I'll tell him when the time is right."

"It's been ten years."

"I hadn't seen him until recently."

"So you're in touch with him again?"

Maggie swallows nervously, wishing she could backtrack. "We ran into each other," she says vaguely. "We were both home visiting. I *am* going to tell him. Soon."

Audrey nods, smiling sympathetically. "What was it like?" she asks. "Being pregnant and knowing you were giving up the baby?"

"I don't really remember," Maggie lies.

"I always feel so bonded with my babies when I'm carrying them."

"I guess I liked the feeling of her inside me."

"*Her?*"

Maggie nods.

"A girl?" Audrey gasps, as though knowing the sex makes it all the more tragic. "Will you try to find her one day?"

"Giving information to the birth mother is illegal," Maggie explains. "So it won't be easy, but yes, I'm going to try. I've already called the foundling home where she was supposedly taken."

Audrey raises her perfectly plucked and penciled brow. "Do you think about her a lot?"

"Every single day of my life," Maggie confides, grateful to finally say it out loud. "I think if it wasn't for what I did—giving away my own child, sending her out into the world alone—things would be all right. I just find it . . . Well, it's impossible to ever feel completely okay, knowing she's out there. The guilt's been so much worse since the pregnancies and miscarriages."

"That makes sense."

"Maybe I don't deserve to be happy, or to have another child."

"Rubbish," Audrey says. "How's Roland handling this?"

"He works a lot."

"They always do. But he's a good husband for you."

The remark reminds Maggie of her days at Simpson's. She'd point out the sturdy clasp and the thick, supportive straps. *This is a good brassiere for you*, she'd tell the customers. *He's a good husband for you.*

"Listen, the other thing I wanted to tell you," Audrey says, brightening, "is I've got a job for you. My uncle's a journalist at the *Gazette* and he mentioned he knows a French-Canadian writer who just had a book published. He needs a translator for the English version. I told him I know someone who could do it."

"I've never translated anything before."

"How hard can it be?" Audrey says. "You're perfect for it. You're bilingual. I don't know anybody as good in both languages as you are. And you were always so good at composition."

"I could never."

"It would be published, Maggie."

Maggie's heart lurches just thinking about it. "I'm unqualified."

"Just meet him," Audrey says. "His name is Yves Godbout. What've you got to lose?"

Maggie's interest is definitely piqued. Perhaps it's an opportunity to do something useful for a change. "All right, I'll meet him," she says, feeling brazen.

"Oh, good," Audrey says, reaching for her hand.

Maggie smiles appreciatively, thinking she's underestimated Audrey all these years.

CHAPTER 26

Yves Godbout is waiting for her at the St. Regis Brasserie downtown. He's sitting at one of the long wooden tables with a pitcher and two glasses, a pack of tobacco and rolling paper spread out in front of him. The tavern is long and narrow, a man's place, with wood floors and wood paneling on the walls, even rows of picnic-style tables lined up like in a mess hall. There's a loud clang and clatter of dishes from the kitchen behind them.

Godbout looks to be in his late thirties. The roots of his brown hair are greasy, and even though it's warm outside, he's wearing a ratty gray sweater with holes in the elbows. He nods as Maggie approaches, but doesn't stand up to greet her. "I'm told you're half French," he says, not wasting time.

"My mother's French."

His eyes narrow. He lights his homemade cigarette, and the smoke that floats into her face makes her gag.

"From where?" he asks.

"Hochelaga."

"Mine, too," he says, warming slightly. "My mother still lives in the same tar paper shack where I grew up."

Maggie isn't sure what's expected of her. Does he want her to commiserate? "I don't have any credentials," she tells him.

"Credentials?" He laughs. "You think I have a degree in creative writing?"

"How long is your book?" she asks him, trying to sound professional.

Before he even finishes his cigarette, he licks the edge of his rolling paper and seals a fresh one without answering her. "About fifty thousand words," he responds. "The publisher pays three cents a word."

She does a quick calculation. The money isn't much of an enticement. "So you married an Anglo," Godbout says. "Larsson."

"Yes."

"Why?"

"Because he asked me."

His eyes dart down to her pearl necklace and then back up to her face. "You know, not so long ago, a small English press wouldn't have considered publishing a book like this," he says, reaching under the table and pulling out a copy of his book. He holds it against his chest, over his heart.

"But things are already beginning to change," he tells her. "With Duplessis dead, there's going to be a revolution in this province. My publisher—he knows this. For an English guy, he's pretty smart. He has vision. Anglos have never wanted to read anything by a Québécois writer unless it was Gabrielle Roy."

He hands her the book. It's called *On Va en Venir à Bout*.

"Is there a deadline?" she asks.

"Hopefully before I'm dead. I think my publisher wants it done as soon as possible, to capitalize on the fervor around Duplessis's death. Things will move quickly now."

Fifty thousand words.

"You don't get any sign credit," he tells her. "Which means your name won't be on the cover of the book, only on the copyright page."

She looks down at the cover and instantly knows what it will be called in English. *We Shall Overcome*. "I'll read it," she says.

"I'll have the publisher call you."

They shake hands, and Maggie leaves the tavern feeling terrified and inexplicably excited.

Less than an hour later, she's standing outside Canadair, where the men are starting to pour out after the day shift. She can't wait to tell

Gabriel about her meeting with Godbout. They've spoken a couple of times over the phone, but haven't seen each other again. She spots him in the crowd, and his face instantly brightens when he sees her. She breaks into a smile. Will it always feel this way with him? Exhilarating, wicked, slightly terrifying?

He takes her in his arms, smelling of airplane grease, not caring who sees them. His reluctance to get attached to her seems to have fallen away as swiftly and completely as the decade of their separation. Their landslide into the old feelings of their youth has taken them both by surprise but, at the same time, feels absolutely right and inevitable. They've acknowledged to each other in giddy whispers over the phone that not being together has become utterly inconceivable.

"What are you so excited about?" he asks her, taking her by the hand.

"I'm going to translate a French book called *On Va en Venir à Bout*—"

Gabriel stops suddenly and faces her, his eyes bright. "*You're* translating Yves Godbout's book?"

"You know him?"

"I know *of* him. I've read the book. You met him?"

"Yes, I just met with him."

"What's he like?"

"Well, he's got brown teeth and yellow fingers and greasy hair and torn clothes, and he was extremely condescending, but besides all that, he's wonderful."

Gabriel laughs. "Maggie, this is incredible. How did it happen?"

"Audrey set it up," she says.

"Audrey did?" he says, sounding shocked. "Can you do it justice?"

"I'm not sure," she admits. "I've never formally translated anything."

"I don't mean it like that. I mean, can you convey his passion for the cause?"

"I hope so."

"I can help you," he says.

"Really? I'd love that."

Gabriel pulls her into his arms. "This is good for you," he tells her. "And for us."

"Let's get started as soon as I'm back," he says. "And I want to meet Godbout."

No mention of the husband and wife who still stand in their way. They continue on arm in arm toward his car. "I'm excited," she says, more to herself.

"Me, too."

"I want to be with you," she tells him, her readiness for it sharpening into focus even as the words form on her tongue. "I want us to finally start our life together."

"I want that, too."

"You do? Really?"

"Of course. It's you I'm worried about," he says.

"But you're the one I want to be with."

"What about everything you'd have to give up?" he reminds her.

"I'm miserable in that big house with all my beautiful things. Roland is a good man, but our marriage isn't what I hoped it would be."

He pulls a pack of cigarettes out of his shirt pocket, offers her one, lights both of them. They exhale at the same time.

"Are you ready to leave Annie?" she asks him.

"I've been ready to leave Annie since the night I ran into you in the field."

"All right then," she says. "Let's tell them."

"Let's just sit with it a while longer, okay?"

"More thinking? We just agreed—"

"We're deciding about our future, Maggie. We're talking about divorce . . ." He opens the car door for her. "You'd be giving up a lot."

"I told you I don't care about any of that stuff."

"I just want you to be absolutely sure," he says, pulling on to the street. "I don't want you to resent me because I can't provide for you the way you're used to. I never want that burden. We're going to move very slowly. Okay?"

Maggie nods, taking her cue from him. Impulsiveness has only ever gotten her into trouble. For the first time, she feels confident and clear about what she wants, and impervious to defeat.

When they get to the apartment, Gabriel orders St. Hubert BBQ and they have a picnic on the floor. Chicken and gravy and red wine. Maggie is euphoric.

"This is the best day," she says, touching his face. "I love you."

"I love you, too."

She climbs over the containers of food and kisses him on the mouth. He pulls her into his arms and lies down on his back, her body on top of his. The moment has no feeling of illicitness or duplicity. Knowing they're going to be together, it feels absolutely perfect.

He lifts her shirt over her head and she does the same for him. He unclasps her bra and it slips onto the wood floor. The moment he lifts his head toward her breast and the tip of his tongue grazes her nipple, she cries out and there's no turning back.

CHAPTER 27

Roland reaches for the pitcher of lemonade and refills his glass. His forehead is glistening with sweat and his cheeks are flushed. Maggie leans across the table and pats him with her paper napkin. "It's muggy for May," he says, aggressively spraying Off! into a swarm of mosquitoes until she can taste it with every bite of her hamburger.

He starts folding and refolding his napkin. "It's been a long time since . . ." He looks up at her nervously. "Since we discussed our situation."

She doesn't say anything.

"You're still not pregnant," he says. "I'm starting to get concerned. Maybe our timing's been off, but still."

She hasn't told him she's been using her diaphragm. She hides it in her underwear drawer under her many "top salesperson" brassieres.

"I think we should see Dr. Surrey again," he says. "He was very optimistic. He might have a tip for us."

The pine trees bordering their land begin to close in on her. The sun is disappearing, bringing more mosquitoes.

"Roland, are you happy?" she asks him.

"About what?"

"In general. With us. Our life?"

"Yes. Of course," he says. "Obviously, it hasn't been smooth sailing, but I think the best remedy is to start a family. A child will be just the thing."

Gazing out at her expansive backyard with the geraniums bloom-ing in clay pots and the manicured lawn ready for a swing set and sandbox, she can't find the words to tell him the truth.

"Is there any Jell-O left from last night?" he asks her.

"Do you really think a child can fix this?"

"'This'?"

"I'll get the Jell-O," she says, dropping it, escaping inside to re-group. She returns moments later with a glass dish of green Jell-O.

"Lime. My favorite," he says, smiling appreciatively.

"I don't think I can do this anymore," she tries again.

"Do what?"

"Be in this marriage."

"I beg your pardon?"

"I'm sorry, Rol. It's just not working."

"You're telling me this *now*?" he says, incredulous. "Like this?"

"I'm sorry. I didn't know how else . . ."

Roland looks confused; his eyes go a bit out of focus. He stabs his spoon into the Jell-O and breaks it up into pieces. "It's obvious your fertility problem is causing you great stress," he says. "I wish you would quit being so stubborn and let me make us an appointment with Dr. Surrey."

"It's not about my fertility problem."

"We'll regain our footing as soon as we start a family," he says confidently. "Let's make the appointment next week."

"Don't you see what's happened to us, Rol? Everything's become about having a baby. There's nothing else."

"That's not true," he defends. "It's not all about that."

"It is for *you*."

"Of course I want to start a family," he admits. "I want to be a father. I'm not going to apologize for that."

"You shouldn't have to," she says. "It's just not the end-all for me." She feels herself getting emotional and wipes her eyes with a paper napkin. "I've been convincing myself that I'm ready to have a child."

"You're saying you're not?"

"You know I loved working," she says. "You pretended to support my independence at first, but it turns out you weren't being sincere."

"I wasn't pretending!" he cries. "I just didn't realize it precluded having children."

"It didn't. It doesn't. It's more like our difficulty trying to have a child has exposed the bigger problem."

"Which is?"

"Isn't it obvious, Rol?"

"Not to me."

"There's no passion between us," she says. "Maybe there never was. I'm not even sure we want the same things anymore."

Roland looks away, hiding his face. "This would all just go away if we had a child," he murmurs obstinately. "The passion would come back, our goals for the future would realign."

"Would they?" she says. "You don't even know mine."

"Tell me then."

"Well, for one thing, I love translating."

Roland lets out an exasperated huff.

"I've been trying so hard to be the person you want me to be," she says. "Trying to give you a baby, ignoring how much pressure it's put on me, pretending not to notice that it's slowly killing our respect for each other and whatever attraction may still be there. I want *more*, Roland. My work with Godbout has helped me get in touch with that part of myself again."

Roland sighs and his shoulders collapse. He looks tired. He must be, from working so hard at denying their fundamental differences, perhaps from the moment they first met.

"Roland, you married me because I came along at the precise moment in your life when you wanted to start a family."

"That's unfair."

"I know you care about me," she concedes. "But becoming a father has always been your focus and the priority in our marriage."

His head drops. She reads his silence as a grim acknowledgment of her point.

"Is there someone else?" he asks her, not looking up.

The question catches her off guard. She didn't think he'd ask, and she hadn't planned on bringing it up, if only to protect him. But she doesn't want to lie. He deserves better.

"Ah," he says, guessing before she even decides how to answer him. "So we're *that* couple. I'm the clichéd cuckold."

"It's not like that."

"Who is it?"

"Does it really matter?"

"Yes, it does," he snaps. "Very much, in fact."

"It's my first love," she admits. "I ran into him in Dunham last fall. We haven't actually spent much time together, but the old feelings are still very much there." She omits the part about having slept with him the one time. Roland would be shattered.

"So you're leaving me for another man," he says. "Let's don't pretend it's about my wanting a child and you wanting to translate books."

"We haven't been happy together in years," she says softly. "How I feel about Gabriel may be the impetus for ending the marriage now, but it's not the *reason*."

"Right. You want to be a full-time translator."

"You're being petty, Roland. Godbout has encouraged me to spread my wings, gain some confidence. And I *like* this feeling. I want to keep exploring it."

"With another man by your side. Your 'first love.'"

"You can't honestly tell me *you've* been happy in this relationship?" she says.

"Who's 'happy' anyway, Maggie?"

"I'd like to be."

"We have a marriage," he states portentously, making it sound as though the marriage is something they own, a possession not unlike their car or their house. "We've endured for this long, through some very difficult situations. It's a damn shame to throw it all away now."

"I don't want to just *endure*," she says wearily.

Roland is quiet for a few moments, defeated. Maggie's heart swells with fondness for him. "You're a good man," she says. "Intelligent and reliable and stalwart. Let's just be honest with each other, for once."

"What's your plan exactly?"

"I thought for now I could move into the house in Knowlton."

"You'd move back to the Townships alone? Or with him?"

"Alone. I'd be near my family. You never go up there anymore," she says. "Hardly ever at all. It's not like you'd miss it."

"I could sell it," he points out.

"You could," she says. "But let's face it, Roland. Even if we stayed together, I'd be alone. You're never here."

"That would change if—"

"We had a child," she finishes, exasperated. "Exactly."

She gets up and carries their plates into the kitchen. Roland follows her inside but goes to the living room. She hears him pouring himself a drink. She cleans the kitchen and then joins him. "I'm sorry," she says, not knowing what else to say.

Sitting here in this grand room, surrounded by her precious Swedish furniture with the ice-blue silk upholstery, flocked wallpaper, white marble fireplace, and view of her sprawling garden through the picture window, she's absolutely certain she's doing the right thing.

"We have nothing to show for our life together," he says mournfully.

She sits down beside him and reaches for his hand. She notices a couple of wiry silver hairs on his knuckles, and for some reason this makes her want to cry.

"But you're right," he says, surprising her. "We're a mismatch, aren't we?"

She squeezes his hand. "We tried valiantly. We really did."

He nods, and what she sees on his face is relief. In spite of his hurt feelings and pride, she can tell he's beginning to wrap his head around the fact that he's free to start over with someone who wants exactly what he wants: a simple, fertile girl with matching aspirations of parenthood and housewifery. It was never going to be Maggie. And although he'd never admit it out loud, she can tell he's cycling through the same realizations in his mind.

CHAPTER 28

⟞⟝⟞

She arrives at the Motel Maisonneuve on Ontario Street breathless with excitement. She has so much to tell him, starting with the news that she's leaving Roland, that it's done and there's no turning back. She's also going to tell him about what happened to her in Frelighsburg—the rape, the pregnancy, having to give up the baby. She wants to rid herself of all her secrets and start this next phase of her life with a clean slate. Fate has brought them back together, and she owes Gabriel the truth. He's been in the dark long enough.

She knocks on the door, in case he's already here. She's smiling just thinking about him. She's got a bottle of wine in her bag, and she's wearing a new lace bra and panties. Gabriel opens the door and then immediately sits down on the bed without actually greeting her. No hello, no embrace. She follows him inside.

The room is a disappointment. It's dingy and has a musty smell. The curtains, mustard-yellow burlap, are drawn. There's a simple pine headboard, a frayed chenille bedspread, and an olive green carpet that needs vacuuming. "I thought it would be nicer," she says, setting her purse down on the bureau and pulling out the wine.

He doesn't say anything, only stares straight ahead with a strange look on his face. She rushes over to him and strokes his blond brush cut, then bends down to kiss him on the mouth.

He turns away.

"What's wrong?" she asks him.

"I went home this weekend."

"Don't tell me your sister talked you out of leaving Annie?" she says, sitting down beside him. "Don't listen to Clémentine. I've already told Roland I'm leaving."

"What did you do that for?" he says gruffly. There's something in his voice that frightens her.

"Why not?" she says. "We agreed it's what we both want."

His eyes are dark, distant. Something is different.

"What's wrong, Gabriel?" she asks him again.

"It's not going to work."

"Since when?" she cries, confused. "You don't love Annie. We talked about this."

"This isn't about Annie."

"What is it about then? I thought it was decided, right before you went home to Dunham. We still love each other. What happened?"

"We almost made a huge mistake."

"I don't understand. Did Clémentine say something? Did my father?"

"It's over."

The bed beneath her feels unsteady. "Don't say that," she says, crouching down in front of him and wrapping her arms around his legs.

He pushes her off and looks her right in the eye, with not a trace of affection.

"What have I done?"

"I ran into Audrey McCauley in Dunham," he says, his voice chillingly calm.

"Where?"

"I went to church with my sisters on Sunday," he explains. "I actually wanted to thank Audrey for putting you in touch with Godbout."

He knows. In that split second, Maggie's world collapses.

"She told me you had quite a heart-to-heart, the two of you."

She feels like throwing up. This isn't how it was supposed to go.

"She told me you gave away our baby," he says, getting up off the bed and moving restlessly around the room.

"Gabriel—"

"I didn't even know you were pregnant."

"Why would Audrey tell you that?"

"She assumed I knew. Why would she think you'd keep such a thing from me?"

"*I told her you didn't know!*" Maggie cries. "She also knew I was planning to tell you."

"When?"

"Today! *Now.*"

He laughs. "Right. What a coincidence."

"She did this to hurt you and to punish me."

"I don't care about *her!*" he shouts. "This isn't about Audrey."

Maggie covers her face with her hands. How could she have made such a colossal error trusting Audrey?

"I told Roland I was leaving him," she says. "And that I'm still in love with you. I was planning to tell you everything today, so that we could have a fresh start."

Gabriel laughs again, a hard, angry noise that fills her with dread. "So it's true," he says. "You gave away our child."

She realizes that no answer will ever bring him solace or possibly even salvage their relationship. The truth is impossible. It's been too long. "I had no choice," she attempts.

He paces the carpet while she cowers against the headboard, watching and waiting. "You gave away my daughter, Maggie."

"My parents made me," she says. "They made all the decisions. I had no say. It was 1950 and I was sixteen and my father threatened to disown me if I ever saw you again!"

"And what about the last few times we were together?" he accuses. "The night we bumped into each other in the cornfield? Or the first time I took you to the Papineau apartment and we talked for hours? Or the day we made love?"

"I came here to tell you today," she repeats dejectedly. "I'm sorry you found out before I had the chance."

"*Sorry?*" He shakes his head in disgust. "We stood outside Canadair the other day and talked about the future and about me divorcing

Annie for you, and you didn't think of mentioning that we had a fuck-ing daughter together?"

"It wasn't like that," she says. "There's more to it."

"What is it like then?" he cries.

"I wanted to tell you everything the moment I saw you in the field that night. But it's complicated. There's more to the story than what Audrey told you."

"I know the story," he says. "You didn't want to spend your life with me, living in poverty with a French-Canadian factory worker."

"I wasn't sure the baby was yours!" she blurts.

This silences him.

"My uncle Yvon raped me when I was living with him," she says. "*That's* the story."

Gabriel's hands ball into fists.

"I was going to tell you, my love. *Today.*"

Gabriel sits down on the edge of the bed, deflated. She waits, hopeful that he'll understand and take her in his arms and they can move forward with their plans. A long time passes, but he doesn't move. He just sits there, staring at the floor.

"Gabriel? Say something. Please."

He looks up at her, his eyes red. "I'm sorry for you," he says. "I really am. And if you had told me back then, I would have killed the bastard. Maybe I still will."

"I know."

"I *know* you know," he says. "That's the problem. If you would've told me the truth back then, we could have managed. We could have raised the baby together. And that's the thing I can't get past. *You didn't want to.*"

"That's not true," she says, but her words lack conviction. There *is* some truth to them—she'd weighed her options back then, and what she was most terrified of losing was her father and his seed store. To that end, she was complicit with her parents' decision.

"That's what hurts most," he tells her. "You knew I would take care of you no matter who the baby belonged to, but when your father threatened to disown you, you chose him."

"I was a child," she says. "I wasn't ready for marriage. So yes, I chose my family. You would have done the same. But I'm a grown woman now."

"I would not have done the same thing," he counters. "Anyway, nothing's changed, Maggie."

"Don't punish me for the decision I made over a decade ago when I was just a kid."

"So it *was* your decision," he says, his rage suddenly reignited. He turns away from her and kicks in the wall with his boot. The plaster crumbles, but it doesn't stop him. He comes at her and grabs her by the shoulders. For a split second, she worries he's going to throw her to the ground. He shakes her once, hard, and then stops. "I would have married you," he tells her, devastated.

"Marry me now."

"It's too much of a risk. We haven't changed enough for it to work."

"We've grown up, Gabriel. We're adults now."

"I can't get past this," he says, releasing her. "You could have come clean about your pregnancy before I had to hear it from Audrey McCauley. But you were still sizing me up, trying to figure out if you could be happy in my world. If I'm good enough for you."

"You're the one who doesn't think you're good enough for me!" she throws back. "That's why you're running."

"I'm not running. I'm leaving, because I don't trust you."

He stands up and moves away from the bed. She follows him, positioning herself directly in front of him and blocking his path. "My love," she says. "Please, don't go."

He tries to hide his face, but she glimpses his expression. Instead of the condemnation and contempt she'd anticipated, she sees tears sliding down his cheeks.

"Don't do this," she pleads.

He stares at her for a moment, his expression cold and resigned, and then he pushes past her. "It's over, Maggie."

"No one can love you like I do."

"Or hurt me as much."

CHAPTER 29

—◦/◦/◦—

Maggie lies in bed, gazing up at the crystal chandelier Roland bought her for their second wedding anniversary. Each of the ten cast-iron arms has a single cut glass bobeche with dangling teardrop crystals. She remembers the day the electrician installed it above the bed, how elegant the room had looked, how pleased she'd been. She'd arrived— that's how she felt. Now it seems to be taunting her, glittering up there in the light through her bay windows, beautiful and meaningless.

She's pregnant again. It was confirmed by her doctor today. The baby is Gabriel's—that's not in question. The only time she's had sex without her diaphragm was at the Papineau apartment a few weeks ago, her first and last time with Gabriel. She hadn't expected to sleep with him that day, hadn't been prepared. In the moment, she'd ignored the little voice in her head. *It'll be fine*, she'd told herself. Whatever happened, she felt it would be fine.

And now she's carrying his baby, due in January. She hasn't spoken to him since that night at the motel. She wanted to give him some space, felt it was essential. He needed time—time to miss her, time to reflect, time to figure out he can't live without her. Time to forgive her. She hasn't given up hope. Not yet.

She is determined to have this baby with him. Staying with Roland is no longer an option; he's already moved out, living temporarily at a hotel until she relocates to Knowlton. He would probably take her back if she asked, maybe even raise this child as his own, but when Maggie contemplates the possibility, she imagines one of those generic family portraits in which everyone is posed in pretty ribbons and crisp white collars, with frozen smiles capturing a single moment of synchronized perfection, but behind the smiles, it's all secrets and disconnection and pain.

She reaches for the telephone on her bedside table and calls Gabriel's house again. It rings and rings, until finally the wife picks up and says harshly, "Who is this?"

"An old friend from Dunham."

Annie is silent.

"Is he there?" Maggie asks.

"Why're you calling so late?"

"I need to speak with him," Maggie says, choosing her words carefully. "It's important."

"He's not here," Annie says. "Stop calling my house."

The line goes dead.

The next day, Maggie decides to drive out to Canadair and confront Gabriel outside work. She checks herself in the mirror and pinches her cheeks to bring some color into them.

Three fifteen. The men begin to pour onto the street, their boots stampeding the pavement, their Zippos glinting in the sun. Maggie gets out of her car and waits. The mob thins. The last stragglers emerge from inside the building, but Gabriel is not among them.

Maggie spots one of his union acquaintances and catches up with him. "Where's Gabriel?" she asks, dispensing with a formal greeting and sounding far more hysterical than she'd intended.

"Gone," he says, pulling a pack of cigarettes from his shirt pocket. "He's driving a cab full-time now."

"He left Canadair?"

"Better hours, better wage."

"What cab company?"

The guy shrugs. "No idea," he says, sounding put out. "I don't keep tabs on him."

The sky suddenly grows dark and a clap of thunder announces

a coming rainstorm. Maggie drives over to the place on Papineau. With her purse over her head to protect it against the now pounding rain, she rushes up to the front door, only to see there's a new name freshly handwritten next to the buzzer. She buzzes anyway and a young woman answers.

"I'm looking for Gabriel or Pierre?"

"Pierre doesn't live here anymore," the woman says.

Soaking wet, Maggie runs back to the car and sits there for a while, her mind scrambling to concoct some new scheme.

The rain is beating against her windshield, and she's growing worried about having to drive home in rush hour traffic. She turns the key in the ignition and pulls onto the street, practically smelling the boy Gabriel once was that day in his pickup when Clémentine drove her home in the storm. Sweat and soil, damp teenage hormones and the smell of rain.

A few days later, Maggie finds herself in Dunham, knocking on Clémentine's door. The Phénix shack looks slightly less dilapidated than she remembers it. The roof and windows look new, and the front door is freshly painted.

Clémentine appears at the door in her overalls. "Maggie," she says, looking surprised. She brushes a strand of loose hair from her eyes and smiles. She's still beautiful in her natural, unfussy way. She doesn't bother with the tricks and tools that most women are enslaved to in order to feel desirable or even adequate. She opens the door wider and gestures for Maggie to come in.

Maggie has to hide her shock. She can't remember ever seeing the inside of it, even when she was friends with Angèle. It's the size of a motel room, and as she takes it in, she wonders how they all managed to live here together. Had Maggie kept her baby and married Gabriel, they would have been five in this place.

Clémentine offers Maggie a cup of tea. She doesn't seem at all embarrassed about her living situation, and it occurs to Maggie that Clémentine may not think there's anything to be embarrassed about.

She brings out a tray with cream, sugar, and two pretty teacups with pink roses on the porcelain. A very English custom, Maggie observes.

"I'm all for change," Clémentine is saying, as she sets the tray down. "As long as this new government doesn't forget about us farmers."

Maggie notices a copy of *The Handbook for Gardeners* on Clémentine's bookshelf.

"I can't complain, though," Clémentine says. "So far it's been a good summer."

"How's Angèle?" Maggie asks her.

"Busy," she says, pouring tea into Maggie's cup. "She keeps having babies."

Clémentine sits down beside Maggie and reaches for the sugar bowl. When they're both settled, the silence they've been staving off with polite small talk settles between them. Clémentine waits. Maggie wonders if she knows about the baby Maggie gave up at sixteen. She's not sure if Gabriel would have confided in his sister after he found out or kept it to himself.

Maggie is still feeling queasy and her tea is too sweet, but she forces herself to have a few sips because it's something to do. "I'm here about Gabriel," she begins.

"I figured."

"Have you heard from him?"

"We had a falling-out," she says. "I haven't heard from him in a few weeks."

Maggie can feel the familiar panic clamping down on her chest.

"We've always had these . . . troubled patches," Clémentine says.

So have we, Maggie thinks.

"He thinks I try to be his mother," Clémentine confesses. "But he's the one who treats me like a child. He tried to convince me to sell the farm—"

"Sell the farm?" Maggie says, hurt that Gabriel obviously does not share her sentimental attachment to the cornfield.

"Is everything okay, Maggie?"

"He's vanished," Maggie says, her voice breaking. "I've tried his house, but he's never there."

Clémentine is quiet for a moment. Finally, she says, "Are you . . . seeing him again?"

Maggie looks away.

"Has he left Annie?"

"I don't know."

"They were never a fit," she says.

Maggie instinctively touches her stomach. What if she does find Gabriel and he wants nothing to do with her or their baby? What if he can't forgive her? She considers now that her hope of reconciliation and living happily ever after as a family may be hormonal delusion.

"I could call Annie and find out what she knows?" Clémentine says.

"Would you?" Maggie says, brightening.

Clémentine takes her cup of tea into the kitchen. Maggie sets her cup down, folds her hands in her lap, and waits. She can feel the saliva collecting inside her cheeks, and she knows what's coming. Her first thought is to run to the kitchen and ask for crackers, but she quickly realizes she's not going to make it. Instead, she lunges for the front door just in time to throw up all over the pretty red geraniums on the front stoop.

When she's done with the first round—and there is *always* a second—she straightens up and looks for a more secluded location. This time she aims for the bushes, projectile vomiting all over a wall of moosewood.

Maggie crumples to her knees on the grass to catch her breath. She feels empty. Her back hurts.

"Are you okay?"

Maggie turns, and Clémentine is standing above her, her hair shimmering in the sunlight.

"I'm sorry," she says, wiping her mouth. "Your geraniums—"

"Don't worry," Clémentine says, retrieving a hose from the side of the house. She turns it on and sprays her front stoop, cleaning away the vomit. "Maybe it'll be good for them," she jokes.

They go back inside, and Clémentine heads straight to the kitchen, returning moments later with a plate of saltines.

"Thank you," Maggie says, stuffing the crackers in her mouth as though she hasn't eaten in days. Clémentine is watching her.

"Did you reach Annie?" Maggie asks.

"He's gone, Maggie."

"Gone?"

"Annie says he left. He took all his things, she hasn't heard from him in weeks."

Maggie is relieved, but now she's run out of places to look for him. "I should go before I . . ."

Clémentine nods and walks Maggie to the door. *Gabriel is gone.* It's slowly starting to sink in. He obviously does not want to be found, certainly not by Maggie. "If he gets in touch with you," Maggie says, "please tell him I need to speak with him."

Clémentine nods, touches Maggie's arm. "I know it's not my business," she says. "But . . . you love him, don't you?"

Maggie can't hold back her tears any longer. Clémentine moves closer and holds her while she sobs softly into the bib of her overalls. "I've lost him for good now."

"I know how you feel," Clémentine says, her chest rising and falling in a commiserative sigh, and Maggie isn't sure she's still talking about Gabriel.

CHAPTER 30

Elodie

Elodie opens the door to the stairwell and hurries down the first flight of stairs on her way to the basement. She's late for work because one of the girls in her dorm got her period and tried to secretly wash the blood out of her sheets before anyone found out. Sister Ignatia caught her and chose ten girls at random to whip with the leather strap. Elodie was mercifully not among the chosen ten, but she had to stay and watch as the other girls were lined up and strapped, one by one.

She got lucky not being chosen, but all Elodie could think about was not being late for work.

As she rounds the corner and continues down the next flight of stairs, she's suddenly aware of footsteps behind her. Nervously, she quickens her pace and doesn't look back. She's sure it's the new orderly who works the night shift on Ward B—a middle-aged man whose innocuous face seemed neither evil nor dangerous at first. She'd never considered for a moment that he might harm her—that was the domain of the nuns—so she was caught completely off guard when he pounced on her in the bathroom in the middle of the night. He put his hand over her mouth, shoved her into a stall, and yanked her nightgown above her knees. Her instinct was to bite his fingers, which were carelessly close to her teeth, and when she did, he cried out.

"*Tabarnac!*" he said, and slapped her.

She screamed for help, and within moments, several girls were outside the stall. Elodie was terrified Sister Ignatia would hear them and come charging in, but by some miracle, she never came.

The orderly flung open the stall door and escaped the bathroom.

"What a pig," one of the girls muttered, cursing after him.

"He tried to—"

"Of course he did," the girl said. "It hasn't happened to you yet?"

"No."

"You're lucky. They all do it."

"Do the nuns know?" Elodie cried, stunned.

The girls just laughed.

Elodie has managed to avoid him for several weeks, but now she's cursing herself. She should have waited for one of the other girls this morning.

Her heart is pounding as the footsteps close in. She keeps moving briskly down the stairs, but as she picks up speed, so does he. She can hear him approaching, the soles of his shoes squeaking on the concrete stairs behind her.

"I'm late for work!" she cries out. "Sister Calvert will come for me!"

But when she turns to look behind her, it's just a doctor. He ignores her and rushes past, down the stairwell with his white coat flapping behind him like a cape.

Elodie stops to catch her breath. "Thank God," she murmurs, relishing her good fortune and forgetting that she neither likes nor believes in God. After she steadies herself, she hurries down the rest of the flights. Sister Calvert—though not nearly as sadistic as Sister Ignatia—does not tolerate lateness.

In the end, Elodie manages to slip into her seat at the sewing machine precisely on time and gets to work on the first sheet hem.

"Psst."

Elodie looks over and Marigot is grinning.

"What?" Elodie whispers.

"I found something."

"What?"

Sister Calvert is moving up the aisles, supervising all the girls' work, commenting here and there. *It's crooked. Start over. You're too slow. There's a pillowcase on the floor.*

When she's out of earshot, Marigot holds out her hand and opens up her palm to reveal a small brown square that Elodie does not recognize.

"What is that?"

"It's chocolate."

"Chocolate?"

"Smell."

Elodie glances behind her to make sure Sister Calvert is still preoccupied reprimanding one of the other sewers, and then she sneaks a furtive sniff. Her eyes roll back. The smell is heavenly, sweet and pleasing in a way that jolts all her senses to life.

"Sister must have dropped it," Marigot whispers. "Here. Quick."

Marigot breaks the small piece in two, pops one half in her mouth and hands the other to Elodie. Elodie puts it on her tongue, closes her eyes, and savors the taste of it as it melts. "It's sweet, but not like molasses," she moans, enjoying the way it sticks to the roof of her mouth while she sucks it.

"Mam'selle de Saint-Sulpice?" Sister calls out.

"Yes, Sister?"

"What are you up to?"

"Nothing, Sister. Just sewing."

Sister Calvert harrumphs and moves on. She's not nearly as interested in goading or torturing the girls as some of the other nuns. She isn't kind or friendly in any way, but her sternness rarely crosses over into abuse. She just wants to get the job done.

"Thank you, Marigot," Elodie whispers.

Marigot winks. Today is a good day.

CHAPTER 31

Maggie

In the middle of a muggy autumn night, Maggie is awakened by a strong wave of nausea. It's her first night back in the Townships as a separated woman, and she opted to sleep at her parents' house instead of alone in Knowlton. In spite of their disappointment over her decision to leave Roland, her parents did not turn her away.

She creeps downstairs and rifles around the pantry for some crackers. She grabs a handful, throws on one of her mother's scratchy cardigans, and goes outside. Her father is standing in the small vegetable garden, surveying it as though it's perfectly logical to be out gardening at midnight in October.

"What are you doing, Daddy?"

He turns and looks up at her, illuminated by the yellow glow of the floodlight above the back door. His eyes take a moment to focus, and she knows he's drunk. "Checking on your mother's herbs," he says, in his twilight slur.

"Now?"

"It's a waxing moon," he says, tipping his head up to the sky. "One must always sow seeds under a waxing moon, never waning."

She sits down on a white wrought iron garden chair and inhales the crisp autumn air.

"The scientists are beginning to discover the effects of lunar rhythms on the earth's magnetic fields," he says. "Which of course affects growth."

He crouches down and digs around in the soil, pulling out a small potato. "They say a potato grown in a laboratory will still show a growth rhythm that reflects the lunar pattern."

He attempts to stand up but wobbles a bit and has to reach for the chair to steady himself. She notices his hands are trembling and his entire body seems to sway with every passing breeze, as though it's not firmly rooted to the ground.

"I love the smell of thyme," Maggie says, inhaling the scent of the herbs. The air is warm and muggy for October.

"I must plant some parsley for your mother," he says, more to himself. "It's good for enhancing the smell of roses, too."

Maggie stands up and stretches. "I'm tired. I'm going to bed."

"You should go back to Roland," he tells her. "This baby is exactly what you two need."

What you two need. As though it's a blender or a vacuum cleaner. A *thing.* That's how Roland described it, too.

"We're both moving on, Daddy. It was mutual."

"You have everything, Maggie. I don't understand you."

"You don't understand that I want to be happy?"

"It takes more courage to stay."

"I disagree," she says wearily. "I'm sorry if that hurts you." She kisses his forehead, which is damp and thinly beaded with sweat.

He reaches into his jacket pocket and pulls out a silver flask. She watches him take a sip and then tuck it back in his pocket.

"Good night, Daddy."

He doesn't answer, just continues staring straight ahead, his face etched with exhaustion and disappointment. There's such despair in his eyes it almost makes Maggie wish she could have made it work with Roland, for her father's sake.

Maggie still hasn't reached Gabriel, nor has he materialized. Her dream of having this child with him is beginning to dim. And yet, in spite of these frequent undulations of despair, a stubborn fissure of faith—or possibly blind delusion—has persisted. She will not give up on him, which is why she will do it alone rather than go running back to Roland for security. She believes it to be an act of faith more than anything.

She leaves her father standing there with his herbs and his flask, and she goes back inside. She wanders past his sanctuary and stops, noticing that the door is slightly ajar. For as long as she's lived in this house, she's never known him to leave it open. Either he's drunker than usual, or he just assumed everyone was asleep and there was no need.

Maggie lightly pushes the door open and slips inside. She stands there for a moment, breathing in the scent of her father. His well-worn book, *Operating a Garden Center,* is open to the chapter called "Attracting Customers," which means the store is having a slow season. Her eyes sweep over the rest of his books, his radio parts, the mess of his papers and pending projects, the steel gray file cabinet in the corner of the room.

Without thinking and before even registering what she's doing, she finds the key in the top drawer of his desk, poorly hidden in an empty cigar box. She kneels in front of the file cabinet and opens it. She flips through the files—mostly bills—until her hand comes to rest on a thick manila envelope in the bottom drawer. There's an address stamped in the corner. Maggie reaches for it just as her father comes up behind her. "What do you think you're doing?" he cries.

She jumps to her feet, dropping the envelope. All she can make out is the name *Goldbaum, LLB* before her father slams the drawer shut with his foot. Her gut tells her it has something to do with Elodie. "What is this?" she asks him. "Why did you have a lawyer?"

He takes her by the wrist and forcibly shoves her out of his sanctuary. It's the most physical he's ever been with her. His cheeks are flushed, and the veins in his nose seem to have suddenly exploded in anger. He closes the door in her face and locks it.

She stands outside his door for several minutes, shocked by his uncharacteristic outburst. She can hear shuffling and banging from inside.

"Daddy!" she yells through the door. He doesn't respond.

CHAPTER 32

Elodie

Elodie wipes a film of sweat from her forehead and turns her face away from the steam. She's been assigned to pressing sheets this month, a task even more tedious than sewing them. It's also a lot more painful on her right arm, which has never been the same since she was bound to that bare bed for a week.

"Take five minutes," Sister Camille says. "Your face is red."

Sister Camille is new. She doesn't look much older than Elodie, but she's now the one in charge of the sewers. She's too kind for Saint-Nazarius. It's only a matter of time before they get rid of her.

"Why do you stay here?" Elodie asks her, replacing the iron in its plate. "You don't belong here any more than I do."

"God put me here for a reason," she says. "Though sometimes I can't think why."

"Do you think He put *me* here for a reason?" Elodie asks her.

"Of course," Sister Camille says with certainty. "We don't always understand what He does or why He does it. We may never, not in this lifetime. That's what faith is."

"That's not comforting," Elodie mutters.

Sister Camille squeezes her hand, a gesture so startling that Elodie flinches and retracts it.

"That's the worst part of being here," Sister Camille says sadly. "Watching children grow up without any affection. It's not normal. I hate not being able to hug the little ones and hold them when they're crying."

"You'd be fired," Elodie says. "Or worse."

"I did once, when I first started. I picked up a little girl who'd been chained to a pipe all night. She couldn't have been more than four."

"What happened?" Elodie asks, wishing Sister Camille had been around when Elodie was little.

"I was caught by Sister Laurence and banished to the cafeteria." She looks sheepish and adds, "And then down here to the basement. I can't be cruel like they tell me to be. I just can't."

"Maybe that will change."

"Of course it won't."

"Then why do you stay?"

"I told you," she says. "It's God's will. But between you and me, I'll be happy when they do get rid of me."

"Take me with you, Sister—"

"I wish I could," Sister Camille says, taking Elodie by the hand and leading her out into the corridor. "Listen to me," she says, lowering her voice. "They're changing the law."

"What law?"

"The law that put you here."

Elodie shrugs, bewildered.

"The government is starting to investigate these hospitals," Sister Camille explains. "They know about the orphans and they're doing something about it. *They know you're not mental patients.*"

Tears spring to Elodie's eyes and she collapses against Sister Camille's chest. "When?" she cries. "When can I leave?"

"The doctors have already started interviewing the children."

A surge of panic charges through Elodie's body.

"What's wrong?" Sister Camille asks her. "It's a good thing, Elodie."

"The last time a doctor interviewed me I wound up here," she whimpers, remembering that day at the orphanage. "I failed!"

"Just be yourself," Sister Camille reassures her. "You're not retarded. We both know that. These doctors are on your side."

Elodie is skeptical. The doctors are never on her side; they only pretend to be.

"They're going to find that most of the children here are of normal intelligence," Sister Camille says. "If anything, you're disturbed from being locked up in here and from all the abuse. You're smart, Elodie, but ignorant."

"What does that mean?"

"It means you don't know anything about the world. Basic things. You're backwards, that's all. But not crazy."

"That's true."

"If you poor things weren't retarded when you came in, you surely will be when you get out."

"Do you think I'll be able to find my mother?"

"Anything is possible with God," Sister Camille says, but the look in her eyes belies her words. Elodie does not see faith in them, only pity. Or maybe it's Elodie's own doubt, her ambivalence about God.

"Where will I go?" Elodie wants to know. "I don't know anything other than this place—"

"The younger kids will probably go into foster homes or proper orphanages. The older ones will just be released, I imagine."

"Released?"

Sister Camille nods. And then, reading the look of alarm on Elodie's face, she adds, "Don't worry, you're not old enough to be on your own."

"Do you think they'll send me back to the orphanage in Farnham?"

"I don't know."

Elodie's mind is buzzing. The very possibility of escaping Saint-Nazarius—of never having to see Sister Ignatia's face again—fills her with a burst of fresh hope, something she hasn't felt in years.

"You're going to have to be patient," Sister Camille warns. "It won't happen quickly."

"But it *will* happen?"

"I believe it will. It's already happening at other hospitals."

Elodie beams, her whole body trembling with excitement and relief. There's a fissure of fear—she still has to convince the doctors she isn't crazy or retarded—and some trepidation about where she'll be sent, but nothing that can possibly outweigh her joy.

CHAPTER 33

Maggie

Maggie arrives at her father's seed store with breakfast for both of them. The window is decorated with fake snow and a shiny red Christmas banner that says JOYEUX NOËL MERRY CHRISTMAS. She hasn't spoken to him in weeks. She tried to reach out several times, but he refuses to speak to her.

Today she's determined to make amends for breaking into his filing cabinet. She's brought the galleys of her first translation as a peace offering. *We Shall Overcome* represents not just the fifty thousand or so words she managed to coax from French into English, but also the successful assimilation of her French and English selves. Godbout's encouragement along the way has surprised and bolstered her. If not for him, she would have quit the project.

"You've captured the struggle," he told her when they were reviewing an early draft of her manuscript. "*I believe you.*"

"You wrote the words," she deflected.

"I wrote them in French, Larsson. You're writing them in English. I was worried your version might come off inauthentic. Or, worse, academic. But your writing is honest and real. *I buy it.*"

"Thank you," she said, blushing. She was thrilled. In the absence of her father's support, Godbout's approval was profoundly reaffirming.

"We're not so different, you and I," he told her, rolling one of his homemade cigarettes. "Being a woman in a man's world is not much easier than being a French Canadian in an English world, is it?"

"I suppose you're right," she said, having never made the comparison before.

She appreciates that he notices such things and consistently credits her for her efforts and resilience. He sees something in her that few men do and genuinely respects her. She attributes this generosity of spirit to his being a man with a deep allegiance to the subjugated and the downtrodden across all walks of life.

Still, in spite of Godbout's praise, she worries what people will think of her work. She still cares too much how people will judge her. She wonders if Gabriel will stumble upon her translation at a bookstore. Say to someone, *Hey, I used to know that woman.* Maybe think she didn't manage to capture Godbout's passion after all.

She opens the door and steps inside the store. The smell of earth wafts around her. Vi no longer weighs the seeds; she works as a secretary at the Small Bros. Company, where they make the evaporating pans for boiling syrup. It sounds so dull, but then Vi never had grand aspirations for herself. She's moved into Peter's old room so she doesn't have to share a bed with the others, and she's still got no prospects for a husband. Nicole is the one who weighs the seeds now.

Maggie's father glances up from a bin of seeds and immediately withdraws his friendly expression. He's still upset with her. She has her own reasons for being angry with him, but right now she cares more about getting answers. She found a lawyer in Montreal named Sonny Goldbaum, but hasn't been able to reach him because of the holidays. In the meantime, she is determined to find out what was in that manila envelope.

Her father looks thinner, pale. He's getting too old to work this hard, she thinks, stomping light snow off her boots. "I brought you something," she tells him.

When he fails to respond, she holds up a grease-stained paper bag in one hand and the galleys in the other. "Breakfast and . . . ta-da . . . my book!"

He offers a wan smile and mutters, "Congratulations."

"It's a peace offering," she says, extending it to him.

Reluctantly, he comes over to her and examines it. "Well done," he says, admiring the thick manuscript.

"Godbout says that what makes me a misfit is exactly what allows me to do such good work."

"Misfit?" her father says. "I never saw you that way."

She follows him to his office and he pulls out a chair for her to sit down. She hands him a fried-egg sandwich. "How's the new saleswoman working out?" she asks him.

"She likes to give discounts to make a sale," he complains. "I keep telling her it cuts into the margins."

Maggie nibbles on a strip of bacon. When she first found out he'd hired a woman to sell on the showroom floor, she was crushed. She felt betrayed, as though he were cheating on her. At least having Godbout's book to translate helped to soften the blow. By then she was well into it, distracted and plodding along with a renewed sense of purpose. Now her father's slight only stings if she lets herself think about it for too long.

"The customers seem to like her well enough," her father goes on. "She's got spunk."

Maggie doesn't say anything. She glances up at a framed slogan above his desk, reading it with a swell of longing. *Whoever could make two ears of corn, or two blades of grass, to grow upon a spot of ground where only one grew before, would deserve better of mankind, and do more essential service to his country than the whole race of politicians put together. —Jonathan Swift*

"What can I do for you?" he asks her, treating her like she's a customer.

"I just wanted to give you the galleys," she says, handing them to him. "Keep them. I have another copy."

He flips through the pages, his expression unreadable. She wonders if he's at all proud of her.

"Maggie," he says, looking up and setting the galleys down. "I don't think you've thought this through. You can't possibly mean to raise this child by yourself. It's just not practical financially or for the child."

"I'll have spousal support," she says. "And whatever I earn from translating."

"I'm sure Roland would gladly reconcile."

"I came here to talk about my book, not my marriage."

"I wish you would be more practical," he pleads. "For once in your life, this is no time to go against the grain." *You always were my wildflower.* "You're having a baby."

"Why did you have an envelope from a lawyer in your filing cabinet?" she asks him.

"You shouldn't have gone through my things."

"You know why I did it," she says. "Why did you have that envelope from a lawyer?"

"I know you think there's some great mystery, Maggie, but there isn't."

He stands up, throws away the garbage from breakfast, and turns back to face her. "I patented my Prévert seed," he says, sounding exasperated. "That's why I needed a lawyer. Satisfied?"

Maggie searches his face for some clue he's lying.

"Anticlimactic, isn't it?"

Maggie can't hide her disappointment. She'd been hoping for something else.

"Take a poinsettia on your way out," he says. "I'm overinventoried."

"They give me a rash," she mutters, leaving his office with the sinking feeling that things between them will never be the same.

CHAPTER 34

Sonny Goldbaum's office is in an old apartment building on Queen Mary Road, nothing like the swanky law offices on St. James Street that she'd imagined. Maggie dusts the snow off her coat and huddles against the radiator for warmth before pressing his buzzer. She's extremely eager to speak to him, given that she's been waiting nearly two months for him to return from Florida.

"It's Maggie Larsson," she says into the speaker. He buzzes her in.

She holds tightly to the railing, maneuvering her large body down the stairs. The hall reeks of cat urine. When she gets to the basement, Sonny Goldbaum is holding his door open for her. "I didn't know you were expecting," he says, as though he should have. "And by the looks of it any minute?"

"Not till the end of the month," she says, unwinding her scarf.

Goldbaum is about forty, much younger than she was expecting, with dark curly hair, black horn-rimmed glasses, and a deep suntan. He's short and wide, wearing a white polyester shirt, through which she can see his white undershirt, and gray slacks that are fastened below his stomach. "Come in," he says.

Inside, he helps her into one of two sagging yellow-and-brown-plaid armchairs in his living room, which doubles as his office. There are half a dozen wooden filing cabinets lined up against the wall and a desk sandwiched between the kitchenette and the hallway, which is strewn with file folders and piles of papers.

"I found your name in my father's things," she begins, still smelling the cat litter from the hallway, along with something fishy. "I just want to confirm what you did for him."

Goldbaum leans back in his chair.

"He told me you handled a patent for him?" Maggie continues. "For a special type of grass he invented. Prévert?"

Goldbaum's face is a complete blank.

"Do you remember doing a patent for a man named Wellington Hughes?"

"Hughes?" he says, still baffled. "That doesn't sound like anyone I'd know."

Maggie shifts around in her chair, trying to get comfortable. Her back is starting to hurt.

"And I don't do patents either, Mrs. Larsson."

Maggie's heart sinks.

"So what's the real reason for this visit?" he asks her, staring directly at her belly. He removes his glasses, lowers his voice, and says, "Because I'm not in that line of business anymore."

"What line of business?"

"The baby business."

"Oh, no . . . I'm not . . ." Her hand goes right to her stomach, where she can feel the baby kicking.

"Then I'm afraid I don't understand," he says. "I don't do patents, and I certainly don't remember your father or his grass. So why don't you tell me why you think I would know him?"

"I had a baby when I was sixteen," she says. "My father must have hired you to arrange an adoption. That is what you do, right?"

"It *was*, in a manner of speaking."

"I thought my father took the baby to a foundling home, but there's no record of her arriving there," she explains. "And then recently I found your name in his files."

"And he told you I worked on his grass patent?"

"Yes."

"Well, he lied to you."

"Did you arrange for her to be adopted?" Maggie asks him.

"It's possible."

"You must have a record of some sort," she says, glancing behind him at all the filing cabinets. "It would have been March 1950."

"I arranged a lot of adoptions," he says.

"Can't you look it up?"

"What good would that do?"

"I want to know if she was adopted."

"Shouldn't you ask your father?"

"I've got a better chance getting the truth from you," she says. "I just need to know for my peace of mind."

"I can assure you that if I was involved, your daughter was adopted. That's what I did. I got babies into the hands of the right parents. So if your father hired me, your daughter found a home."

Maggie begins to relax. She already feels lighter. "Can you confirm he hired you?" she asks, ever more hopeful. "Would you mind checking your files just so I can be sure?"

"You signed the agreement when you were paid," he explains. "Forfeiting your rights to her and to all information about her."

"When I was *paid*?" Maggie cries. "I never signed anything. Or got any money."

"I assume you were at the home for unwed mothers?" he says, reaching for a pen and tapping it on his desk.

"No. I wasn't," she says, confused.

"Look, I'm sorry," he tells her. "I don't remember. There were a lot of babies back then. Most of them came from that home for unwed mothers in the East End. I always dealt with the nuns. There were only a few cases where I dealt directly with the birth mothers or, in your case, the parents of the birth mother. But my hands are tied. It was a closed adoption and the records are sealed."

"You can't even check for my father's name?"

"It's illegal, Mrs. Larsson. I've had enough legal woes. Besides, I don't have any files that predate the kerfuffle in '54."

"What kerfuffle?"

"You're too young," Goldbaum tells her. "Some of us lawyers in the baby business came under scrutiny a few years back."

"For what?"

"The government doesn't like it when people sell babies," he says. "The politicians don't mind institutionalizing them and turning the other way when the priests and nuns abuse them, but God forbid you want to sell a baby to a decent family."

Sell a baby? Maggie opens her mouth to say something, but he stops her.

"Mrs. Larsson, it looks to me like you're back on the right track," he says. "Believe me, if your father had correspondence from me, chances are I'm the guy who placed your baby. In which case, she's in good hands and you leave here with what you came for. Peace of mind."

Maggie drives straight to her father's store and waits for him outside, pacing in the cold while he finishes up for the day. It's dark out and she can see her breath, but the winter air feels good in her face. She watches him usher out the last customers, those end-of-day stragglers, and then the lights go off. As he's about to lock the door, Maggie pounds on the glass.

Her father lets her in, puzzled. "What are you doing here?" he asks, locking the door behind her.

"Why did you tell me you brought my baby to the foundling home?" she wants to know. "Why did you lie to me?"

Her father's shoulders slump ever so slightly, enough for her to notice. He still doesn't look well. "If you've spoken to that lawyer," he says, "I'm sure you know why I lied."

"Because you sold her."

"Not exactly."

"What does that mean?"

"We were supposed to," he admits, rubbing his temple with his thumb. "How could I tell you that? It was better that you thought she went to an orphanage. Still, Maggie, selling illegitimate babies was common practice."

"It's horrible!" she cries.

"It wasn't even my idea. Yvon knew how to go about it. I guess he'd gotten a girl pregnant."

Maggie scoffs in disgust.

"I thought it would ensure an adoption," her father says. "And I was always in need of extra money. It was win-win, Maggie. But then it all fell through."

"Why?"

"The baby was sick. She was supposed to go to a Jewish couple from New York," her father explains. "Everything was arranged. I was going to deliver her to one of the Grey Nuns at Mercy Hospital—"

"The *nuns?*" Maggie cries. "They were involved with selling babies?"

"It was big business," her father says. "The lawyers would arrange the documents and then give the baby to a nun or a doctor at the home for unwed mothers. They were all in on it. Goldbaum was arrested a few years after I dealt with him. It was in the news."

The kerfuffle in '54. Goldbaum made it sound like he'd been unfairly persecuted.

"There were all kinds of charges," her father says. "Forgery. Falsifying birth certificates. But he got off the first time. The second time he had to pay a fine. That's when the whole story came out in the paper."

"How much were you going to sell her for?" Maggie wants to know.

"Three thousand dollars, but the nuns were to get most of it. After the lawyer got his share, we would have had five hundred dollars. Half of that would have gone to Yvon for letting you stay on their farm while you were pregnant."

"My daughter was worth two hundred fifty dollars to you?"

Her father doesn't answer.

"So what happened?"

"Goldbaum assured me they were good people who couldn't have a child of their own," he continues. "But when they found out the baby was premature and had jaundice, they changed their minds. They didn't want a sick baby."

"So where did you take her?" Maggie asks him, wiping her tears.

"She stayed at the hospital. The nuns were going to take her to the foundling home as soon as the jaundice cleared and she put on some weight. She was barely four pounds."

"So you just left her there?" Maggie cries, not wanting to imagine her tiny baby girl being abandoned at the hospital.

"I left her in the care of the doctors and nuns, yes."

"So she did go to the foundling home, but later? Maybe in April?"

"Maybe," he says. "It was common practice, Maggie. I'm sure she got adopted in the end."

"How can you be sure?" Maggie accuses. "You have no idea what's become of her. Not that you even care."

CHAPTER 35

On her way back to Knowlton, Maggie obsesses over what to do next. Visit the foundling home? Call back and inquire about any baby girls who arrived in the weeks following Elodie's birth date? She starts to feel twinges of pain in her groin, so she pulls over and takes a few deep breaths, waiting for the pain to pass. When it does, she continues on her way, relieved to feel the baby stretching inside her.

She almost makes it back home, but then feels something warm between her legs. She looks down and discovers she's sopping wet. The water. She remembers the water.

Yvon's carving knife being sharpened for the carving of the roast beef. "Is there any horseradish?" And then the hot rush of water between her legs, the shame of her ignorance.

She's not due for another three weeks. After another sharp pain, she decides to drive straight to the hospital. The water continues to pour out onto the seat. She keeps checking to make sure it's not blood. *Don't let it be blood.*

She pulls up to the Brome-Missisquoi-Perkins Hospital and nearly falls out of the car.

"She's in labor!" someone cries. "Get a wheelchair."

Her attention comes back to the present. People are around her. The wind and the snow on her face feel good. "It's too early," she mutters.

Even as she's saying the words, a contraction comes, sharp and brutal. "Your baby disagrees," the stranger says.

These things can't be conveniently arranged.

"Is something wrong?" Maggie asks.

No one answers. The present dims again. Another contraction, another memory. *Dr. Cullen's sturdy hips. The enamel basin. The blood. The broken cord.*

"Will she be okay?" Maggie asks.

"Everything is fine. Let's get you inside."

A wheelchair is slipped beneath her, and someone—a nurse—pushes her toward the hospital. In between contractions, she's able to relax. She takes a deep breath of cold air and feels lucid.

"Just keep breathing deeply. It's just a contraction."

"I don't remember it being this painful."

"You've done this before then," the nurse says. "You're a pro."

"It's too early," Maggie moans, stroking her stomach, trying to keep the baby inside. "I still have a few weeks—"

"It's plenty long enough," the nurse assures her. "I have a cousin who gave birth eight weeks early and the baby was perfect. Tiny, but perfect."

Maggie can feel the pain in her rear, a hard pressing sensation that's wretchedly uncomfortable. Inside, she's rushed to the maternity ward. There are no available rooms, so she's left on a gurney in the hallway. A nurse wants to know if she should call Maggie's husband. "My mother," Maggie grunts in the grip of a contraction.

Even in the fog and confusion of labor, she can't get Elodie out of her mind. Each contraction brings a sharp stab of guilt over the fact that she left her daughter in this very hospital—sick, alone, and unwanted. When Maggie starts to cry, it's not from pain but from remorse. *Where is she now?*

"Elodie . . ." she sobs.

"It'll be just fine," the nurse assures her. "We're going to give you a shot for the pain."

There are no spaces left between her contractions, just intolerable, unrelenting agony. "It's coming!—" she wails, slipping in and out of consciousness. "Call my doctor. It's *here*—" She can feel the baby now, pushing its way out into the world. She keeps weaving in and out of the past, one moment here, the next she is sixteen again.

"A doctor is coming."

Dr. Cullen appears next to the bed. "It's crowning."

She's vaguely aware of her hand in someone else's. Pushing, pushing. Her head flopping back on the pillow. A nurse standing above her. The white uniform.

She jams her feet into Dr. Cullen, squeezing her aunt's hand.

"You're doing a great job." It's the nurse again. The white uniform.

"One more!" Dr. Cullen encourages. "Last push!"

And then her screams are suddenly joined by the piercing screams of a newborn. Her baby, the one she gets to keep this time. She tries to sit up, but the nurse gently pushes her back down.

It's a girl.

"Can I see her?" Maggie says, half delirious.

"It's a boy, hon. You have a son."

A bolt of clarity in the haze of the flashbacks. *A boy.* She looks around the room, and her mother and Deda are not here. Neither is Dr. Cullen. There's a nurse in a white uniform, a doctor she's never seen before. And her son.

Her son. Even as he's wrapped in a thin blue cotton blanket and gently placed on her chest, she can't help but grieve for the baby girl she gave away. Grieve and laugh with relief as she kisses his damp golden scalp.

"He's perfectly healthy," the doctor says.

"He would have split you in two if he'd gone full term," the nurse says.

The baby is staring up at Maggie, surprisingly alert. She touches his nose and lightly kisses his forehead. She searches for Gabriel in his face. She's accepted his absence in her head, but not yet in her heart.

The nurse leans in to take him.

"What are you doing?" Maggie says, tightening her grip on him.

"Just taking him to the nursery."

"Please, not yet."

She refuses to let him go. She made that mistake once and never saw her daughter again. She won't let this one get too far out of her reach.

"What's his name?" the nurse asks her.

Maggie thinks about it for a moment, and then, as though she's known it all along, says, "James Gabriel."

> *Gabriel,*
>
> *I tried my best to get in touch with you, but all my efforts have come up short. I know you're estranged from Clémentine, and Angèle won't respond to my letters or return my calls. She was always ferociously loyal to you. She must be as disappointed with me as you are.*
>
> *Since I can't find you to tell you everything I want to say, I'm going to write it down so at least you'll have a record. Maybe I'll send this to Clémentine one day, trusting that eventually the two of you will patch things up. I know how much you love each other. I remember that afternoon during the rainstorm, when she drove us home from school, the tender way you spoke to each other, the affection that was so apparent between you. I remember I was jealous. I wished you would talk to me that way. I was already in love with you.*
>
> *The reason I'm writing this is to tell you about our son. I found out I was pregnant right after you ended things and disappeared. What irony, eh? You left me over the child I gave away, only to miss the birth of the child I chose to keep. Our child, which I know for certain.*
>
> *As I stare into his sleeping face, I can't think who I'm sorrier for: you, for not being here to see and hold and love him, or our son, James Gabriel Phénix Hughes, who, it seems, is going to grow up without a father. We're not completely alone, though—no need to worry. My sisters*

come over every day and fawn all over him. He's even managed to melt the ice wall around my mother's heart. My father hasn't seen him since the day of his birth, but I'll save that story for if I ever see you in person.

Not a day goes by that I don't think about you, regret how things turned out, or hate myself for messing things up so badly. And yet, I did do one thing right. I had this baby, this perfect, beautiful boy with blond hair like his papa and dark blue eyes. His legs are like white sausages, and his tiny pink feet and hands make me weep. He smells like talcum powder and sour milk.

I rock him to sleep with his white-clothed bum in the air and his rosy cheek flat against my chest. I hum lullabies in his ear and rub his back. His body is no bigger than a football and fits perfectly between my breasts. When he's in a deep sleep, he smiles to himself and his mouth twitches, as though he's having a funny dream or speaking with people from another life. His cries wake me up every hour, all night long, and sound exactly like an angry goat.

That's everything I can think of for now. I wish you were here with us. And I'm so sorry.

Love,
Maggie

PART III

The Families of Flowers

1961–1971

Birds have wings; they can travel, mix and standardize their populations . . . On the other hand, flowers are rooted to the earth. They are often separated by broad barriers of unsuitable environment from other "stations" of their own species.

—A FIELD GUIDE TO WILDFLOWERS

CHAPTER 36

Maggie answers the phone wearing an oven mitt. It's her mother, which is not unusual, though they typically speak Sunday nights after dinner. "Why're you calling so early?" Maggie asks, shoving the chicken back in the oven.

"He's sick," Maman says.

"Who's sick?" Maggie asks, her heart quickening.

"Your father. He has cancer."

"Cancer?"

"He wouldn't go to Dr. Cullen. You know how he hates doctors. Now it's spread. He waited too long."

Maggie's father has always been deathly afraid of doctors. She can't recall a single time he's ever gone—not for a checkup, nor for an ailment or an illness. His way is to battle it on his own and hope for the best.

"How long has he been sick?"

"Last year he noticed a small lump right below his ear," Maman says. "He lied and told me he went to the doctor and that it was nothing. He said it was just a cyst, so he ignored it until it was the size of a meatball. That's when I told him he had to get it removed, that it was growing as big as his head. I took him myself and Dr. Cullen sent us straight to the hospital. The damn idiot! He never even told me how bad he was feeling. And now—"

"Now what?"

"Now it's too late. He's going to die."

"Surely something can be done," Maggie cries. "There's always something to be done. What kind of cancer is it?"

"It's rare," Maman says. "The doctor called it gardener's cancer."

"What the hell is that?"

"From pesticides probably."

How many times has Maggie heard her father defend pesticides to his customers? *They are friends of the seed, gentlemen!*

"He's been having tests at the hospital all week," her mother says. "He wouldn't let me tell any of you. Not till we knew how bad it was. They've sent him home to die."

Maggie puts a hand over her mouth to suppress a sickening gasp. "How long did they give him?"

"Months. A year at most."

"They don't know Daddy," Maggie says, her voice breaking. "If anyone can fight something like this, he can. He won't give up."

"Maggie. This isn't a business problem. It's *cancer.*"

Maggie leans against the oven and cries quietly. She hasn't spoken to her father since James Gabriel was born. She was planning to wait a lot longer, too, to punish him for what he did with Elodie. She's been making her mother and sisters visit James at her house rather than going to her parents' place. Now she's gutted.

She knew her father wasn't right. He hasn't looked well in months. He's only seen his grandson once, at the hospital when he came to visit with cigars for anyone who happened to be there. Maggie didn't say a word to him.

"Did you hear me?" her mother says.

"No."

"I said he's asked to see you."

Her mother is waiting for her in the kitchen when she arrives, looking old and weary. She's only in her fifties, but she looks twenty years older. She's put on more weight and has a double chin now. The first thing she does is take the baby from Maggie. She gazes into his sleeping face and smiles, a smile that lights up her dark eyes and softens the deep lines around her usually frowning mouth. *"Bonjour, mon p'tit choux,"* she coos.

Maggie watches her mother cradle James Gabriel in her arms, murmuring baby gibberish and staring at him in adoration, and she wonders if Maman ever held *her* that way, looked at her with those same besotted eyes, cooed softly in her ear.

"How's Daddy?" she asks.

"He's in terrible pain. He's got morphine, but it doesn't help. The cancer's already in his liver."

Maggie climbs the stairs. The room is pitch-black and ominously quiet. As she approaches the bed, she can make out a slight mound under the chenille bedspread. "Daddy?"

Her father stirs. "Maggie?"

She sits down beside him.

"Turn on the lamp," he croaks.

With the light on, she can see how much he's already deteriorated. She has to fight back tears so as not to alarm him. Whatever anger she's been holding on to over the past couple of months instantly vanishes. He looks like a sick old man. Skeletal, gray, helpless. Gone is the solid, reliable man. Not a trace remains of his vitality or passion or arrogance.

"Maggie," he wheezes. He's got dark pouches under his eyes and his limbs are like branches. He coughs into a handkerchief and Maggie cringes. "How are you?" he asks, his voice rattling with mucus.

"I'm fine, Daddy."

He attempts a smile. Years of cigar smoking have yellowed his bottom teeth. "You've got your son to look after now," he says.

Maggie reaches for his hand.

"If I had a dying wish . . ."

"Please don't say it."

"The boy needs a father," he says. "Roland would take you back in a snap. I know he still loves you."

Maggie is silent.

"The store has to go up for sale," he says.

"I know. I can help with that."

"Just make sure it doesn't wind up in the hands of a Frenchman, eh? I don't want Superior Seeds getting a bad reputation after all my hard work building it into something."

She laughs. He always did believe himself to be cut from a superior cloth.

"Unless you take it over," he adds.

"Take over the store?"

"You always had a good mind for business," he says. "It *has* to be you. You could run it. Keep it in the family."

Maggie's mind goes off in all directions. Running her father's seed store was her childhood dream, but she's got the baby now and she's come to enjoy translating . . .

"I need to sleep," he murmurs. "Think about it, hm?"

She nods, knowing she won't be able to think of anything else.

Maman grabs the pan of spaghetti from the oven and hands it to Vi to set down on the table, and then she drops a couple of sausages into a fry pan. Watching her mother expertly maneuver around the kitchen, Maggie experiences a small surge of fondness. She's always taken good care of them. She's never done it with affection or tenderness, but she's always tended to their basic needs. They were well fed, smartly dressed, sparkling clean; their home was always spotless, pretty, and comfortable. It's probably the only way her mother knows how to love anyone.

"You made his favorite," Maggie remarks. Baked spaghetti and sausage.

"After thirty-five years," Maman says, turning the sausages in the fry pan, "it's strange not having him at the table."

James Gabriel stirs in his basket at Maggie's feet. Maman drops the sausages on top of the spaghetti casserole and sits down. Maggie, Vi, and Maman eat in silence. It's just clinking cutlery, Patti Page on the radio.

"The farmers used to warn him," Maman says, suddenly break-ing the silence. "About those goddamn pesticides. *They* knew. But he never listened to anybody. He always knew best. He always had to be right."

"No one knows for sure it was the pesticides," Vi says, adjusting her browline glasses on her nose.

"That ghost up there," Maman goes on. "That's not my husband anymore." She pauses, reflecting. She hasn't touched her supper. "He used to boast about his fancy diploma, his plans to open his own plant store. He was so full of himself." She laughs, remembering. "The day I met him he was wearing an Irish tweed vest. He actually made a point of telling me it was Irish. As if *I* cared about goddamn Irish tweed!"

She roars with laughter. Maggie leans over and pulls the blanket up over James Gabriel.

"He made an effort," Maman concedes. "I'll give him that. He lived in L'Abord-à-Plouffe, but he'd ride an hour and a half on the streetcar to come see me with a bouquet of fresh-picked flowers. He didn't seem to mind at all that I lived in Hochelaga."

The back door suddenly swings open and Nicole appears in the mudroom, looking flushed and exuberant. Her dark hair is cut very short in that new Jean Seberg pixie style from *À Bout de Souffle*. She's as pretty as Maggie, but with more confidence. She grabs a sausage on her way out of the kitchen.

"She's a pain in the ass, that one," Maman complains.

"It's no wonder," Vi says. "You let her get away with murder and she's not even sixteen yet."

"What's the point of trying?" Maman says. "None of you turned out the way I thought you would. Except for Peter and he's the one I left alone the most."

"Geri's at university," Vi reminds her.

Maman shrugs and gets up to clear away the dishes. She puts on a pot of coffee, lays some homemade icebox cookies on a plate, and brings three mugs to the table. When the coffee's ready, she stirs Fry's cocoa and a drop of milk into the bottom of the mugs and then pours the coffee on top.

"After your father and I were married," she says, sitting back down at the table, "that's when he started trying to change me. All of a sudden he couldn't stand my Frenchness. He was like that. He hated himself for wanting to be with someone like me."

"What did you like about him?" Maggie asks her.

"He had good manners," she says. "All the other boys I grew up with drank and swore, but your father had some class. I suppose that's why he liked hanging around in the East End with the French girls."

"That doesn't make sense," Vi says.

"Your father had no confidence," she tells them. "His father died when he was young and he was raised by his mother. She was a total snob, you know. She didn't come from money either—she lived in the country, for God's sake—but she acted like a queen. Talk about putting on airs."

Maman rolls her eyes at the memory of her mother-in-law. "Everything your father did was wrong in her eyes," she says. "She wanted him to go to McGill, not to horticulture school. She wanted him to be a doctor or a banker. She was always making fun of him for becoming a 'gardener,' as she put it. He hated that."

Maman snaps a cookie in two and pops a piece in her mouth.

"He didn't think very highly of himself when I met him," she resumes. "But in the East End, he was always the best dressed and acted like he was better than all the rest of us. He was a king in the slums. He wore those expensive suits that made the French girls worship him. He loved the attention, but he was afraid of his own kind. His mother planted that in him. Everyone was beneath her. I think he married me to punish her. Or to escape her ridiculous expectations."

"He loved you," Maggie states. "I know you fought a lot, but you loved each other."

Her mother waves a dismissive hand in the air, but her cheeks flush a deep pink. "Anyway, his mother disowned him when he married me," she says, gloating.

Maggie sips her coffee, bittersweet from the cocoa, and she's struck by how common a thread it is—the rejection of a parent, a lifetime spent trying to patch up the ensuing feelings of deficiency.

"He tried to turn me into an English doll," her mother goes on. "He did the same with you girls, which of course is exactly what his own mother did to him."

"Can't you say something nice about him for once?" Vi says. "Now that he's dying, for Christ's sake, can't you just say you love him?"

"To tell you the truth, I've never given it any thought," Maman answers. "We didn't think about things like that when I was growing up in Hochelaga, and we still don't. We thought about survival. *You* girls think about love too much. You always did."

"You and daddy must have stayed together for a reason," Maggie says.

"We could hear it from your bedroom," Vi mutters, surprising Maggie. They never talked about it when they were young.

"That was just sex," Maman says.

"Well, that's more than most."

CHAPTER 37

Maggie tiptoes across the room and stands over her father, watching him sleep. She spent the night here again last night and doesn't want to go home to Knowlton yet. She's worried if she leaves, he'll die.

"Maggie," he rasps, sensing her there. "That you?"

"I didn't mean to wake you."

"Sit."

She sits down on the bed and he attempts to prop himself up. She helps him by raising the pillow behind his back. The effort leaves him spent.

"Maggie, I just want you to know I'm sorry." He squeezes her hand and she's surprised by the strength of his grip.

"It's okay," she says.

"No. Listen to me. I'm sorry I forbid you to be with Gabriel Phénix. I know you loved him."

Maggie wipes her eyes and then strokes her father's thin, damp hair.

"And I'm sorry about your baby," he says. "I didn't lie to you for any other reason than to spare you unnecessary pain."

"I know that."

"We made the decision to put her up for adoption to protect your future, Maggie."

"I know."

"It was the times," he says. "It's what families had to do back then.

Otherwise your life and your reputation would have been ruined at sixteen." He pauses then and clasps her hand. "We wanted you to have a chance. Look how Clémentine's life turned out and she was just a divorcée."

Maggie knows he's right. The moral climate of Duplessis's Quebec was the integral backstory to what unfolded in their family. Her parents were merely reacting out of fear and panic, doing the only thing they knew to do in order to shield their child from public humiliation and disgrace. How can she stay angry with him? He's a dying man. She has no desire to punish him on his deathbed or carry a grudge after he's gone, which would only serve to poison her life.

"Have you tried to find her?" he asks.

"I haven't had a chance to do anything since James was born."

"I can't bear the thought of you hating me," he says.

"I could never hate you, Daddy."

His eyes flutter shut and his breathing becomes even more strained. His head lolls to the side, his body convulsing with quiet sobs. Tears are collecting in his sunken cheeks. "She was so beautiful, Maggie. Just like you." He starts to cough. "I'm sorry I didn't save her when I had the chance."

"Save her?"

"Enough," her mother says, coming into the room. "Let him be, Maggie."

"Hortense," he chokes. "Get me a drink."

"Wellington, don't be an idiot."

"Please."

Hortense begrudgingly leaves the room, muttering to herself, "*Maudit ivrogne.*" *Goddamn drunk.*

"I gave her that name you liked," Maggie's father reveals, once they're alone.

"What name?"

"Elodie."

Maggie lets out a small noise and covers her mouth with her hand. "Maman told you?"

"Deda did."

"Why didn't you ever tell me?"

He shakes his head helplessly, his eyes clouding. "It was an impulsive decision," he admits. "I had no intention of doing it, but at the last second I just couldn't let her go without at least some connection to you. Some way back."

Maggie lays her head on his chest. It doesn't erase what he did, but giving her baby that name was as close to a gift as he could have given her.

"What if she was never adopted?" Maggie says, lifting her head. "What if she grew up in an asylum?"

"If only that couple had been more honorable," he laments. "They should have taken her, sick or not. They're the ones to blame."

"Why did you choose people from New York? Why so far away?"

"It was hard for Jews to get babies back then," he explains. "They were desperate and started buying babies in Quebec. I thought it was our best bet to ensure an adoption."

"Couldn't you find another family here in Quebec after they decided not to take her?"

"That was the plan," he says. "She was to be transferred to the Saint-Sulpice Orphanage near Farnham. I'm sure they eventually placed her with a family, Maggie. She was perfect."

His eyes close and he starts to snore unevenly. "That's how it worked," he murmurs, half awake again. "We didn't think we were doing anything wrong. But then nothing worked out how I thought it would."

Before long, he's snoring loudly, his throat rattling. As Maggie steps out of the room, she collides with her mother. She's got a Crown Royal bottle in one hand and a glass of ice cubes in the other.

"He's asleep," Maggie says, closing the door.

"What did he tell you?" her mother wants to know.

"Everything."

"We didn't think we were doing anything wrong," her mother defends. "We were just trying to clean up your mess the best way we knew how, Maggie."

"*My* mess? It's possible it was Yvon's fault!"

Maggie may be able to forgive her father for having taken Elodie to the orphanage, but she won't afford her mother the same courtesy for having chosen to believe Yvon over her own daughter. "I guess it's more convenient for you to blame Gabriel instead of your beloved brother-in-law," Maggie says.

"He's my sister's husband, Maggie."

"*I'm* your daughter."

Maman looks away.

"I'm going to find her," Maggie says.

"You won't be able to," her mother warns. "They probably changed her name, wiped away her history. No one in this province wants you to know where that child is, or what's happened to her."

Maggie glares at her mother for a moment, and then repeats with authority, "I'm going to find her."

CHAPTER 38

Maggie brings the car to a stop in front of the Hôpital Mentale Saint-Sulpice, and sits there for several minutes, trying to collect herself. Its redbrick facade and inviting front yard make Maggie think it was probably quite a charming home once. If not for the bars on the dormer windows, it still could be.

A quick phone call to the foundling home in Cowansville revealed that a three-week-old baby girl had arrived there in April of 1950 and was transferred a month later to Saint-Sulpice, as her father had guessed. In 1954, its name—and, with it, its vocation—was officially changed to the Hôpital Mentale Saint-Sulpice.

Maggie gets out of the car and stands at the front door for a long time, imagining her infant daughter being brought here all those years ago in the arms of a stranger. She takes a breath and bangs the knocker. Almost immediately, someone opens the door.

"Can I help you?"

Maggie is surprised to find herself facing a middle-aged man with an Elvis pompadour. She'd been expecting a nun.

"Is there someone in charge I can speak to?" she asks him. "One of the sisters?"

"I'm the caretaker."

"I'd like some information about my daughter."

The man frowns. He has tired eyes, a hard expression. He must get women like Maggie showing up all the time looking for their long-lost children, especially since the commissions of inquiry are just being made public. "We don't give out information," he says. "It's against the law."

She steps toward him and presses a fifty-dollar bill into his hand. "Please accept this donation," she says nervously. "Anything you can tell me would be appreciated."

He hesitates a moment and then quickly pockets the money. "Come with me," he says.

Maggie follows him inside, noting the grim interior—dim lighting, neglected furniture, a strong odor of mildew—as they make their way to an office at the back. He tugs on a cord, and a bare bulb illuminates a narrow room lined with wooden filing cabinets. Maggie scans the cabinets, envisioning their sanctified contents—babies' names, birth parents' names, adoptive families' names, dates of birth, places of birth, hospital records, birth certificates; all of it off-limits to the very people who most want access.

"Name?" the man says.

"Maggie Larsson."

"The *girl's* name," he says impatiently. "Did she have one?"

"Elodie."

"Date of birth?"

"March 6th, 1950."

He kneels down in front of the cabinet marked *1948–1950* and flips through the manila file folders until he finds what he's looking for. Maggie holds her breath.

"Here," he says, handing her the file. He leans back up against the cabinets and lights a cigarette. "Hurry up before Sister Tata and the others get back. Most of them are still at the morning service."

Exactly what she was hoping. Maggie opens the file with shaking hands. There are two documents inside. The first is a copy of the birth certificate. *Name, Elodie. Date of birth, March 6th, 1950. Place of birth, Brome-Missisquoi-Perkins Hospital. Cowansville, Quebec. Mother: unknown. Father: unknown.*

The other paper in the folder is a Record of Transfer. "What is this?" Maggie asks. "It's dated October 1957."

"A lot of children were transferred to the mental hospitals in Montreal," he says. "After the conversion."

"Does that mean she wasn't adopted?"

"Not if there's a Record of Transfer."

"But why would she have been transferred?"

"To make room for more patients," he responds. "After '55, they started sending real mental patients here. They had to start shipping orphans to the asylums in the city to make space. We weren't equipped to handle them all."

"Were you here then?" she asks him. "Do you think you might remember her?"

"I've only been here two years," he tells her. "I was working at an orphanage in Valleyfield before that, but I remember the day the nuns there told the children."

He stubs out his cigarette in a nearby ashtray and opens his pack for another. He hands her one and lights it. It feels good in her lungs. It's the first deep breath she's taken in hours.

"I remember one of the nuns going from classroom to classroom that morning, announcing to the children that they were all going to be declared mentally deficient. Imagine? The nuns were upset, they knew they were doing something wrong."

He shakes his head at the memory. "One day they were all sitting in class, getting an education," he says. "The next, just like that, no more school. They were treated like retards from then on. Bars went up on the windows, as you can see. Gates around the property. It wasn't long after that when they started sending them to asylums in Montreal, cramming them into wards already overcrowded with real mental patients."

The small room is cloudy with their cigarette smoke. "Why?" she asks, knowing the answer. Hating it.

"Why is the easy part," he says. "The province paid the nuns a pittance to care for orphans, and more than three times as much to care for mental patients. That's why Mount Providence turned itself into a mental institution, and why so many orphanages in Quebec followed suit. It's always about money, isn't it?"

"That can't have been legal?"

He lets out a hard laugh. "Legal?" he says. "Who do you think benefited most from the whole thing? The moment those kids' records were changed to classify them as mentally deficient, the church *and* Duplessis started to line their pockets. The province got giant subsidies from the federal government to build hospitals, so it could certainly afford to pay the church more than triple for taking care of mental patients than it used to pay for orphans."

"Where was she taken?" Maggie asks him. "Why doesn't it say on this Record of Transfer?"

"They wouldn't have included that information. Nothing that might lead someone like you to your child was ever kept."

"Where are the rest of the documents?" Maggie wants to know. "Shouldn't there be more?"

"A lot of the records were destroyed after the orphanages were converted. It's possible hers were transferred to the asylum with her, but as you can see, if there *was* a Record of Transfer left here, it would be quite vague."

Maggie closes the file and hands it back to him. She feels as hollow as she did the day Elodie was taken from her eleven years ago. "Do you have any idea where she might have been sent?" she asks him. "Any idea at all?"

"Maybe Saint-Nazarius or Mercy. Those were the two where most of our orphans were transferred. I doubt you'll find her, though. They're all fortresses, those places. Besides, most of the records on that end are all lies anyway. I've seen files describing normal, healthy kids as severely retarded, a danger to themselves and others. All made up. Real records were expunged. A lot of those orphans were given new names when they got to the hospitals—starting with A for the babies born in January, B for February, and so on."

Maggie's spirits plummet. How will she ever find Elodie if Elodie was given a new name? If her records—her *identity*—were wiped clean?

"The church has to keep covering this up," the caretaker says. "You won't be able to pay them off the way you did me."

"What *can* I do?"

"You could write to Quebec City."

"Where will that get me?" she sniffs. "Since when does the government get involved with helping orphans?"

"Since Duplessis died," he says. "A commission of psychiatrists has been investigating some of the province's mental hospitals. At Mount Providence they've already concluded that most of the five hundred children they examined are perfectly normal. Big surprise, heh?"

"What are they doing about it?"

"I'm not sure. I think the plan is to put the younger ones into foster care. Let the older ones fend for themselves." He shrugs, his expression cynical. "The new government has only just revealed these kids don't belong in mental institutions. There are still hundreds of hospitals to investigate."

"My God. So I may be able to get her back," Maggie says.

"If you manage to find her," he says. "But believe me, the nuns will do everything in their power to stop you."

Outside, Maggie takes several deep breaths before jumping in her car and driving home, where she immediately starts firing off letters to the provincial government, demanding to see her daughter's files and to learn where she was transferred in 1957.

CHAPTER 39

Maggie's breasts are engorged; she's hoping the baby will wake up soon so she can offload some of this milk. She's been reading Godbout's latest manuscript to distract herself, making notes here and there, mulling over how she might handle it. She asked for sign credit this time and Godbout promised to discuss it with his publisher. He's become a champion of her literary career.

She's still trying to decide what to do about her father's store. She's certainly tempted to take over the reins, but Peter wants to sell it and give the money to their mother. He doesn't seem too interested in what their father wants, given he's never thought the business had the potential to turn a substantial profit. Although Maggie is inclined to believe keeping it in the family would be a better long-term investment, generating a decent income for their mother, she hasn't fought for it yet. She's still not sure how she would manage motherhood and running a very demanding retail business. Her father was never home, which is not an option for Maggie, but the thought of selling the store to a stranger doesn't sit right.

James Gabriel is plump and solid now, with fine golden hair, eyes that hover between blue and gray, and bright pink cheeks. Maggie's mother even declared him to be cuter than Peter was as a baby. Life since his arrival has become one long sequence of breastfeeding, sleep deprivation, hormonal madness, stunning confusion, loneliness, and ferocious, almost painful devotion to this self-centered little creature.

There's been scant time to prepare for her father's death, if such a thing is even possible. There's also been no time to ruminate over Gabriel or Elodie's whereabouts. In many ways, Maggie is grateful for her zombielike state and the suspension of reality.

Her sisters have been a great help. Now that Vi has her driver's license, she visits almost every day, often bringing Nicole with her, Geri, too, if she can get away from school. Sometimes one of them will stay by their father's sickbed so that her mother can visit the baby, too. They fight over who gets to hold James and change his diapers and fetch him from his naps, especially Maman, who lavishes him with affection. Maggie and her sisters think she's going soft in her old age.

Violet comes into the kitchen carrying a laundry basket filled to overflowing with freshly washed diapers, burp cloths, layettes, and baby blankets.

"Oh, Vi, you're a lifesaver," Maggie says.

Vi sets the basket down and removes her glasses, which are fogged up. "I love folding his little things," she says.

"You're such a natural with him."

"I don't know how you do it without a husband," she says. "I'll drop by tomorrow after work." And then the door slams behind her and the house falls silent. James Gabriel sleeps on, undisturbed.

Maggie returns to Godbout's book. About half an hour goes by and there's a knock at the door. Maggie notices Violet's glasses sitting on the edge of the table and grabs them as she gets up. She quickly pats her nipples with a dish towel and rushes to the door.

More knocking.

"Coming, Vi!" she says, exasperated. She reaches the door and opens it, glasses in hand. "I just noticed them, otherwise I would have called to—"

She stops midsentence when she realizes it's not Violet. Instinctively, she looks down at herself—her leaking breasts and stained shirt—and regrets opening the door.

"Maggie," Gabriel says.

Maggie makes an effort to compose herself, but her entire body is shaking.

"I'm sorry I didn't call in advance," he says. "I wasn't sure you'd want to see me."

"Of course I want to see you," she says, her voice choked with emotion. At the same time, her eyes sweep over him, taking a quick inventory from head to foot. He's wearing an army jacket and jeans with a Montreal Canadiens tuque pulled down low over his brow. Still gorgeous. His shoulders seem broader, his eyes bluer, his lips fuller. Or does she just imagine it to be so? Part of her wants to fling herself into his arms; the other, to smash her fist into his face. She has no idea where they stand.

"Come in," she says, opening the door.

"Nice place," he comments, following her to the kitchen. "You've done a good job decorating it."

Maggie's like her mother that way. She likes to sew her own curtains and buy vintage fabrics and use lots of ruffles; she buys antiques from flea markets and auctions, and paints and restores them.

"New translation?" he asks, eyeing her notes on the kitchen table. "I read your last one. You did a brilliant job."

"I'm glad you liked it," she says, feeling her anger mounting.

"How have you been?" he asks, as though he's just gotten back from a fishing trip.

"A lot's happened."

"I heard about your father. I'm sorry."

"Where have you been?" she blurts out. "Do you know the lengths I went to trying to find you? How often I harassed your sisters? You just vanished!"

Gabriel pulls off his cap and tousles his hair, which has grown out since she last saw him, but he doesn't say anything. He sits down at her kitchen table without waiting to be asked.

"I called everywhere," she says, sitting down as well. "I even spoke to your wife. I went to Canadair, the place on Papineau—"

"I know."

"You quit the factory and didn't tell anybody? You just disappeared. Why?"

"Everything fell apart after it ended between us. I left Annie. I couldn't stand being there, couldn't stand driving the cab anymore, the factory. I had to get out."

"Why didn't you call me?"

"It was you I had to get away from most of all," Gabriel admits. "I believed it could never work between us. You were used to a different kind of life. You had expectations I couldn't meet."

Maggie looks away.

"But I've made my peace," he says.

"What does that mean?"

"With who I am."

"I see," she responds, not sure what he's trying to tell her.

"You were still married, Maggie. What did I have to offer? I had nothing."

"You could have come back to Dunham, to your family's farm."

"To have to answer to my big sister for the rest of my life? To have absolutely no say while she makes all the decisions, like I'm still four-teen? Or to steal you away from your wealthy banker husband and support you? *How? With what?*"

"I left him," she says. "I'd already told him I was going to. I didn't care about the stuff. I only wanted you. I waited and waited for you."

"It just didn't seem like such a great plan at the time."

"Where did you go?"

"Gaspé."

She glances up at him, allowing herself to really look at him for the first time.

"I got a job cod fishing," he says.

"You didn't even tell your sisters where you were?"

"Clémentine and I weren't speaking. Angèle knew, but she would never tell anyone if I asked her not to. Not even Clem. I just needed to be alone."

"You did a good job."

"That was the point." He adds some milk to his tea. "But I feel okay now," he says. "Pretty good, actually. The physical work is good. I love living by the sea, working outdoors. Far from Montreal."

"And from me."

"At first. I needed to get some clarity, absorb everything."

"And now?"

"I bought some land in the Gaspé."

Hearing this, Maggie feels the same acute sense of loss she felt the first time he left her. She wants more than anything to beg him to stay, but he's bought land, extinguishing their second chance at love.

"I don't want to drive a taxi or spend the rest of my life at Canadair," he tells her. "It's the one thing I was able to get really clear about while I was gone."

A loud cry from the nursery startles both of them. Gabriel nearly jumps out of his seat. Maggie is used to the baby's waking screams, his inconvenient sense of timing. She waits for a moment, hoping he's up for good and she can finally feed him and relieve the pain in her breasts, but the crying subsides. He's fallen back to sleep.

"Angèle told me you had a baby," he says. "Congratulations."

She pauses. "He's yours, Gabriel."

Her revelation visibly knocks the wind out of him. His mouth opens, but no words come. He sits there for a moment, absorbing it. His eyes like glass.

"I tried to find you," she reminds him. "I wanted him to have a father."

"I know," he murmurs. "I can't . . . I don't know what to say."

She lets him sit with the news for a little while.

"Do you want to meet him?" she finally asks, breaking the silence.

Gabriel's face lights up. "Yes," he says. "Please." He gets up and takes a few steps toward Maggie, then pulls her in for an unexpected hug. "I've wondered," he admits, releasing her. "When Angèle told me, I thought the baby might be mine."

"You should have come back then."

"It could have been your husband's, too. I didn't want to fuck things up any more than they already were. And I was still upset, Maggie."

"I'm going to feed him and then I'll bring him down."

James Gabriel beams the moment he sees her face. He adores her. She is the grounding, nurturing centerpiece of his universe. "Hi," she says. "Hi, little man."

Maggie scoops him up and presses her lips to his warm cheek. "Time to eat," she whispers, putting him back in his jammies. He grabs a fistful of her hair and yanks hard. She lets out a small shriek, marveling at how strong he is. She sits with him in the rocking chair while he sucks on her nipple, draining her breasts of milk, and tries to calm herself before she introduces him to his father. How many times has she played that scene out in her mind? She can hardly believe it's actually happening. She almost gave up.

After the baby pulls his face away and spits up on her shoulder, she holds him against her chest and says, "Now let's go meet your daddy."

She carries him downstairs and takes a deep breath before entering the kitchen. "Here he is," she says, bursting into tears before Gabriel even has a chance to hold him.

"What's his name?" Gabriel asks her, reaching out his arms to take him.

"James Gabriel."

Gabriel's eyes widen, and he manages a smile.

The baby burps as he's passed from his mother to his father, and Maggie quickly leans in to wipe his chin with her shirtsleeve. Gabriel takes the baby in his arms with surprising confidence. "*Mon Dieu*," he murmurs, rubbing his nose on top of James's downy head and kissing his fat cheek. "He's beautiful."

Gabriel looks up at Maggie and their eyes lock. He's crying. "My son," he says proudly. "*Mon gars*."

Maggie laughs, feeling happier than she's felt in a long time.

"*Bonjour, mon homme*," he says softly, bouncing him in his arms. James is smiling at him. Love at first sight.

Gabriel starts singing to him in French. *"Fais dodo, bébé à Papa . . ."*
Maggie's heart is beating fast. James is cooing and giggling.
"Si bébé pas fais dodo, grand loup-loup va manger."
The phone rings and Maggie reaches for it.
"Your father's dead," her mother says. Just like that.

CHAPTER 40

The Seed Man is buried in the cemetery behind the Protestant church. Just about every farmer from Frelighsburg to Granby shows up to honor him. Maggie barely recognizes any of his customers in their dark, formal trench coats and solemn faces. The men she knew always wore overalls and muddy boots, had suntans and dirt in their fingernails. But here they all are—Blais, LaPellure, O'Carroll, Cardinal, Loriot. They toss seeds at the coffin as it's lowered into the ground, and when it's fully immersed, swallowed whole by the earth her father loved so much, Maggie weeps.

She thinks about his catalogues, his unrealized garden, his smoky sanctuary in the maid's quarters; she thinks about his homemade radios, his cigars, his Dale Carnegie seminars and self-improvement books, and all the ways he ever attempted to hide from his wife and blot out the grim reality of his home life, all the while never failing to support his family no matter what toll it took on him.

Maggie was surprised to learn that he'd made her the sole executor of his will. He also had a clause put in that gives her say as to whether the business will be sold, which felt to her like a sincere gesture of conciliation. Much to Peter's shock and chagrin, no one in the family has a vote—not even their mother. The decision is entirely Maggie's. It was a smart move on her father's part, knowing Maggie as he does. He understood that she would never—*could* never—sell his store.

And he was right. She never will.

The men approach the family one by one, shaking hands and offering condolences. When it's over, Maman takes hold of Geri's arm and they walk purposefully back to the Packard. Gabriel and the baby follow after them, leaving Maggie to linger behind and take a moment alone with her father.

She can't quite believe he's gone. A numbness has settled over her, which has diffused the grief and emptiness just enough for her to get through each day. She kneels down and touches his stone with her gloved hand, silently promising to carry on his legacy with equal passion and dedication.

When she finally rises and turns away from his grave, Clémentine Phénix emerges from the shadows of the trees, clutching a silk paisley handkerchief to her face. She catches Maggie's arm and gazes at her beseechingly. Her eyes are puffy and red as she comes close enough for Maggie to smell the Yardley soap on her skin. "I'm sorry for your loss," she says, her voice broken.

Georgette is lurking behind her, her cheeks flushed from the cold, her nose running. She's gotten so tall, Maggie observes. She must be about seventeen, with the same freckled nose and golden hair as Clémentine. She's wearing a tattered coat, which looks like one of Vi's old coats from years ago. Yes, she thinks, looking more closely. It *is* Vi's coat—she can tell from the missing button.

"He was a good man," Clémentine says.

"Thank you," Maggie responds cordially, still staring at the coat in confusion. How did Georgette wind up with it? she wonders.

"Your father may have known seeds," Clémentine states, looking Maggie directly in the eye. "But he understood nothing about flowers, did he?"

Maggie takes a step back, not knowing what to say.

"Our condolences to your family," Clémentine adds, and then walks off with the snow crunching beneath her boots and Georgette trudging behind.

Maggie returns to her parents' house after the burial, but doesn't stay long. Still troubled by her encounter with Clémentine, she can't face more condolences, small talk over party sandwiches, and the absence of her father. Instead, she sends Gabriel back upstairs to put the baby down for a nap and heads where she always goes for solace, the cornfield.

The sun slips behind the Phénix house, and the sky quickly changes from bright hyacinth blue to navy as she makes her way down. Wandering through the frozen field, Maggie adds up all the inconsequential bits and pieces that on their own have always seemed benign, but taken together now paint a picture of something far more incriminating. The signature smell of Yardley soap on Clémentine's skin, the *Handbook for Gardeners* in her book shelf, the English tea set, Violet's hand-me-downs on Georgette.

Maggie remembers a young Clémentine fondly tending her crops, one hand on her hip, the other caressing the corn, the way Maggie has seen her do a hundred times—a woman Maggie's father would not have been able to resist, especially right under his nose.

It wasn't just the one time, Maggie realizes. It must have gone on and on, long after that day Maggie caught them.

She turns and heads back toward the Phénix shack. She knocks on the door and Clémentine appears. "Come in," she says, expecting her. She's still in her black dress, still puffy-eyed and hanging on to that handkerchief.

"Is Georgette my father's daughter?" Maggie asks, barely through the door.

Clémentine draws back, startled.

"*Is she?*"

"Of course not," Clémentine responds, with a perceptible undertone of defiance.

Maggie sits down on the couch without being invited to do so. "But you've been with him all these years, haven't you?"

"Yes."

"All this is him," Maggie says, pointing to the books on her shelf, the tea set. "Our hand-me-downs . . ."

"He was just trying to help us."

"Does my mother know?" Maggie asks coolly.

"Of course not," Clémentine responds. "I wouldn't be alive."

"And Gabriel?"

"Absolutely not."

"He made you beg for credit at his store," Maggie reminds her. "Even though you were lovers."

"I'm the one who wouldn't take his money," she says. "I was young and stupid, full of pride. He offered and I said no. When I asked for credit at his store that day, I think he was angry with me for doing it in front of people, instead of just letting him quietly support me. He was angry with me for being so stubborn and proud."

She fixes herself a Scotch and pours one for Maggie, without even asking her if she wants one.

"Did he love you?" she asks.

"In his own way," Clémentine says, her eyes finally dry. "Not the way he loved your mother. Not enough to leave her. He was always driven by lust. He didn't really understand love. He tried, though. He really did try."

Maggie laughs at that and Clémentine blushes.

"*I* loved him," Clémentine admits. "It's a relief to finally say that out loud."

Maggie gets to her feet.

"I'm sorry," Clémentine murmurs.

Maggie doesn't respond. She's too tired. She's not even angry, just drained.

She walks back to her parents' house, feeling heavyhearted and alone. Once inside, she wanders into her father's sanctuary and pulls on the light cord, startled to discover the room is practically bare. It smells of cleaning products and bleach. The wood floor is gleaming and freshly polished and all of his homemade radios are gone. He's gone. He's been scoured and scrubbed away. Maggie recognizes her mother's handiwork right away. There are no scattered papers on the desk, no half-finished catalogues, no ashtrays, no sign of any of his hobbies. His books, which were usually piled everywhere depending on which three or four he was currently reading at the same time, are now arranged by height on the shelf. The agriculture mixed in with the business books. She skims over their spines with her finger, resting on one of his old catalogues. She makes a note to bring all of them to the seed store and keep them in what will soon be her office.

She kneels down and opens his toolbox, which is full of his personal mementos: his diploma of horticulture, the homemade cards and drawings they've given him over the years, a frayed sepia portrait of his mother. She tries the file cabinet in the corner, but it's locked. This time, the key isn't in its usual spot.

Maggie's mother suddenly appears in the doorway.

"Why did you clean out his room already?" Maggie asks, ready to take her revenge and tell her everything about Clémentine. "It smells like bleach! It doesn't smell like him."

"What did you want me to do?"

"You could have waited."

"For what?" Maman cries, tears springing to her black eyes. "He's not coming back!"

"Do you even care?" Maggie accuses.

"Of course I care," she says. "I loved him."

"Did you?"

"I know I could be mean to him sometimes—"

Maggie laughs. "Yes," she says. "You could."

"Come out of there now," her mother manages, wiping her eyes and nose with the bottom of her apron. "We still have guests."

"Where's the key to the file cabinet?" Maggie asks her.

"I don't know. It wasn't here when I cleaned the room. He probably hid it after you went through his things."

Of course he would have done exactly that.

"What are you looking for anyway?" her mother asks. "You know everything there is to know."

Maggie turns off the light and follows her mother out of the room. She closes the door behind her, wondering where he would have hidden that key and how she will ever find it.

She goes upstairs to Peter's old room, where James is sleeping peacefully, surrounded by pillows to keep him from falling off the bed. She watches the small mound of his body rise and fall with every sweet breath, and she's overcome with a powerful swell of love and inexplicable optimism. This spirit of resilience was inherited from her father, a man who never gave up; a man who endured and persevered, snatching handfuls of pleasure wherever he could.

CHAPTER 41

The sunlight spilling through the gauzy curtains gently wakes her. Everything from the day before slowly comes back—the funeral, her conversation with Clémentine. Maggie stretches, rolls onto her side, and curls up against Gabriel.

He presses her hand to his chest and she can feel his heart beating beneath her palm. "I want you to move to the Gaspé with me," he says, his voice hoarse from sleep. "I bought that land for us, Maggie. That's why I came back. For a fresh start."

"I can't just leave."

"Gaspésie is the most beautiful place," he says, turning around to face her. "It's the best of both worlds. Countryside by the sea."

"My life is here."

"You can translate books anywhere."

"My father left me the business," she tells him. "And I want to run it. I've always wanted to."

Gabriel sighs and flops onto his back.

"You completely disappeared from my life," she says. "You can't just come back a year later and expect me to give up everything. I want to be with you, but *here*."

"I want to raise my son," he says, lighting a cigarette. "A boy needs a father in his life. My land is on the water. I can teach him to fish . . ."

"Fatherhood is more than fishing."

"I know that."

"You don't understand," she says. "I want to stay here and run my father's seed store. I was always meant to do it. I'll be good at it."

"How can you work and take care of James?"

"I'll find a way," she says. "Violet has offered to help me."

"We're a family, Maggie. We should be together."

"You mean where *you* want to be."

"I love you," he says. "I always have. Goddamn it, Maggie. Have some faith in us and choose me over your father."

The baby lets out a loud cry from his nursery and Gabriel instinctively jumps out of bed to get him.

"You can't smoke while you're holding him!" Maggie scolds.

"Why not?"

"It's not healthy! It's bad for his lungs."

"Says who?"

"He was premature. His lungs are fragile."

Gabriel stubs out the cigarette and leaves the room, returning moments later with James in his arms. "Do you want to come live in Gaspésie, little man?" he asks the baby, kissing his head and cheeks.

A breeze comes in through the open window, rustling the eyelet curtains and blowing Maggie's translation notes off her bedside table and onto the floor like softly falling leaves. She crouches down to pick them up, grateful for something to do. When she's got them all back in order on the table, she allows herself a quick glance at Gabriel.

He caresses his son's fine hair. "Isn't it strange, Maggie, how you miscarried all your husband's babies, but mine is the only one that survived? How can we not believe this is right?"

"I can't move to the Gaspé."

"Everything that ever got in the way is behind us," he tells her. "Your father is gone. You don't need his approval anymore. Let go of his plan for your life already, Maggie."

"That's what you don't understand," she says. "Running the store *is* my plan for my life. It always has been."

Gabriel looks unconvinced.

"It hasn't only been about pleasing him," she states, with more clarity than she's felt in a long time. Her reason for staying now is to fulfill *her* life's purpose, not her father's. "You belong here, too," she says. "You just won't admit it."

"I've already bought the land there, Maggie. I have a good job—"

"Then you can see James whenever you visit."

"So you've made up your mind?" he says, staring at his son.

"Haven't you?"

She turns away, not sure she can withstand another ending. After all this time, neither one of them is prepared to make the sacrifice to be together. Gabriel wants to be with her on his terms, on his turf, which is exactly what *she's* always wanted from *him*. She realizes, as he hands the baby over to her, that she feared it would end this way the moment she opened her door to him. When it's really mattered, neither one of them has ever been able to commit to the other. Maybe love doesn't always prevail over who a person is at the core.

He pulls on his black pants from the funeral, buttons up his white shirt, and stuffs his tie in his pocket without saying a word.

"Gabriel?" she says. "Before you go back to Gaspé, there's something I'd like us to do together."

CHAPTER 42

It's Sunday morning, sunny and cold. Maggie looks out the window at Saint-Nazarius Hospital and knows it's a long shot. All she got from the government in response to her inquiries was the official copy of Elodie's Record of Transfer from October 1957, confirming that she was one of dozens of girls between the ages of seven and twelve transferred to an unnamed institution in Montreal that year. After doing some research, Maggie was able to narrow down the three primary hospitals that bore the brunt of most of those transfers, one of which was Saint-Nazarius.

Maggie and Gabriel went to Mercy Hospital first—an unpleasant experience in which they were rebuked and stonewalled by a team of nuns, and Maggie made to feel like a criminal for having gotten pregnant at fifteen. Afterwards, Maggie understood how Clémentine must have felt in her own hometown.

Saint-Nazarius is set back on a vast campus surrounded by at least a dozen separate pavilions. The main entrance is housed in a stately gray stone building, U-shaped, with endless rows of white dormer windows. The center of the main building resembles a church, with two stone pillars on either side and a prominent cross on the roof.

"Ready?"

She looks over at Gabriel and gives him an unconvincing nod.

They get out of the car and he reaches for her hand. They enter through the front gate and approach the building in silence.

The psychiatric pavilion, with its barred windows, cavernous hallways, and strong stench of bleach, gives Maggie a terrible feeling of dread. She does a full sweep of the floor, which is ominously clean and quiet, and wonders where the children are.

At the front desk, Maggie introduces them as the parents of an orphan who might have been transferred here in '57. "She was born on March 6, 1950."

The nun, thin-lipped and bespectacled, cuts Maggie off. "I can't help you," she says. "All the patients' records are sealed."

"I have her Record of Transfer," Maggie says, retrieving it from her purse and holding it out to the nun. "I know most of the orphans from outlying towns were sent here or to—"

"You gave her up, did you not?"

"Yes, Sister, I did, but I was sixteen at the time," Maggie explains. "I'm in a position to take care of her now."

"The records are sealed, madame. You gave up your rights to them."

"But if she's here," Maggie says, her voice rising, "isn't it the best possible outcome for all of us if we take her home?"

"Can't you check the records," Gabriel intervenes, "and tell us if she's here?"

"We know the exact date she was transferred," Maggie adds, pointing to the Record of Transfer.

"You're wasting your time, madame."

"But we're her parents," Maggie cries, losing control. "Besides, this barbaric experiment is about to come to an end anyway. Dr. Lazure has already declared that the orphans don't belong in mental hospitals."

"It doesn't work that way," the nun interrupts. "We still have laws in Quebec. If the girl was ever here, it's because she's mentally deficient."

Gabriel places his hand on Maggie's forearm to calm her.

"Can't you just confirm if she's here or not? Or if she ever was?" Maggie pleads, softening her tone. "A quick peek at her file?"

"I will not," the nun snips indignantly.

Gabriel is glaring at Maggie, silently admonishing her to keep her cool. She ignores him. "I'll come back with a lawyer if I have to," Maggie threatens as another nun approaches the desk.

She's short and broad-shouldered, with a round face and wide-set brown eyes. "Hello," she says warmly, taking over from her colleague. "My name is Sister Ignatia. Is there something I can help you with? I'm one of the ward supervisors."

Her friendly demeanor immediately puts Maggie at ease. "Yes, Sister," she says, relieved. "Thank you. I'm looking for my daughter, Elodie. She was transferred here in '57—"

An unmistakable flash of recognition crosses Sister Ignatia's eyes. Both Maggie and Gabriel catch it and exchange hopeful looks.

"Elodie de Saint-Sulpice," Sister Ignatia says, and the other nun gives her a sharp look.

"Yes!" Maggie cries, her heart pounding.

"I knew little Elodie."

Maggie's heart stops. "'Knew'?" she manages.

"She was seven when she was transferred here."

"Yes," Gabriel says. "She's not here anymore? Was she adopted?"

"Elodie was very sick when she got here," Sister Ignatia explains. "She died not long after. I'm sorry to be the one to tell you."

Maggie collapses against Gabriel. She feels his hand enclosing hers, hears the nun saying something about Elodie being very weak from birth. All Maggie can think is that she failed her daughter.

"I can make you copies from her file," Sister Ignatia offers.

When Maggie doesn't respond, Gabriel says, "Yes, please. That's very kind."

Sister Ignatia disappears down the hall, her shoes squeaking on the linoleum, her habit sweeping behind her. They wait about twenty minutes in bereaved silence before she returns with a Saint-Nazarius envelope.

Maggie numbly opens it and glances down at some of the scribbled notes. Even through the blur of tears, some of the words leap off the page.

Profound mental retardation. Danger to herself
and others. Paranoid delusions. Violent outbursts and
convulsions. Influenza.

The diagnosis is signed by someone at the Hôpital Mentale Saint-Sulpice. The name is illegible. A scribble.

"She wasn't mentally retarded," Maggie says, looking up.

Sister Ignatia smiles sympathetically, but doesn't say anything. Her look—full of pity and recrimination—says plenty.

"This can't be right," Maggie says. "Is it possible there's been an error? A mix-up?"

"I knew her, madame," Sister Ignatia says softly. "She had many problems. Not only health issues, but grave mental and emotional problems, too. Those notes were written by a doctor."

"Where's the death certificate?" Maggie wants to know. "There's nothing in the file after 1957. Not even a mention of her death."

"If there was a death certificate," Sister Ignatia responds calmly, "the government would have it."

"What do you mean, 'if'?"

"Your daughter was mentally deficient and born out of wedlock," Sister Ignatia says gently, her voice as sweet as syrup. "It's unlikely there's any record of her death, let alone her life, other than what you're holding in your hand."

Outside, Maggie picks up a rock and throws it at the hospital's brick facade. "I don't believe her," she says, turning to Gabriel.

"Maggie—"

"My daughter is not dead. I'm going to write to the government and request her death certificate."

He pulls her close and tries to hold her, but she fights him off. "I'm not just giving up."

"That nun has no reason to lie," Gabriel says softly. "It's time to let go."

"I'm not letting go," Maggie states. "I don't believe that woman. She had a sinister face."

"I get that you need to keep believing—"

"My daughter is alive and I'm going to find her."

CHAPTER 43

Elodie

1961

One afternoon in the final days of winter, when the outside world is gray and colorless through the barred windows, and all the snow has melted, Elodie is called away from her sewing machine in the middle of her shift. She gets up from the Singer and follows one of the nuns down the corridor in silent consternation. *Swoosh. Swoosh.* Never will she forget the portentous sound of the nuns' habits sweeping the floor.

They go up the six flights of stairs to the main lobby of the mental ward, but instead of going through the locked doors that lead to Elodie's ward, the nun stops in front of one of the offices and knocks.

"*Entrez,*" comes a man's voice.

The nun opens the door and gently nudges Elodie into the room. "Elodie de Saint-Sulpice," she says, before disappearing.

"I'm Dr. Lazure," the man says, reaching for a file on the desk. Barely looking up. "Sit, please."

Elodie doesn't move. As she realizes what's happening, her body goes numb.

"I won't bite," he says.

She opens her mouth to speak, but nothing comes. She's frozen. Whatever she says and does in this office will decide her fate. She messed up last time. She said the wrong things, and they thought she was dumb or retarded or difficult. Whatever mistake she made, it ruined her life. She can't let it happen again.

The doctor is watching her. She feels herself trembling. Still, she can't budge.

"There's nothing to be scared of," he says. He seems kind enough, but she knows better than to trust him. Twice she's been fooled by doctors; both times she paid dearly for her poor judgment.

"Sit," he repeats, more firmly.

Finally, her legs move and she does as she's told.

"I'm part of a psychiatric team investigating institutions like Saint-Nazarius," he explains. "We're examining hundreds of children like you—"

"Why?"

"Because we're part of a commission tasked with determining whether or not you and others like you belong in a place like this."

"What's a commission?" Elodie asks, and then regrets it immediately. Terrified he's going to think she doesn't know anything; that she's retarded or ignorant, like Sister Camille said.

"It's a duty or a project assigned to a group of people," he answers neutrally. "I don't work at this hospital, you see. This isn't my office. I'm just visiting. I'm here to ask you some questions."

She nods, taking a nervous breath. She notices the file in front of him and can't help but stare at it. It's her file. She can see the numbers 03–06–50 on the front cover and recognizes them as her date of birth.

"Shall we start?" he asks her.

"Yes, monsieur."

"Remember, I'm here as an ally."

She has no idea what that means—*ally*—but this time she doesn't dare say so.

"How long have you been here, Elodie?"

"Four years," she says.

"And before that?"

"The orphanage."

"And you're now . . . ?"

"Eleven?" she says tentatively, wondering if it's a trick question.

"It's not a test," he says, reading her mind. "Elodie, do you know why you're here at Saint-Nazarius?"

"No, sir."

He scribbles something in her file.

"Because the doctor from the orphanage thought I was retarded?" she ventures. "Or crazy?"

Dr. Lazure continues scribbling in her file.

"On Change of Vocation Day," she explains, "Sister Tata told us we were all mentally retarded, but me and Emmeline and a couple of other girls, we were the only ones sent here to Saint-Nazarius. So we must have done something wrong—"

Dr. Lazure looks up at her, but doesn't say anything.

"I'm not retarded," Elodie says, her voice rising. "I don't belong in here."

"I don't disagree with that."

"I'm an orphan," she tells him. "Not a mental patient. Sister Camille says I'm backwards from being here so long, but that doesn't mean I'm crazy."

"Indeed not."

"So I may not know all the answers to the questions you're going to ask me," she says. "But I'm not crazy."

Dr. Lazure nods, frowning. She can't tell if she's displeased him or said something wrong. *Shut up*, she silently reprimands herself. "I didn't know the answers to the other doctor's questions and that's why they sent me here. But I was only seven—"

"This isn't a test you can fail."

"Isn't it?" she says. "I want to get out of here. *I have to*."

"I understand."

She shakes her head. "No, you don't."

"Tell me," he says.

"They killed my friend," she blurts. "Emmeline de Saint-Sulpice. We came here together. She wasn't the first one they killed either."

Elodie stops and covers her mouth with her hand. She's done it again. Said too much, the kind of reckless babbling that already got her into terrible trouble with Sister Ignatia. What if this doctor tells on her like the last one did?

"That's a very serious accusation," Dr. Lazure says.

"It's true, though," Elodie continues, unable to stop herself. "They gave Emmeline an overdose of Largactil. Another girl was killed for singing. They weren't retarded either. They were just orphans, like me—"

Dr. Lazure is nodding. There's a deep crease between his eyes. Elodie knows she's made another serious mistake. She looks down at the floor, trying to hide her trembling lip and tears.

After a moment, in which the crease in Dr. Lazure's forehead softens, he says, "Can you tell me what this is, dear?"

He holds up a picture of what looks like a box with knobs.

"No, sir," she responds.

"It's a radio," he tells her. "What about this?"

"No, sir."

"It's an accordion. And this?"

"A car," she says, recognizing it at once.

He holds up more pictures of different objects, asking her what each one is. She knows some, but not all.

"This is a refrigerator," he tells her, when she fails to guess.

This is a pineapple, a telephone, a present. A tractor, a heart.

"It's just like last time," she interrupts, her voice breaking. "I've never seen these things, but it doesn't make me crazy!"

"Of course not," he agrees.

"I'm ignorant," she tells him. "That's all."

He smiles sadly and writes something in her file.

"If you're letting us out of here," she says, "do you think you can arrange for me to go back to Saint-Sulpice? In case my mother comes back for me?"

His expression clouds. He looks away, avoiding her.

"That's all for today," he says.

She sits there for a moment, not wanting to leave without something concrete to latch on to, a promise or some shred of hope to get her through the remainder of her days here. "I don't belong here."

He nods in response and gets up from the table.

The days trickle by lethargically, each one gloomier than the one before. Girls from Elodie's ward start disappearing, but she remains. Sister Camille assures her that her day will come, but she's beginning to wonder. The older girls—the ones who are eighteen, nineteen, in their early twenties—are being sent out into the world with a single suitcase and a prayer. They'll have to find work and places to live, a mandate that to Elodie seems insurmountable given their limited skills and knowledge about the world. Elodie is grateful she's only eleven.

"What do you think you're doing?"

Elodie's head snaps up to find Sister Ignatia standing above her.

"I'm just sitting here rocking," Elodie responds, her tone slightly more defiant than usual.

"The toilets and floors in your dormitory bathroom need scrubbing," Sister Ignatia says, her black eyes hard. "Now that Yvette is gone, it's your job."

"I already have a job—"

The back of Sister Ignatia's hand lands squarely against Elodie's temple before she can finish her sentence.

Elodie clutches her head to stop the ringing in her ears. She can feel hot tears burning her eyes. "When I get out of here—"

"You're *not* getting out," Sister Ignatia interrupts.

"I'm an orphan," Elodie says, emboldened. "That's why the doctor interviewed me."

"And where do you think you're going to go?"

"Back to a real orphanage or a foster home, somewhere my mother can find me."

"Your mother's dead," Sister says, her tone almost triumphant.

Elodie feels her pulse start to pound. "No, she's not," she says, her voice a tremor. "You're just saying that."

Sister Ignatia's expression is void of pity. "It's in your file."

"I don't believe you," Elodie manages, her mouth dry.

Sister Ignatia turns suddenly and leaves the room. Elodie rocks back and forth, trying to calm down. Could it be true? Her mother dead?

The girl in the rocking chair beside her—one of the real mental patients—lets out a loud yelp.

"Shut up," Elodie mutters.

The girl yelps again, baring her teeth like an animal.

"I said shut up!" Elodie cries, tears spilling down her cheeks. The retarded girl grunts something and whimpers.

The next thing Elodie knows, Sister Ignatia is back, waving a file in her face. "Here," she says, holding it up. "Just so you know, once and for all."

Sister opens the file. "'Mother deceased,'" she reads aloud, and then she turns it so Elodie can see for herself. Elodie can make out the word "mother," but the other word—"deceased"—is just random letters. She doesn't remember how to read very well.

"She's dead," Sister says. "She died in childbirth—God's punishment for her sins. You have no father. You're a bastard, and you've nowhere else to go. You're too young to go out on your own, and too old for an orphanage or a foster family. *No one* wants a pubescent girl. You've fallen between the cracks, so this is where you'll be staying."

"It's not true," Elodie says, her voice catching.

Sister Ignatia smirks. "It's right here," she says, pointing to the elegant script, permanently recorded in black ink. "'*Mère décédée.*'" *Mother deceased.*

"But you've never said so before!"

"I'm saying so now."

CHAPTER 44

———

Maggie

Maggie steps inside the seed store and turns on the lights. She hasn't felt up to being here since her father died, but tonight she was inspired to come back and reconnect with him. She looks around with a stab of grief. Her father will never set foot in here again, never roam the floor or ring up a sale or engage in another political debate with the French farmers he derided and adored so much. It's Maggie's place now.

She passes the bins of seeds on her way to the attic, stopping to open one of the drawers and let a handful of Indian strawberries slide through her fingers; then she climbs the stairs, thinking how one day James will weigh the seeds on Saturdays, just like she did.

Upstairs, it's unchanged. The scale, the stack of tiny yellow envelopes, the metal scoop. She gazes out into the alley, remembering who she was back then, the pubescent girl with high ambitions and a crush on Daddy's worst nightmare. Even the smell is the same—damp earth, mildew.

She goes back downstairs to her father's office, which is now hers: the place where her father agonized over his bills, tallied his invoices, ordered the seeds; where Maggie caught him with Clémentine. She sits down at the big desk. There are neat piles of file folders laid out for her: *Accounts Payable. Inventory. Overdue Invoices. Orders Pending.*

Tomorrow she will meet with the store manager to review her father's systems and learn the ropes. He's the one who's been in charge while her father was at home dying. He's the one who's kept the business organized and afloat. Maggie will have to be careful not to step on his toes, or anyone else's. Her biggest challenge will be the saleswoman. One of the last things her father said to her was, "If you decide to stay and run the store, do it with humility. Give them all time to adjust to you."

A funny thing to say, coming from him. Humility was never his strong suit, but she understood it would have to be hers if she was going to earn the respect of her employees and her customers. Sitting here now, with the reality of the task laid out before her, she feels nervous and slightly sick. What if she fails? What if the business goes bankrupt in her inexperienced hands?

She reminds herself that her father had enough faith in her to leave his most prized possession in her care. She has a mind for business and she's always loved a challenge, and now she's poised to take it over before the age of thirty. She opens the top drawer of his desk, which smells musty, like wet wood, and there in the otherwise empty drawer is a seed envelope with her name on it, *Maggie*, written in her father's neat, square handwriting. She opens the envelope. Inside, she finds the key to his filing cabinet with a short note. *You always were my wildflower.*

She wastes no time getting back to Dunham. The house is dark and everyone is asleep. She quietly lets herself into her father's sanctuary and opens the filing cabinet.

In the bottom drawer, she discovers a neatly folded white flannel baby blanket. As she unfolds it, she sees the words PROPERTY OF BROME-MISSISQUOI-PERKINS HOSPITAL printed on the fabric. She shakes it out, and a tiny plastic hospital bracelet lands in her lap. There's no name on it, only a date: 03–06–50. She presses the blanket to her nose and smells it. Elodie's blanket.

Her father was more sentimental than she realized.

Beneath the blanket, there's a large manila envelope from Sonny Goldbaum.

She sits cross-legged on the floor and tears open the envelope. There's a birth record from Brome-Missisquoi-Perkins hospital and a number of letters on thin blue stationery.

FROM THE DESK OF SONNY H. GOLDBAUM

Sept 9 1949

Thank you for driving into the city for our appointment, Mr. Hughes. It was a pleasure to meet you. I will start my search immediately for a suitable placement. Please keep me informed as to the progress of your daughter's pregnancy, health, due date, etc. As per our conversation, the adoptive family will be Jewish, but rest assured the families I agree to represent are of the very highest caliber.

Dec 12 1949

Good news, Mr. Hughes, I've found a young couple thrilled to adopt your daughter's baby. They have not been able to conceive and have had a difficult time going through the usual channels. You are helping to make their dreams come true. They've agreed to your fee. I will be in touch with more details. How is the pregnancy progressing?

Feb 4 1950

Mr. Hughes,

Here are the logistics: you will deliver the infant to Sister Jeanne-Edmoure at Mercy Hospital. She will bring the infant to me. You will be paid in advance, as will the doctor and nun at Mercy. No money is to be exchanged between you and any of the parties. You will not see the adop-

tive parents or know their names. It's understood
there is to be no contact.

March 18 1950
   Mr. Hughes,
   I have not succeeded in convincing the couple
to take the baby, due to her poor health. I will
continue my search for a new placement, though
as per our earlier conversation, the jaundice and
low birth weight are both obstacles. I will keep
you informed.

Maggie sifts through the correspondence and finds a yellowed
newspaper clipping from *La Presse*, dated February 1954.

Montreal lawyer Sonny Hyman Goldbaum was taken into custody
yesterday and arraigned on charges of falsifying birth certificates
and giving counsel in an indictable offense, in association with an
international ring dealing in black market babies. Goldbaum, 31,
pleaded not guilty to the charges, but evidence so far reveals that
more than 1,000 French-Canadian babies born in Montreal have
been sold illegally to Jewish families in the United States.

   According to sources, a family wishing to adopt a child in New
York would contact a lawyer there who would then refer them to
Goldbaum. Once the financial details were agreed upon, the ring
would obtain a baby from a home for unwed mothers, with or without the birth mother's consent. The baby would then be delivered to
its destination with a falsified visa and passport. More arrests are
expected in what sources describe as a multimillion-dollar ring of
doctors, lawyers, nurses, and others.

Maggie rifles through the filing cabinet and retrieves the re-
maining items her father left for her. Among them, some business
books—*The Entrepreneur's Bible*, Drucker's *The Practice of Man-*

agement, Napoleon Hill's *Think and Grow Rich*—as well as some gardening books and old catalogues, and an essay Maggie wrote in third grade.

The Person I Admire Most
My father is called the Seed Man in town because he has the largest selection of seeds in the Eastern Townships. His store is called Semences Supérieures/Superior Seeds. The sign is written in French and English . . .

Sniffling and wiping tears, she comes upon the galleys of her first translation, *We Shall Overcome.* When she reaches for one of the gardening books, *Wildflowers of Eastern Canada,* she discovers pressed between its pages the dried rosinweed flowers she gave her father the day she moved to Montreal. She remembers him setting the bouquet down on the front counter at the store and thinking he would forget about them.

She presses Elodie's blanket to her face and pulls her knees to her chest. Sitting amidst the precious tokens and mementos her father saved for her over the years, Maggie realizes just how much he really loved her. He didn't often express it or even seem to approve of her, but her findings today prove otherwise.

Flipping once more through the worn pages of the wildflower book, Maggie comes upon two envelopes tied together with an elastic band, both addressed to Wellington Hughes in swirling, old-fashioned script. She opens one of them, and a small black-and-white photograph slips out onto the floor, of a little girl standing in the middle of someone's backyard. She has a bowl haircut and is wearing a pinafore dress with saddle shoes; she's holding a bedraggled baby doll in one hand and what looks like a drawing in the other. The date on the white border of the photograph is June 17, 1953.

Maggie stares at the picture for a moment, and then pulls out the letter.

Dear M. Hughes,

The child you and your wife have expressed interest in is a bright, friendly girl who has been with us since birth. She is in perfect health, progressing nicely through all the milestones. As you requested, I am enclosing a photograph. If you would like to visit her again, we would be happy to welcome you at your convenience and discuss possible arrangements for her adoption.

Sincerely,
Sister Alberta

Maggie reaches numbly for the other letter, which is dated November 1955.

M. Hughes,

You may not be aware that as the result of a recent government mandate, the former Saint-Sulpice Orphanage is now L'Hôpital Mentale Saint-Sulpice. The child to whom you are referring is no longer here. I am not at liberty to disclose any other information.

Sincerely,
Sister Alberta

It takes Maggie a little while to absorb what she's just found. She returns to the photograph, staring at that little girl in awe. *Her daughter.* All at once the pieces fall into place.

Her father not only found Elodie, but also visited her at the orphanage and pretended to want to adopt her so he could find out . . . what? That she was alive, healthy, "progressing nicely through all the milestones"? Was he merely curious about her, or had he been in search of some solace or reassurance that she was okay to assuage his own guilt?

Once he had seen her for himself and he was satisfied that she was thriving and would likely get adopted, he seems to have abandoned interest in her until 1955, right around the time the orphanages were converted to mental hospitals.

I'm sorry I didn't save her when I could.

He'd tried to get her back, but it was too late. She'd already been declared a mental patient. Sister Alberta lied in the letter; Elodie wasn't transferred until 1957. Were they all liars, those nuns? Destroying the lives of helpless children to make as much money off them as possible and protect the church at the same time?

Maggie clutches the picture of her daughter to her chest and folds herself over it, crying softly.

A knock on the door startles her. She gets up, wipes her nose and eyes, and crosses the kitchen to find Gabriel standing outside. "What are you doing here?" she asks him, unlocking the door and letting him in.

"I went to your house and you weren't there. I figured you'd be here."

The door closes behind him and he follows her back to her father's office.

"You look like you've been crying," he says, touching her cheek. "It's been a hard week for you."

"You could say that."

She looks away so he won't see a fresh outpouring of tears.

"I'm not sure how long it will take me," he says.

"How long what will take you?" she asks him.

"To quit my job, pack up my things, and sell my land."

She looks up at him, confused. "Sell your land?"

He nods.

"But you love your job," she says. "You love the seaside—"

"I can fish here, Maggie. It's just land. I want to be with you, and I want to raise our son. I've thought of nothing else since I got here."

"Really?"

"We belong together. *Here*, in the Townships, just like you said. We always did."

Without a word, she falls into him, sobbing.

"Are these happy tears?" he asks her, brushing her hair from her face.

Maggie pulls away and hands him the photograph.

"What's this?"

"It's a picture of Elodie," she says. "I found it in my father's things. There was a letter, too. Gabriel, she wasn't sick."

He looks confused.

"That nun at Saint-Nazarius lied to us. Look."

She gives him the letter to read for himself.

"Elodie was never sick," she says fiercely, rereading it over his shoulder. "The government has no death certificate. Why would we believe she's dead?"

CHAPTER 45

Elodie

1967

Elodie is lying awake on her cot, looking up at the ceiling she's come to despise. It doesn't matter that Ward A is called the Freedom Ward and living here is a huge improvement over Ward B; she still hates every square inch of this hospital. And although life on Ward A—where she's been since 1964—has afforded her more freedom to come and go within the hospital, more independence and no more physical abuse, Saint-Nazarius remains what it has always been for her: a prison.

Tonight is her last night in this prison. Sister Camille has arranged for her to share an apartment with another Saint-Nazarius girl who's been out on her own for almost a year. The girl, Marie-Claude, currently rents a one-and-a-half-room basement apartment in Pointe Saint-Charles. Elodie remembers her from Saint-Nazarius—a tall, quiet girl whose accommodating, subservient disposition spared her at least some of the torture and punishments suffered by the others. Marie-Claude and Elodie were not exactly friends, but they knew each other from Ward B and coexisted without incident.

Elodie rolls onto her side and closes her eyes. Tomorrow, she will walk out of this place into her future. As surreal as it feels, her dominant emotion tonight is fear. The truth is, she'd almost rather stay here. *Almost.*

She knows what to expect here, what's expected of her. There's a certain simple rhythm to her days, a familiarity and predictability she's not quite ready to leave. Who knows what awaits her out there in the world?

After Sister Camille found her a place to live in the city, the medical superintendent at Saint-Nazarius invited Elodie to his office and tried to convince her to stay. "What can you possibly do in the world?" he asked her.

She shrugged; she had no idea. He offered her a private room—not on the mental ward—and a job with pay at the hospital pharmacy and the freedom to come and go as she pleased.

It was a tempting offer and Elodie promised to think about it, which she did. His question plagued her for days. *What can you possibly do in the world?*

She has no education, no skills, no money, no family or friends. Aside from the orphanage and a couple of outings by bus into a nearby town, she's never left the Saint-Nazarius grounds. She's been institutionalized since the age of five, most of her seventeen years.

At least here she has Sister Camille. Sister Camille has become her best friend, advocate, and confidante. The one who taught her to read again by practicing with the Bible, the one who got her transferred to Ward A. And now the one to set her free.

What if the real world is no better than Saint-Nazarius? Certainly she won't be able to hide her stupidity and lack of experience, and everyone will know she's grown up in a mental hospital.

When the sun finally rises in the west window of her dorm, Elodie rises with it. She removes the small suitcase Sister Camille gave her last night from beneath her cot and lays it on the mattress, taking care not to wake the others. Into it she neatly places her two dresses, nightgowns, undergarments, and socks—all donated over the years—and the Bible Sister Camille gave her. She pads softly to the washroom to change out of her nightgown, brush her teeth and hair, gaze at herself one last time in the chipped mirror above the porcelain sink.

The girl she sees staring back at her fills her with self-loathing. Her short bobbed hair lies flat and colorless against her scalp; her skin is sallow, her eyes lifeless. That's the first thing people will notice— that she looks crazy.

She adds her nightgown and toiletries to the suitcase and closes it. *You should be happy today,* she tells herself. *This is the day you've dreamt of your whole life.*

She pulls the blanket up over her bed and has one last look around the room.

The corridors are quiet. Elodie half hopes one of the nuns will appear so she can look her in the eye and say, *None of you will ever tell me what to do again.* But not one of the sisters shows up to see her off. In some ways, this final display of indifference is almost as upsetting as some of the crueler punishments she endured.

She contemplates dashing over to Ward B to bid Sister Ignatia a triumphant good-bye and then spit in her face, but she wisely concludes that Sister Ignatia would probably have her thrown in a cell and locked up, left to rot. With that in mind, Elodie hurries to the stairwell.

Downstairs in the lobby, she remembers the night she first arrived, how terrified she'd been, how unsuspecting. Throwing open the doors, she steps outside into the cold morning, gasping for breath. She squints against the brightness of the sun reflecting off the snow.

I'm free.

"Elo!"

It's Sister Camille, waving from the car. Elodie buttons her coat to the neck; she's forgotten how cold the winter days can be. She hasn't been on an excursion in a long time, and they were usually in the summer. How will she afford to buy a hat? Mittens?

Her chest tightens just thinking about it. The practical things of life.

She doesn't look behind her as she walks down the steps.

"Elo! Hurry up!" Sister Camille is waving. Her brother is waiting in the driver's seat to take them to Pointe Saint-Charles. "Are you ready?" she asks.

Elodie swallows. She knows this is Sister Camille's day off and she's grateful to her, but she can't find the words to express it. She's seventeen years old and broken. She isn't ready to face the world at all. As the car pulls away, she weeps.

"Cry," Sister Camille tells her, reaching around to take her hand. "Cry all you like."

And she does, loudly and without restraint, as they drive off into the bewildering unknown.

CHAPTER 46

⟨✦⟩

Her new home is in the basement of a flat redbrick row house on Rue de la Congrégation, in an industrial part of the city. "You're going to like it here," Sister Camille says, trying to fill the silence with her usual bubbles of optimism.

"There's a park nearby," Sister Camille's brother adds. "Right there on the corner of Wellington and Liverpool."

"Wellington and Liverpool?" Elodie repeats in broken English.

"It's mostly Irish around here."

"And French, too," Sister Camille adds, glaring at her brother. "Griffintown over on the other side of the canal is all Irish, but don't worry, here in the Pointe there are just as many French."

Elodie stares out the window. The neighborhood beyond her street is a mix of factories, row houses, looming smokestacks.

"There's still work being done for the new Métro," Sister Camille explains. "That's why there's so much debris from the construction."

"The Métro?"

"It's an underground train. They're building it for the world expo this summer."

Sister Camille may as well be speaking a different language. Underground train? World expo? Elodie is staring at her, fighting back tears.

"We can tell you all about that when you're settled," Sister Camille says. "Don't worry, Elo. It will get easier."

Elodie nods, not believing her.

"The city is blossoming," Sister Camille goes on. "It's a wonderful time to live here. Just wait till summer."

Elodie forces a smile. She can see how hard Sister Camille is trying. "I like it," she says, staring at the red row house. The rent is seventy-four dollars a month, including heat, of which Elodie will pay half. "Let's go inside," she says, taking a breath.

"And it's yours," Sister Camille reminds her. "You don't have to answer to anyone. Except God."

Elodie ignores the remark. She doesn't have a sense of humor about God.

Marie-Claude is waiting for her inside. The apartment is clean and sparse. One room with a pullout couch and a dresser for them to share, a tiny bathroom, and a kitchenette with just enough room for a square table and two fold-up chairs.

"It's not much," Marie-Claude apologizes. "But it's better than Saint-Nazarius."

Elodie smiles and sets down her suitcase.

"Here," Sister Camille says, handing her a note.

Elodie opens it. "Dominion Textiles?"

"They're hiring sewers," she explains. "I saw the sign in the window. The factory is in Saint-Henri."

"Isn't that where that FLQ guy got blown up last summer?" Marie-Claude says.

"Blown up?" Elodie repeats, feeling faint.

"He was trying to blow up the Dominion Textile factory, but his bomb detonated."

"Why would he do that?"

"He was FLQ," Marie-Claude says. "They're terrorists who want Quebec to separate from Canada, so they attack English companies like Dominion Textiles."

Elodie looks nervously at Sister Camille.

"They still need sewers," Sister Camille says firmly. "It won't happen again. Not there anyway. It's perfect for you. Saint-Henri is easy to get to from the Pointe."

"How will I get there?" Elodie wants to know.

Sister Camille sighs. "You'll figure it out, Elo. You're not helpless."

"I am, though!" she cries. "That's exactly what I am."

Sister Camille looks her in the eyes. "You don't have to be," she says. "You're free now."

"That's easy for you to say," Elodie mutters.

"You must forgive the other nuns," Sister Camille says sharply. "Some of us had fifty children to look after with no help. The decent among us were forbidden to treat you with kindness or affection. *But we weren't all bad.*"

Elodie looks down at the ground. "I'm sorry," she murmurs. "You've been so good to me, and I have no way to repay you."

"Repay me by forgiving the others."

Elodie holds her tongue. She will never forgive the others—least of all Sister Ignatia—but she won't disappoint Sister Camille by saying so.

"I have to go," Sister Camille says.

"Already?"

Sister Camille pulls Elodie into her arms and hugs her—a short, quick embrace—and then hands her some money. "To tide you over," she says. "I'll be back in one week." And then she leaves the two girls to their new life.

It doesn't take more than a minute before Elodie bursts into tears again. Marie-Claude hands her a tissue. "I was the same way when I first got out," she says, sitting down on the couch. "I couldn't stop crying."

"How am I supposed to find this place?" Elodie cries, holding up the note. "I have no idea where I am, let alone where Saint-Henri is. And what if someone tries to bomb it again? It's crazy, isn't it?"

"I'll come with you," Marie-Claude says. "I'll make sure you find it."

"Thank you."

"You have to get a job right away," she adds. "I can't pay the rent on my own."

Elodie nods, feeling overwhelmed.

"Do you want to unpack? There's a drawer for you."

Elodie opens her suitcase on the floor and removes her few belongings. All of them fit into the bottom drawer with room to spare.

"Are you hungry?" Marie-Claude asks her. "There's some food in the refrigerator which I'll share with you until you have money for your own."

The refrigerator. Elodie looks over at the white metal box in the kitchen and remembers being asked by the doctor at Saint-Nazarius if she knew what it was. She did not.

Marie-Claude jumps up, full of nervous energy, and goes to the kitchen. "I have some leftover pork," she says. "And we can boil some potatoes."

Elodie nods mutely.

"Come and help."

Elodie reluctantly joins her new roommate in the kitchen. She watches dumbfounded as Marie-Claude fills a pot with water, covers it, and places it on the stove. "This is how you turn the stove on," she explains, twisting the dial. "Now we peel the potatoes."

She reaches for one of the mismatched knives in the drawer and begins to expertly carve the dirty brown skin off the potato.

"Why are you doing that?" Elodie asks her.

"Because you don't boil the potato with the skin on."

"Why not?"

"You just don't."

Marie-Claude continues peeling the potatoes. The skin comes off in a perfect coil. "Want to try?"

"No."

"You'll learn all of this stuff," Marie-Claude assures her. "I did."

Elodie nods, tears streaming down her cheeks. "I'm sorry—"

"Don't be. You know what? Never mind this. Let's go out."

"Out?"

"For lunch."

"But there are so many people—"

"Yes, there are people in the world. You can't hide from them."

"I'm too scared."

"Of what?"

Elodie shrugs. "That they'll know."

"Know what?"

"That I've just come out of a mental institution."

"Only you and I know that."

"I feel like it's stamped on my forehead—"

"Well, it's not. How much money did Sister Camille give you?"

Elodie reaches into her pocket and pulls out a few dollar bills.

"We won't use much," Marie-Claude says. "Fifty cents at most. Just enough to celebrate."

The girls bundle up in their coats, and Marie-Claude loans Elodie her scarf to wrap around her head instead of a tuque. They head out into the cold, flinching at the sharp bite of the air against their cheeks. The wind whips around them, and Elodie pulls the scarf up to her eyeballs. *"Tabarnac, y' fait fraite,"* Marie-Claude curses.

Snow crunches underfoot as they come to the Parc Marguerite Bourgeoys. Elodie glances up and notices a group of children running around in their snowsuits, laughing and yelling, playing in the snow. What shocks her most is how free they are. They don't seem the least bit afraid to laugh out loud or raise their voices or enjoy themselves.

They turn onto Wellington and the sound of the children's laughter lingers, following Elodie down the street.

"Here," Marie-Claude says, coming to a stop in front of a place that says PAUL PATATES FRITES in the window. "My favorite greasy spoon."

Inside it's warm and smells like fried oil, the way it did in the cafeteria at Saint-Nazarius when they served fried perch for special occasions. They stomp their boots to shake off the snow and sit down side by side at the counter on red leather stools that spin. At first Elodie worries she might fall off, but soon she's spinning around like a child on a merry-go-round.

Marie-Claude orders two *steamés* and two Pepsis. Not more than five minutes later, the waitress delivers a plate that smells like heaven.

"What is this?" she asks Marie-Claude, leaning over it and inhaling the pleasing smell of grease.

"That's a hot dog and french fries," Marie-Claude says.

Elodie reaches for a french fry and shoves it in her mouth, not caring that it burns her tongue. She closes her eyes and savors the taste and texture of it—crispy on the outside, mushy inside, perfectly greasy—and then grabs another handful.

"Try this," Marie-Claude says, pouring a glob of red goop from a glass bottle that says HEINZ. "Dunk the French fry in the ketchup. That's it."

"*Mon Dieu,*" Elodie gasps, reaching greedily for the hot dog. "It's delicious."

"Put ketchup on that, too," Marie-Claude instructs.

"*Mon Dieu!*" Elodie exclaims again, biting into the pink sausage wrapped in a blanket of warm, squishy bread. "Why couldn't they feed us like this at Saint-Nazarius?"

"This is *real* food," Marie-Claude says, her mouth full. "You have ketchup all over your face."

"I don't care."

The waitress sets down two glasses of a dark liquid. Elodie puts the straw to her lips and takes a sip to wash down the hot dog. "*Oh, mon Dieu,*" she repeats, her lips tingling and her tongue fizzing. "It's so sweet!"

"Pepsi," Marie-Claude says. "Beautiful, isn't it?"

Elodie laughs, delighted. "Yes," she says, taking another long slurp. "Beautiful."

CHAPTER 47

※

Maggie

Maggie sits down on her porch swing with a cup of coffee and her stationery, barefoot and still in her nightgown. The sun is already up, and the air has the lovely, dewy smell of summer mornings. Gabriel and James are asleep, a rare moment that's nothing short of sacred. If not for the chorus of the magnolia warblers in her yard, it would feel like she had the planet to herself.

She pulls out a fresh sheet of paper and her good pen. There's a new premier in office, which means it's a new opportunity to make her case. She starts to write.

> *Dear M. Bourassa,*
> *I'm writing on behalf of my daughter, Elodie de Saint-Sulpice, an orphan born—*

"Good morning, my love."

Maggie looks up, and Gabriel is standing in the doorway, hair disheveled, naked but for his briefs. He lights a smoke and comes out onto the porch. "It's warm," he says, joining her on the wooden swing he built.

Maggie sets her letter aside, and they rock quietly for a while.

Gabriel reaches for her mug and takes a sip of her coffee. "You're writing Bourassa, aren't you?"

"Yes."

He nods and she detects a note of pity in his eyes. "Poor bastard," he teases. "He has no idea how often he's going to hear from you. He probably wouldn't have run for premier if he'd known."

"I know you think she's dead," Maggie says, reiterating the same conversation they have every time she sends one of her letters to the government.

"It doesn't matter what I think," he says.

"It does to me."

"I know you need to believe she's alive, Maggie."

"And you?"

"I just don't think the government is going to help you get her back," he says pragmatically. "*They're* the ones who put her where she is."

"Bourassa is new," she says. "It's a fresh start. He hasn't heard our story. Maybe if we go to Quebec City in person."

"And do what? Knock on the door and ask to speak with him? We couldn't even get past the goddamn nuns!"

Maggie looks away. "She's twenty this year," she reminds him.

"She would have been."

"You read the letter from Sister Alberta to my father," Maggie says sharply, not for the first time. "She was perfectly healthy. Profound mental retardation? We both know that's not true, and we have proof."

"But it doesn't mean she didn't die, Maggie. Who knows how her health might have deteriorated by the time she got to Saint-Nazarius? Are you going to keep sending letters to the government for the rest of your life?"

"I don't know what else to do."

"Let's have another baby," he says.

Maggie looks at him like he's gone mad.

"I'm serious."

"Why? So I'll forget about Elodie?"

"No," he says. "So James has a little brother or sister."

"He's nine."

"So?"

"I'm too old for another kid."

"You're thirty-six."

"It won't fill the void," she tells him. "James didn't. You didn't. Nothing can, except her."

"And you may have to live with that for the rest of your life," he says. "We all have our crosses."

CHAPTER 48

Elodie

1970

Elodie drops four plastic menus on the table and smiles without making eye contact. "Something to drink?" she asks, pulling an order pad from the pocket of her white apron.

The boys in the booth stare up at her with blank expressions. One of them says, "English?" and points to his baseball cap. "We're from Boston."

"Drinks?" Elodie repeats in English, still not looking up from her pad. "Four Cokes."

She nods and rushes off to get the Cokes. She's been working downtown at Len's Delicatessen for more than a year. She applied on a whim—walking along St. Catherine Street the previous summer, she noticed a sign in the window and went in. She liked it immediately because it reminded her of the diner she went to with Marie-Claude, the first time she ever tried a Pepsi and french fries. Looking up at the towering glass counter crammed with slabs of smoked meat at Len's, she knew it was the right place. Behind the counter, a man wearing a white doctor's coat—so she thought at the time—was singing as he sliced meat with a machine that purred like a car. In a refrigerator at the front of the deli, there must have been a dozen enormous cakes all decorated with white icing and chocolate shavings and topped with shiny red cherries. An older woman in a beige waitress uniform kept tossing sandwiches on top of the counter, where they sat for a few minutes under the buzzing heat lamps before getting swept away by the other waitress. Those dumbfounding sandwiches, with their thick walls of shaved pink smoked meat, were so big they looked like yawning mouths.

Every booth at Len's Deli was full that day, the din of cutlery and conversation just loud enough to drown out the doctor's singing. The smell of smoked meat and french fries made Elodie deliciously woozy. She had to wait a while for the lunch crowd to disperse before anyone could speak to her, but when things quieted down in the late afternoon, the doctor (who turned out to be the owner and not a doctor after all) sat her down in a booth and interviewed her.

Although she could barely look him in the eyes or speak a word of English, he must have taken pity on her because he hired her on the spot. "You're adorable," he said. "We don't get many French girls applying."

She quit Dominion Textiles the next day, which was an enormous relief. She hated sewing, hated factory life even more. It reminded her too much of Saint-Nazarius. She'll be happy if she never has to hear the whir of a sewing machine again. Besides, she was constantly looking at the windows, worrying that a Molotov cocktail was going to come smashing through the glass. It's 1970 and a lot is happening in the province—the War Measures Act, political kidnappings—but Elodie feels much safer at the deli.

She's managed over the past few years to adjust to the outside world as best she can. She finds ways to be inconspicuous among people, to fade into the background without being noticed, to draw very little attention to herself. She likes being downtown, where the moving throng of people can swallow her whole. She's good at disappearing in plain sight, blending in, becoming invisible. Relationships are more challenging—intimacy, looking people in the eyes, one-on-

one conversations. She prefers the obscurity of strangers. She has little confidence in her intellect and is perpetually afraid of calling attention to her ignorance and lack of education. At least at Saint-Nazarius, she didn't stand out. She was just one of many unfortunate girls, no worse off than any of them.

Out here in the world, though, the real or imagined scrutiny of others plagues her. Apart from when she's home with Marie-Claude, Len's Deli is the only place Elodie enjoys a reprieve from her crippling insecurities. She owes that to her boss, Lenny Cohen, whose warm and gregarious personality set her at ease from day one. Lenny is a large, hulking man, with a booming voice and an even louder laugh. He wears a white butcher's coat for cutting the meat, sings Johnny Cash songs all day. He eats the leftover smoked meat and french fries from the customers' plates without even a hint of shame and encourages his employees to do the same. "I pay for this stuff," he always says. "Why should it go to waste?"

The other two waitresses are Len's cousins, elderly women who mother Elodie and teach her English, the way Sister Camille once taught her how to read from the Bible. They not only accept Elodie; they seem to like having her around. They don't ask questions about her limp or her scars; they know she's an orphan and have likely deduced the rest. She, in turn, is like a little French refugee they've taken in to nurture and mend.

Elodie sets down four glasses of Coke at the booth by the window, and retrieves her pen and pad. "You know what you order?" she says, in her terrible broken English.

"Four smoked meat sandwiches," the one with the cap says.

She glances up long enough to notice his blue eyes, his freckled pink cheeks, his bright white teeth. They all smell of beer, which is not unusual. Len's is open until midnight to accommodate the partiers who stumble in drunk and craving smoked meat. Elodie likes the nighttime crowd—a sprinkling of college kids, hippies, bums, and tourists. The stranger and more marginalized they are, the more comfortable she is.

"I'm not sure I can serve you in that cap," she deadpans, surprising herself with the uncharacteristic quip. She's learned enough living in Montreal to know of the long-standing hockey rivalry between the Montreal Canadiens and the Boston Bruins.

The boy grins and obligingly removes his Bruins cap. His hair is pale orange, buzzed close to the scalp. These days, almost everyone has long hair—including Elodie. She parts hers in the middle and lets it fall over the sides of her face.

"Better?" he says, tossing his cap on the table.

She turns and hurries away, flushing. She can hear them laughing behind her. *Feisty French gal.* She shouldn't have said anything.

When she returns a few minutes later with their food, the boy with the cap asks her name.

"Elodie," she says, sliding his plate at him.

"Elodie," he repeats, closing his eyes. "Like Melody without the *M.*"

When she responds with a blank stare, one of his friends says, "She doesn't understand English, Den."

"What time do you finish work?" Dennis asks, gazing up at her with an undeterred expression.

"Midnight," she says, her face growing hot.

Dennis checks his watch, a shiny Timex on his thick, freckled wrist. "That's in half an hour," he says. "Can I wait for you?"

"*Bien, non,*" she says, dismissing the offer. Not because she wants to, but because it's the proper thing to do.

Other customers are arriving to get their smoked meat fixes before Len's closes, and Elodie rushes over to grab a handful of menus by the cash register. No sooner has she deposited them at the other booths then Dennis and his friends beckon her back.

"Dennis has a crush on you," one of the friends confides.

"Crush me?"

"He *likes* you."

"He don't know me—"

"But he wants to. He has a thing for French girls."

"Let me walk you home," Dennis chimes in on his own behalf.

"I live in Pointe Saint-Charles," she says, as though he should know where that is. "It's too far."

"We'll take a taxi. Or the streetcar."

"*Non*," she says, confused by the attention, knowing she can't let him walk her home. He's too fresh and clean-cut, out of her league.

"Let him walk you home," one of his friends says. "He's going to Vietnam next week."

Elodie has heard about Vietnam. Marie-Claude always has the radio on, and you can't walk past a newspaper without seeing it in the headline. This lovely orange-haired boy with the clearest eyes she's ever seen is going to war.

"I'm sorry," she says. "But—"

"Don't be sorry. Just let me take you home."

Elodie hesitates. The other boys are pleading with her, hands clasped in mock prayer. She can't quite believe this boy likes her enough to go to this much trouble for a walk home.

"You really go to Vietnam?" she asks.

"I really go."

Even before she acquiesces, he smiles triumphantly. She wonders, with a swell of sadness, what war will do to someone like him.

Dennis waits for her by himself in the booth until the lights go off in the delicatessen. They walk out together, ignoring the raised eyebrows and good-natured winks of Lenny and Rhonda.

"Where did your friends went?" she asks him, as they step out onto St. Catherine Street, which is still brightly lit and crawling with revelers.

"They went back to Cleopatra," he admits sheepishly. "Do you know what that is?"

Elodie nods. Café Cléopâtre is a strip club in the red-light district. She knows about it because her neighbor on Sébastopol is a go-go dancer there.

"It was my first time," Dennis adds. "I was so uncomfortable, that's why we left. It's not my thing. I wanted to try smoked meat instead."

"But your friends?"

"They liked the strippers," he laughs.

"Why you came to Montreal?" she wants to know. What she means is, *Why is Montreal your last destination before going to war?* But she doesn't speak enough English to formulate the sentence; she understands considerably more than she can actually communicate.

"Montreal is so European," he says. "Your bars are open later, your women are more beautiful, and I'm legal drinking age here," he explains. "Also for the strip clubs and smoked meat."

"You said you don't like strip clubs—"

"I didn't know that till tonight."

Elodie smiles and he reaches for her hand. Her body tenses at his touch.

"Don't worry," he says. "I'm just being gentlemanly."

She lets him hold her hand and they walk like that to Ontario Street.

"You have a limp," he remarks.

"I was born with it," she says, coming to a stop.

"I thought it might have been polio."

"This is where I take my streetcar," she says. "You can ride with me, but then you turn back."

"Scouts' honor," he says, holding up a hand.

"Who?"

"Boy Scouts. It's an expression."

She shrugs and they both laugh.

Dennis talks easily as they sit side by side on the empty streetcar. Elodie strains to understand him, listening attentively, content to let him have the spotlight while she sneaks sidelong glances at his lovely profile. He has a straight nose and round, peach-fuzz cheeks. She wonders if he shaves. He doesn't seem grown-up enough to be a soldier.

The more he talks, the more she likes him. He admits to being a lover of sports but not a great athlete. He has two younger sisters, both still in high school. His father is a plumber. His mother wanted him to go to college, but school wasn't his thing. He says that a lot. *His thing.* Strip clubs and school are not his "thing." French girls are.

Instead, he spent the last year apprenticing with his father. And then he was drafted.

"I'm trying to stay positive about it," he says, his eyes clouding over. "I didn't even mind basic training that much. I spent eight weeks at Fort Lewis, and then another eight weeks at Fort Polk doing my AIT. I'm in the best shape of my life, although I've put some weight back on in the past couple of weeks of my leave."

Elodie nods, pretending to understand everything he's saying.

"Eight weeks of basic and another eight of Advanced Individual Training, and I'm evidently ready for war. I leave for Da Nang next week."

"You must be scared."

Dennis shrugs, looking out the window. "I'd be an idiot not to be," he mutters. "But, hey, I get to defend democracy." In spite of the language barrier, Elodie is still able to detect the sarcasm and bravado in his voice.

They get off on Wellington and cross through Parc de la Congrégation. It's a gorgeous autumn night, with a touch of humidity in the air. The ground is covered ankle-deep in damp red and yellow leaves. Elodie doesn't take any of it for granted. Fresh air, a starry sky, a maze of majestic trees, a cool breeze, the heat, snow on her face, the splash of a rain puddle, the sun on her back, the buzz of mosquitoes in her ear, the perfume of a flower—all are gifts, she knows that.

"What are you thinking?" Dennis asks her.

She smiles to herself. There are no words to communicate the bittersweetness of a night such as this, certainly not in a language she has not yet mastered. Without answering Dennis, she bends down, scoops up a pile of leaves, and throws them up into the air above her head. As the leaves rain down on her, she wonders if these rare happy moments will always be lined with sadness, never one without the other.

Dennis retaliates with a pile of leaves of his own, laughing as they cling to Elodie's uniform and come to rest in her long hair. "You look like one of those flower children," he says, brushing a leaf from her shoulder.

She throws another batch of leaves at him before she takes off through the park, loving the feeling of her feet on the pavement as she runs, the breathlessness in her chest. This is freedom, she thinks, as Dennis catches up to her and pulls her to him. Before she can stop him or panic or think too much about it, he kisses her.

Her first kiss. As his lips press softly against hers, she's overcome with emotion. Tears spring to her eyes. He tastes like beer and smoked meat and mustard, and it's wonderful.

"You're not really going to send me back to my hotel, are you?" he says, touching her cheek.

She averts her eyes.

"Well? Can I come in?"

Marie-Claude is visiting her boyfriend's family in Valleyfield for the long weekend, so she has the apartment to herself until Monday night. And it's not like she's a virgin; she hasn't been for years, thanks to one of the orderlies at Saint-Nazarius.

"Next week at this time, I'll be in a jungle," he reminds her.

"Is that really true?" she asks. She's still not sure if she can trust him. She's not sure if she can trust anyone.

"I wouldn't lie about going to war," he says, sounding slightly offended.

The pros and cons of letting him in are churning in her mind as he waits for her to make up her mind. Cons: She's terrified.

Pros: He's leaving for Vietnam, so he won't abandon her when he realizes how much better he is than she, or how much better he could do for himself. She'll never see him again, so she really doesn't have to worry about what he thinks of her. Emboldened by the fact of his looming deployment, she's free to be anyone she wants tonight, and even if he does uncover the worst about her—her ignorance and darkness—he could be dead soon anyway. Tonight, she can pretend to be a normal girl with a normal boy before he goes off to war.

The nuns are closing in on her. She can hear their snickers, smell the soap and cigarettes on their rough hands, but she can't see them with the pillowcase over her head.

"*Don't!*" she screams as one of them grabs her by the wrists and another by the ankles. They throw her onto a chair and bind her to it with leather straps. There are at least six of them, their habits swooshing like crows flapping their wings.

"Please, *no!*" she wails.

Someone rips off the pillowcase, and Sister Ignatia appears, glowing white, terrifying. There's a small knife in her hand. "I'm going to cut your brain out now," she says calmly.

Elodie wakes up, gasping for breath. She turns, startled to see Dennis's face beside hers on the pillow. "I forgot you were here," she manages, her voice thick.

"Are you okay? You're soaking wet—"

"Did they give me the lobotomy?" she asks him, disoriented.

"Huh? What are you talking about?"

He's been at her place for three days. They've talked for hours, deep into the night and well into the early mornings, sharing things new lovers share. They've discussed their hopes for the future—his to be a plumber like his father, get married and have kids; hers to find a living relative, her father perhaps or an aunt. And although they've traded some scars from the past, she hasn't said a word about Saint-Nazarius. All she's told him is that her parents are dead and she grew up in an orphanage in the Townships. He hasn't probed about why every little noise—a car horn, a bus, the heater, a mouse—makes her jump; why she has so many scars; why she has nightmares and wakes up in a cold sweat. She assumes he's drawn his own conclusions about the hardships of life in an orphanage. He doesn't need to know that her orphanage was really a mental hospital.

"You sounded like a crazy person in your nightmare," he says.

"I'm not crazy," she snaps, turning her face away from him.

"Hey," he says, laying a hand on her shoulder. "I didn't mean anything by it. I was joking."

He pulls her back, and she rests her head on his shoulder. He strokes her hair. She looks up at him, knowing these are their last hours together. They haven't talked about seeing each other again. There's an unspoken understanding that this is simply a moment in time, a lost weekend. If he survives the war, he'll have a fond memory of the French girl who devirginized him. As for Elodie, she'll always remember the first person—man or woman—to show her physical affection and tenderness.

"You have the saddest eyes," he says. "And you're not even twenty-one."

She quickly looks away and turns on the TV. "*Tabarnac*," she says, sitting up. "They killed him."

"Who?"

"The politician," she says. "He was kidnapped by the FLQ. They just find his body in the trunk of a car."

"The FL-who?"

"FLQ. They want Quebec to separate from Canada, so they blow up building and kills people," she explains, struggling with her English grammar. "They throw a bomb into the place where I used to work."

"Were you there?"

"No."

"How does that help their cause?"

"I don't know. I just know they 'ate the English."

"They ate the English?" he teases.

"*Hate*," she clarifies, emphasizing the *H*.

"Do *you*? Hate the English?"

"*Bien non.*"

"But you're French," he says, plainly confused.

"We don't all 'ate the English," she says.

The truth is everyone who ever harmed her was French. Maybe that's why she doesn't feel any real connection to her own people, why she's more comfortable with the likes of Len Cohen and Dennis from Boston.

She turns up the volume to hear the news anchor from *Le Télé-journal*.

"He's not even English," Dennis points out. "The dead politician has a French name, which means they just killed one of their own."

"But he's Libéral," Elodie explains. "They're also the enemy."

"You're pretty smart for a—"

"For a what?" she cuts him off, bracing for the dagger. *For a retard. For a lunatic.*

"For a Canadian," he says innocently. And she laughs, relieved.

"I like when you smile," he tells her. "It makes your eyes less sad."

CHAPTER 49

Maggie

Maggie throws open the front door and steps inside the mudroom. "Hello?" she calls out, going into the kitchen. "Ma?"

The house is quiet. She grabs a handful of saltines from the pantry—she knows her mother always has the familiar red box on hand—and stuffs one in her mouth to quell the nausea. As with the last pregnancy, saltines bring instant relief.

"Ma?"

She finds her mother on the couch in the den, staring vacantly into space.

"Ma?"

"Yvon is dead," her mother says, shell-shocked.

Maggie's heart skips. *Good*, she thinks, feeling nothing at all. "How?"

"He hung himself."

In spite of the shock, Maggie experiences a jolt of triumph. "Why?" she asks her mother, sitting down on her father's worn ottoman. "Did he leave a note?"

"No. A girl came forward saying he'd raped her."

Maggie wants to scream, *I told you so!* But she holds her tongue. She wonders how many others there were.

"The girl's father was one of their farmhands," Maman says. "She was twelve. Her father beat Yvon nearly to death and threatened to go to the police. Yvon would have gone to jail."

"How did you hear?"

"Deda's neighbor called me," she says, sobbing into her handkerchief. "Thank God Deda isn't alive to see all this."

Deda had a heart attack last year, died in her sleep. Maggie didn't go to the funeral.

"Other girls came forward, too," Maman says. "From all over Frelighsburg."

Her shoulders collapse and she starts to wail loudly, expressing more anguish than when her own husband died. Maggie's back stiffens and she stands up. "You're obviously very upset that he's dead," she says coldly. "I'll leave you."

Maman stops crying at once and looks up at Maggie. "It's not him I'm upset about!" she cries. "It's *you*. You tried to tell me . . ." She breaks down again. Maggie has never seen her mother like this.

"It's all right," Maggie says awkwardly. "It was a long time ago."

"I didn't believe you," Maman sobs. "You tried to tell me and I cared more about protecting Deda than I did you."

Maggie looks away, remembering the pain of that same realization all those years ago.

"Can you forgive me?" There is a vulnerability in her mother's eyes that is hard to reconcile with the woman she has known all her life.

Maggie can't bring herself to say yes. While she feels vindicated, it's not enough. Not yet.

Maman jumps to her feet and pulls Maggie into a too-tight embrace. "I'm so sorry, *cocotte*," she murmurs, her breath warm against Maggie's hair.

Maggie's body remains stiff in her mother's arms. How strange it feels to be held like this, she thinks, as Maman's thick arms squeeze her with surprising vigor. More than three decades' worth of love poured into one well-intentioned but belated gesture.

"Don't crush the baby," Maggie tells her.

CHAPTER 50

Elodie

1971

Elodie pulls up her skirt in the bathroom, and it occurs to her as she's wiping that she hasn't seen blood in a long time. She tries to remember the last time she had her period—a challenge, since her memory is terrible—and realizes she hasn't had one since the fall, possibly even as long ago as September. She had terrible cramps, she remembers, and had to go and buy more pads late at night and it was still warm outside. It's January now.

She looks down at her protruding stomach, and it's suddenly so obvious she actually gasps out loud. She chalked up the weight gain to too many french fries and smoked meat sandwiches at Len's, even mentioned to Marie-Claude that she should cut back because she was getting a *bédaine*.

She rushes out of the bathroom and returns to the kitchen, where Marie-Claude is washing dishes. "I think I'm pregnant," she blurts.

"Heh?"

"I haven't had a period since the fall."

"Who the hell is the father?"

"Someone I met at the deli," she admits. "He was going to Vietnam the following week. I don't even know his last name."

Marie-Claude's cheeks turn red.

"It was just . . . a weekend," Elodie murmurs.

"*Here?* You did it here? In our apartment?"

Elodie looks down at the floor, ashamed.

"Are you sure you're pregnant?" Marie-Claude says, her voice crisp with self-righteousness. "You haven't been throwing up in the mornings—"

"I don't know."

"Do you know *anything?*"

"I've been a bit tired and queasy," Elodie admits.

"*Oh, mon Dieu.* You obviously can't keep it."

"What do you mean?"

"You can't have a baby by yourself."

"You think I should give it away?" Elodie cries. "Are you serious?"

Marie-Claude sighs. The water is still running, and her rubber gloves are dripping suds on the linoleum.

"You of all people should know I could never give up my baby," Elodie says.

"But how can you be a mother, Elo? You *can't.*"

"I'm tired of people telling me what I can or can't do. I've had enough of that."

"You don't know how to do anything. How can you take care of a kid?"

"At least it'll have a mother."

Marie-Claude turns around and resumes washing dishes in silence. Elodie stands there for a few minutes, reeling. She didn't think Marie-Claude would react this way. Didn't think much at all.

"You can't stay here," Marie-Claude says at length, her voice barely audible above the water.

Elodie is frozen, speechless.

"I can't help you raise a child," she says. "I just can't."

"I didn't ask you to."

"You have to find your own place."

Elodie's mind is racing. She still has the suitcase from Saint-Nazarius and everything she owns still fits inside. But where will she go?

"When do you want me out?" she asks coldly.

Marie-Claude doesn't answer, just slumps against the sink and turns off the water. She's quiet for a long time. Elodie leaves the kitchen, retreating to the pullout couch in a daze. She lies there for a long time with her hand on the gentle slope of her belly. *A baby*. It's surreal. She closes her eyes, not wanting to contemplate tomorrow, let alone the next few months.

"I'm not trying to be cruel," Marie-Claude says, suddenly appearing beside the couch. "I just can't do this with you."

"I understand."

"You can stay for a while," she concedes. "But you have to go after it's born."

"Thank you."

"I'm sorry, Elo."

"This is my fault," Elodie says, sitting up. "I don't expect you to help me raise my kid."

"Jean-Marc and I will probably be getting married anyway—"

"You don't have to explain."

Marie-Claude nods, looking away, unable to meet Elodie's gaze. "How could you let this happen, Elo? You should have known better than to repeat history."

Elodie knows she's right, but she'd felt so happy that weekend. She'd let herself get thoroughly caught up in the charade of being normal.

"You sure you don't remember his last name?" Marie-Claude asks her. "Maybe he could help you."

"I never knew his last name. He's probably dead by now anyway."

"Oh, Elo," Marie-Claude says, shaking her head. "How could you let this happen?"

The months of her pregnancy fly swiftly by—*too* swiftly. Her approaching due date feels more like doomsday. She's still waitressing—day shifts only—but her swollen ankles are making it a living hell, as are the summer heat and her flaming heartburn. Len and the waitresses have been mercifully nonjudgmental. One night, when she was beginning to show, Rhonda came up to her and said, "The redhead from Boston?"

Elodie nodded.

"Is he going to marry you?"

"He's in Vietnam."

Not another word was said about it. Elodie let them assume there's an ongoing, long-distance courtship and that he might be coming home to marry her at the end of his tour.

On a particularly sweltering afternoon in her final trimester, Elodie lets herself inside the apartment after work and shuffles down the hall, stopping in the kitchen to get something cold to drink. Marie-Claude is sitting at the table, smoking a cigarette and fanning herself with an *Allo Police* magazine.

"How're you feeling?" she asks Elodie. "You look a little pale."

"I'm tired."

"You're going to have to stop working soon."

"I can't," Elodie says, grabbing a Pepsi from the fridge and lowering herself into a chair. "Not till the baby comes."

"That's in less than a month."

"I need the pay."

She's already made arrangements to move into Mme. Drouin's basement apartment next door at the end of the month. Mme. Drouin has agreed to mind the baby while Elodie is at work, charging her a reasonable monthly payment that she's rolling into the rent. With tips and welfare, Elodie figures she should be able to manage.

"I know you think I'm making a huge mistake," Elodie says, tearing open a May West and biting hungrily into the cream-filled cake. "Raising the baby by myself."

"I don't actually," Marie-Claude says, surprising her. "I'm an orphan, too, remember? I know what it's like to grow up without parents. I know you could never give it away."

Elodie washes the cake down with a swig of Pepsi.

"I do think you made a mistake getting pregnant in the first place," Marie-Claude adds sharply. "Especially with a stranger."

"I'm scared I won't know what to do," Elodie confides.

Marie-Claude reaches across the table and taps her hand. "You won't," she says. "But you'll figure it out. You're smart."

Marie-Claude has been kind to her over the years. After Sister Camille was transferred to a hospital in Repentigny, Marie-Claude became her one and only confidante, letting Elodie stay here through her pregnancy and forgiving her for her mistake. She may not be the easiest person, but she has a spirit of compassion.

"I'm going to have a nap," Elodie says, taking the Pepsi over to the pullout couch.

She lies down on her back with a pillow under her legs and closes her eyes. The bed has never felt so comfortable. The baby presses a foot or elbow against her. Strange little creature, she thinks as it continues to kick and tumble inside her. It's always most energetic when Elodie settles down to sleep. She finds it strangely lulling, all that motion and activity.

The next thing she knows, Marie-Claude is shaking her awake. "Elodie!" she cries. "The bed is drenched!"

Elodie opens an eye.

"Feel the mattress."

Elodie touches the bed and it's saturated. She sits up, confused. "What's happening?"

"Didn't they tell you at the clinic that your water would break right before you went into labor?"

"Yes, but—"

"That must be what this is," she says. "You have to get to the hospital."

"I'm not ready!"

"I'm calling a taxi."

Elodie starts to cry. *"Mon Dieu!* What have I done?"

"Now is not a good time for that."

"I don't know how to be a parent! I'll never know what to do!"

Marie-Claude ignores her, dials the phone, and requests a taxi.

"Will you come with me?" Elodie cries, panic rising.

"Of course," Marie-Claude says. "I just have to be at work by seven.

It better be out by then." Marie-Claude still works in the secretary pool at the Grand Trunk Railway.

"I'm scared," Elodie whispers.

"You should be."

Thirteen hours later, Elodie finds herself alone in a hospital bed, wondering how she's going to be a mother to the baby girl she's just delivered. When the nurse placed the baby on her chest, Elodie felt nothing. Not joy or relief, nor any significant kind of connection. Certainly not love. She felt what she always feels. *Empty.*

She wasn't able to relax until the nurse scooped up the baby and whisked her away to the nursery. "You can visit her later," the nurse said, smiling as she left.

"When can I leave?" Elodie called after her.

The nurse gave Elodie a strange look and said, "In two days."

Two days in the hospital. She'd rather be on the street than trapped in here. She hasn't been inside a hospital since the day she left Saint-Nazarius; everything about it makes her squeamish. The smell, the fluorescent lights, the horrible cafeteria food.

Now what?

Sister Ignatia's words come back to her. *Imbecile. Retard.* How is someone like her supposed to care for another human being?

She wipes tears from her face with a corner of her bedsheet. For a split second, she contemplates running. How easy it would be to escape! But then she imagines her daughter and reconsiders. Surely that would be worse than a life with Elodie.

All this is pounding in her skull when the nurse returns to clear away her tray—the food beneath the cloche untouched. "You have to eat, Mam'selle de Saint-Sulpice," she says. "You're going to need your energy."

"It's inedible," Elodie mutters.

"Have you picked a name yet?" the nurse asks, her voice upbeat and perky. "She's a little angel."

"No."

"Is your family coming to see her?"

Elodie turns away, not answering.

"I'll let you rest," the nurse says, her chipper tone never waning.

Marie-Claude shows up after her shift, holding a handful of pink carnations. "How is she?"

It takes Elodie a moment to figure out Marie-Claude is talking about the baby. "I don't know," she says. "I haven't been to see her yet."

Marie-Claude lays the flowers on the table and sits down on the edge of the bed. "You have to get on with things," she says. "You can't stay in the past."

"I have no feelings for her," Elodie confesses. "What kind of mother am I?"

"You have to get to know her, that's all."

"I can't do this."

"Stop feeling sorry for yourself," Marie-Claude snaps. "You have a baby now and she needs you. Did you give her a name yet?"

Elodie shakes her head no.

"Well, you better think of something."

Elodie turns away, ashamed.

"She's better off with you than in an orphanage," Marie-Claude says sharply. "You can't possibly do *more* damage than the nuns."

"How do you know?"

"A shitty mother is still better than no mother at all."

"Do you remember the way Sister Ignatia used to line us up and give us the strap, always for another girl's mistake?"

"Of course."

"One time she strapped a bunch of us because Sylvie saw a mouse and screamed. When it was over, she said, 'This is to teach you all how to behave.'"

"What's that got to do with now?" Marie-Claude says impatiently.

"That's all I know about raising a child."

"Is that what you want for your daughter then? For her to grow up like that, without a mother?"

"What about a good family?" Elodie says, perking up. "I could give her to a family. People *I* pick. Rich and kind."

"Get up," Marie-Claude says.

"Heh?"

"Get out of the bed and come with me."

"Where?"

"To see your daughter."

Elodie does as she's told, slowly sliding her legs around and easing herself off the bed. She shuffles down the hall alongside Marie-Claude, her chest filling with dread as they approach the nursery.

"Think how much times have changed," Marie-Claude says, linking her arm in Elodie's. "Our mothers weren't allowed to keep us and raise us on their own. They *had* to give us up. At least you have a choice now. It's okay for a woman to have a child without being married."

They stop in front of the nursery window and press their noses to the glass. Elodie scans all the cribs until her eyes light on the name *de Saint-Sulpice*, which seems officially to have become her last name. Seeing it written there on her daughter's crib—not her name at all, but the name of the orphanage where she spent the first seven years of her life—she breaks down sobbing.

Nestled inside the crib is her daughter, wrapped in a pink blanket and no bigger than a doll. A pink face, long lashes, perfectly bald.

Marie-Claude brings a hand to her mouth and gasps. "She's beautiful, Elo!"

Elodie stares at the baby. "Is she?"

"Of course she is. What's wrong with you?"

"I don't know what I'm supposed to feel."

Marie-Claude turns to face Elodie, grabs her by the shoulders, and gives her a hard shake. "Give that baby a name and *get on with it*," she says. "Do you hear me? You need to find a way to let go of what happened to you."

"Have *you*?"

"I try," Marie-Claude cries, releasing Elodie. "At least I try."

"I don't know how to let go."

"Then tell people what they did to us at Saint-Nazarius," Marie-Claude says. "Write it down, talk to someone from a newspaper. They print stories like that all the time in the *Journal de Montréal*. Tell the world about Sister Ignatia and how we were treated in there. Do *something* and then give your daughter a goddamn name."

PART IV

Planting

1974

How fair is a garden amid the trials and passions of existence.

—Benjamin Disraeli

CHAPTER 51

Maggie

Maggie looks up from her typewriter and gazes out the window at her beloved view of the water. She sips her coffee, enjoying the peaceful Sunday morning. The subtle licorice smell of the wildflowers Stephanie picked for her—a lovely homemade bouquet of goldenrod, aster, thistle, and snakeroot—wafts around her. She loves her new home, her life here in Cowansville. After they had Stephanie, they decided to sell the house in Knowlton and move closer to the store. Gabriel never could get comfortable living in Roland's discarded house.

Roland let her sell the place without a hassle. He'd remarried by then and had children of his own, and he was happy to let her keep the money from the sale of the house. She and Gabriel bought a white 1830 Georgian on two acres of land, overlooking Lac Brome. Gabriel can fish in his free time and still run the farm back home in Dunham. Clémentine has a fiancé now and has relinquished control over the day-to-day operations. Gabriel is finally doing what he was always meant to do—working his field on his own terms. He's been able to increase revenue on the farm thanks to the expansion of Route 10 into Magog and Sherbrooke, and with the seed store also faring well, they live a better life than either of them ever thought possible.

It's not lost on Maggie that in many ways she is also living her father's life. She spends her days serving the sons of the farmers she grew up around, talking seeds and crops and earworms with them, warning them about the pesticides for which her father has become a cautionary tale. Like her father, she is known to engage in long political conversations and the occasional argument (or sermon, if warranted) for she is still an Anglo at heart. Like her father, Maggie isn't afraid to make her opinions known. She is respected for that, as much as for her knowledge and expertise of seeds.

At the end of each day, before she goes home to prepare supper for the family, she locks herself in her father's office—she still refers to it as her father's office—and takes a quiet moment to review the day's sales or double-check Fred's bookkeeping, and then to make her to-do list for the next day. She understands now her father's reluctance to let go of the reins even a little bit. Having her hand in every facet of the business gives her a feeling of security, especially since that new garden store opened up in Granby. It's called Seed World—the sign doesn't even include the name in French—and it's one of those gigantic, industrial-looking warehouses where the customer has to push a cart through the aisles and fend for himself. It smells of hardware, not gardening. At least Maggie's store still smells of things growing.

Out in the yard, Gabriel and the kids are sprawled in the grass, a bucket of fresh-picked blueberries between them. Maggie watches Gabriel toss a blueberry at James, and then another one at Stephanie. The kids both retaliate, and before long the three of them are engaged in a blueberry fight, their screams of laughter coming in through the windows.

Maggie chuckles to herself as James sticks his hand in the bucket and launches a handful of blueberries at his father. It still confounds her to observe him on the brink of manhood—long-limbed and gangly, almost as tall as Gabriel, with a square jaw and shaggy hair that is too "hippie" for her taste. He's thirteen and his handsomeness is just budding, his features readjusting themselves within this new larger frame. Seemingly overnight his body shot up, while the rest of him is still scrambling to catch up. She finds herself searching frantically for that little boy she knows once existed somewhere beneath those broad shoulders and big hands and feet that go clomping clumsily around the house, but all traces of her baby are gone.

Maggie's attention drifts back to her typewriter, and she resumes planning the contents of the spring catalogue. Although corn season is barely underway, by the time her mock-up goes to print, the November deadline will have arrived. She tends to stick to her father's original layout, dividing it into categories of seeds—grasses and legumes; herbs; fruit and vegetables; grains; flowers—with separate sections for packaging and transport, tools and pesticides. She's added a section called Tips of the Trade, where she discusses how to identify abnormalities in the seedlings, how to test for moisture, ultimate conditions for germination, and other fascinating topics of that sort.

Corn typically gets the spotlight. She always does very well with the original grow strain of Golden Bantam, and as she starts typing the blurb that will accompany her photographs, she decides to do a special promotion. Thirty cents for a package of a hundred seeds.

When she's done, she double- and triple-checks for typos—her father abhorred errors in the catalogue and passed down his obsession to Maggie—and then she pulls the paper out with a dramatic flick of the wrist, as though she's just completed a novel.

As she's getting up to replenish her coffee, the phone rings. Maggie's mood dips; she assumes it's her mother calling to complain about her pending move into the seniors' home. She contemplates ignoring the call, but guiltily grabs the phone at the last minute. With all the siblings moved away—Geri and Nicole in Montreal, Peter in Toronto, and Violet in Val Racine—Maman has no one else left to make miserable.

"Maggie? It's Clémentine. Have you read today's *Journal de Montréal*?"

"No, why?" Maggie asks, realizing her heart is pounding. Something about the urgency in Clémentine's voice.

"There's a story on page three," Clémentine says. "About the Duplessis orphans."

"I'll call you back."

"Maggie. I think it could be her—"

Maggie hangs up and goes off in search of the paper. She finds it untouched on the bathroom vanity, where Gabriel has left it for his after-dinner reading. She doesn't even bother going into another room, just sits down on the cold tiles beside the toilet and turns straight to page three.

Grown-Up Duplessis Orphans
Transition Back Into Society

On a warm spring day in 1967, seventeen-year-old Monique (not her real name) stepped outside the doors of Montreal's Saint-Nazarius Hospital to claim her freedom. Monique grew up behind the barred windows of the Saint-Nazarius mental ward, not because she was mentally deficient but because she was an orphan. Monique is but one of thousands of healthy, illegitimate children who were diagnosed mentally incompetent in the 1950s under Premier Maurice Duplessis's government and sent to psychiatric hospitals across the province.

In 1954, Duplessis signed an order-in-council converting the province's orphanages into hospitals as a way to provide more federal funding to the religious orders that were caring for the orphans. At that time, the Quebec government received federal subsidies for hospitals, but almost nothing for orphanages. Financial contributions for orphans were only $1.25 a day, compared with $2.75 a day for psychiatric patients.

These children weren't just orphans; they were the province's abandoned "children of sin," born out of wedlock, with no one to advocate for them. Monique's earliest memory is of life at the Saint-Sulpice Orphanage in Farnham, where she lived until she was seven. In those days, it was known as the Home for Unwanted Girls. "But it wasn't a bad place," she recalls. "I have no bad memories of it, until they turned it into a mental hospital."

Monique remembers the day the bus pulled up and a group of elderly mental patients debarked and moved into the place Monique called home. School stopped abruptly that day, and Monique was given the job of caring for the mental patients, right up until her transfer to Saint-Nazarius in 1957.

What was life like for a normal-functioning child growing up in a mental institution? At her basement apartment in Pointe Saint-Charles, Monique pulls out a notebook filled with detailed documentation of her experience there—her drawings, journal entries, and dreams. If not for the benevolence and quotidian care of the Sisters of Saint-Nazarius, it's hard to imagine what would have become of children like Monique. The nuns in charge of the overcrowded mental wards had their work cut out for them. It was the norm to have just one nun overseeing at least fifty children on a ward without any assistance. Stretched to their limits, they had to run a tight ship and could be strict disciplinarians.

"I was put to work right away," Monique says. "Cleaning toilets, sewing. We were harshly punished for even the smallest mistakes."

But there were happy times, too. Christmas concerts, excursions to nearby towns, friendships that will last a lifetime. After she left the hospital, Monique lived with a former roommate from Saint-Nazarius, who was also released as a result of a commission in the early sixties tasked with investigating these institutions. It was reported in 1962 that more than twenty thousand patients did not belong, after which followed the steady release of many of the now grown orphans, who were sent out into the world to find work and live normal lives.

Like most of the orphans in her situation, Monique left Saint-Nazarius with few life skills. Describing herself as childlike and "backwards," Monique says, "I didn't even know how to peel and boil a potato."

And yet thanks to the diligence of the Sisters of Saint-Nazarius, Monique could sew and was able to find work almost immediately as a seamstress. She's been able to support herself and transition back into the fold of regular society. Time will tell the full story about the ramifications of Duplessis's initiatives, but for now, Monique is leading a quiet, normal life, which, she says, is all she ever wanted. "I'm not crazy," she says. "I never was. I'm just like everyone else you see on the street."

Maggie finishes the article and gets up off the floor. She doesn't bother calling Clémentine back; instead, she runs outside, wildly waving the paper in her hand and calling out to Gabriel.

CHAPTER 52

———

Elodie

Elodie stares at the sketch in her notebook and realizes she's made a mistake. She erases what she's drawn and makes the correction: there were three buckled straps that ran across the front of the straitjacket, not four. The fourth buckle was actually at the bottom; it was for the strap that went between her legs and fastened behind her back.

Satisfied, she closes her notebook for the day and tucks it safely inside the drawer of her nightstand. It's become quite a tome, this book containing page after page of hand-drawn sketches and detailed notes about what happened to her at Saint-Nazarius—chronicled with agonizing precision, the memories still raw and vivid in her mind.

She has no plans to show the notebook to anyone else. She bared her soul to that journalist, and instead of telling the truth, he wrote a fairy tale with a happy ending. The morning the piece was published, she could hardly wait to read it. It was a week ago Saturday. She thought, *Finally, I'll get my revenge.* She figured the whole province would soon learn about what the nuns had done to the orphans and consequences would follow at last.

By the time Elodie was finished reading the article, she was sobbing on the floor, devastated. The story made no mention of the torture and abuse she'd suffered on a daily basis, no mention of Sister Ignatia's name or the fact that "Monique" was raising her own illegitimate child now. That would have interfered with the journalist's happy ending; it would have sullied the idea he'd put forth of her leading a "quiet, normal life."

It was bullshit, all of it. Lies by omission—and worse. "Christmas concerts"? "Friendships that will last a lifetime"? Elodie wanted to throw up reading that part. And most egregious of all was his description of the nuns' "benevolence" and "quotidian care."

That's when she tore the newspaper to shreds and set it on fire in her sink and then stood there watching the flames destroy her first, but not her last, attempt at retribution.

She's not a good enough writer to tackle her own autobiography, but she's vowed to herself that one day she will tell her story to someone willing to expose the truth: not some whitewashed fluff piece that continues to protect the church, but an unsparing, graphic account of the horrors the orphans endured. She only hopes Sister Ignatia will still be alive when the world finds out what she did.

"Maman?"

Elodie looks up to find Nancy standing there, watching her with those worshipful blue eyes. She's almost three now, with fine blond hair and a round, rosy face. It still amazes Elodie that she's somehow managed to create this exuberant angel, this spark of light and joy who doesn't sit still, laughs at everything, stomps her feet when she doesn't get her way; this child who is fearless and confident and inherently happy.

Not a day passes that Elodie does not wonder, *How did I make this creature?*

They're nothing alike. Nancy is curious and clever, optimistic. Elodie's passing dark moods hardly seem to deflate the little girl's buoyant spirit or deter her from her mission to explore, entertain, or get her way. In fact, very little dampens her zest, other than being told no. Compared to her own childhood, Nancy has had a marvelous life so far, which is a point of great pride for Elodie.

She may not be the best mother; she'll be the first to admit it. She waitresses five nights a week and they're still on welfare. When she's home, she spends far too much time with her nose buried in her grievance notebook, obsessively trying to record every single abuse she ever suffered. But Nancy is safe and well fed, has no bruises or scars, has never been locked up. She's been snuggled and kissed and tickled and told "I love you" a thousand times. Elodie has surpassed all her expectations for the kind of mother she'd be and managed, in spite of everything, to transcend her many limitations.

"Maman, *up*," Nancy says, raising her plump arms above her head.

Elodie lifts her onto the pullout couch they share, and Nancy curls up in her lap like a kitten. "*Je t'aime, Maman*," she coos.

Elodie still finds it jarring to hear those words so freely uttered. *I love you.* She's had to do so little to earn them. "I love you, too," she says, lighting a cigarette.

"When am I going to Grand-Maman's?" Nancy asks, looking up at Elodie with unfiltered adoration.

"Who?" Elodie says. "You don't have a grandmother."

"Mme. Drouin told me she's my *grand-maman* and that's what I'm supposed to call her."

Elodie has a long drag from her cigarette and tries to calm her racing pulse. "Well, she's not," she says angrily.

"Then who is?"

Elodie opens her mouth to tell Nancy the truth, but quickly reconsiders. Nancy is watching her expectantly, the way children do. "Mme. Drouin is not your grandmother," she says carefully.

"But she takes care of me."

"It doesn't work that way."

"All the other kids on the street have grandmothers and aunties and uncles and cousins," she says. "Where are mine?"

Elodie stubs out her cigarette in a mug by her bed, blinking against the threat of tears. "Aren't I enough for you?" she asks the little girl.

Nancy looks thoughtful, her golden brows adorably furrowed. "Can't I have both?" she says.

"Maybe one day, *chouette*," Elodie says, never giving up on the possibility of one day finding a relative. "Now go get Maman a Pepsi."

Nancy scrambles out of bed, singing "Frère Jacques" on her way to the kitchenette.

"Don't shake the can!" Elodie calls out.

Moments later, Nancy returns with a can of Pepsi. She holds it out and Elodie opens it, and sure enough, it explodes, the frothy soda spilling out like lava all over her shirt and sheets. Nancy bursts out laughing, completely unafraid of any consequences. Elodie laughs with her, knowing for certain that Nancy must be the universe's gift for the terrible childhood she endured.

The phone rings and Elodie slides across the bed to grab it. *"Allô?"*

"Elodie, it's Gilles Leduc from the *Journal de Montréal.*"

Elodie tenses and her face feels hot. "Your article was bullshit," she says. "You're as bad as them, protecting the nuns like that. You call yourself a journalist, but you're just a liar. You left everything important out. My 'quiet, normal life'? Are you blind?" She hears him sighing on the other end, but she goes on. "You made it sound like I had an enchanted childhood in that place, for Christ's sake. Why didn't you just tell the truth? It would have made for a much better story!"

Nancy is watching her with her big eyes.

"Do you read the classifieds?" he interrupts, silencing her rant.

"No."

"Maybe you should."

"I won't ever read your paper again, asshole. You don't write the truth!"

"I really think you need to buy today's paper."

"Why?"

"A copy editor I know in the classifieds department mentioned there's someone who's been running an ad for years, the first Saturday of every month. I think it could be you he's looking for."

"Me? What are you talking about?"

"Your story matches the details in this classified ad. Just go buy the goddamn paper."

He hangs up. In spite of her vow never to read a newspaper again, she drags Nancy to the corner store to pick up the *Journal de Montréal.*

She scans the entire classifieds section right there, until she comes to the ad that just about stops her heart.

> I am in search of a young woman with the given name Elodie, born March 6, 1950, at the Brome-Missisquoi-Perkins Hospital in the Eastern Townships. She was transferred in 1957 from the Saint-Sulpice Orphanage near Farnham to Saint-Nazarius Hospital in Montreal. I have information about her birth family. Please call—

And just like that, everything changes.

Her birth family. She repeats those words over and over in her head as she rushes home, clutching the newspaper to her heart.

"What's wrong, Maman?" Nancy asks, trying to keep pace with Elodie.

"Nothing's wrong," Elodie says, crouching down to her daughter's eye level. "It's just the opposite. I think everything might finally be all right."

CHAPTER 53

⟡

Maggie

It's the usual Saturday evening chaos. Gabriel is over at the farm, and Maggie is by herself with the kids. The phone is ringing and Stephanie is having a tantrum because she wants to wear her rain boots in the bath. James is at the kitchen table watching an Expos game and eating his third supper of the night—he's a bottomless pit these days. The TV is blaring.

Maggie grabs the phone, ignoring Stephanie, who's pulling on her bell-bottoms and wailing about needing to wear the boots in the bathtub so she can pretend it's a puddle.

"*Allô?*" Maggie answers.

"I saw your ad in the *Journal de Montréal* today," a woman says.

"I'm sorry, what ad?"

"It said you have information about my birth family? My name is Elodie."

Maggie's knees buckle. She reaches her arm out to the counter to hold herself up.

"Madame?" Elodie says.

"Yes. I'm here. Sorry."

"The ad said to call this number."

"Of course," Maggie manages, reeling. Gabriel must have placed it. All this time he's let her do the crusading, but quietly he's been looking for Elodie, too.

"So this *is* the right number?" the woman says.

"Yes," Maggie manages. "Yes."

She's not dead. It's her.

When she read the article in the paper last week about "Monique" and the Duplessis orphans, she felt a resurgence of hope. She thought there was a strong possibility that Monique could be Elodie. The problem was Maggie still didn't know how to find her. She suggested to Gabriel that they drive around Pointe Saint-Charles, patrolling up and down the streets in search of a twenty-four-year-old woman they might hopefully recognize, but Gabriel put his foot down, told her she was being irrational and manic. They did visit every sewing factory in the Pointe, Saint-Henri, and Griffintown, but no one fitting Elodie's description worked at any of them. Maggie even went to the Centre de Retrouvailles, but all she could do was leave her own information and hope that Elodie would show up there one day looking for her birth mother.

"The ad says you have information about my birth family?"

"I—Yes, I do," Maggie stammers, trying to sound normal.

Stephanie is still tugging on Maggie's bell-bottoms, whining about the goddamn rubber boots. Maggie holds the phone away from her mouth and says to James, "*Get her out of here!*"

James ignores her.

"Do it *now*," Maggie hisses. "Put her in a bath."

"With my boots on?" Stephanie wants to know.

"Yes," Maggie says impatiently. Stephanie immediately perks up and skips off. James turns off the TV and follows her begrudgingly out of the kitchen, leaving Maggie alone.

"Do you know anything about your background?" she asks Elodie, hoping to establish it's really her.

"I was born in 1950," Elodie says. "I don't know the date. Nobody adopted me because I was small and sickly. I don't know much else. My mother died giving birth to me."

Maggie clamps a hand over her mouth to keep from crying out. *Died giving birth?* Why the hell would the nuns tell her that?

"Who am I?" Elodie asks her again. "What's my family name?"

"Your name is Elodie Phénix," Maggie says, trying to steady her breathing and stay calm.

"And who are you?"

Maggie hesitates, not sure how to respond. The poor girl thinks her mother is dead. How can Maggie tell her the truth over the phone?

"I'm Maggie," she says, at last. "I think I might be your aunt."

"My mother's sister?"

"Yes," Maggie lies. "She had a daughter born March 6, 1950, a few weeks early. The baby was at Saint-Sulpice until 1957, and then transferred to Saint-Nazarius. My sister gave her the name Elodie."

"Before she died?"

Maggie squeezes her eyes closed. "Yes. Before she died. It was on the birth certificate."

"I have so many questions."

Me, too, Maggie thinks.

"I want to know all about her," Elodie says. "And do I have other relatives? What about my father?"

"Would you like to meet in person?"

"Yes," Elodie says, and Maggie surges with excitement.

They arrange to meet next weekend. Maggie was hoping for sooner—she'd drive to her apartment now if she could—but she senses that Elodie is more apprehensive about how quickly everything is happening and she backs off.

She tries reaching Gabriel at Clémentine's, but he's already left and is on his way home. Maggie doesn't mention anything about her conversation with Elodie. Gabriel has to be the first to know.

Maggie paces around the kitchen, desperate to get her hands on that newspaper. She needs Gabriel to walk through that door. Still shaking, she sits down at the table, her head pounding with a burgeoning migraine.

My daughter is alive. She never really believed Elodie was dead, but it still makes no sense that Sister Ignatia would have lied to her that day in 1961. Who would deliberately keep a mother from her own child? The inhumanity of it, the sheer cruelty, is something Maggie will never be able to comprehend or forgive. She robbed Maggie of thirteen years with her daughter.

The back door opens and Maggie jumps up, flinging her body into Gabriel's arms.

"What's going on?" he asks. "Kids asleep?"

The kids. She completely forgot about them. They're being quiet upstairs, probably thrilled she's forgotten about them and they're getting to stay up late. "I don't know."

"You don't know where the kids are?" he says, placing a bucket of blueberries on the counter.

"Elodie called."

Gabriel stops and turns to face her. "Heh?"

"Elodie called here," she repeats. "She's alive."

The color drains from his face.

"She read your ad and she called!" Maggie cries. "How long have you been running it? It means that nun did lie to us, which I always knew. Do you remember her telling us how sick Elodie was when she was transferred to the hospital?"

"Wait. What ad?"

"In the classifieds. The *Journal de Montréal.*"

Gabriel shakes his head, his expression blank. "I have no idea what you're talking about."

They stand there for a moment, staring at each other. "Go to the store," Maggie says. "Go get the paper."

"What about Elodie? What did she say? How did she sound?"

"It was a very short conversation," she says, and gives him a quick summary.

Brushing tears from his eyes, Gabriel disappears out the back door. The store is just at the corner of their street, so it doesn't take long. Maggie stands by the door until he returns and hands it to her. Silently, frantically, they tear through the paper to the back pages.

"There," Gabriel says, pointing to it.

> I am in search of a young woman with the given name Elodie, born March 6, 1950, at the Brome-Missisquoi-Perkins Hospital in the Eastern Townships. She was transferred in 1957 from the Saint-Sulpice Orphanage near Farnham to Saint-Nazarius Hospital in Montreal. I have information about her birth family. Please call—

They stare at the ad, more baffled than before. "That's our number."

"We have to call the paper," she says. "Find out who placed this ad. Someone who knows our number."

"It's Saturday night. We won't reach anyone till Monday."

"Could it be Clémentine?"

"She wouldn't interfere," he says. "Not with something like this."

"My mother?"

Gabriel rolls his eyes.

"No one knows about Elodie other than my mother," she says. "The only people who knew are dead. Who else could it be?"

Gabriel quickly pulls a cigarette from his pack and lights up. "What if this is all a hoax?"

"It's *our* phone number in the paper!"

"How do you even know it was really her on the phone? What if it wasn't?"

"Who else would it be?" Maggie says. "Another orphan named Elodie? She knew things."

"What if it's another girl from the hospital? Someone who knows the facts about Elodie's life and is looking for a handout? We have to be careful here, Maggie. No matter how much we want it to be her, none of this makes sense!"

"She has nothing to gain by pretending to be our daughter."

"Of course she does. A family, possible financial support. Any girl could say her name is Elodie."

"Since when are you so cynical?" Maggie accuses. "Why can't you just let this be the miracle that it is?"

"Goddamn it, Maggie," he cries, banging his fist on the table. "I'm scared to let myself believe it might be her! This isn't only about you. As far as I'm concerned, she's mine."

"I'm sorry."

He sits down and runs a hand through his hair. "We're going to have to wait until Monday."

"She thinks I'm dead," Maggie tells him. "They told her I died in childbirth. It's probably in her bullshit file."

"But why?"

"God only knows. I went along with it over the phone," she confesses. "I didn't know what else to do. I said I was her aunt."

"*Calice.*"

"I should call her back and tell her I'm alive. I shouldn't have lied."

"You can't tell her over the phone," he says. "*You gave her away,* Maggie. It's going to be a big enough shock for her to find out you're alive, never mind that you gave her up."

"You're right," she says, defeated. "She's going to hate me."

"*If* it's her, she's going to need time."

"It *is* her," Maggie says, sounding a bit like Stephanie when she's not getting her way. "Think about this, Gabriel. That day we went to Saint-Nazarius and asked about Elodie? She was *there*. We were probably just a few feet away from her on the other side of those doors. And what did the nuns do? They told us she was dead, and they let her go on believing *I* was dead."

Gabriel stands up again and circles the kitchen table. She watches him scan the room, knowing he's looking for something to punch or throw, a way to vent his anger. His eyes light on the vase of Stephanie's wildflowers, but he manages to restrain himself.

Maggie gets up and goes over to him, touches his cheek, which is wet.

"Do you really think it's her?" he says softly.

"We're going to meet her," she tells him. "And then we'll know for sure. We have to focus on that right now. And we have to find out who placed this ad."

"Call your mother."

Maggie goes to the phone. While she's dialing, Gabriel says, "I'm going to fucking murder that nun. And all of them who did this to us. If it is Elodie and they told us she was dead, it's *sick*. And why? So they could keep her locked up in that fucking mental institution rather than give her back to us? Why the hell would they do that?"

"I don't know," Maggie says, trying to stay grounded for both of them. "I don't understand either. But listen to me. Listen. We're going to have her in our lives after all. That's what matters now."

Her mother answers after about a dozen rings. "Ma!" Maggie cries. "Are you the one who placed the ad?"

"I'm watching *La Petite Patrie*!"

"Did—you—place—the—ad—in—the—classified—section—of—the—*Journal—de—Montréal*?" Maggie repeats.

"What ad?" her mother says. "What are you talking about? My show is about to end."

"You didn't place an ad looking for Elodie?"

"*Bien non!*" she says. "Why would I do that?"

"I don't know. I just thought . . . Doesn't matter. Go finish your show."

Maggie hangs up, disappointed. "It wasn't her," she says, joining Gabriel at the table.

"Of course it wasn't her."

"Who then?"

Gabriel shrugs.

"I don't think I can wait until Monday."

"I wonder if she's mine," Gabriel says, exhaling a ring of smoke. "We'll know right away, don't you think?"

"Probably."

"Twenty-four years."

"She's suffered," Maggie says, her voice breaking. "If she grew up in that awful place?"

"It didn't sound so bad in the article."

"Maybe it didn't tell the whole story," Maggie points out. "You know how the French papers like to protect the church. Remember that book I read a few years ago? *The Mad Cry for Help?* That sure painted a different picture."

"No sense torturing yourself," Gabriel tells her. "You'll be able to ask her yourself soon."

"That's what I'm afraid of," Maggie says, reaching for the cigarette he's left burning in the ashtray.

CHAPTER 54

———⋘⊙⊘⊙⋙———

First thing Monday morning, Gabriel calls the newspaper. Maggie hovers behind him. "Make sure you get a name," she insists. "They may not want to say."

"I haven't even been transferred to classifieds yet."

"Ask if it was a man or a woman," she says. "And how long has the ad been running? And how often?"

"*Bonjour, madame,*" he says, gesturing to Maggie to stop talking.

Maggie steps away to give him some space. She chews on a nail, kills a fly buzzing around the windowsill, opens the back door to toss it outside. It's a beautiful morning, the sun already blinding, the air thick and perfumed by her garden. She examines her hollyhocks, which are in full bloom, forming the towering wall of pink, coral, and white flowers she'd envisioned two years ago when she planted them.

She goes back inside, and is disappointed to see that Gabriel is still on the phone. "Who placed the ad?" she mouths.

Gabriel glares at her and puts a finger to his mouth.

"Don't forget to ask if it's going to run again," she says.

"And is it scheduled to run again?" he asks, motioning for Maggie to hand him his coffee. "I see," he says. "Please go ahead and cancel it. No need to run it anymore." After a beat: "Yes. She did."

Maggie signals maniacally for Gabriel to wrap up.

"Thank you," he says. "You've been very helpful."

As he puts down the phone, Maggie throws up her hands in exasperation. "So?" she cries. "I'm surprised you didn't invite her over for dinner."

"The ad was paid for by a Mr. Peter Hughes."

"*Peter?*" She shakes her head. "My brother? I don't . . . That doesn't make sense."

"Call him."

Gabriel hands Maggie the phone and she dials his number at work.

"Peter Hughes," he answers, in what Maggie perceives as a rather self-important tone. He recently made partner at a large architecture firm in Toronto—as per the photocopied letter he mailed everyone in the family at Christmas.

"Elodie called me," she blurts. No preamble. No greeting.

Peter is quiet.

"Did you hear me?"

"Yes," he says. "That's a good thing, isn't it?"

"Yes," she says. "But why? I'm stunned, Peter."

Peter laughs good-naturedly.

"Really," she says. "Why? And why not tell me?"

"It wasn't me, Maggie. It was Daddy."

It takes a moment for his words to land.

"He started running the ad years ago," Peter explains. "Before he got sick. The first Saturday of every month."

"He never said—"

"He made me promise to keep doing it after he died. And not to tell you."

"I can't believe it."

"*I* can't believe she actually saw it and called you," he says. "After all these years. I never thought she would. I told Daddy I thought it was futile, but he could be stubborn, as you know."

"Does Ma know?"

"Are you kidding? Of course not."

Maggie leans over the sink and turns on the tap, splashes water on her face. It's hot in the kitchen. She tucks the phone between her ear and shoulder and opens the window for some air.

"Will you meet her?" Peter asks her.

"Yes," Maggie says. "Next week."

The week crawls by. Maggie and Gabriel go through the motions of each day, feigning normalcy for the kids. They don't discuss Elodie much among themselves, preferring instead to process it alone. Maggie can think of little else, but with two children, life keeps moving forward whether she likes it or not. There are meals to prepare, moods to manage, tantrums to quell; fights to break up, baths, housecleaning. At work, it's catalogue season, on top of which her publisher just sent her a book to consider for translation. It doesn't end, and certainly doesn't leave much time for anguishing over her fears.

Still, the knot in her chest doesn't go away. Not for a minute. Beneath every word or movement courses an unrelenting strum of anxiety; her thoughts stubbornly drift back to Elodie. What will she say to her when they finally meet?

She keeps imagining that moment over and over in her mind— the way Elodie will react, the possibility of her anger and hatred, the withholding of forgiveness. Maggie can't bear the thought; the dread in her body is visceral, as if Elodie were already standing in front of her, accusing and rejecting her.

When Maggie's mother gets wind of the reunion, she calls Maggie in a panic. "Some things are better left alone!" she cries.

"She's my daughter, Ma. This isn't even a conversation."

"This is not a good idea, Maggie. You gave her up."

"It's the seventies, Ma. No one gives a shit that I had a baby at sixteen."

"You can't tell the kids. What will they think of you?"

"They'll understand. I told you, times are different now. They don't judge like your generation did."

"What will *she* think of you?" Maman says. "What if she hates you? Have you thought about that?"

"It's all I've thought about," Maggie says, and hangs up.

The night before she's to meet Elodie, Maggie wakes up with a racing heart. She snuggles against Gabriel. To calm herself, she tries to remember the stories her father used to tell her to help her fall asleep. One of his favorite aphorisms comes into her mind, and she can almost hear his voice, as if he's speaking to her now. *He who plants a seed plants life.*

At least she did that. She gave Elodie life, though not much else.

CHAPTER 55

⸻⟨ø/ø⟩⸻

Maggie pulls her cake out of the oven and sets it down on the counter to cool. The house is quiet. The kids are at her mother's for the afternoon; it was easier than trying to explain everything. Gabriel is out in the yard, building a tree house for the kids, trying to keep his mind off everything. She watches him from her kitchen window, hammering and sawing, his Canadiens cap pulled down over his brow. She loves him as much as she did when she used to watch him working his cornfield.

"Your cake sank," Clémentine says. She's here for moral support.

Maggie looks over at the sad cake and her heart sinks with it.

"You're a terrible baker, Maggie."

"It's this oven!" Maggie defends, and they both laugh. The cake goes in the garbage.

"I brought crackers and cheese," Clémentine says. "And cookies."

"Cookies from a package?"

Clémentine rolls her eyes.

"My mother would never serve packaged cookies to a guest," Maggie mutters, and then regrets it immediately.

Clémentine's face falls and she quickly turns away. Sometimes Maggie forgets; she's become so close to her sister-in-law over the years, she can hardly remember that Clémentine was her father's lover first, her mother's nemesis.

"I'm sorry," Maggie says, grabbing Clémentine's hand. "I didn't mean it like that."

"Course not," Clémentine says, tossing cheese on a platter. "Will Red Rose tea be good enough? Or would your mother have brought the leaves in from China?"

Maggie bursts into laughter and Clémentine joins in, the awkwardness quickly dispelled.

And then a knock at the door. They look at each other. Neither of them moves until Clémentine says, "Let's go meet your daughter."

Maggie is frozen. Clémentine squeezes her hand, and they go to the front door in silence.

She's a few feet away, Maggie tells herself, trying to convince herself this is really happening. *She's on the other side of that door.*

The moment has a surreal quality to it, as though it's just another one of her silly fantasies. It feels as if Clémentine is opening the door in slow motion.

And then she's there. Maggie hears herself gasp. *It's her.* Her face has an unmistakable stamp of Hughes and Phénix.

"*Allô,*" Elodie says. She attempts a smile, but doesn't meet Maggie's eyes.

"Come in," Clémentine says, stepping aside.

Elodie enters the house. Maggie wipes her eyes, not wanting to frighten the girl with an emotional outburst before she's even through the door. She has to keep reminding herself that Elodie has no idea who she is.

"I'm Maggie," she says, her voice sounding strange. "And this is my friend Clémentine."

Elodie says hello, again without making eye contact with either of them. She has a nervous, skittish energy, but who could blame her?

Clémentine takes Elodie's macramé poncho and shows her to the living room. Maggie notices she walks with a slight limp. She's wearing jeans and an olive green tank top—she's very thin—but it's her face Maggie can't stop staring at, even though it's mostly hidden behind a curtain of long hair, parted in the middle. There's an undeniable resemblance to Maggie's side of the family, certain subtle traces of her sisters—the curve of Geri's mouth, the wide space between Vi's eyes, the thick Hughes eyebrows they all share. She's fair and dirty blond, and her body—lanky and long-limbed—is pure Phénix.

"Would you like a cup of tea?" Maggie asks her as she gestures to the couch. "Or a Pepsi?"

"Pepsi, please," Elodie says, sitting down.

"Yes, of course," Maggie says. "I'll be right back."

She goes to the kitchen and splashes water on her face. She's trying hard not to hyperventilate. She throws open the back door and calls out to Gabriel. He stops hammering and turns to her, his face ghost-white. He approaches slowly.

"It's her," Maggie says, before he can even ask. "See for yourself."

Gabriel takes a long breath, bracing himself, and they go inside together.

"This is my husband, Gabriel," Maggie says, returning to the living room and handing Elodie a glass of soda. "Gabriel, this is Elodie."

Tears come to Gabriel's eyes the moment he sees her. He knows he's her father, Maggie can tell. She sees it registering in his eyes. He pulls her brusquely into his arms and squeezes. He never was one to hold back.

"Let her breathe," Maggie says softly.

Gabriel releases the girl and stands back, gawking at her. None of them can stop staring at her. Maggie can't quite believe this is the infant she first laid eyes on in an enamel basin more than two decades ago. And in some ways, she isn't. She looks a little malnourished, like she doesn't eat well. She doesn't have good teeth or skin, a sign of poverty. There's a scar over her eye.

"I can't believe I'm here," Elodie says, echoing Maggie's thoughts. "That you're my *aunt*."

"The ad's been running for years," Maggie says. "How did you finally come across it?"

A shadow passes over her eyes. "There was an article about me in the *Journal* a couple of weeks ago," she explains. "The journalist who wrote it recognized my story in your ad. He told me to buy the paper and read the classifieds."

"A miracle," Clémentine whispers.

"We read that article," Maggie says. "I thought there were a lot of similarities."

"It was all lies," Elodie states, her tone turning harsh. "He left everything important out, like all the *facts*. He made it sound like a fairy tale, which it wasn't. I don't exactly lead a 'normal, quiet life.'"

Maggie feels heartsick. She had her suspicions that the article made Elodie's life sound too good to be true, compared to some of the other accounts she'd read.

"The article said you work as a seamstress?" Clémentine asks her, changing the subject.

"I used to," Elodie clarifies, biting her nails. "When I first got out of the hospital. I'm a waitress now."

Maggie suppresses disappointment, reminding herself she has no right to judge. She glances over at Gabriel and can tell by the pulsing vein in his forehead and the set of his mouth that he's holding back a deluge of emotion.

"Sewing sheets was the job I had at Saint-Nazarius," Elodie continues. "It was pretty much all I knew how to do when I got out. But I'm much happier at the deli."

Maggie shoots Gabriel a look, but he doesn't meet her gaze.

"I have so many questions," Elodie says, turning to Maggie. "Were you close to my mother? Did you know about me?"

"Yes, I knew about you," Maggie answers, uncomfortably.

"What was she like?"

"She was very young."

"Her parents made her give you up," Gabriel adds.

"They thought you'd be adopted right away," Maggie says. "Everyone did. But that was before they converted the orphanages."

"That part of the article was true," Elodie says. "Change of Vocation Day was the day my life may as well have ended."

They all fall silent. Maggie has to squeeze back tears.

"They told us we were crazy," Elodie tells them. "And that was it. From then on we were."

"What made you go to the newspaper with your story?"

"It was my friend Marie-Claude's idea. She thought it would help me with my anger." She laughs out loud then, not a happy laugh. "Instead that stupid article made me angrier." She takes a cigarette out of her purse. "You mind?"

"Of course not."

She lights up and inhales deeply. "Marie-Claude meant well," she says, waving a cloud of smoke away from her face. "And it turned out all right in the end because you found me."

The whole time she's talking, Maggie can think of nothing other than how she's going to broach the truth with her.

"Do you have a boyfriend?" Gabriel asks her, probably hoping that the care and protection of a good man might somehow redeem her tragic life. A man would think that way, Maggie reasons. It would make him feel better.

"No. I have a daughter, though," Elodie says, matter-of-factly. "Her name is Nancy."

A daughter?

"She's three."

The same age as Stephanie. Maggie is numb. *Three years of my granddaughter's life missed,* she thinks with a stab of grief.

"Her father was going off to Vietnam when we met," Elodie explains. "He doesn't even know about Nancy. I'm not even sure he's alive."

"Did you try to find him?"

"No. I don't know his last name."

Maggie observes Gabriel's jaw tightening and says, "Do you have a picture of her?"

"No. She's very pretty and confident. She's nothing like me at all."

"I'm sure she's very much like you," Maggie says, finding her voice.

Elodie looks down at the floor, her knee bouncing nervously.

"Who takes care of her when you're working?" Clémentine asks.

"My neighbor."

"And you earn enough to support the both of you?" Maggie prods, unable to stop herself.

"We manage," Elodie responds. "I'm on welfare, which helps."

Maggie nods, not knowing what to say. She doesn't dare look in Gabriel's direction or she might burst into tears.

"I'm so grateful you found me," Elodie says. "I didn't want Nancy to grow up without any family like I did. I hoped she might wind up with some cousins or something, a nice aunt or uncle." She looks directly at Maggie. "Do you have any children?"

"Yes," Maggie responds. "A boy and a girl."

"Wow. I have cousins."

Maggie doesn't say anything.

"So how old was my mother when she had me?" Elodie asks her.

"Sixteen."

"Were you close? You didn't say."

"Yes."

"Did you know my father?" Elodie pursues.

"No," Maggie answers, not daring to glance in Gabriel's direction.

"Do you know anything else about your parents?" he asks Elodie.

"Just that my mother is dead," she says.

"Who told you that?"

"Sister Ignatia. She was in charge of our ward. She showed me my file and told me my mother died of her sins."

Maggie's heart clenches. She bites down on her lower lip to stay silent.

"When did she tell you that?" Gabriel asks her, impressively controlling his temper.

"When I was eleven," Elodie says. "Right after the doctor interviewed me. That was when they started sending a lot of the orphans into foster care. Turns out we weren't crazy after all."

Gabriel has guzzled his beer. His fingers on the can are trembling.

"I had to stay at Saint-Nazarius because my mother was dead and nobody wanted a teenage girl," Elodie adds, her tone flat.

"Will you excuse me?" Maggie says, standing abruptly. "I'll be right back."

Upstairs in her bedroom she sits down on the bed. Gabriel joins her a few minutes later.

"If what Elodie remembers is true," she says before he's even through the door, "then Sister Ignatia must have told her I was dead *right after* we showed up at Saint-Nazarius looking for her."

Gabriel shakes his head helplessly.

"She told me that Elodie was dead," Maggie goes on. "And then she told Elodie that *I* was dead, just to keep us apart. *Why would she do that?* Why?"

"I'm going to throw a Molotov cocktail into that fucking hospital ward," he says, sitting down beside her.

"I don't know what to do, Gabe."

"We're going to go downstairs and tell her we're her parents."

"I'm too scared."

"Of what?"

"That she'll hate me. Look at her, Gabe. She's . . . Did you notice her eyes? I've never seen so much sadness in someone so young. That article in the *Journal* was all lies."

"She's had a hard life, Maggie. We always knew that. But she's strong. She's a fighter, like her mother."

"I can't even imagine what she's been through. I don't want to. She has a limp, you know. And that scar over her eye? It's my fault."

"What happened to her in that place is not your fault."

"The fact that she was ever there *is* my fault," she argues. "And you know it, and I'm sure some part of you hates me for it, too."

Gabriel sighs, lights a cigarette. "We've had this conversation, Maggie. I made my peace with your choice a long time ago."

"She's suffered and it can't ever be undone. This is who she is now."

"You don't know who she is. You don't know anything about her yet."

"I'm afraid to know," Maggie says childishly.

"I'm going to get her," he says, standing up. "It's time."

Maggie doesn't respond, but she doesn't stop him from leaving.

Moments later there's a soft knock on the door frame and Elodie steps into the room with obvious trepidation. "Is something the matter?" she asks, her voice small and scared.

"Come in," Maggie says, forcing a light voice.

Elodie approaches.

"Here," Maggie says, sliding over. "Sit."

Elodie blinks nervously, hesitating. She doesn't trust Maggie. Probably doesn't trust, period.

Maggie stares at her for several long seconds without speaking. She would give anything to just take her in her arms and hold her. "I know this is an important day for you," she begins. "Meeting your aunt—"

"Not as important as if I was meeting my mother."

Maggie shifts nervously on the bed and looks down at the floor. "I have something to tell you," she says, her voice wavering. "You *are* meeting your mother."

"Heh? What do you mean?" Elodie cries. "That other lady, Clémentine. Is she my mother?"

"*I'm* your mother, Elodie."

Elodie doesn't move. Her eyes register passing clouds of shock, disbelief, incredulity.

They sit for a long time in silence, tears sliding down both their cheeks.

"I don't believe you," Elodie says, finally. "You can't be."

"I'm your mother," Maggie states, more firmly this time. "You were born March 6, 1950. It was a Sunday night."

"It's not possible. My mother died—"

"That's what the nun told you," Maggie explains gently. "But it wasn't true."

A strange noise comes out of Elodie—guttural, from deep inside, a tortured sound that breaks Maggie's heart.

"That nun told me the same thing," Maggie says. "That you were dead."

"Sister Ignatia? When?"

Maggie reaches for her daughter's hand. It flops limply in her own. "Elodie," she says. "First, can I just hold you in my arms?"

Elodie nods, tears rolling down her face, and they collapse into each other. Maggie's body surrenders wholly to the embrace, heart surging, muscles unclenching, limbs loosening with indescribable relief. There's an instant release of tension, deliverance from a lifetime of chronic worry that's become as natural and constant as breathing. Not since the day she gave birth to this child has she ever felt whole or fully at peace.

"You don't know how long I've waited for this moment," Elodie sobs, her voice muffled against Maggie's neck.

"Yes," Maggie says, releasing her. "I do. Not a day has gone by in twenty-four years that I haven't thought about you, my daughter."

"When did Sister Ignatia tell you I was dead?"

"We went to Saint-Nazarius in '61 to find you," Maggie tells her. "I'd been looking for you for a long time. First I went to the orphanage."

"Saint-Sulpice?"

"Yes. But it was a hospital by then."

"Did you speak to Sister Alberta?" Elodie asks her, her eyes filling with fresh tears. "She was kind to me. I loved her. I remember the nuns used to call it the 'Home for Unwanted Girls,' but it wasn't a bad place before it became a mental hospital."

Maggie struggles to hold back the anger that's stuck in her throat. That word again, "unwanted," like she was some discarded doll.

"Was she there?" Elodie asks. "Sister Tata?"

"I spoke to the caretaker," Maggie says. "He suggested I write to the government for information, which I did. I finally got hold of a document showing that two groups of orphans had been transferred to Mercy and Saint-Nazarius in '57. Gabriel and I went to both."

"And she told you I was dead?"

Maggie nods.

Elodie reaches for the pack of cigarettes in her front pocket and lights one, fingers trembling. "She was a monster, that woman. But to tell us both the other was dead, when she could have let you take me home—"

"I can't comprehend that kind of cruelty either," Maggie murmurs. "I just . . . There aren't words."

The pain has a suffocating quality, the kind that leaves you gasping for breath. Maggie suddenly remembers that scratchy wool blanket at Deda and Yvon's house, the way it felt on her body when she was being raped. Like she was being smothered and couldn't breathe. "I know this is a lot to take in," she says. "You must have a million questions for me."

"Why did you give me up?" Elodie asks, her voice cutting through their shared grief.

The air goes out of the room. *Here it is*, Maggie thinks.

"I was fifteen when I got pregnant," she says, looking directly into her daughter's desolate blue eyes. "I wasn't allowed to keep you. It's not a very original story, but it's the truth. My father made arrangements to—" She almost blurts, *sell you*, but corrects herself in time. "—to have you adopted by a couple who couldn't have children of their own. But there were some complications when you were born and the couple changed their minds. You were sent to Saint-Sulpice when you were well enough."

Elodie stubs out her cigarette in the ashtray next to the bed. She sniffles and wipes her nose. How hard this must be for her to hear, even harder than it is for Maggie to say.

"I named you Elodie," Maggie continues. "It's a type of lily. It's very hardy . . ."

Her voice trails off. Elodie is watching her, waiting for something else.

"I started trying to find you after my third miscarriage," Maggie says. "It was 1959. I blamed myself for the miscarriages. I thought God was punishing me for having given you away. I never stopped thinking about you. I never felt whole. Ever." She dabs her eyes with her shirtsleeve. "I know how much you've suffered, but—"

"No," Elodie says. "You don't."

Maggie bites her lip.

"Who is my father?"

Maggie takes a long, nervous breath. "It's Gabriel," she says, trying to keep her voice and gaze steady.

Elodie's back straightens. "Him?" she says, pointing to the door. "Your *husband*?"

"Yes."

"You married him?"

"Yes, but—"

"Why couldn't you have kept me then?" she asks, obviously wounded. "If you were together and you loved each other?"

"It was complicated," Maggie attempts, persevering in the face of her daughter's shock. "My parents sent me away to live with my aunt and uncle in another town so I couldn't be with Gabriel."

"Why?"

"My father wanted someone else for me," she says. "Someone educated, from a better family. I found out I was pregnant while I was living with my aunt and uncle, so I had to stay there until you were born."

"Did Gabriel know you were pregnant?"

"I didn't tell him," Maggie confesses.

"Couldn't you have married him?"

The way Elodie puts it makes it sound so simple, so logical. Perhaps it should have been. "I didn't think I had a choice," Maggie explains sheepishly. "I was only fifteen."

Elodie considers this, but the hurt and bewilderment on her face is rebuke enough.

"They told me I couldn't keep you and that was the way it was," Maggie says. "It was 1950. I couldn't go against them."

Elodie remains silent.

"I broke it off with Gabriel that summer," Maggie continues. "He moved to Montreal, and that was the last I heard from him. We both ended up marrying other people."

"How did you find each other? And when?"

"Our families were neighbors," Maggie explains. "We reconnected about ten years later. We rekindled a friendship and then . . . Well, things got quite messy for a while, but eventually we both got divorced from our spouses and started a life together."

"So your children are my brother and sister?"

"Yes," Maggie says, almost guiltily. "James and Stephanie."

"*Mon Dieu.*"

"I know this is a lot to absorb," Maggie says, reaching for her daughter's hands again. "If only I could convince you how guilty I've felt every single day of my life since I gave you up. I wish I'd kept you and stayed with Gabriel and that we would have been together all along. I wish I hadn't been so afraid. But I was. I was so terrified."

"I understand," Elodie says, but her voice is small.

"I hope you can," Maggie whispers, her voice breaking.

They sob together for a little while, Elodie's hands locked inside Maggie's.

"Do I look like them?" Elodie asks, wiping her eyes. "Your kids?"

"I think there's a resemblance," Maggie says. "Would you like to meet them? I wasn't sure."

"Of course," Elodie interrupts. "All my life I've longed for a big family. Sisters and brothers, grandparents, aunts and uncles, cousins . . . *Of course* I want to meet them."

Maggie pulls Elodie into her arms and clings to her. Elodie lets Maggie hold her like that for a long time, until Maggie finally pulls away and stares into her daughter's haunted eyes. She strokes her long blond hair and cups the girl's chin in the palm of her hand. "You're so beautiful," she whispers.

"No, I'm not," Elodie says. "But you are. I never imagined you with black hair."

Maggie stands up and pulls Elodie to her feet. She leads her across the room to the mirror above the dresser, and they stand side by side, staring at their reflections. "There's definitely a family resemblance," Maggie says. "Not our coloring, but look here." She points out their eyebrows and noses. "And the shape of our eyes is exactly the same."

"Maybe," Elodie concedes, clearly unconvinced.

"You look a bit like my sisters, too," Maggie says. "I have three of them, and a brother. You wanted a big family, that's what you're getting."

Elodie hasn't taken her eyes away from the mirror, as though she can't quite believe what she's seeing. "Is it really you?" she asks. "I'm afraid if I look away, you'll be gone."

"I'm here, and I'm not going anywhere," Maggie assures her.

Elodie reaches out and touches the mirror.

"I know this is a lot to ask," Maggie says, still looking straight ahead into the mirror. "But do you think you can ever forgive me?"

Elodie hesitates before responding, taking her time to think about it. The silence is interminable. Finally, she says, "You were young. What else could you do? No one knows better than me that it's a sin to have a baby out of wedlock."

"That's more than I could have hoped for," Maggie says. "Thank you."

Elodie leans her head on Maggie's shoulder. Maggie doesn't budge; she barely breathes. She wants to stay exactly like this as long as possible.

"*Maman,*" Elodie says, and Maggie understands that she's just saying the word out loud to test it, that no response is required. *Maman.*

"I see your father in your face, too," Maggie says softly. And then, after a few more minutes in the mirror, "Should we go back?"

They leave the bedroom and go downstairs. Elodie approaches the chair where Gabriel is waiting for them. "*Allô, Papa,*" she says.

Long after everyone has gone to sleep, Maggie climbs out of bed and creeps down the hall. She stops at James's room to peek in on him, and she can see by the blue and green light of his lava lamp that his legs are dangling off the bed, his body rising and falling beneath his quilt. In the next room, she finds Stephanie sleeping horizontally across her bed, with her Raggedy Ann doll on the floor. Maggie picks it up, tucks it under Stephanie's arm, and kisses the little girl's warm cheek.

Finally, Maggie reaches the end of the hall and stops outside the guest bedroom, where her other daughter—her firstborn—is spending the night. She stands there for a moment, overcome with emotion. Never would she have imagined all her children sleeping under one roof.

She opens the door as quietly as possible and freezes when she hears the soft sobbing from inside. She considers going in to comfort Elodie, but quickly dismisses the idea. Elodie might prefer to be alone; she's always been alone, after all. A stranger barging in on her in the middle of the night might make her uncomfortable. And Maggie *is* a stranger, mother or not. She has to remind herself of that. She has to remember to go slow.

And so Maggie backs away and heads downstairs to the kitchen. She pours herself a glass of wine, lights one of Gabriel's cigarettes, and sits down at the table. Her mind is wired. A welcome numbness has washed over her, subduing some of the intensity of the day's events, but she can't shut down her thoughts.

What have I let happen to her? The question beats like a drum in her head.

Elodie is upstairs crying into her pillow—how many tears has she already shed in her lifetime? how many nights has she cried herself to sleep? how deep are her wounds? how bereaved is her soul?—and all Maggie can do is sit here helplessly, knowing she is the cause of it.

Her worst fear is that all the love in the world—which Maggie and Gabriel are prepared to give—can't possibly be enough to neutralize what's been done to Elodie or restore what's been destroyed.

Maggie gets up and grabs the bottle of wine from the fridge. May as well finish it. It's the only one left over from dinner. They all drank too much. Part celebration, part tension reliever. She refills her glass and notices the box of her father's things sitting on the floor by the pantry. She hauled it out the other day in anticipation of Elodie's visit.

She goes to it now and settles on the floor with her wine and her ashtray, and starts making neat piles of the contents—old agriculture books, business and inspirational books, cards and drawings his children gave him over the years.

Someday she will tell Elodie about her grandfather, maybe even take her to the seed store, where he was larger than life. She would like Elodie to know that he was so much more than just the person who took her away from her mother, that he was fundamentally a good man trying to protect his own daughter. Over and over again, he attempted to redeem what he'd done, always with quiet, meaningful gestures that ultimately yielded fruit. First, he sent Elodie into the world with her name—a seemingly small detail, but momentous enough to have made their reunion possible; then he tried to get her back from the orphanage; and finally, he conceived of the ad that brought them back together.

There's really a perfect symmetry to it all, Maggie thinks, a sweet, symbiotic full circle that's led them to this moment. Her mother used to say, *The Lord gives and the Lord takes away.*

Maggie is reminded of that now. Her father took away, and then he gave.

Your grandfather was known as the Seed Man . . .

In spite of everything, Maggie has managed to turn out all right. She is a mother of three children—all of them here tonight in the house she loves so much; she is a wife, a lover of seeds and language, a French woman with English blood, an English woman with French blood. She is neither fully one thing nor another, as she's always wanted to be. She is arrogant and humble, audacious and timid, alive. She is still growing and always will be.

She pulls Elodie's baby blanket and hospital bracelet out of the box, and then retrieves an elastic-bound stack of photographs. She lingers over them for a while, lost in bittersweet nostalgia, until she finds herself staring at a picture of her father standing in the middle of a garden she doesn't recognize. He's knee-deep in flowers, with a wooden rail fence behind him. He's in his late thirties, wearing suspenders and a white Panama hat that conceals his premature baldness. He has a round face, a curly moustache, and he's holding a cigar between his fingers. He looks content, as though there's nowhere else on earth he'd rather be but in that garden, communing with nature in all its wild splendor.

It's an expression Maggie recognizes from when she used to observe him working at the seed store—fully and wholly in his element. A place Maggie has found herself in many times over the last few years, and where she knows she will be again.

CHAPTER 56

―――⸗⸗――

Elodie

Elodie hears the door open and holds her breath. She knows it's her mother. Her *mother*. Over and over again, she's been repeating that word in her head. No longer some hypothetical idea or childhood delusion. Her mother is here to hold her in the dark, to wipe away her tears and take away her pain and terrors.

"Maggie?" she whispers, but her voice is too meek, not quite loud enough.

And as suddenly as the door opened, it closes, and Elodie can hear Maggie retreating down the stairs. Her heart sinks. Maggie must have heard Elodie crying and fled.

Elodie lies very still. She hadn't realized how much she'd been longing for her mother to comfort her. Even in a house full of people, in this pretty room with its floral wallpaper and grand brass bed and red patchwork quilt, she still feels frightened and strangely hollow. Resentment starts to bubble up inside her, and she reminds herself that for all their kind words and hospitality, she is probably just a nuisance to them.

She wonders what it would have been like to grow up in this lovely, warm house full of love. That girl in there, Stephanie—her sister, the same age as Nancy, with her fat pink cheeks and her fearlessness and her happy disposition—will grow up with everything that was taken away from Elodie. *It should have been me*, she thinks, with a stab of acrimony. *I came first.*

She lies there stewing for what feels like a very long time. She can hear the crickets outside, and it reminds her of her early years at Saint-Sulpice—a memory she'd forgotten until now. She used to love them chirping outside her window. There were no other sounds to drown them out, only the perfect silence of a country night. Sister Tata told her the chirping noise came from the males rubbing their wings together. How could she ever have forgotten that?

She doesn't fall asleep. How could she? All she wants is to go home to Nancy. She misses Nancy's warm little body curled up against her, her sweet breath against her skin.

And then the door opens again, and this time, Maggie enters the room. The floor creaks as she approaches the bed. Her weight on the edge of the mattress, her hand on Elodie's damp cheek. "Elodie?" she whispers. "Do you want to be alone?"

"No," Elodie blurts, her voice childlike.

"Good," Maggie says. "I'm here."

Elodie reaches for her. "Don't go," she says, and as she listens to Maggie's heartbeat, she feels the bitterness fade.

"Of course not," Maggie promises. "I wasn't sure you wanted me."

"I've always wanted you."

Maggie settles in beside her and rests her head against a propped-up pillow.

"Will you write my story?" Elodie asks her. "Will you tell it exactly the way it happened?"

"Yes," Maggie answers without having to give it any thought. "Of course I will."

"And will it be published?"

"Absolutely," she says, knowing it will. She will fight for that; Godbout will help her if need be. The idea feels as right as anything she's ever set her mind to.

"We have to do it soon," Elodie says. "I want it to be published while Sister Ignatia is still at Saint-Nazarius. And I want you to use her real name, and for us to bring it to her in person."

"Yes," Maggie agrees, her heart racing with excitement. The prospect of a new project that will require them to work together for many months—their lives intertwined, their connection deepening—while at the same time outing Elodie's abuser is exhilarating.

"Thank you," Elodie says. "I'll give you my notebook to start. I've written absolutely everything in it."

"Maybe you could live here with us while we work on it," Maggie suggests. "I don't want to pressure you, but Stephanie and Nancy are about the same age . . ."

Elodie can't quite believe the offer. "Nancy would love it here in the country," she says. "It must be a beautiful place to grow up."

"And you could be home with her," Maggie says. "At least until she starts school, and then there would always be a job for you at my store."

"It sounds nice," Elodie says, thinking about her apartment in Pointe Saint-Charles and Len's Deli, and how much she would miss working there.

"I don't want to overwhelm you," Maggie adds. "We have all the time in the world for you to decide." She puts her arms around Elodie and strokes her hair. They lie like that for a long time, wide-awake in the dark.

"I'll never sleep tonight," Elodie says.

"When I was little, my father used to recite this poem to help me fall asleep," Maggie whispers softly.

"Tell it to me," Elodie says.

"Let me see if I can remember it. 'Johnny Appleseed, Johnny Appleseed . . .'" she begins, using the French translation, Jean Pépin-de-Pomme.

In that pack on his back
In that talisman sack
Tomorrow's peaches, pears, and cherries,

Tomorrow's grapes and red raspberries,
Seeds and tree-souls, precious things,
Feathered with microscopic wings . . .

Elodie closes her eyes. *Maybe I've died,* she thinks. The feelings inside her are too good, unfamiliar. There's sadness, too, of course. This she accepts as the most natural, inevitable aspect of her life. Sadness lives in her cells, alongside her sense of injustice and outrage toward Sister Ignatia and God. These things cannot be transcended. They are as much a part of her being as her limbs and her organs and Nancy. But tonight there's something else: *hope.*

She has a family now, at the helm of which is a beautiful, living, breathing mother. A mother who wants to be in her life, who tried to find her more than once and wants forgiveness and a second chance; a mother who was forced to give her up and then tried to get her back.

Elodie can live with that. She will never get those twenty-four years back—she knows she will carry the burden of her past for as long as she is alive—but at least now she has a future as part of a family.

"'All the outdoors the child heart knows, and the apple, green, red, and white,'" Maggie continues. "'Sun of his day and his night, the apple allied to the thorn, child of the rose—'"

Elodie doesn't understand the poem. She doesn't need to. Nothing is diminished by the not knowing.

ACKNOWLEDGMENTS

Much of the insight I gained into the emotional story of the Duplessis orphans came from Pauline Gill's magnificent book, *Les Enfants de Duplessis* (Quebec Loisirs Inc., 1991). The heartbreaking true story of Alice Quinton helped me to understand the physical, spiritual, and emotional toll these orphans endured throughout their lives, long after they were freed. I owe a tremendous debt of gratitude to Alice Quinton for sharing her story with Pauline Gill, and for her candor, honesty, courage, and resilience.

My biggest debt of gratitude is to the one and only Billy Mernit, my mentor and first reader-slash-editor extraordinaire: without your vision and insight as to what the *real* story was—and challenging me to *tell* Elodie's story—this book would still be in my drawer. Twenty years in the making, it took your gift for storytelling and editing to steer me in the right direction. Again. I've said it before, every writer should have a Billy.

Another enormous thank you to my resilient, relentless, beloved agent and friend, Bev Slopen, whom I met twenty years ago when I showed her the very first version of this manuscript. We've toiled on the "Seed Man" together, on and off, for two decades, *and you never ever fired me!* I am so blessed that you've stood by me all these years. Not many agents would. I think we are officially family now.

Thank you SO VERY MUCH to Jennifer Barth, my magnificent editor at HarperCollins. I feel so blessed to have your support and guidance, and it's always a delight to work with you. Again, thank you for taking such good care of this book in particular—it means everything to me. You set it free with its new title and all your brilliant insights, and allowed it to soar above and beyond what I ever hoped it could be.

Thank you to the most wonderful marketing team ever, both at HarperCollins US and Canada: Mary Sasso, Katherine Beitner, Sabrina Groomes, Cory Beatty, Leo Macdonald, and Sandra Leef. The past year has been full of excitement, surprises and joy, truly. I can't wait to see where this one brings us.

To my "live-in" editor and best friend, Miguel, let me copy and paste the last book's acknowledgements (they still apply): thank you for picking up the kids and driving them all over the city and basically taking care of my entire life, so I can continue to be The Writer. I love you. Jessie and Luke, you didn't contribute much to the process, but your snuggles helped. A lot.

Finally, thank you to my mother, Peggy, the inspiration for Maggie. All those interviews and long talks, everything you shared with me about your childhood in Montreal, all your feedback and read-throughs, have finally come to fruition. I only wish you were here to experience our book finally coming into the world. I'm just going to assume that you are, somewhere. I miss you.

ABOUT THE AUTHOR

JOANNA GOODMAN lives in Toronto with her husband and two children. Originally from Montreal, she based *The Home for Unwanted Girls* in part on the story of her mother. She is also the author of *The Finishing School*.

ALSO BY
JOANNA GOODMAN

THE FINISHING SCHOOL
A Novel
Available in Paperback, eBook, and Digital Audio

"Both a coming-of-age-story and a literary mystery but ultimately culminating in an addictive read full of skillfully conveyed characters." —*Library Journal*

In this suspenseful, provocative novel of friendship, secrets, and deceit, a successful writer returns to her elite Swiss boarding school to get to the bottom of a tragic accident that took place while she was a student twenty years earlier. An unputdownable read as clever as it is compelling, *The Finishing School* offers a riveting glimpse into a privileged, rarefied world in which nothing is as it appears.